Santa's Baby

A Hilarious Holiday RomCom

CHANTAL ROOME

Book Cover by Chantal Roome

1st edition 2023

ebook ISBN 9781777914967

print ISBN 9781777914974

Dedicated to my mother's obsessive love of Christmas decorations and her insistence on decorating earlier and earlier each year. You inspired me to give up my official Scrooge designation and now my house rivals yours in gaudy excess when it comes to decorating for the holiday season.
You still have me beat with your Christmas village, though. It's truly a sight to behold.

No butt plug trees, though.

Shame.

Contents

Chapter 1

WHAT A HO HO HO

Phoebe

OF ALL THE WAYS I ever imagined spending the Christmas of my thirty-first year, I can say, with certainty, tracking down the Santa Claus who impregnated me was not one of them.

Yet, here we are.

"Oooh, this place is nice, Phoebe." Gavin walks into the living room and sets down a box marked *Lincoln*. "Maybe the owners will decide to stay overseas so you can buy the place. The furniture is pretty sick." My idiot brother flops face down on my furnished rental's overstuffed blue velvet couch and groans obscenely into the cushion. "Oh, man. You don't want to know the dirty things I'm thinking of doing to this couch."

It's not every day I rent a place sight unseen, so you can imagine the relief I felt when we got here and the place looked precisely like it had in the photos. That I found a furnished place on such short notice, right before the holidays, could be considered a miracle in itself. Finding a nice place in a safe neighborhood? Yeah, there had to have been some divine intervention involved for that to happen. Maybe I've had a visit from the Ghost of Christmas Present. Heh. Get it? Because finding this place had been a gift. A gift that I don't want defiled by my disgusting brother and whatever he plans on doing to my new couch, regardless of how temporarily it's in my possession.

"Ew, don't be gross, Gavin. And get your stinky ass off the couch. You're filthy."

"Hey! Is that any way to treat the guy who spent one of his infrequent days off both school and work carrying all your boxes into the house?" He drags himself off the couch. "Speaking of carrying boxes, didn't you promise me pizza and beer as payment for helping you move?"

"Ha! Nice try, kid. I'll order pizza, but you're sticking with soda until you're of legal age. Plus, you still need to drive home so I wouldn't let you drink even if you were old enough."

Gavin is only eighteen, my much younger sibling from my mom's second marriage. Two days after my mom gave birth to Charlie, and with a few months left to go before my second birthday, my biological father decided being a father wasn't really his thing, and he left. It took Mom a long time to find another man worth taking a chance on after that. She started dating Warren ten years later, and they married a couple of years after that when Gavin was born.

Like most teenage guys, Gavin is all raging hormones and unrestrained snark. But, despite his many annoying traits, he has a huge heart, and that's why he's one of my favorite people. No one was angrier than Gavin when I found myself waiting at the altar for a man I knew in my heart wasn't right for me. He spent that night a year ago storming around the hotel, hoping to run into my former fiancé so he could unleash his teenage fury. It's probably a good thing he never found him, though. I doubt it would have been a fair fight. Webster kept himself in excellent shape and would have been more than a match for seventeen-year-old Gavin.

Seventeen-year-old Gavin was a short, scrawny little shit. Eighteen-year-old Gavin is almost six and a half feet tall and packed with muscle. He's never said so, but I'm pretty sure he started working out after the wedding disaster, so he'd be ready if he ever saw my ex again. After a year of protein shakes and lifting weights, not to mention a huge growth spurt, Gavin is formidable. It still wouldn't be a fair fight, but the advantage would go to Gavin, not Webster. He took it pretty hard when I told him Webster did me a favor that day.

I almost felt guilty for not being as upset as Gavin about the situation. It had been a shock when I got the text telling me he wasn't coming, but not marrying Webster Day turned out to be the best thing that could have happened. It seemed like a dick move at first, but in the end, he made the best decision for both of us. I'd been considering making that same decision that morning as I sat through the hours of hair and makeup appointments required to turn me into a blushing bride. I should have done it, too. If we'd both skipped out on the wedding, I bet we'd have been able to get past it a lot faster. To this day, I've yet to speak to Webster face to face. The failed wedding incident has forced me to connect with my lifelong best friend through phone calls and the odd video chat only. Which sucks. I could have used his support when I found myself pregnant and alone.

"No way. Charlie said she would do the driving on the way home." Gavin jumps up off the couch and yells down the back hallway, "Isn't that right, Charlie?"

Oh, shit. Despite being one of my favorite people, I will still murder Gavin if he wakes up Lincoln. That thing they say about never waking a sleeping baby? Yeah, that's not just an old wives' tale.

"Shhh. Will you shut up?" I slap my hand over his mouth. "Lincoln is sleeping."

He looks so sheepish I could almost believe he felt bad about waking my baby if I didn't already know better. There's no way Gavin would leave here without saying goodbye to his nephew, even if that nephew is a baby who still hasn't figured out things don't disappear when he can't see them. Gavin is sure he has a special bond with my baby, though, and it's something he's incredibly proud of. I believe they have a bond, too. Lincoln always seems calmer when his Uncle Gavin is holding him. And

Gavin never misses a chance to hold him, even when he has to make his own chances.

"Too late," Charlie says, coming out of the back hallway with a tiny baby snuggled in her arms. "The little guy was awake when I tried to sneak into the room to drop off a box. I think he sensed me because as soon as I walked in, an unholy rumbling started coming out of his little rear end. You'll need to do laundry, by the way. I rinsed everything and left it to pre-soak." She looks down at Lincoln with a grin and singsongs, "Isn't that right, Linky? Mommy has to do laundry. Yes, she does. She's lucky Auntie Charlie changed you and the sheets instead of running away and letting her deal with it."

My heart swells while I watch my little sister snuggle my baby, and not for the first time, I second-guess my decision to move back to Westborough. What am I going to do without my family around to help me for the next three months? Why did I follow through with this terrible idea? Oh, right. If I want Lincoln to have the chance to meet his father, this is where I need to be. And my sense of right and wrong won't let me entertain the thought of not trying to find his father. There's a man out there who doesn't know he has a son, and that doesn't sit right with me. There's still a possibility he will decide not to, but I want him to have the option to be involved in Lincoln's life. So, even if he ends up being a dickhead like my own biological father who wanted nothing to do with me or my sister, I'm going to find Lincoln's father and give him a chance to do better.

"Hey, hey. None of that now. I can see your brain working from here." Gavin is back on the couch, getting his sweaty teenage boy smell all over it. Whatever, I'll use a fabric refresher on it when he leaves. He can't stink it up too badly in such a short time, can he? "Everything is going to be fine. Tell her your news, Charlie. I can't handle seeing Fifi cry."

I rub my fingertips over my cheeks, and sure enough, they come away wet. "Sorry if my feelings offend you, you little twerp. I'm going to miss you guys, that's all. I'm allowed to be sad about that."

He jumps up off the couch and wraps me in a sweaty hug. "I'm going to miss you too, Fifi," he says. "But you won't have to miss Charlie."

I blink a few times and pull myself out of his embrace. "What's he talking about?" I ask Charlie, then repeat my question to Gavin. "What are you talking about?"

Gavin takes Lincoln from Charlie, snuggling him to his chest, and takes him into the kitchen. I hear the cupboard doors open and close and the water running in the sink. Sounds like Uncle Gavin is making his nephew a bottle.

"I didn't tell you because I knew you'd try to talk me out of it, but I'm staying with you. You have the third bedroom I can sleep in. I even got myself a part-time job at a coffee shop. I'm staying to help you with Lincoln so you can focus on finding his dad. It will be easier to track him down if you don't have to bring Lincoln with you everywhere you go. Plus, I can't be away from you guys for that long." Charlie's eyes are shiny with unshed tears. "You know I can't get enough of those midnight feedings," she jokes.

I chuckle. "Are you sure? You don't have to put your life on hold for me, Charlie. I love you for wanting to do this, but you don't have to stay."

"I know that," she says, wrapping her arms around me. "I want to stay."

"You're the best sister I could ever ask for," I choke through a sob. "I couldn't have made it this far without you."

And it's true. The seemingly endless months of my pregnancy would have been so much harder if it hadn't been for the help of my brother and sister, and, of course, my mom and stepdad. I'll never admit it to them, but after living back home with my parents for the last year, and having my family around all the time, I was a little scared to be on my own with Lincoln. I loved living here with Webster, but being on my own with a baby is different. The excitement of Westborough seems almost scary when I think about protecting my son from unseen dangers. I tried to play it cool, but I'm thinking I didn't do such a good job of it if Charlie covertly arranged to move here with me.

I've never been so happy to be such a shitty liar.

"Are you guys done with all the girly feelings out there? Me and the big guy want to come chill on that sweet-ass couch, but we don't want your emotional breakdowns cramping our style. It's hard to relax with all this crying going on."

Charlie and I both burst into laughter. After one more squeeze, I let her go.

"Yeah, we're done," I call out. "I'll order that pizza now so you can get on the road."

"Oh, yeah. About that," he says, walking back to the living room with my son in the crook of his arm. "Mom told me to spend the night and drive back in the morning. She doesn't want me driving alone at night in the winter. I don't know what she thinks I do after work at home. It's usually pretty late by the time I get out of the market."

Charlie sits next to him on the couch, her eyes on Lincoln. "There's a huge difference between driving five minutes in Fallbridge at ten at night and driving on the highway at two in the morning. Especially in the middle of winter."

"Yeah, yeah. Okay, *Mother*," he teases. "I'm already staying the night. Happy?"

"You bet," she says while ruffling his hair, taking advantage of the fact that he has his hands full feeding Lincoln. "We just wuv you so much, Gavvers," she adds in a baby voice. "It would devastate us if anything happened to you."

"Hey, no fair. Hands off the hair. Do you know how long it took to get it like that?"

They sit side by side, alternating between cooing over Lincoln and bickering with each other while I busy myself with ordering the pizzas. After I do that, I focus on unpacking my few boxes. The best part about finding a furnished rental is how little I had to pack to come here. It would have sucked if I'd had to move my furniture out of storage for such a temporary stay. Three months isn't long enough to justify renting a moving van.

I only hope three months is long enough to find Lincoln's dad.

The doorbell rings, and Gavin hops up to grab the pizzas. "Oh, thank god. I'm starving," he says, spreading the boxes down on the coffee table and flipping one open. "I'm a growing boy, you know." He grabs two slices and stacks them sandwich style.

I bring plates and napkins out from the kitchen. "We know, Gavin. You tell us every time you get even the tiniest bit hungry."

He wiggles his eyebrows, and grins before shoving the makeshift sandwich in his mouth.

"So, Phoebe. Why don't you tell me how you're going to find this guy? You didn't go into much detail when you announced you were moving here for three months to look for him. Do you even have any idea where he is?"

I heave a sigh. We've hit on the biggest problem with my plan. It sucks. Getting drunk and hooking up with a stranger after skipping your own wedding would be a lot easier to get over if you didn't get yourself pregnant in the process. Failing that, it would be nice if you remembered the name of the guy or any detail about him other than he'd been dressed as Santa Claus for a Christmas party being held at the same hotel as your wedding. The only things I have to go on are the luxurious red velvet coat I stole when I crept out, and a blurry photo I took of his face mashed into the pillow. Not great clues.

Why did I take his jacket, you ask? I guess I thought my walk of shame would feel less shameful if I covered my wedding dress with Santa's jacket. It didn't. But I made it back to my room without being seen, packed up, and headed home with no one finding out I spent what should have been my wedding night with a stranger.

Until a month and a half later, when two pink lines gave me the shock of a lifetime, ensuring that everyone would know exactly how I spent that night.

That's right.

My fiancé left me at the altar and the first thing I did was run out and get knocked up by Santa Claus.

Talk about Ho Ho Ho.

Chapter 2

Christmas Party Do-Over

Archer

"You're sure you want to do this again? I recall it didn't work out so well for you last year." My best friend, Eric Baxter, sits on the couch in my hotel suite, arms spread wide across the back, looking more relaxed than I've ever felt, as he waits for me to get ready for the company Christmas party.

Truthfully, I don't know if I want to do this again, but I have a feeling that replacing a shitty memory with a better one is the best way to put this past year to bed. A last farewell, if you will.

I step out of the bathroom, sporting a fake stomach strapped to my front and a pair of red velvet pants held up by wide, black suspenders. I spin the luxurious white beard dangling from my fingers and walk over to grab my scotch from my desk.

"Yes. I need to do it. It will be fun for the staff and their families, and it's my way of putting everything that happened with Annabelle to bed." She didn't ruin Christmas for me, despite her ill-timed wish during last year's party for Santa to destroy the sex tape she'd made with her trainer so her rich boyfriend wouldn't see it. The rich boyfriend in question? Yeah, that was me.

Eric bursts into laughter. "Her eyes, man. You should have seen her eyes when she realized you were in the Santa costume! I've never seen eyes get that wide. I honestly thought they were at risk of popping right out of her head and rolling across the floor. It was the funniest fucking thing I've ever seen."

Yeah, looking back, I can see the humor in the situation. Not that I found it funny back then. Considering I'd hoped she would ask Santa for a proposal, her wish to hide a sex tape she made with someone else set that ring in my pocket on fire. But it also did something else: set free the stirrings of relief.

No matter how it came about, I dodged a bullet. That's what I need to remember.

"I'm glad my pain entertained you. But really, she did me a favor. We were never right for each other."

Truthfully, I'm not getting any younger. I've always wanted a family, and I thought Annabelle would be an acceptable choice for a partner. Turns out I couldn't have been more wrong. Looking back, I realize now that she would have been a terrible mother and an even worse wife. We hadn't even seen each other for almost three months because of our conflicting schedules before the fateful Christmas party. I honestly do not know why I thought I should ask her to marry me. I was settling, and I knew it.

"Maybe you'll get lucky tonight and your runaway bride will be running away again. You could make it a yearly thing." Eric lifts his glass to me and shakes his head. "Only you could pick up a woman while dressed as Santa."

After Annabelle's confession at last year's party, I took myself to the hotel bar while security escorted her from the building. I planned to drink top-shelf whiskey until I passed out while Eric and my assistant, MaeLynn, removed every trace of Annabelle from my apartment. I would never entertain the thought of reconciliation with someone who could cheat on me so easily and then ask Santa Claus for help to cover it up. I'm not that desperate.

I may have been planning to drown my sorrows in whiskey, but when a curvy brunette in a wedding dress sat beside me and ordered three shots of tequila and a double margarita, plans changed. After that, figuring her out became my new plan. A more appealing prospect than ruminating over Annabelle's confession to Santa. I sat there transfixed as she swallowed the shots like they were water, asked the bartender for three more, then turned, looked right at me and said 'What's up, Santa?' with a single lift of her chin. For some unknown reason, I replied, 'Hey there, Bride.' The sheer ridiculousness of the exchange caught me off guard and, with the help of the several whiskeys I'd already consumed, I completely lost it. I'm not sure how long I laughed, but when I finished, she was still there, smiling at me and sipping on her margarita.

The rest of the night is a bit of a blur, but bits and pieces have come back to me over the past year. I know I laughed harder that night than I ever had before in my life, and I know I ended up back in my hotel room with the bride. I never even learned her name. I called her Bride all night, and she called me Santa. I'm not sure what I called her when we had sex, but the fuzzy memory of the words "Yes, Santa" being moaned in my ear still gets me hard when I think of it. By the time we made it back to the hotel room, we were so hot for each other that our clothes practically flew off. Even the six hundred or so buttons on her dress didn't slow us down.

When I woke up the next morning, she was gone, and she'd taken the jacket of my Santa costume with her. The costume shop was not pleased that I'd lost it, and I was not pleased that she took it and didn't leave her phone number. It wasn't like I was in a position to start a new relationship right then, and I doubt she was, either, what with the wedding dress and all. Even so, it would have been nice to have a way to contact her later on.

That night is still the best I've ever had.

"I highly doubt she'd be running away from another wedding only a year later," I say to Eric. "She didn't seem like the type to run in the first place, let alone to do it on multiple occasions."

"What do you know, man? You would have proposed to that witch, Annabelle, if you hadn't found out about her cam girl debut. Your judgment is clearly flawed."

"Yeah, yeah. Not my finest hour." And it really wasn't. I was proposing more out of the sense that that's what I should do in my life at my age, and not because I loved her. Again, thank god she was so drunk she didn't realize it was me in the Santa costume or I might never have learned her secret.

Eric throws back the rest of his drink and stands up. "Well, I'm heading back to the party," he says, placing his glass on the desk. "Shoot me or MaeLynn a text when you want me to announce your entrance."

Once I'm alone in my room, I take a seat at the desk. Thinking back on that night almost a year ago, all I can do is smile. Truthfully, Annabelle hasn't crossed my mind in months. The only person from that night who crosses my mind these days is the beautiful bride who made me forget my problems. She crosses my mind more than I'd like to admit.

I looked for her the next day, but without a name, I had little to go on. This is a giant hotel, with a few large ballrooms and several smaller ones, and there were several weddings, not to mention other parties, that night. Plus, no matter how much I pleaded, the hotel staff wouldn't give me the names of the couples who were having weddings. Something about protecting the privacy of their customers. I couldn't even find anyone who was willing to take a bribe, which was equally impressive and frustrating. All I have left are some blurry, disjointed memories, and the lingering certainty that it was the best night of my life.

Still, as far as relationships go, even my runaway bride proved they're not all they're cracked up to be. She ran away from her wedding, after all, and then she ran away from me. If that doesn't scream relationships never work, I don't know what does.

"Is this what happened at the end of the party last year?" I yell to Eric as I walk through the ballroom looking for any items my staff may have forgotten. "You wandered around looking for lost toys?"

As if the embarrassment of last year's failed proposal weren't bad enough, it was my first experience hosting the company Christmas party since I'd taken over. We'd had Christmas parties before, of course, but when my father ran the company, they tended to be uptight affairs full of his golf buddies and other uptight society pricks. The asshole didn't even bother to invite the staff to the party. If that doesn't tell you what kind of man my father is, then nothing will. When I took over, one of the first things I did was to dismantle the party-planning committee that my father had staffed with his friends' mistresses and hire an actual event-planning company. I also gave them strict instructions to make the party family-friendly.

I volunteered to play Santa because I wanted to see the faces of my staff when they finally got to attend the party. That and I wanted to see the kids' faces when they got all the latest toys and gadgets. With their parents' permission, of course. I didn't want to step on anyone's toes by giving their kids video game systems and electronics without telling them first. I wanted to make my staff and their children happy and to see the smiles on their faces while I did it. Annabelle nearly ruined that for me, too, by jumping to the front of the line and sitting on Santa's lap before any of the kids had the chance.

I should have thrown her on the floor then and there, instead of waiting for her to spew her betrayal in the form of a wish from

Santa. What kind of idiot asks Santa Claus to help her lie about cheating? If that's not naughty list material, nothing is. Once again, I'm reminded of how thankful I should be that I decided to surprise Annabelle with a Christmas proposal and that her powers of observation are so abysmal. If she'd recognized me, I'd never have known she'd cheated, and we'd probably be married already.

Eric laughs at me from across the room. "Not exactly. If you'll recall, MaeLynn and I moved every trace of Annabelle out of your apartment while you went out with your runaway bride. Some of the other guys took care of rounding up lost items."

At least this year, I got to enjoy the rest of the party. Last year, after having Annabelle escorted from the premises, I forced myself to stay and hand out the gifts to the kids because I couldn't bear to disappoint the kids, but I left soon after. Compared to that, I'm doing great this year. Hell, I even made it out of the costume.

I've already been back to my hotel room to remove the Santa costume and I'm wearing the burgundy three-piece suit I bought specifically for the party. Well, most of it anyway. After playing Santa and handing out toys to all the kids and cash bonuses to the adults, I needed to get out of that damn Santa suit so I could be myself and enjoy the party. I didn't count on it being so warm in the ballroom even without the costume, though. My jacket came off almost immediately and I haven't put it back on since. It's still hanging on the back of a chair backstage where I left it.

"You coming out for drinks after this? We're hitting that new club that opened up downtown. I hear only the most beautiful women get in. What do you think? Isn't it time you ended your dry spell?"

Another effect of being humiliated by the woman I'd planned on proposing to? I've been celibate since that night. After my runaway bride ran off the next morning, I had no interest in looking for another hook-up. I let everyone think it was because of Annabelle, but the more time passed, the more I realized she had nothing to do with it. After my runaway bride, I gave up.

But it might be time to get back on the horse.

Or a woman, as it were.

"You know what? I think I will join you," I say, trying to muster up some excitement at the prospect of meeting someone but falling short. "Who else is going?"

"Just the guys. Mason knows the owner, so they're in the VIP section. He's already there with Damien and Lucas." He scans the ballroom. "Looks like we're done here."

I look around. He's right. There's nothing left but the cleanup and the hotel takes care of that as part of the fee I paid for the ballroom. Nothing is stopping me from going to that club, finding a willing woman, and taking her home for what will most likely be a mediocre time.

But for some reason, I'm having trouble getting excited about that. It's like my dick couldn't be less interested. Maybe he'll rally when we get to the club and find someone interesting. It's worth a shot, at least.

"Yeah, looks like you're right."

"Well, okay then, Mr. President, let's go get you laid."

I force a laugh and follow him to the door. "One thing at a time," I say. "This is the first time I've been out in a year. Maybe let's just let me get acclimated to the scene again, hey?" As the words leave my mouth, I can taste how awful it's going to be. The last thing I want is to get acclimated to the scene again. I'm thirty-four, well past the age of going to clubs and hooking up with random strangers.

Fuck, I hate being in this position. Annabelle may not have been the ideal match for me, but at least she was someone.

Eric stops inside the doors and grabs my arm. "Archer," he says seriously. "You don't have to do this, you know? If you don't want to hook up with someone, then don't. No one is forcing you to move on if you're not ready. If you need more time after the whole Annabelle thing, take more time." He's breathing heavier by the time he stops talking and takes his hand off my arm.

"That hurt you, didn't it?" I joke.

He snorts a laugh and shakes his head. "You have no idea."

I give him a brotherly clap on the back. "I appreciate it, man. And you're right. I'm not ready. But I will come out with you and the boys. Maybe a little fun is just what I need." I take a step toward the door.

"Aren't you forgetting something?" Eric asks, looking pointedly at my shirt. "I know it's not exactly cold in Westborough in the winter, but you should probably still get your jacket."

"Shit." I walk toward the backstage area. "I'll grab it and meet you in the lobby. Go find us a cab, or order an Uber or something."

"You know, you have enough money to keep a driver and car on staff. You should think about that," he calls out after me.

"Yeah, yeah. Fuck off." I laugh. "You know I hate that kind of shit."

I can hear his laughter echoing down the hall. Eric understands why I feel the way I feel about my family's money, but he still likes to give me shit about it from time to time. He wouldn't be my best friend if he didn't.

I find my jacket right where I left it earlier this evening and I'm sliding my arms into it when I hear a panicked-sounding voice from the main ballroom.

"Shit! No, no, no. Why is the party over so early? It wasn't supposed to be like this. Fucking Gavin. Fucking Charlie. Fuck my life. The hotel doesn't have any more parties booked. How will I ever find him now?"

I chuckle at the sudden burst of colorful vocabulary. When I step out of the backstage area to investigate, I spot a woman so dejected-looking I long to hug her. Her bright carrot-orange hair is in a large knot on top of her head, the stray curls sticking out at odd angles. She's buried her face in her hands. The leggings and hooded sweatshirt combo she's sporting tells me she likely wasn't an attendee at the party. My staff aren't rich, but they did dress up for the event tonight. And if her clothes weren't enough to call attention to her, she's sitting on the floor, elbows balanced on her knees, curled up in a tight ball. She must be lost. Inexplicably, the only thing I want is to help her.

"Hello? Are you looking for someone? Maybe I can help you?"

Her head jerks up at the sound of my voice and she stares straight at me, her eyes wide. "Holy shit, it's really you."

Chapter 3

Santa Sighting

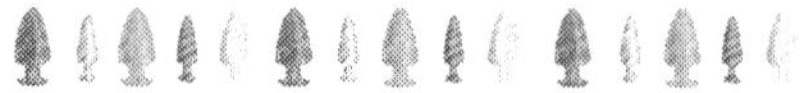

Phoebe

"Holy shit, it's really you."

I can't believe it worked.

I found him.

Now what?

"Excuse me? Are you a new hire? Did I miss you? I'm afraid I don't have the bonus checks on me, but I can let HR know and they'll have it deposited directly into your account. I was about to head out, but let's try to get this straightened out first."

What? Does he *really* not recognize me?

His concern about having missed giving me a bonus check seems genuine. I wonder if he could get in trouble for something like that. A Santa not handing out all the gifts would probably be reprimanded by their talent company, I bet. Or maybe even fired. I'm surprised at how calm he is. He found a crazed woman sitting on the floor in a ballroom about to burst into tears. I don't even look like I belong here, yet his first instinct is that I'm an employee he doesn't recognize who's upset about not getting a bonus check. God, I hope he's this nice when he finds out the reason I'm here.

I'm nervous, which makes me even more self-conscious about my far too casual attire. For all the other Christmas parties I dressed up, but Charlie and Gavin were so late getting home that I didn't have time to get ready. I managed a quick shower and styled half my hair, but it was impossible to get everything done with Lincoln wanting constant cuddles. I had to throw my hair up in a huge messy bun on top of my head and spread some lip balm on my lips and call it a day. Hell, I'm even still wearing the leggings and hooded sweatshirt from when I gave Lincoln his bath. It's still sporting a few damp spots, some of which I know for a fact are puke, not water. Frankly, I'm a mess.

You know who isn't a mess? Mr. Santa himself. He's standing there in a perfectly tailored three-piece suit and a pair of obviously very expensive dress shoes. He's dressed to impress, and he's so much hotter than I remember. The blurry candid picture I have on my cell phone doesn't do him justice. The wavy brown hair is shorter than last year, and not nearly as messy, probably due to not having just spent the entire night having wild monkey sex, but it's easy to see it's him. The chocolate brown eyes I've seen in my dreams for the last year gaze on me with concern now.

"Miss? Are you alright?"

Shit. I've been staring at him while he's waiting for an answer. Why did I think I could do this? I shove my hand in my pocket and finger the thick envelope I put there earlier, my backup plan giving me courage.

I've spent the last three weekends trawling through the various Christmas parties hosted in this hotel. Each night I'd get myself dolled up, make sure Charlie and Gavin had everything they needed to babysit for the evening, kiss Lincoln, then go crash holiday parties looking for a man whose name I didn't even know. I never thought I'd be the one pulling Santa beards at Christmas parties, but when you're looking for your baby's Santa daddy, you do what needs doing. And no, I didn't do it in front of any kids. I'm not a monster. Of course, the one night I didn't have time to make myself presentable would be the night that I finally find him. I straighten up and square my shoulders, feigning a confidence I don't feel. *Get it together, Phoebe. You came here for one reason and it wasn't to win a beauty contest.*

I wouldn't mind if I looked a little less lived-in, though. It turns out that my memories of my Santa's good looks were inaccurate, but not in the way I'd assumed. I had convinced myself that I'd exaggerated his sex appeal thanks to beer goggles and a spotty memory, but this Adonis standing in front of me has proven that to be a lie. The man is cologne advertisement sexy, the perfect mix of brooding and approachable, gloomy and joyous, mysterious and captivating. And the way he fills out a suit? If the image that flashed through my mind is correct, I'm positive he's hiding a pair of those sexy V-lines that only exist on men in fitness magazines and firefighter calendars. So yeah, I didn't exaggerate his looks at all. If anything, I downplayed them. If I'd remembered the truth of it, I would have thought the entire night had been a dream. You know, if not for the whole impregnated-by-Santa thing I had as proof.

Because, seriously, no one should be this good-looking. It's too distracting, too mesmerizing, too...much.

When I look up, he's standing right next to me in all his sexy Santa glory.

I look down again, fiddling with the envelope in my pocket some. "I...I don't know. Wait. What did you say?"

He offers his hand, pulling me up off the floor, sending a riot of tingles flying through me. When he lets go, it takes everything in me not to rub my fingers together to prolong the aftershocks.

"Are you looking for someone from HR? Did I miss you when I was handing out the bonus checks? I'm sure I can have that in your account tomorrow at the latest."

I shake my head, finally understanding what he's been saying. He doesn't recognize me. He thinks I'm an employee. "Oh, no. That's not it."

He draws his brows in confusion. "Oh, well, were you looking for someone who came to the party?"

I shake my head. Then nod my head. Then shake it again. Geez, talk about confusing.

The man, my baby's father, the guy I've been looking for at all these Christmas parties, takes in my appearance, looking me up and down. A look of what I'm sure is recognition comes across his face. *This is it, Phoebe. He remembers you.* All that's left is for me to tell him. After that, it's in his hands.

I open my mouth, ready to confess everything, when a voice from the doorway cuts me off.

"Oh, my god. There you are, babe. I've been looking everywhere for you." A feminine voice calls out from somewhere behind me, and I jump away from the man, guilt gnawing at me. "Who's your little friend?" She asks, wiggling her fingers in my direction.

One look at the woman who has joined us in the ballroom leaves me breathless. She's gorgeous. Like walking-down-the-runway-in-her-underwear-with-wings-strapped-to-her-back gorgeous. And it's obvious she had time to get dolled up before coming here. Not that she needs much to make her look beautiful. Her long legs, lean dancer's body, delicate features, and long blonde hair take care of that all on their own. Everything else just enhances what she already has.

I cringe when I look down at my spit-up-stained outfit and the messy bun to end all messy buns flops over my forehead. A lump forms in my throat when my mind catches up with what she's said.

She called him babe.

Ah, shit. My heart drops into my stomach. He has a girlfriend?

The woman is glaring at me for all she's worth. She looks me up and down, a smirk on her face, and my skin crawls. I don't think she likes me very much. Not that I can blame her. She caught me standing here making heart eyes at her boyfriend, after all.

Well, I guess I know what I need to do now. Good thing I prepared that backup plan.

I don't want to out him in front of her. There's no need to blow up his life in case he decides he wants nothing to do with Lincoln, so I slide the fat envelope out of my pocket and hold it out to him. "Here. I came to give you this. It's personal, so maybe wait until you're alone to open it. Read it when you can and get in touch. I've included all the, uh, pertinent information."

He takes it and opens his mouth to say something, but I turn on my heel and run out of that ballroom like my ass is on fire, tears stinging my eyes before I've made it out the doors. Luckily, the elevator is still on this floor when I get there, so the doors open as soon as I press the button. I'm slamming my hand on the close door button before my body is inside the cabin, looking behind me the whole time, hoping no one has followed. When the doors finally close, I slump against the wall and release a breath.

Well, that...sucked.

How fucking stupid could I be?

When I imagined meeting Lincoln's father again, it had somehow never occurred to me he would have a girlfriend. And why would it? I've spent the last year growing, birthing, and then caring for a baby. Lincoln kept me so busy that it didn't even cross my mind to think about relationships.

Looks like the same can't be said for Lincoln's dad.

His beautiful girlfriend showed up as I was about to spill my guts. How could I possibly stick around after that? I mean, I should have, but as soon as she arrived, guilt started eating at me. I couldn't get out of there fast enough.

It isn't until I'm back home, sitting at the kitchen table alone with a fresh cup of tea, that the disappointment really hits me. It's not like I'm looking for a relationship or anything—just look how the last one turned out—but somewhere deep down I harbored a tiny feeling of what if?

We had so much fun the one night we were together that my clearest memories are of us laughing. On what could have been the worst night of my life, I'd laughed harder than I ever had before. And came harder than I ever had before, too. Our chemistry was off the charts. I'd have to be insane to not have at least a little hope that we could be something more.

But I should have known better. A guy like that doesn't stay single for a year. Hell, I doubt he stayed single for a month.

Shit. Wait.

I jerk with a sudden realization, bumping my tea and spilling it on the table. What if he was never single at all? Was I the other woman? Some random chick he got pregnant while cheating on his girlfriend? His wife? Suddenly, my stomach is roiling too much for tea.

"Hey," Charlie says, pulling a mug out of the cupboard. She grabs a tea bag from the canister on the counter and uses the remaining water from the kettle to fix her own cup. She hands me a few paper towels to clean up my mess. "You're home early. How did it go? Do we need to expand our search to include mall Santas?" She chuckles. "I'm pretty short. Put me in a hoodie and a baseball cap and I'm sure I could pass for a kid. I don't mind pushing little brats out of the way to get us to the front of every line."

I hiccup a laugh. "No. I won't need you to assault any children." I look away and take a deep breath. "I found him."

Charlie's mouth works noiselessly as she drops heavily into the chair next to me. "Seriously?"

I lean back. "Yeah."

"So...now what?"

I chuckle dryly. "Well, considering he had no idea who I was? I guess we wait and see if he contacts me after he reads the letter I gave him." If his girlfriend had held off for five minutes, I think he might have figured it out. It looked like recognition was dawning on him, anyway.

"He didn't recognize you?" She looks me up and down. "That tracks, actually. Have you seen yourself? You've let your hair go back to its natural red and you're covered in freckles. When you were with Webster, you always hid the two most recognizable parts of yourself. Lincoln's father met you when you had brown hair and a face full of makeup. To him, you were a beautiful brunette with porcelain skin. Not to mention you were wearing a wedding dress. And didn't you say he'd already been drinking before you got to the bar? I'm not that surprised that he didn't recognize you."

"Yeah, I guess you're right."

She raises her eyebrows and gestures for me to continue. "Well, what did he say when you told him? Did he seem angry or upset? Do we need to sic Gavin on him?"

I snort a laugh and choke on a sob simultaneously. "I didn't get the chance to tell him."

She raises an eyebrow. "Why the hell not?"

I drop my head to the table and groan. "His super-hot girlfriend showed up, and I panicked. I shoved the letter at him and ran."

"No! A girlfriend? What the hell?"

I lift my head and drop it against the table, the cold wood soothing against my skin, though the impact fails to knock any sense into me. Ever since I saw him, the previously fuzzy memories of our night together keep flashing through my brain with his face front and center, highlighting the hope I didn't want to acknowledge before tonight.

I never wanted a fairy tale ending, but I couldn't suppress a glimmer of hope that something would come of seeing Lincoln's father again. At the very least, I thought I would learn his name during our first reunion, even if I didn't get to broach the subject of him being Lincoln's dad. I certainly never thought he would look at me with confusion, not even remembering who I am. It comes as a bit of a blow to realize how forgettable I was.

Shit. I still don't know his name.

I'm not any farther ahead. I still know nothing about him.

"It doesn't matter if he has a girlfriend, Charlie." I had no business hoping for anything, anyway. "I found him, and that's what matters."

"How long are you going to wait for him to call before you call him? We only have the house for a couple more months."

My laugh is brittle as I shrug. "It's in his hands now, Charlie. There's nothing more I can do."

"Well...shit," she says before standing abruptly, pushing her chair halfway across the room. "I think this calls for cookies. Time to bake something. I found a recipe for bacon chocolate chip cookies. I have a good feeling about it."

I sigh. It's been a long night, and it looks like it's about to get longer.

Charlie's instinct is to bake when she's stressed, and if she could ever accomplish it without setting off the smoke detectors, it would be a kind gesture. But she's a hazard in the kitchen, so now I'll have to stay up to make sure she doesn't burn the house down. Or worse, wake up Lincoln with the alarm.

Chapter 4

Feeling Nostalgic

Archer

I STARE AFTER THE woman, a sense of familiarity warming in my chest as she runs past Annabelle and out of the ballroom. Stunned, I slip the thick envelope she gave me into the inside pocket of my suit jacket. That will have to wait until later. Right now, I have something more pressing to deal with.

"What the fuck are you doing here, Annabelle?"

I haven't seen Annabelle since her ill-fated request to Santa. Not that she hasn't tried to see me a few times, but I've always had security escort her from the premises. After she showed her true colors last year, I wanted to keep her as far away from me as possible.

Looks like my good luck has finally run out.

"Aw, baby. Don't be like that," she pouts. When she steps toward me on sky-high stilettos, the slit in her dress shows more leg than most people consider acceptable in polite company. I don't recall her being this thirsty before. Has she changed that much?

"What are you doing here? After what happened last year, I would think my company's Christmas party is the last place you'd want to show your face. How'd you even know where I would be tonight?"

She trails her long manicured fingernails down my arm and a shudder racks my body. I take a step back. This is not the same Annabelle I remember.

She huffs a breath and the scent of vodka wafts past my nose. "Your mother told me where you were. I came to tell you I still love you, and I forgive you." She flutters her eyelashes, the extensions so long and thick I'm pretty sure they make their own breeze. Those are new, too.

"My mother? What the hell are you doing talking to my mother?" And what is my mother doing talking to her? "What do you mean 'you forgive me'? You're the one who cheated on me. What the hell do I need your forgiveness for?"

She sighs and rolls her eyes. "She kept in touch with me after that unfortunate incident last year. But enough about her. Don't you miss me?"

I bark a laugh. "Miss you? You made a sex tape with another man, Annabelle. Why would I miss you? Where is he tonight, anyway? Don't you have some filming to do?"

She pops a hip and crosses her arms in front of her, examining the nails on one hand. "I never meant for you to find out," she whines. "I wanted Santa to help me make sure you never saw the video. But it doesn't matter. I don't even go to that trainer anymore." She drops her arms to her side and fixes me with a sultry stare. "So we can be together again, baby. Isn't that wonderful news?"

"You fucking cheated on me, Annabelle. What on earth makes you think I would take you back?" I take a deep breath, willing myself to calm down. *What the fuck? Is she for real?* I swivel my head, looking for cameras because even on her drunkest day, Annabelle had never been like this. "Okay, but really. Is this a prank? You can't be serious. Where's Ashton?" She glares at me. "You're serious? Oh. Well, then. Yeah." I clear my throat, thanking the powers that be, yet again, for showing me that Annabelle and I were not right for each other. She would have driven me insane within a year. "Annabelle, no. We are never getting back together." The Taylor Swift song plays in my head and I smile.

Would it be too cruel to play it for Annabelle right now? Probably. I pull my phone out of my pocket and open my music player, you know, in case I decide cruelty is the way to go.

"But we were so good together," she whines. "We look amazing in photos."

"No, we really weren't. You were always traveling and we were both too busy with work.. In the six months we were together, we saw each other so infrequently that I wonder how I ever thought we were dating. And who cares about photos? That shit doesn't matter. You're a model, Annabelle. It's literally your job to look good in photos, regardless of who's in them with you. No, I think this worked out for the best."

"Doesn't it matter what I think?" She stamps her foot like a petulant child. "What if I want to get back together?"

I laugh again. If she thinks this is going to work out in her favor, she's delusional.

Fuck. I need a drink.

"What you think stopped mattering to me the minute you hopped into bed with another guy."

She huffs a laugh at me. "Well, it's not my fault you dressed up like Santa Claus. I thought you were one of his official helpers."

I snort a laugh, appreciating the joke until I look at Annabelle and see she's not joking. "Wait. Do you...? Annabelle. You don't think Santa is real, do you?"

She scoffs and rolls her eyes. "No, Archer. I'm not stupid. I said I thought you were a real Santa's Helper. Like a trained Santa impersonator. I couldn't get in touch with my therapist and I thought that a Santa impersonator would be the next best thing. Instead, it was you. I'd never have asked for what I did if I'd known you were in that costume."

I shake my head, still not sure if she believes in Santa, but not really interested in finding out the answer. If she believes there is such a thing as official Santa's Helpers, it's entirely possible she believes in old Saint Nick. I don't care either way, though.

No, the only thing I want to know right now is, who was that woman I was talking to earlier? Her tear-stained face, wild red hair, and wide smile are stuck in my brain.

Her ass in those leggings wasn't bad, either.

"Archer. Are you listening to me?" Annabelle snaps her fingers in front of my face to get my attention. "I said, you can take me out tonight and we'll talk about this."

I scoff. "You can't be serious. I'm not going anywhere with you."

"Look. You're not being rational right now. I get it. You've had a long day. You deserve some time to yourself after hosting this ridiculous party for the...people in your company." She shudders. She never agreed with what I wanted to do for my staff. Annabelle figured they weren't important enough for me to talk to or spend time with, let alone invite to the company Christmas party. I don't know what I ever saw in her. "They're so lucky to have a nice boss like you. Of course, you know you can't afford to throw these parties for them every year. When you go back to the lovely cocktail parties your father used to host, you'll need someone like me on your arm. A powerful man deserves a beautiful woman to help him look good to investors." She reaches out to smooth my tie, but I yank it from her hand and step away. "At least you've dressed appropriately. I'm so glad you skipped the whole Santa thing this year."

I shake my head. She always did care more for appearances than anything else. "I didn't skip it. I changed earlier so I could enjoy the party after I passed out the gifts."

She rolls her eyes again, as though she can't believe how stupid I am. "Well, you're certainly not going to be doing that next year. Throwing them a party is one thing. Spending time with them is another thing altogether. You're better than them, Archer. What will people think if they know you fraternize with your employees? It's weird."

"Says the woman who has her naked ass posted all over the world wide web."

She waves me off. "That's a non-issue. Your mother got me in touch with someone that specializes in wiping things like that from the internet."

There she goes, bringing up my mother again. "What does my mother have to do with this? Why would she care if you're flashing your pussy all over the internet for the world to see?"

She cringes. "Must you speak like that? I told you I didn't mean for you to find out. I said I was sorry. And it's not like I was that recognizable in the video. If people had known it was me, there would have been no stopping its spread. I contained the situation. What more do you want from me before we can move forward?"

What the hell? I want to shake this woman. Why doesn't she get it?

"Annabelle. I want you to listen carefully. We will not be moving forward. Nothing is going to happen between us ever again. Please leave me alone."

She scoffs again, tossing her hair. "Your mother is already planning the engagement party, Archer. Why would she do that if we weren't getting back together?" She holds her hands up. "But okay, I will leave you be for now. Call me when you get yourself sorted out. Don't wait too long, though. It will be a summer wedding and you're going to have to pull strings to get me the venue I want." She spins and flounces out, hair flowing behind her while she puts an extra wiggle into her ass.

My mind races. My mother is planning an engagement party? What the hell is she thinking? She knows I broke up with Annabelle a year ago. I thought I made it plain that it was over for good.

With a resigned sigh, I take one last look around the ballroom, giving Annabelle time to get downstairs and leave the building before I go to the lobby. I step off the elevator in time to catch Eric jogging into the hotel from the main entrance.

"Hey, man. You might not want to leave yet. I just saw Annabelle out there. Looks like she's waiting for her driver or something."

I heave a sigh and rub my hand down my face. "Yeah. She ambushed me. That's why I took so long to come down. Look, I'm going to cancel on you tonight. I'm not in the mood for the club after all. Turns out my mother's been meeting up with Annabelle behind my back. Somehow, they've both gotten it into their heads that I'm going to take Annabelle back and that we'll be getting married soon."

"What? That's ridiculous. Your mom knows there's a video out there of Annabelle fucking some other dude, right? Doesn't that go against her whole make-the-company-look-respectable crusade?"

"She knows. Apparently, she put her in touch with a company that makes that kind of stuff disappear. Annabelle seems to think there's no trace left." I wouldn't know. I didn't watch it when I first found out about it, and I'm certainly not going to look for it now.

"So what now?"

"I need to find out what my mother has to say for herself, I guess. I'm too fucking exhausted to deal with it tonight, though." I tilt my head toward the hotel bar. "Grab a drink with me before you head to the club?"

He nods and slaps me on the shoulder. "Yeah, man. Let's go. I'm buying."

Eric takes the lead and walks into the hotel bar ahead of me, leading me to the counter before pushing me down onto a stool. "Sit."

"Dude, I'm fine. It's not that serious."

"I know. I just like pushing you around." He laughs and signals to the bartender. "And if you're not coming to the club tonight, I need to get my hits in now."

I turn on my stool to face the bar, and a memory floats into my brain. This is the stool I was sitting on last year when the runaway bride stormed up and ordered her tequila. Her puffy white ballgown, elaborately styled hair, and face full of makeup screamed fruity cocktail more than straight tequila, and I couldn't tear my attention away from her after that. I can't help but smile as I remember the way she threw those shots back, like they were nothing more than water.

"Two scotch and sodas, please," I hear Eric.

"Actually," I say, turning back around to face the bartender, "I'll take three shots of tequila and a margarita, please."

"It's your funeral," the guy says as he grabs the tequila from the shelf behind him. "Don't come crying to me when this tequila comes back to visit you later tonight."

Eric raises an eyebrow, and I shrug. "It's nostalgic."

Eric laughs. "I can't wait to hear how nostalgic you feel tomorrow morning."

He's probably right, but I can't bring myself to care about tomorrow morning. For now, I'm going to enjoy my tequila and attempt to remember the best night of my life.

The bartender drops off the drinks and returns to the other end of the bar.

"Bottom's up" I tap my shot glass to Eric's drink before swallowing it back. The liquid burns its way down my throat, making my eyes water. "Fuck," I splutter. "What the hell? That shit's just not good."

So much for nostalgia. How did my runaway bride drink this shit with no reaction? It burns like gasoline all the way down.

Eric laughs and smacks me on the back while I cough. "Want that scotch and soda now?"

I shake my head and force out a raspy, "No, I'm good."

He chuckles into his drink. "Sure you are, buddy."

He's right. I'm not good. I need to get to the bottom of whatever my mother is up to, and the thought of confronting her has me reaching for my next shot. It goes down more smoothly than the last one, and the next is even better. I signal to the bartender for another round.

Before I know what's happening, Eric is pouring me into a cab and sending me home. The next thing I remember is stumbling into the elevator at my building and heading up to the penthouse. In my apartment, I strip, leaving a trail of discarded clothing on the way to my bedroom before dropping face-first into my bed.

I pass out to the nagging thought that there's something else about the redheaded woman that I'm supposed to remember, but the tequila-induced blackness pulls me down before I puzzle out what it is.

Chapter 5

Investigating Santa

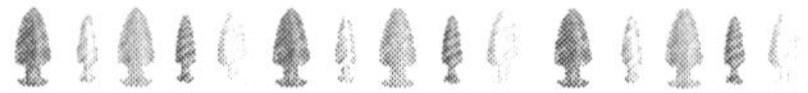

Phoebe

"I still can't believe he didn't recognize you." Charlie sets a giant mug of steaming cappuccino on the table in front of me. After my early wake-up, caused by yet another of her failed attempts at baking, I couldn't care less what I drink as long as it's caffeinated. "No, wait. That's not exactly true. I can believe that." I give her a disbelieving look. "What? Cut that out. You know you look different from the way you did last year. What I can't believe is that after all the trouble you went through to find him, you didn't even introduce yourself. You should have introduced yourself, Phoebe. That's the whole reason you were there. That's the reason we're in Westborough at all."

She has a point. I used to color over my copper hair and slather makeup on to cover my freckles, and the first day I met Lincoln's father was no different. Still, while my hair's longer and redder, and I have a few freckles, and I've undoubtedly gained some weight, it's not like I'm not completely unrecognizable. At least, I wouldn't have thought so before last night. What I don't understand is how he seemed on the verge of recognizing me when his girlfriend walked in.

Like he was about to figure out how he knew me.

But that's just wishful thinking. Maybe I'm not as memorable as I thought.

"Who doesn't recognize you?" Xena, the owner of Bump & Grind, the adorable coffee shop and bakery where Charlie works, asks while pouring a coffee for her friend, Devon.

Every time I pick Charlie up at the end of her shift, Xena and Devon have been here. Xena I can understand, considering she owns the place, but I can't figure out why Devon is always here. He's fun to talk to, though, so I usually sit with him for a few minutes before Charlie and I leave.

"You remember I told you Phoebe moved here to find her baby daddy? Well, she found him, but instead of talking to him and finding out anything about him, she panicked and ran away."

"Charlie," I huff. "That's not what happened." She raises an eyebrow at me. "Well, not exactly." I turn to Xena and explain, "His girlfriend showed up. I didn't want to put him on the spot, so I gave him the letter and information I had prepared and left." Okay, so maybe I left in a hurry, but to say I was running away is putting it a little too strongly. The quick-step, shuffle-walk I did could hardly be called running. Maybe one could consider it a slow jog, but even that's pushing it.

"A girlfriend?" Xena yells, reaching under the counter and pulling out a familiar-looking sword. "Tell me where that bastard is. I do not condone cheating."

Devon steps around the counter and, much to the surprise of the few customers waiting in line, hoists Xena with one massive arm. "That's enough, sweetheart," he says. "You've already had the cops called on you six times this month. You know how your brother gets when he has to come deal with you."

Xena struggles in his grip, kicking her legs in the air. Devon's well over six feet tall, an enormous beast of a man, and Xena is barely five feet, making it look like he's carrying a squirmy kid. Her frantic energy is no match for his calm, controlled demeanor, though, so she cannot free herself. It's ridiculous how cute they are together.

She huffs and stops wiggling, crossing her arms over her chest. "Pshh, what good is having a brother who's a cop if he can't take care of some of silly charges every once in a while? It's a rubber sword, for the love of ducks. It's not like I could do any actual damage."

Devon sets her down and takes her sword, putting it back under the counter. "That's not the point, Princess. You know, he has to put money in the sword jar at the precinct every time they get a call about you. He's single-handedly funded the last five staff events because of you and your sword."

Charlie looks over at me with wide eyes and we both burst out laughing. Imagining Xena, who looks like an innocent little pixie with her slight frame and short, messy blonde hair, threatening random people with her sword, is too hilarious.

"You guys suck," she mumbles, moving over to help the next customer in line. "You better sleep with one eye open, Tiny Dancer," she says to Devon. "I know where you live."

"Looking forward to it, Princess." He chuckles and takes a drink of his coffee. "So, tell me more about this guy. Where'd you finally find him?"

Devon and I take a seat at a nearby table and I spend the next few minutes telling him about my evening. I spare no details regarding the embarrassment of having remnants from Lincoln's dinner all over my shirt when I finally met his dad.

"And you think you won't be able to find him again?"

I sigh, sliding down in my seat. "What are the chances that I could find him anywhere else? The hotel has no further bookings, a fact I had to bribe a bellboy to learn, by the way, and there's only a few days left until Christmas. The best I could hope for would be to track him down at a mall or something."

Charlie yells from the counter, "Again, I would totally go undercover dressed as a kid and force my way to the front of every line to make things go faster."

Xena hops up and down, an excited grin taking up half her tiny face. "Ooh, ooh. Me too! I'm not sure if you've noticed, but I'm also pretty short." She stands back to back with Charlie. "Quick, Tiny Dancer. Who's taller?"

Devon chuckles and shakes his head. "She is, Princess."

Xena's grin turns into a pout. "Not by much, though. It could be her shoes."

Lincoln fusses in the stroller he's been napping in, so I lean over and pick him up, snuggling him against my chest. Charlie comes over to dig a bottle out of the diaper bag, taking it to the kitchen to heat it without even being asked. My heart swells with how much I love her. She really is the best sister and auntie we could ever hope for.

"What makes you think he's a career Santa?" Devon asks. "Aren't those guys usually the ones who look like Santa? You know, chubby old guys with white beards? Unless you're saying Lincoln's dad is a chubby old guy?"

My mouth drops.

It hadn't even occurred to me he might not be a Santa all the time. He had such a high-quality Santa costume, I sort of assumed being Santa was his job. Even when he thought he'd forgotten to give me a bonus check, I thought it was him being a good Santa. Could he work for the company that threw the party? Did he say something about HR cutting me a check?

"What did you say he looked like last night?" Charlie asks, coming back with Lincoln's bottle. "He wasn't in a Santa costume, was he?"

I shake my head, my cheeks heating when I remember the way his suit pants hugged his ass so deliciously. "No. He was wearing a nice three-piece suit. Like, a really nice suit. He looked gorgeous."

Devon raises an eyebrow and takes a drink of his coffee. "And you think his Santa salary is enough for him to afford to buy a nice suit?"

"I mean, maybe?" I groan with the realization that Santa impersonators probably aren't raking it in. "Ugh. Probably not."

Charlie comes back and hands me Lincoln's bottle, pulling out a chair to sit with us. She gets comfortable, then takes Lincoln and his bottle and begins to feed him.

Devon chuckles. "Okay, so he probably isn't a career Santa. Maybe he works for the company? Did you happen to get the name?"

"Uhhh," I stall, trying to force myself to remember something I'm pretty sure I didn't see in the first place. I was running late, so I didn't pay attention to the name on the sign outside. I ran right past it with barely a glance. What did it say? "It's some kind of toy store, I think. The sign had the word Toys on it, at least. I was in a hurry, so I didn't read it properly."

Devon pulls out his phone and starts typing. "Leave it with me. I'll find him." He gets up and walks to the door. "See you later, Princess," he yells to Xena. "I'll talk to you soon, Phoebe. Don't worry. We'll find him."

Xena comes over to the table and picks up Devon's cup.

"He doesn't need to do that," I tell her. "He barely knows me."

She shrugs. "Let him. He's still kicking himself for not finding his buddy's first girlfriend a couple of years ago when they'd bumped into each other and immediately lost contact again. He figures that having police training and working security for a local band means he should also be an amazing private investigator. He's always looking for ways to redeem himself. Trust me, he loves doing this kind of thing. You're doing him a favor by letting him find Lincoln's dad."

I think for a second, finally realizing why Devon looked so familiar the first time I came in here. "Wait a minute. Does he work for Sleeping Dogs?"

Xena nods. "Yeah. How'd you know?"

"I worked for their record company before I had Lincoln. I used to handle social media for them and a bunch of other bands. I saw Devon in the background of some photos. He looks way different when he's not wearing that black suit."

Xena laughs. "No way. That's awesome. I can't wait to tell him. So why aren't you working there anymore?"

I roll my eyes and shrug. "No idea. Someone at the record company decided they didn't need me anymore. I moved back home to live with my parents because of the pregnancy anyway, so I didn't fight it."

"She didn't fight even though our whole family thinks she should have," Charlie says, throwing one of Lincoln's blankets over her shoulder before resting him against it and firmly patting his back. I should have done that last night when I burped him. Then maybe I wouldn't have had puke stains on my shirt when I met his dad. "Those bastards fired her for being pregnant." She spears me with a pointed look. "Which is so wrong."

"Hella wrong." Xena nods in agreement. "You shouldn't have let them get away with it."

"I know, I know." I hold my hands up in surrender. "I should have done something when they let me go. But you remember what it was like for me back then, don't you, Charlie? I had more than enough to worry about without adding taking on a record label for wrongful dismissal to the pile. Plus, they never really blamed it on my pregnancy. There's no proof."

When I found myself pregnant after a one-night stand with Santa Claus, I decided it would be easiest if I moved back home with my parents. When faced with an unplanned pregnancy so soon after I'd walked away from the man I thought I'd be spending the rest of my life with, I wanted to be around family. I had so many things to think about with the drastic turn my life took that worrying over losing a job I was planning to quit anyway wasn't even on my radar. At the time, I was just relieved I'd have one less thing to do. Xena and Charlie are right, though. I shouldn't let them get away with it.

I release a shuddering sigh and reach for Lincoln, wanting to snuggle my baby. "So, what can I do about it now?"

"Yes! I knew you would come around." Charlie jumps up, pumping her fist in victory. "Let me look into some things and we'll figure it out."

I chuckle, dipping my head to nuzzle Lincoln. I'm not sure there's anything that can be done, but I enjoy seeing Charlie happy like this. It's been too long since she's shown this much excitement for anything that wasn't directly related to Lincoln. This last year has been full of heartbreak for both the Fox girls, something I plan to address with Charlie's scumbag ex-boyfriend if I ever get my hands on him.

Xena runs back behind the counter and grabs her sword again. "Yeah!" She yells, thrusting the sword up in the air. "Count me in. I am amazing at revenge."

Oh crap. What have I gotten myself into? How likely is this scheme to end up with someone going to jail?

"Hey, Xena?"

She stops swinging her sword around and turns to look at me. "Yeah?"

"You said your brother's a cop, right?"

"Yeah, why?"

"Just checking."

She laughs. "We have nothing to worry about. He hardly ever arrests me. Plus, for this kind of revenge, I have just the thing. My best friend's husband is a petty revenge specialist."

I snort a laugh. "Oh? I need to know, what do you mean by 'hardly ever'? And what the hell is a petty revenge specialist? I didn't know that was a thing."

"He's only arrested me twice. And our parents gave him so much shit for it, that he's scared to do it again for anything short of murder. And a petty revenge specialist is someone who exacts revenge in non-permanent, mostly irritating ways." She ticks off on her fingers. "Think dick glitter, biodegradable vandalism, and gigantic penis sculptures. Trust me, if we secure his help, there's no way that label won't gain an intimate understanding of what dickheads they've been." Xena cackles a laugh and swings her sword in a sweeping arc one last time before placing it back under the counter. "Now. Who wants a doughnut? I tried a new recipe that I think might end up being my best seller. Peanut Butter S'more." She runs back to the kitchen without waiting for an answer.

"You'll feel better when you give the label a taste of its own medicine," Charlie says, sitting next to me again. "They were wrong to fire you for being pregnant."

I know she's right, but with everything else I've got going on, taking on the label seems like more trouble than it's worth.

The petty revenge idea sounds like something I could get behind, though. I might have to look into that.

Chapter 6

SANTA'S TOY SHOP

Archer

Beep... Beep... Beep... Beep... Beep... Beep... Beep... Beep... The unwelcome sound of my alarm shocks me from a dead sleep, setting my head to throbbing. I throw out an arm, fumbling around on my nightstand for my phone to shut the damn thing off, knocking over the lamp and throwing my wallet onto the floor before I manage to find it. Finally, my fingers land on the smooth face of the phone, but I can't get the alarm to turn off without dragging it over to me and cracking an eye to look at the screen. It flashes with a reminder:

```
Talk to your mother about Annabelle.
```

I groan and squeeze my eyes shut against the bright light of my room. Probably should have closed the curtains before I passed out last night.

I have to get up and go talk to my mother. I set my alarm for eight before I fell into bed last night, thinking I'd have plenty of time to get ready and head out to see her, but that task seems impossible now that a marching band has taken up residence in my head. I'm pretty sure it's a marching band made up of only drums. Huge booming bass drums keeping time that has no real rhythm. That's the only logical explanation for the pounding currently forcing my brain to scrape against the inside of my skull.

Of course, the marching band doesn't explain why the sun seems bright enough to burn a hole through my eyelids. Or why I can smell the old banana peel in the trash from yesterday's breakfast over the smell of the alcohol seeping from my pores. No, the only thing that can explain these things is a raging hangover from what must have been the excessive amount of alcohol I drank last night.

So much for nostalgia. I do not have what it takes to drink substantial amounts of tequila, I guess. Lesson learned.

I roll to the side of my bed, throw my legs over the edge, and fall to my knees, needing to rest my head on the mattress for a moment longer before attempting to stand upright to walk to the bathroom. I need to get moving if I'm going to meet my mother before she heads out for the day. She doesn't work, but she keeps to a strict schedule of shopping, lunching, and gossiping. If I'm not there before ten o'clock, I'll have to track her down when she's with her friends, where she's unlikely to talk to me at all.

After what Annabelle told me yesterday, I think my mother owes me an explanation. And the sooner I get it, the better.

With a deep breath, I heave myself up to my feet, trying to hold my head parallel to the floor in a feeble attempt at keeping the pounding to a minimum. It doesn't work, but somehow I drag my ass into the shower and wash away the stink of last night's tequila, anyway.

The cool water helps, but not much. I still feel like I got hit by a flaming garbage truck. A garbage truck driven by the, at my last count, six shots of tequila and two margaritas I stupidly drank.

While I wash, my mind wanders. Was my bride this hungover last year when she snuck out of my hotel room? Somehow, I doubt it. She doesn't seem like the type to be taken down by something as minor as a hangover. No, she's the type to steal Santa's jacket and then sneak away without a trace.

I chuckle a little, imagining her holding up her wedding dress under the red velvet coat, creeping around the hotel, trying not to be seen. I'm sure her makeup and elaborate hairstyle were a little worse for wear by then, too, if the number of hairpins she'd discarded on the nightstand was any indication. She had so much metal in her hair that she'd have been at risk of being struck by lightning if she were out in a storm. I can only imagine she was quite the sight when she left my room.

Not unlike the way I look now, I'm sure. Finished with my shower and standing in front of my mirror, I wipe the fog away to take in my pasty skin and bloodshot eyes. The throbbing in my head has lessened, but it's not gone entirely. I take it back. There's no way she could have looked anything like this. Even hungover, she would have been beautiful.

Yeah. No more tequila for me.

I lurch back to my room to finish getting ready before heading out to confront my mother. She's going to complain about the jeans and button-down I'm wearing like she always does, but I can't find it in me to care. The woman is likely going behind my back to arrange my wedding to a woman I dumped a year ago, so sue me if her opinion of my clothes is not high on my list of concerns today.

I'm pulling my luxury SUV out of my building's parking garage when my phone rings. I push the hands-free button to answer, Eric's name flashing across the built in display in the dash.

"What do you want, Eric?"

"Hey, man. How're you feeling this morning? Nostalgic?"

Eric's deep laugh spills from the speakers and fills my car, sending another painful throb through my head. Guess that shower didn't help as much as I'd hoped.

"Haha, you're hilarious."

"I know. Listen. I wanted to see if you wanted to meet up with the guys and play some ball. I need to blow off some steam."

"I'm on my way to my parents' house now. Later?"

"Oh, shit. You're really doing that today? I thought you were talking out of your ass last night. Are you in any shape to throw down with Mommy and Daddy Warbucks? You drank a lot last night. Like, a lot, a lot. Your mom is going to have a shit fit as soon as she sees your hungover face."

"I need to catch her before she heads out to meet her friends for their daily shopping-slash-looking down on the poor folk excursion."

"Ah, yes. I wonder if my mother will join them today. She said she's been sad lately and nothing makes her happier than belittling the poor retail workers who need to serve her to make a living. It amazes me how quickly they forgot where they came from."

Eric and I grew up together, but we're not really from the world our parents have been trying to force us into. My parents are what the society types in Westborough like to call "new money", and his parents are the same. The Baxter's shoe empire started bringing in the big money around the time I was ten. My family's toy company took off right around my twelfth birthday, which means it hasn't been much longer than twenty years since my mom had to serve tables at Maggie's diner for grocery money. For a long time, the other rich families worked to keep us out of their inner circle, but our parents chased them so relentlessly that they eventually gave in. Both Eric and I wish they never had. Now it seems that in order to keep in their good graces, our mothers have to be the worst of all of them. It's sad, really, because my mom isn't necessarily a bad person. She just wants to fit in.

I have a strong sense that this whole Annabelle scheme is something my mother thinks she needs to do in order to look good to her so-called friends. She's always trying to compensate for our money coming from somewhere other than oil and long-dead ancestors by attempting to make us look *respectable* in the eyes of Westborough high society. Never mind that I'm positive the toys we sell are in ninety-nine percent of those other families' homes, more than likely several times over.

Fade Toys is a household name, after all.

"I'm sure she will be. They're never far from each other."

"True enough. When there's a dumb plan afoot, you can bet our mothers are in it together. Which begs the question: does my mom know what's going on with this Annabelle situation?"

"Even if she does, there's nothing they can do about it without my participation. And if there's one thing I know, it's that I'm not marrying Annabelle, regardless of who is planning the whole thing. Listen, I'm almost at my parents' place. I'll call you later to let you know how it goes."

I hang up as I pull onto the road that leads to the richest neighborhood in Westborough, deliberately slowing down for the rest of the drive, because I don't actually want to deal with this situation. They had a house built out here a few years back and they've been trying to sell it ever since. Some famous musician already lived out here in his ultra-modern mansion and my mom has the misguided notion that living so close to someone like that is unseemly. There was a commotion not long after they moved in where an obsessed fan attacked the guy in his home and the media attention that followed was too much for my parents. They worried the scandal would bring down property values. What I'm sure they don't realize is that he no doubt has way more money than we ever will. He's famous enough that having him in the neighborhood increases property values.

I pull up to the gate at the end of my parents' driveway and key in the code on the control panel. The garish golden gate swings open silently and I creep my car inside. The house looms as I get closer and a sense of dread fills me. This house is so different from the one we lived in when I was a kid. At least back then, it felt like a home. Now they have an enormous house reminiscent of the one in that old movie *Addams Family Values.* You know, the one Debbie forces Fester to move to after he refuses to die on their honeymoon. Yeah, my parents are the Debbie Jelinsky of Westborough. I refuse to stay here long, so I drive around the ridiculous fountain in the center of the drive and park in front of the house. With a deep breath to fortify myself against whatever crap I'm about to face, I step out of my car and walk to the door. As I raise my hand to knock, it swings open, revealing my mother on the other side.

"Archer, my beautiful boy." She holds her arms out to me and thrusts her cheek out. "I've missed you."

"Mother," I say, bending to kiss her. "I see you were expecting me."

I didn't tell her to expect me, so it's interesting that she's here at the door waiting for me to arrive.

"Oh, yes. I spoke to Annabelle this morning, and she told me you might stop by." She smiles sweetly, like she didn't just let it slip that she's been conspiring with my ex.

My features harden at the mention of Annabelle. Despite her being the whole reason I'm here, hearing her name out of my mother's mouth makes me tense. "Annabelle? Would you mind telling me why exactly you're still talking to Annabelle a year after we broke up?"

She waves me off and walks back into the house, her heels clicking on the marble tile. "You're right on time for a quick breakfast before I'm off to meet the girls. Come. Your father is already waiting on the terrace."

I roll my eyes at her use of the word *terrace.* She's even changed her speech habits throughout the years she's spent trying to fit in. I never could figure out what exactly was wrong with the word porch. It's always seemed plenty fancy to me.

"Hey, Dad." I seat myself across the table from him and pour a cup of coffee from the thermal carafe in front of me. "What have you been up to?"

Dad's always had different ideas about fitting in than my mother, but he's always gone along with her plans. In my younger years, Mom's schemes would have me playing nice with the entitled assholes. Now, it seems she wants me to marry one. If there's one thing I regret, it's dating the daughter of someone my parents have spent years trying to impress. I should have known my mother would get something like this in her head.

"Oh, you know. The usual. Golf. Taking your mother to dinner. Trying to keep Fade Toys away from scandal."

"Always so dramatic, Dad," I say, rolling my eyes. "There's no scandal. Fade Toys is as well-respected now as ever. More so, since the staff is all properly compensated and happy to be working for us."

My father huffs. "In my day, people were happy to even have jobs. If they needed more money, they would pull themselves up by their bootstraps and get a second job instead of expecting the first job to fund their extravagant lifestyles."

"Their extrav—Do you even hear yourself? Since when is having a roof over your head and food on the table extravagant? Jesus, Dad." I rub my temples, as my hangover headache comes roaring back in full force. Just as I was feeling better, too, damn it. "What happened to you? Why are you like this?"

I don't expect him to answer, and he doesn't disappoint. He's never been able to back up his ridiculous claims, and he's learned it's better not to try.

"Right." I take a sip of my coffee and turn to my mother. "Well. I suppose you're wondering why I'm here?"

She takes her time adding butter to an English muffin, not taking her eyes off me. She takes a small bite, chews, swallows, then wipes her mouth with a cloth napkin before finally speaking. "No, I know why you're here."

I raise my eyebrows, waiting for clarification. "And? Do you care to explain yourself?"

"Explain what, my dear? You were going to propose to Annabelle a year ago. It makes sense for you to get back together now. You two look so lovely standing side by side. I don't care for the false lashes and gaudy fingernails she's been fond of lately, but there's no denying she's still a beautiful woman."

"Mom! She cheated on me, filmed it, and the video got posted online. Then she got drunk and asked Santa to help destroy the evidence. It was me dressed as Santa Claus, mom. She asked me!"

"Pssh," she scoffs, waving her hand. "That's been taken care of. There's no trace of that video. Besides, none of that would have happened if you hadn't canceled the traditional Fade Toys party to play dress up as Santa Claus. I don't think it's fair to place all the blame on Annabelle, do you? But that's all in the past. Now you can marry her and be part of a respectable couple. It doesn't look good for the business to be run by a single man in his thirties. Fade Toys and family values go hand in hand. Maintaining a good public image is essential to our continued success in the community. In our business, you can't be too careful."

"You're not making any sense. What does me marrying Annabelle have to do with any of this?"

"Your father and I have worked too hard to maintain the respectable, professional image of Fade Toys to allow you to destroy it by remaining a bachelor for the rest of your life. What will our customers think?"

I let out a humorless laugh. "What on earth makes you think our customers care about that? They're buying sex toys, Mom. I don't think they give a shit about whether or not I'm married."

"Okay, fine. Maybe the customers don't care," she admits. "But our friends do. They already look down on our business. At least having it run by a married man gives it"—she waves her hand—"oh, I don't know, a hint of respectability. If I'd known you'd be this stubborn about it, I would have had Annabelle trick you into getting her pregnant last year when she came to me for help with the videotape."

"I'm sorry, you would have what?" I ask incredulously. Did I hear that correctly? My mother wanted Annabelle to trick me into getting her pregnant? "Tell me you're kidding."

The way my mother ignores my question and continues speaking leads me to believe she's lying, which is a lot more likely than Annabelle wanting to get pregnant. As a model, her body is her livelihood. The only thing she ever worked hard at was keeping her body in shape for work. I doubt she'd want to risk that to be tied to the likes of me. I'm not *that* rich.

Her face reddens, and I can tell she's getting frustrated. I almost feel sorry for her. Almost. "A child born out of wedlock to a beautiful couple is much more respectable than an eternal bachelor who...who...bangs his way through the female population of Westborough."

I bark a laugh. "Is that what you think I do? Jesus, mom. That's not who I am."

Her eyes slide to my father and back to me. "I know what men are like, Archer. But as long as you get married and keep your...exploits private, I don't care. Get married. That's all I ask."

I get up and stand next to the table. "Well, I hate to break it to you, Mom, but I won't be marrying Annabelle. I don't know why I ever thought about proposing to her. We never loved each other. Hell, the more I think about it, the more I realize we barely even liked each other. I won't marry someone just because she's beautiful, and you think she'll make our family look good. And in case you weren't aware, marrying someone who cheated on me probably wouldn't look that great."

"You say that now, son. But I know you'll change your mind once you realize what's at stake." My father doesn't look up from his paper to issue his warning. "Don't worry your pretty little head about it, darling," he consoles my mother. "He'll come around. I'll make sure of it."

Fuck this. I'm not wasting any more time talking to these two. They're obviously delusional if they still think they can convince me to marry Annabelle.

And they're even more delusional if they think marrying a cheater will make our business look more respectable to anyone.

Chapter 7

Old Friends and New Headbutts

Phoebe

"COMING!" I YELL TOWARD the front door as I dry my hands on a towel. I was in the kitchen washing Lincoln's bottles when the doorbell rang. And rang. And rang again. "Be right there."

I throw the door open to find a beautiful woman in a vintage Rolling Stones t-shirt cinched at the waist by a skintight leather pencil skirt. *Even after having a baby, she still looks like a pin-up model.* A pissed-off pin-up model if the way she's tapping the toe of her six-inch heels means anything. Next to her is a dark-haired, tattooed, bad-boy rocker of a man carrying a squirmy toddler in one arm and a large green diaper bag on the other.

"Denise. Good to see you." I narrow my eyes at them, curious why they're standing on my doorstep looking mad. "How do you know where I live?"

"Phoebe. You remember Ryder, right?" Than man behind her tips his head in greeting. Denise breezes past me, walking directly into the living room, and arranging herself primly on the couch. "Xena and Devon mentioned you. I didn't think there were too many Phoebe Fox's kicking around. I love the hair, by the way. You should have gone with your natural color ages ago. Why didn't you tell me the label fired you? Also, why didn't you call me when you came back to town?"

I sigh and follow her to the couch, readying myself for what sounds like it's fixing up to be a fine lecture.

Denise was one of the best people I knew in the entertainment industry, but she was also tough as nails. As the manager of one of the more popular bands I worked with, she liked to keep in contact with me for everything, taking care to keep me informed of all the band's comings and goings so I'd have good stuff to post and promote online. The pictures she sent after every show were the best candids I'd ever used. I've always liked her.

But I never considered us more than work acquaintances. When I left town, I simply told her I would be moving back home to be near my family and she wished me luck. I never would have guessed she'd be upset if I didn't call her when I came back to Westborough.

"Okay, first off, babe. We're not here to bombard Phoebe with questions about her old job. We're here to visit with her and to meet the baby. And second," he says, turning to face me, "yeah, why didn't you call Denise and tell her? You should see the shit the new social media person is posting. It's worse than tabloid trash."

I grimace. Of all the guys in the band, Ryder had the worst reputation before he married Denise. Thinking of ways to spin his exploits into funny anecdotes and delightful banter was almost a full-time job all on its own. Almost like bailing him out of jail could have been Denise's full-time job before he came to terms with how in love with her he was and settled down. If he's saying the label's been handling social media poorly, then you know something's really wrong.

Denise waves him off. "He's right, but it's merely one more thing the label's been doing to piss us all off. Can you believe they want to stage some scandals to draw more attention to the guys? As if any of them would agree to fake an affair for the tabloids. Not anymore, anyway." She pins Ryder with a pointed glare before turning back to me. "It's ridiculous."

"But not unheard of. It's the music industry. *Sex, drugs, and rock n' roll, baby*. They do that shit because they know it will sell records. People love a scandal." I never enjoyed using that method, despite some of my colleagues swearing by it. I preferred to paint the bands in a more favorable light, as much as that was possible with a bunch of guys in the music industry. Because, let's be real, some of them come by their tabloid coverage honestly.

Denise nods in agreement. She's been around long enough to know how frequently it comes up. It's actually a pretty common tactic used by media managers. Nothing says "look at me" more than an illicit affair. It also encourages the illusion of availability that some labels insist is necessary to attract female fans. As though women don't like music if they can't imagine themselves in a relationship with someone in the band.

"We're too old for that shit," Ryder says. "We all have wives and kids. We want to make the music, but we don't want the drama anymore. Isn't that right, baby?" He leans over and kisses Denise on the head. She looks up at him with a dreamy smile. "Hell, we're all pushing forty. Aiden's already there."

Aiden plays drums for Sleeping Dogs and he's the oldest member of the band. If memory serves, he got married this last year. In fact, in the year since the label fired me, I think all the guys in the band have gotten married. Not that I found any decent social media coverage about any of them. I saw some blurry tabloid photos of a Vegas wedding for one of them and relied on the rumor mill for the rest of my information. I'm sure you can guess how much I trusted that source.

"Have a seat, Ryder. I'll get us some coffee and we can chat." I leave my guests in the living room and head to the kitchen to make some coffee. I've got the pot started brewing when I hear a commotion from the other room.

"Holy shit, you're Ryder Sullivan." It's Gavin's voice, squeaking as it hasn't done since he started puberty, chased by a brief cry from Lincoln. "Ryder Sullivan is in my sister's living room. Ryder Sullivan is sitting on the sexy blue couch. I'm so going to it marry that thing now. Let Phoebe try and stop me."

I can hear Ryder and Denise chuckle.

"It's good to meet you. Why don't you take a seat, man?" Ryder says. "Stay here and keep us company while your sister gets coffee."

Gavin makes some sort of noise before the murmur of conversation continues at a lower volume. Ryder always seemed to be the most personable member of the band and the way he's engaging with my brother proves it. I finish with the coffee, load the carafe, cups, and cream and sugar onto a tray, and make my way back to the living room where I find Ryder standing with Lincoln in his arms. Gavin is sitting on the couch with the squirmy toddler holding his hands and standing on his legs.

"They traded," Denise tells me with a chuckle. "Your brother loves babies almost as much as Ryder does."

I laugh, setting the tray on the coffee table and taking a seat on the couch. "He surprised me when I had Lincoln. I wasn't aware how much he loved babies before that. He's a teenage boy. How many teenage boys do you know that love babies?"

"Hey," Gavin protests. "None of that. You know toxic masculinity has no place here. Lots of guys love babies. Not all guys are comfortable saying anything about it, that's all."

"He's right," Ryder says, lowering his head and inhaling the sweet baby scent of Lincoln. "When a man says he loves babies, there's always a possibility someone is going to think there's something...weird about him. Women love it, of course, but men can be dicks about it. It's obviously complete bullshit, but it can be hard for us enlightened men sometimes." He chuckles. "Good thing I don't give a fuck what people think. I love babies and kids. They're awesome." He bends and sniffs Lincoln's head again. "Especially that new baby smell. I can't get enough of it." He looks at Denise and wiggles his eyebrows.

"Forget it," she says with a laugh. "I'm not having another baby just so you can smell to your heart's content."

"It's science, babe," Ryder pouts. "Babies have an addictive smell that triggers the dopamine pathways in the brain to light up. I can't help myself."

I laugh. "Well, Lincoln might smell pleasant right now, but before Gavin brought him in here, he'd shit himself from top to tail so badly he needed a bath. The smell coming off him was anything but addictive, let me tell you."

Denise bursts out laughing and looks at Gavin. "And you took care of that? Damn, kid. You *are* a good uncle."

"No kidding," Ryder adds. "Our little Cole there was the blowout champion and no one ever stepped up to take care of it. Never mind my brother, I've known the guys in the band for twenty years and they never even offered."

"That settles it, then. I am officially the best uncle." Gavin looks at me. "Told you." He turns back to the raven-haired little girl who's squeezing his hands while standing on his legs. "I'm sorry you've had such crappy uncles, kiddo. But you know me now, so all is not lost. I can fill in when necessary."

Cole giggles a little toddler laugh and abruptly headbutts my brother in the face, a loud crunch sounding on impact. I snort a laugh before I can stop myself.

"Cole!" Denise scolds. "Not again, sweetie. How many times do I have to tell you, we don't headbutt our friends?"

"Ow, shit," Gavin groans. "What's your head made of, kiddo? Rocks?"

Ryder laughs and passes me Lincoln so he can lift Cole off of Gavin. "Sorry, dude. I forgot to warn you to watch out for that. She comes to the gym with me when I teach self-defense, and so far that's her only move."

"I can see why she sticks with it." Gavin pinches his nose and wiggles it, grimacing. "It's very effective," he says, sounding stuffed up. "I think I better get some ice."

"Sorry about that," Ryder says. "The good news is, you've clinched that best uncle spot for sure now. She rocked you and you didn't even drop her."

"See?" Gavin says, that nasal tone still in his voice. "I knew I was the best uncle."

I chuckle. "I never doubted you for a second."

He laughs, then groans and holds his nose again. "It was nice to meet you guys," he tells Denise and Ryder. "And especially you, kiddo." He reaches out and shakes Cole's hand. "Even if you did try to break my nose."

Cole giggles and buries her face into Ryder's neck.

"So, now that we've assaulted your brother, we should get down to what we're really here for." Denise grabs a coffee mug and takes a sip, raising an eyebrow at me. "I have a proposition for you."

"Aww, babe. You said we were coming to see the baby."

Denise makes a tsking noise. "And we saw the baby. He's right there," she says, pointing at Lincoln in my arms. "You can still see him now."

I snicker.

"How about you get some toys out and play with the babies while I talk to Phoebe about this brilliant idea I have?"

Ryder smiles and bends to kiss his wife. "Yes, dear." He turns to look at me. "Is it alright with you if I take them out to the porch to play? It's the perfect time of day for them to get some fresh air."

Lincoln loves being outside, so I immediately agree, getting up to gather his outdoor clothes and a blanket to spread out for him to lie on. Ryder takes over, insisting he can get everything ready and sending me back to the living room to talk to Denise.

"He's a wonderful dad," Denise tells me with a smile. "I really lucked out."

"Is Cole's biological father involved at all?" When she got pregnant with Cole, Denise had been involved with someone other than Ryder. When she dumped him and started seeing Ryder, he snapped and attempted to hold Ryder's Gran and her friend hostage to get revenge. The guy turned out to not be a match for two little old ladies, and they wound up catching the guy and tying him up before the police arrived. According to the news reports, Ryder's Gran and her friend became heroes at their nursing home after the ordeal.

She chuckles. "No. He disappeared after spending some time in jail. Thank god."

"Well then, good riddance to bad rubbish."

Denise barks a surprised laugh. "Definitely," she says, before picking up her coffee again. "Alright. Let's get to it then. I want to hire you to take care of all the band's social media. The label is fucking it up and not listening to us when we say we want to go in a different direction. Thankfully, their contract is up soon and they'll be going independent, possibly creating their own label, so this is the perfect time to bring you on board. What do you say?"

Shit. That sounds fantastic, and I'd love to say yes, but there's one thing holding me back. "I'm only here until the end of February," I blurt with a grimace. "So I'm probably not the best person for the job."

Denise grins broadly. "We can work around that," she says, reaching over to shake my hand. "Welcome to the Sleeping Dogs family."

Chapter 8

Santa Gets Some News

Archer

WELL.

That was a complete shitshow.

I left my parents' house with no assurances that my mother would drop her ridiculous plan for me to marry Annabelle. She's too attached to her idea of respectability for the company, as though my being married would change anyone's opinions about our sex toy factory.

Ring on my finger or not, we still make dildos, vibrators, butt plugs, and all the other toys that uptight society folks act like they're too good for. Never mind that they have some of our offerings in their bedrooms. And if they don't, they know someone who does.

I don't know why it's so hard for people to understand that toys in the bedroom are your teammates, not your enemies. If you can use something to help your partner achieve greater pleasure than you can provide alone, why wouldn't you? Seems to me like only a selfish, insecure man would deny his partner more orgasms simply because his ego can't take the assist.

I get pretty worked up thinking about how selfish some people are, and by the time I get home, the tension is bunching in my shoulders and there's an ache in my jaw from grinding my teeth. The hangover headache from this morning is once again pounding in my temples, reminding me of last night's poor decisions, and forcing me to squint my eyes against the light. Against the light, but unfortunately also against the trail of clothes still left lying on the floor directly in my path.

Before I've taken three steps into my penthouse, I stumble on last night's shoes, trip over my discarded pants, and perform a clumsy somersault before coming to rest face-down on my jacket. That's sounds a lot more graceful than it is. Really, I trip over my clothes and land on my face. More specifically, I smash face first into some sort of thick padding inside my jacket.

Ouch.

That fucking hurt. But it probably could have been a lot worse. What do I have to thank for saving my face?

Rolling over, I groan and pull myself into a sitting position, dragging my jacket to me and reaching into the inside pocket for the mystery item that cushioned my fall. I pull out a thick white envelope and turn it over in my hands. There's no address, name, or any sign of what could be inside. Whatever's inside has been stuffed so tightly into the letter-sized envelope there's no way I'll be able to remove it without ripping it open. A fuzzy memory pops of me absentmindedly grabbing the envelope from a red-haired woman right after Annabelle ruined my evening pops into my head. Frantically, I rip it open and unfold the contents. I'm left holding a stack of paper and right on top is a letter addressed *"To whom it may concern,"*.

"I'm sorry. I don't know your name or I would have addressed this to you directly. If you have this letter, it means I chickened out and didn't tell you in person. This is so hard for me to write, but I have to do it because it's the right thing to do. So here

GOES NOTHING. I'M NOT SURE IF YOU REMEMBER ME, BUT WE SPENT A NIGHT TOGETHER A YEAR AGO."

Wait a minute.

No.

She must be mistaken. The only person I've been with in over a year is the runaway bride, and she looked nothing like this woman.

Are you sure about that? There was something about her you couldn't put your finger on, remember?

I thought the woman from last night was just a new hire who got missed when I handed out the bonuses. Wasn't she? I close my eyes and try to recall every detail of the runaway bride from the best night of my life and compare it to what I remember about the redhead from last night. On the surface, they are complete opposites. The bride had been a fully made-up brunette wearing a huge white ball gown, whereas the woman at the party was a freckle-faced redhead wearing a stained hooded sweatshirt. But something about the tilt of the redhead's lips when she smiled seems familiar. That, and the way her hips swayed when she walked away.

She looked familiar, but I assumed I'd seen her at work when she interviewed for the position or filling out paperwork. I thought she was an employee. Thinking back on it, though, did she even confirm that when I asked her?

Fuck.

Can it really be?

Is the reason she looked familiar...because she gave me the best night of my life?

I flip through every blurry memory I have from that night, forcing myself to focus on my runaway bride's smile. We laughed so much that night, it burned her smile into my brain. The redhead from last night was wearing the same smile. At least, she was before Annabelle came and ruined everything.

Holy shit.

It's her.

I can see it so clearly now. Despite the difference in hair color and the abundance of freckles on her face, she looks the same. Same heart-shaped face, same lush mouth, same button nose. If only I'd had more time to look in her eyes, or if I'd heard her laugh last night, I would never have assumed she was an employee. I would have known she was my runaway Bride.

She's been looking for me? But then...why didn't she just tell me who she was?

I groan. She must think I'm such an asshole for not recognizing her. No wonder she gave me the letter instead of telling me why she was there.

"My name is Phoebe Fox,"

Phoebe Fox. That's an adorable name. It suits her much better than *Bride* does. Even if she was an especially beautiful bride.

"and we met at the bar in the Hotel Westborough on what should have been my wedding night. You might recall I was wearing a wedding dress?"

I chuckle. Yeah, I definitely remember the dress. It was huge and puffy and had approximately a million layers of fluffy material. I'm not positive, but I have a fuzzy memory of helping her hold it so she could go to the bathroom. Not something one would normally do with a one-night stand, I'm sure, but that night it seemed normal for me to help her with whatever she needed.

"You were in a Santa Claus suit and I'm guessing you'd just finished working for the evening at one of the parties held at the hotel that evening. We sat together and had several drinks before leaving the bar. The rest of the evening is a little spotty (probably thanks to the many excellent margaritas I drank), but I remember at the end of it all, we went to your hotel room and we slept together."

I grin. *Yes, we did.* Several times, in fact. I can't wipe the grin from my face. Fuck, that was a great night.

"I left early the next morning while you were still asleep, and I'm sure you noticed I took your jacket. Sorry about that. I couldn't exactly wander around the hotel in a half-buttoned wedding dress, and wasn't ready to be arrested for attempting to do it in only my underwear. I still have it if you need it back. I had it dry-cleaned and everything."

I knew it! Initially, I had briefly entertained the notion that I simply lost the jacket, but the idea of the runaway bride taking it just felt right. I can't remember much, but I have a strange recollection of it taking a lot of work to get her out of that dress. How on earth would she get it back on by herself? I also recall all that work being so worth it, but that's beside the point. I can't imagine she'd have wanted to put it back on by herself in the morning. So yeah, her taking the jacket made sense. I can't blame her for not wanting to wander around in her underwear.

Jealousy burns in my chest at the mere thought of anyone seeing her half naked. Which is ridiculous, right? I have no right to be jealous of someone else seeing her in her underwear. Except I almost feel like I should be the only one seeing her in that state of undress. But that's absurd. It was one night.

And yet... I physically shake myself free of that line of thought and turn my attention back to the letter.

"But that's not the reason I'm writing this letter. I thought about you a few times after I left that morning, but I had so much going on with my relationship ending that I didn't have the time, or the energy, if I'm being honest, to do anything about it. I'm not sure you would have wanted me to, anyway. If not for the positive pregnancy test I got six weeks later, I doubt I would have tried to track you down at all, regardless of how much fun I had that night. I'm sure you can imagine my surprise when I discovered Santa Claus had knocked me up."

What? Wait a minute. That doesn't say what I think it does, does it?

"You can imagine my surprise when I discovered Santa Claus had knocked me up."

I let the stack of papers fall from my fingers and lower myself to the floor in a daze. A positive pregnancy test led her to find me. She said Santa Claus had knocked her up.

I was Santa Claus.

I knocked her up.

A hysterical laugh creeps its way up the back of my throat and I force myself to swallow it down.

I have a kid? I got a woman pregnant when I didn't even know her name. The laughter bubbles up, threatening to take over as I wonder what my mother's society friends would think about that. Would my mother think this more or less respectable than marrying a cheater?

I take my phone out of my pocket and type up a message as an edge of panic colors my laughter. I need reinforcements.

Archer

I have news. Come over. Bring alcohol.

Eric

Uh, okay? What kind of alcohol?

Archer

Any kind. And lots of it.

Scratch that. Anything but tequila. Bring tequila and you're getting dick-punched.

Chapter 9

WAIT. WHO GOT SANTA PREGNANT?

Archer

"OKAY, I CAME AS fast as I could." Eric closes the door behind him only to find me sitting on the floor, the papers exactly where I dropped them after I read about the baby. "What's your problem? Why are you on the floor?"

I haven't moved from this spot since I read the letter. After I messaged Eric, I continued to laugh hysterically in startling surges until I finally got myself under control a few minutes ago. By then exhaustion weighed so heavily on me I couldn't be bothered to even think about moving, so I stayed on the floor. Now that Eric is here with alcohol, I find the motivation to get up. I grunt and force myself off the floor, bringing my jacket but leaving the letter. "So, it turns out my mom really is trying to get me to marry Annabelle."

Eric's face darkens. He walks to the kitchen area of my open-concept penthouse and places three bottles on the counter. All whiskey, by the looks of it. Thank god for that. I'm not sure I'll ever be able to stomach tequila again, not after last night. "What the fuck?"

I shrug, trudging behind him to the kitchen. "It doesn't even matter. I have bigger things to worry about now."

He looks at me with his eyebrows drawn. "Worse than your mother trying to make you marry Annabelle?"

I sigh and shake my head. "Yes. Worse than that. Or…maybe not? I don't know."

Still confused, he looks around. "What could be worse, or not, than that?" he asks, mirroring my confusion with his choice of words.

I gesture at the papers on the floor in the entryway. "See for yourself."

He does a double take, then walks over to gather up the papers and holds them at his side. "What is this about, Archer? Are you okay?"

"I found her. I found the bride." I mutter, grabbing a bottle and removing the cap.

Eric makes a choking noise deep in his throat. "What the fuck, dude! Way to bury the lede. Who the fuck cares about your mom and Annabelle's bullshit? Tell me about your bride. What did the wedding dress look like this time?" He comes back to the kitchen and sets the papers on the counter, going around the other side of the island to grab a glass from the cupboard. Suddenly, his hands freeze and he fixes me with a stare. "Wait. What the hell are you doing here with me if you found her?"

I nod at the stack of papers and take a drink from the bottle in my hands. "Read that."

While Eric reads, I take myself to the living room and drop onto my couch. Thoughts are still swirling through my mind. I have a kid? I can't believe it. We used protection, didn't we? I think back, trying to recall what my hotel room looked like that morning. I'm positive I saw condom wrappers next to the mess of hair pins she'd left on the nightstand.

So what, then? Why wait this long to find me? Was it so she could find me at a Christmas party? What the fuck am I going to do?

More importantly, when do I get to meet my kid? Because despite the strangeness of the situation, nothing could stop me from being involved in my kid's life.

When Annabelle betrayed me last year, I gave up on the idea of having a family. After her, I pushed the idea of having children to the back of my mind. But now I have another chance. I can't be with this Phoebe woman, obviously. That would be crazy. We don't even know each other. But I want to be involved in my kid's life. No, I *will* be involved in my kid's life. Should I call a lawyer?

"Shit, man." Eric comes and sits next to me on the couch, the stack of papers in one hand and a glass of amber liquid in the other. "You have a kid."

I chuckle and take a long drink from my bottle. Whiskey, my usual drink. No more tequila for me. That shit is bad news. "Yeah. I got that."

"How much did you read?" he asks.

"I only got as far as *knocked up by Santa*. After that, I stopped reading and messaged you."

"Listen to this," he says.

Eric reads the letter, starting with *To Whom it May Concern,* and not stopping until he gets to the part where it reads *"His name is Lincoln and I'd love for him to get the chance to know you."*

"Wait, stop. What?" I rub my eyes, like that will help me hear better. "What's Lincoln?"

"Dude, were you even listening?"

Truthfully, I'm having a hard time concentrating. Maybe it's time to slow down on the drinks. I thought I'd fully recovered from last night before I started drinking again, but now I'm not so sure. "I think I missed a part in the middle."

"Lincoln is the baby. She's saying you have a son."

"A son? I have a son?"

He waves the letter at me. "According to this letter, you do."

"Lincoln," I whisper. "I like that name."

"Here," he says, passing me something. "This fell out of the stack of papers."

A picture of a newborn baby in a hospital bassinet stares at me from my hands and my heart stops.

"He's cute," Eric says. "You know, as far as babies go."

I laugh thickly, an unfamiliar stinging in my eyes. "They look a little odd when they're this small, don't they?"

"So, when are you going to see her again?" Eric asks, putting the papers on the coffee table.

"I don't know. I have a lot on my mind right now."

Eric barks a laugh. "I think this might have to take priority."

I nod and take another deep drink, the bottle feeling oddly light. "Did I tell you what my mom said?" So much has happened since last night when Eric sent me home soaked in tequila that I can't remember what he already knows. "About wanting me to get married, so Fade Toys appears more respectable?"

He takes the bottle from me and refills his drink. Ahh, that must be why it felt so much lighter. Either that or I'm drinking more than I thought.

"You mentioned she was conspiring with Annabelle to get you married. Is that why? She's ashamed of the Fade sex toy empire?" He laughs. "I don't know why she would be. Most of the women I've been with have had your toys in their nightstands. You make a quality product."

I shake my head. Eric is exactly the kind of guy my mom accused me of being. I bet he's already banged his way through the entire population of women between the ages of twenty and fifty in Westborough, or at least close to it. "She'd be happier if we had your family's shoe empire, I'm sure. I don't think the other rich ladies have as much of an issue with someone who makes sneakers as they do with someone who makes dildos and butt plugs."

"Which is hilarious, considering they all act like they have something up their asses." He chuckles. "You think they'd be happy to have the hook-up to replace the uncomfortable sticks with well-made, high-quality butt plugs."

I shake my head, my brain sloshing with the movement. "Jesus, man."

"What? You know I'm right." He chuckles. "Those women are so uptight they ought to run to buy your toys instead of turning their noses up at them. I bet they'd be a lot happier if they had more orgasms."

The bottle is back in my hand, and I take another big drink. "Wanting me to get married isn't even the worst part," I say, yet another slug of the warming liquid finding its way into my mouth. "My mother said Annabelle wanted to get me pregnant..." I shake my head again, ignoring the sloshing. "No, that's not right. They'd discussed having me get Annabelle pregnant after the sex tape fiasco, but ultimately decided against it. I could have been stuck with her for my whole life. If that story is even true. I still don't think Annabelle would ruin her career to trap me."

"What the fuck?" Eric says. "They did what? Shit, man. Your mother is way too involved in the details of your life."

I sigh. "You're telling me."

We sit on the couch, staring at nothing for several minutes, before Eric asks. "Do you think that's what's happening with this Phoebe woman?"

I turn slowly. My vision blurs, leaving the details of Eric's face nearly indistinguishable. "Is what happening?"

"Is she trying to trap you? Get you for your money?"

Shit. Is that what she's doing?

Who does she think she is?

Eric bolts forward and grabs the letter, flipping through it. "What if it's not even your kid? Didn't you say some guy left her at the altar? What if it's his baby? It would make more sense for it to be her ex-fiancé's baby, wouldn't it? More than some random one-night stand, anyway. Maybe she just wants to say it's yours so she doesn't have to stay in contact with the man who dumped her on her wedding day? There's no mention of money in this letter. That might mean nothing, though. She could still be looking for a payday."

I jolt upright, fighting through the swimming sensation that rolls through my brain, and put the nearly empty bottle on the coffee table. "You're right. I won't let her do this without a fight." I stand up, swaying a little before patting my chest and pockets. "Where's my phone?"

"Wait," Eric says, standing and putting his hand on my shoulder. "Hold on a second. Let's think this through. You're beyond drunk, Archer. You're not thinking straight. I'm probably mistaken. Why don't you sober up before you talk to her?"

I find my phone in my back pocket. "I'm plenty sober enough to make this phone call. She needs to know this plan of hers won't work."

Eric drops the letter to the table and throws his hands up. "I was speculating. I'm not saying this is her plan. It's a possibility to consider. When. You're. Sober." He punctuates the last three words with a poke to my chest.

I grab the letter from the top of the stack of papers and locate her phone number. "I'm sober enough. I'm calling now." I put the number in and press the call button while Eric shakes his head at me. "It's fine, man. I know what I'm doing."

Chapter 10

That's It. You're Going On The Naughty List

Phoebe

"No. fucking. way. What an asshole." Charlie stabs at the end button on my phone and passes it back to me. "Who the hell does he think he is? How dare he say those things to you?"

After a sleepless night, thanks to a baby who wouldn't settle and a brain that wouldn't either, I woke up to a voicemail from the man I gave my letter to. A pretty shitty message, all things considered, and Charlie's just finished listening to it.

I listened to it so many times this morning that I know it by heart.

"Listen here, you, you, you not-very-nice lady. You can't trick me. How do I even know this baby is mine? Maybe it's your ex-fiancé's? Hmmm? Did you ever think of that? Yeah, I thought so. So you found yourself pregnant and alone and figured you'd hit me up for money. Or did you find yourself alone and decide to get me pregnant? Huh? Is that it? Poor bride, all alone. Oh, here's an innocent Santa. I'm going to sleep with him and get

him pregnant? No, wait. That's not right. Get you pregnant? Get pregnant? Whatever. I don't think so, lady. Someone else tried that, and it didn't work and it won't work for you either. No way. I don't fall for these kinds of scams, babe. So you can take your letter and...No, Eric. I will not shut up. First Annabelle, and now Phoebe? Do I have dollar signs on my head or something? A billboard that reads 'sucker'? Anyway, what was I saysing...sayings... saying... What was I saying? I don't know...But I know, that I don't know, that who knows if this baby is mine? He is cute, though. So, so cute. Well, as cute as babies that age can be, anyway. They're kind of weird looking when they're so small, aren't they? Like wrinkly little old men. Wrinkly little old alien men. But Lincoln is a, a, a distinguished name. But you know who knows? No one, that's who—" the message cut off after that, but I'm sure he continued his rant. I'm guessing from his accusations that he didn't make it past the letter to the stack of information about paternity testing and the labs in the area that do it.

Charlie is right. What. An. Asshole.

"That dickhead. How dare he insinuate you got pregnant on purpose? Or that the baby isn't even his. Why on earth would you do something stupid like that? It's not like he's famous. Or rich. Who finds a random Santa impersonator and says *'oh, yeah. I'm going to let him get me pregnant so I can cash in'*? Gah!" She throws her hands up. "I'm so mad. What a fucking dick." She storms into the kitchen, her body tense with anger. "It was pretty hilarious when he said that you found an innocent Santa and got him pregnant, though," she yells with a laugh.

I snort a laugh. I suppose I can see the humor in it. And as far as insults go, calling me a not-very-nice lady is one of the tamest I've ever received. Pretty sure I'd been called worse names in grade school. Little girls can be vicious.

That's not to say his message didn't shock me at first. Oh no, it left me flabbergasted. Not so much at what he said, because that makes sense. He doesn't know me and has no reason to trust that what I'm saying is true. What shocked me was how he said it. He slurred his words and rambled so much I could tell he was beyond drunk. I could hear someone in the background yelling at him to hang up, to wait until he sobered up, and that he'd found more than my letter in the packet.

He should have listened to that friend. Instead of hanging up, he continued on a hilarious and expletive-free rant about my *scam* and what a horrible person I'd been for taking advantage of a man in his time of need.

Umm, excuse me? Pretty sure I was the one getting drunk in a wedding dress because my fiancé failed to show up for our wedding. Despite my second thoughts about getting married that day, it was still *my* time of need. He was just a sad Santa.

Come to think of it, he probably had an ulterior motive for being there that day. Sad Santa, my ass. I bet prowling local bars for women is something he does every year after playing Santa for Christmas parties. He takes advantage of the suit, and the trust it inspires, to prey on unsuspecting women. I'm sure he's your average dude-bro, jobless other than at Christmastime when he's hired to play Santa Claus.

What an asshole.

Lincoln snuffles in my arms, finished with his bottle. Even though his eyes are closed, he has an adorable grin on his face. A grin which would be a lot cuter if the cause of it rumbling against my arm. It never fails with this guy. He finishes eating, then he poops. He's cute, though, so I won't hold it against him.

I release a long, slow breath, and force my shoulders to retreat from my ears, trying to release the tension gathering between my shoulder blades. I guess all my hopes of Lincoln growing up with his dad in his life were just that. Hopes. Wishes. Dreams. A bunch of fantasy bullshit dreamed up by someone who never got over her dad leaving her at such a young age.

Maybe I can do what my mom did and find him a good stepdad. If I can do it before he notices his real dad isn't around, even better. Preferably, before it dawns on him that his father didn't want him. Stepdads can be great. My stepdad is amazing.

I only wish my mom would have found him sooner. Maybe if she had, I wouldn't have this inexplicable drive to give Lincoln's father a chance to know him.

Still, as far as Daddy issues go, I suppose it could be worse. At least I waited until my thirties to get knocked up by a loser.

Ugh. Dating sounds awful, though. That's why I'd agreed to marry Webster in the first place. We'd been best friends for so long before the wedding that never happened. It was... comfortable. I was looking forward to a boring, suburban life. So what if we weren't exactly romantically compatible? We were best friends, and being married to him would have been so easy. I'm glad he had the guts to call it off, because I'm not sure I would have. I can't even blame him. Once he told me why he couldn't go through with the wedding, it all made sense.

And after that night with my Santa, a passionless marriage sounds like the worst kind of torture.

I can't deny it would have been nice if we'd called it off before we paid for the wedding. It's going to take a long time to replenish my savings.

Gavin storms out of the kitchen, clutching his phone in one hand and a protein shake in the other. The angry look he's sporting tells me Charlie must've told him all about the message. "What's this guy's name?" he asks, phone poised in front of his face. "I won't hurt him. I only want to talk to him."

I snort a laugh. "Nice try, Gav. Even if I knew it, I wouldn't tell you. You'd show up at his next Christmas party and make a scene. No. I said I'd give him the option to get to know Lincoln and that I'd accept his choice, whatever it was. I think he's made it clear he doesn't want to know him."

He snorts. "He's made it clear he's an asshole who needs to be taught a lesson, you mean?"

"He probably does, but I'd prefer you not be the one to teach it to him. I can only imagine the guilt trip Mom would lay on me if I let you get arrested while you're visiting for the weekend. It's not something I want to deal with."

He sits right next to me on the couch, grabbing Lincoln's foot and absentmindedly give it a gentle squeeze, an instinct I completely understand. Who could resist squeezing a baby's chubby little feet when presented with the opportunity? I know I can't.

"How anyone could not want to know this guy is beyond me." He takes a deep breath and affects a serious tone, "I'm sorry to break it to you, Fee, but it turns out you went and procreated with a dumbass."

A laugh bursts from my throat before I can hold it back, and Lincoln squawks his displeasure at being disturbed. His cry lasts *maybe* a millisecond before Gavin takes him from me and snuggles him against his chest. It happens so quickly I don't even feel guilty about the little diaper surprise he's about to discover.

Hey, it's not my fault he didn't give me a chance to warn him.

"Aw, come here, little dude. Let Uncle Gavin rock you to sleep." He passes me his protein shake so he can use both hands to soothe Lincoln. "Did that mean old mommy wake you up? Shh, shh. It's okay, kiddo. I got you." He stands up and bounces Lincoln in his arms while making shushing noises. He pauses, and his face goes a little green before he lifts the baby high enough that he can sniff his backside. "Dude. Seriously?"

I snicker as he takes Lincoln back to the bedroom to change him. Ever since I brought Lincoln home, my siblings have tried to take him for snuggles so frequently that I had to implement a sort of *you break it you bought it* rule, where if you're holding him and he poops, it's your job to change him. It's worked out well for me since I'd otherwise be the only person changing diapers around here. And if it occasionally works out in my favor when they grab him from me while he's actively pooping? So much the better.

With a sigh, I heave myself off the couch and head into the kitchen, where I find Charlie laying out the ingredients for what look to be a batch of cookies.

"Stress baking again?" I ask, reaching into the cupboard above her head to grab a coffee mug. One great thing about Lincoln being formula fed is that I don't have to worry about whether what I eat and drink will adversely affect him. That, and anyone can take a nighttime feeding if I'm too tired, not that I let that happen very often. He's my responsibility, not theirs.

It would be nice to have a partner throughout this whole thing, though. I swear, the next baby I have will be with an actual partner, not a random Santa Claus impersonator I hook up with when I'm feeling sorry for myself after being left at the altar by my best friend.

I've been so lucky to have my family around to help with Lincoln. I don't know what I would have done without them beside me throughout my pregnancy, and now, helping with this trip to look for his dad. Without Charlie and Gavin, I would have had to find a babysitter, or worse, bring Lincoln to all the Christmas parties I went to while looking for his father. I need to buy them thank you gifts. Good ones.

The doorbell rings as I grab the creamer from the fridge. "I'll get it. You know, since out of the three of us, it appears I'm the only one with my hands clean at the moment."

"Har har," Gavin calls from the back bedroom. "My hands are clean, but this kid definitely isn't. Are you sure he's still only eating milk? Because this diaper is fu-ull." He stretches the word, making it two syllables. I can hear his fake retching all the way from the kitchen. "*Heurgh.* Oh, god. *Heurgh.* It's all the way up his back. Noooo! It's down inside the toes of his sleeper. Again, dude?"

I shake my head and walk to the door, reaching it as the doorbell rings again. "Alright, alright. Hold your horses. What's the fucking russshhh..." My mouth drops open, the last word dragging before fading to silence. Standing here on my front porch is the last person I'd expected to see today. Or ever again, to be honest.

He's attempting to hide behind a slightly shorter, dark-haired man with a grin plastered on his face. Not that the dark-haired man matters. No, the person who matters right now is the man I found two nights ago. He looks pale and sweaty, and more than a little guilty. And right now he's inspecting my porch floor so thoroughly, I'm tempted to ask if he wants to see a work permit.

Good. He should be afraid.

At least, he should be if I could figure out how to be mad at him for his insane message. Sadly, I can't seem to muster up the will to be angry. All I am is sort of sad and disappointed. I hadn't realized how much I'd built up meeting Lincoln's father in my head before he called and told me his thoughts on the situation in a drunken message. I thought I'd kept my expectations reasonable, but he proved me wrong. I had high hopes, and he crushed them. And because I have Lincoln to think about, I have to pick myself and keep going. This mom stuff is hard.

"Everything okay here?" Gavin walks up behind me, a freshly changed Lincoln wiggling in the crook of one arm as he eyes the two men at the door. "Who are these assholes?"

I snort a laugh when my Santa flinches at being called an asshole.

"Hello. You must be Phoebe. I'm Eric Baxter and I believe you've already met my friend, Archer Fade." He steps to the side slightly, allowing us to see my Santa better. Huh. Archer Fade. I suppose it's nice to finally know his name, even if he's proven to be an asshole. "May we come in?"

"I don't fucking think so." Gavin places Lincoln in my arms and Archer's eyes follow the movement. "You've said your piece. You can fuck off now." My little brother reaches around me and grabs the edge of the door, closing it slowly, a smirk on his face. Right before the door closes he glares at Archer. "Oh, and just so you know, Lincoln is the coolest baby ever. You're missing out," he says, then slams the door.

"Fuck that guy." Grabbing me by the shoulders, he leads me back to the couch. "You and Lincoln are better off without him."

The doorbell rings again, followed by a sharp knock.

Gavin raises an eyebrow at me, but I shake my head. I'm tired of this whole situation. This entire trip has been such a letdown. I don't know what I was thinking would happen, but it wasn't this.

I get up. "I'm going to take Lincoln back and we're both going to take a nap. I'm done with this day."

I go to the bedroom without waiting for an answer. I wasn't expecting Archer to be happy—not exactly, anyway—when he found out about Lincoln, but I certainly wasn't expecting to be accused of lying. He has a girlfriend, though, and I'm sure she's pissed off about this surprise, too. Maybe even more than he is.

Not that it matters. I'm not here to get into a relationship, especially not with the one-night stand I had when I walked out on my wedding. He deserves to know he has a son, that's all. I did what I came here to do. I found Lincoln's father and gave him the opportunity to know his son. It's not my fault if he doesn't want to, no matter how much that sucks. I lived most of my childhood without a dad, and I survived, but I always sort of wondered what it would have been like if my dad had stuck around.

Then again, if my dad acted anything like Archer, I'm probably better off not having had him there.

Chapter 11

Santa Sees His Baby

Archer

"I TOLD YOU NO good would come from making that phone call yesterday." Eric's arm swings out and he smacks me on the back of the head. It hurts like a bitch because of the massive hangover I'm presently dying of, and I flinch away. It's dawning on me that piling a day of drinking on top of the hangover I already had may not have been the best idea I've ever had. "You were way too drunk to be making phone calls, especially not in this delicate of a situation. Jesus, man. I'm your fucking friend. One of these days, you're going to have to listen to what I say."

"I listen plenty. Usually it's the listening to you that gets me into trouble."

"Well," he huffs with a laugh. "You've gotten yourself into it this time."

He doesn't have to tell me that. I know it. I feel it. And this hangover isn't letting me forget it anytime soon.

This morning when Eric dragged me out of bed and force-fed me coffee, water, and painkillers, I thought I was already experiencing the pinnacle of self-pity. When he showed me the paperwork that came with Phoebe's letter, I knew I couldn't have been more wrong. I felt like the world's biggest asshole because that's what I was. What I am.

Turns out I should have listened to Eric when he told me to hang up instead of leaving a message, or better yet, when he'd told me not to call at all. The packet of information Phoebe gave me included her letter, a picture, details of Lincoln's birth, and information about his doctor and general health. But that's not what made me want to crawl into a hole and never come out. The contact information for every lab in the city that conducts paternity testing that she gave me did that. She included everything she could to make this easier for me.

Conspicuously absent? Any sort of request for money.

The whole thing showed me I was a giant fucking asshole, which I think was Eric's plan. I knew I would need to apologize, but I wasn't ready to face Phoebe yet when Eric dragged me out under the pretense of going to get food. Needless to say, I was dumbstruck when I saw her at the door, and haven't been able to do much other than stand around filled with shame ever since.

Eric, however, continues with his plan of forcing her to listen and bangs on the door again. We've been out here for almost half an hour and he's been banging on the door every few minutes, his way of reminding them we're still here, I suppose. If we're lucky, they haven't called the cops on us yet. I can't imagine what would happen if they came up to find him banging on the door and me sitting on the step, looking sick as a dog.

"Give it a rest," I tell him. "You saw that monster. He's not changing his mind. If he opens the door again, I'd get ready to duck."

He rings the doorbell several times in a row, then bangs on the door in a steady cadence. *Bang-bang-bang-bang-bang. Over. and. over. and. over.* If it's fucking annoying to me, I can't imagine anyone inside appreciates it. Especially not with a baby in the house.

Oh fuck.

The baby.

"Shit, dude. Stop. You're going to wake the ba—"

The door flies open and a small, red-faced woman with short, wild hair stands there glaring up at Eric. "Would you fucking stop that? I've already had to triple my cookie recipe because every time you knock, I get distracted and add too much of a different ingredient. You need to leave. Phoebe doesn't want to talk to you." She pushes her glasses up her nose with a flour-covered finger, leaving a dusty print on them. Standing there with her fists on her hips, her hair stuck up at odd angles, and looking between us with narrowed eyes, I'm reminded of an angry pixie. Finally, when neither of us says a word, she huffs. "Which one of you is the idiot who left that moronic message?"

I wait for Eric to take over, like he's been doing since he dragged my ass out of bed this morning, but he's frozen to the spot, staring at this little woman who is now looking between the two of us expectantly. She taps her foot, the frilly apron she has over her clothes turning her into the perfect picture of a scolding housewife.

"Well? Out with it."

I duck my head and raise my hand. "Me," I say with a resigned breath.

"Alright, dickhead. I have some things to say to you starting with, how dare you take advantage of a woman whose wedding had just been called off? Have you no shame? Seeing you now, you're not completely ugly. I'm sure you don't need to resort to preying on emotionally vulnerable women to get lucky." She stares at me, arms crossed, foot still tapping.

What the hell am I supposed to say to that? I'm not completely ugly? I'd like to think I'm not ugly at all, but that's not the point. I do not prey on vulnerable women. That night, Phoebe was as drawn to me as I was to her. She ripped my clothes off just as enthusiastically as I ripped off hers.

I stare right back, no answer forthcoming. A minute, maybe two, passes, with neither of us saying a word.

The high-pitched squeal of a smoke detector shatters the strange silence and the woman's face drops into a shocked grimace.

"Shit," she mutters, running back into the house. "My cookies."

Eric shakes himself out of his stupor and jogs into the house after her. Ah, shit. What the hell is he doing?

I hesitate, but it only takes a moment for me to jump to my feet and follow him inside, where I'm promptly met by the behemoth from earlier. Fuck, this guy is huge. And he's looking at me like he wants to knock my teeth down my throat. Not that I blame him. Eric gave me a quick rundown of the message I left for Phoebe last night, and I'm not surprised that anyone who knows her is pissed off at me. I was a huge asshole.

"No," the woman wails from the other room when the alarm finally stops. "Not again. Everything was going so well this time. I was hoping to bring these to work tomorrow."

I hear Eric say, "They don't look so bad. I'm sure they'll be fine."

The woman laughs. "You can't be serious. They're rock solid, not to mention burned beyond recognition. Despite how they appear, it wasn't my intention to make little hockey pucks. They were supposed to be shortbread cookies."

The big guy raises an eyebrow before turning away from me and walking toward the voices. Not sure what else to do, I follow.

In the kitchen we find Eric putting the smoke detector back up on the ceiling and the woman staring down at a tray of tiny, black cookies. They don't look like any shortbread cookies I've ever seen.

"Aww, Charlie. Not the cookies. I wanted to have some of those after the gym. You know it's my cheat day."

The woman, Charlie, evidently, rounded on the big guy, their height discrepancy no match for the anger flashing in her eyes.

"Go away, Gavin. I don't care if it's your cheat day. I wouldn't have given you any of these cookies, anyway."

Gavin presses a hand to his chest and a shocked noise comes from deep in his throat. "Charlie, is that any way to treat your favorite little brother? I'm a growing boy, you know."

Eric shoots me a bemused look. We've walked into some weird sibling twilight zone where the older sibling is tiny and the younger sibling is a giant. She looks a little older than he does, not that she looks old at all. That must mean this Gavin guy is young. Really young.

My stomach churns as I wonder if he's Phoebe's boyfriend. I don't know how old Phoebe is, but this guy looks much younger than she does. There's nothing wrong with women hooking up with younger guys, even settling down with them if they want, but I don't want Phoebe with any of them. I'm struck with the sudden conviction that Phoebe shouldn't be with anyone but me, and I can't tell if the nausea I'm experiencing is from that or if it's my hangover making a comeback.

It's too late for me to be thinking anything like that, though.

The message I left last night made sure of it.

God, how could I be so stupid? I should have listened to Eric. I know I've done something truly moronic when Eric is the voice of reason.

"Why are you still here?"

I spin around to see Phoebe standing behind me with arms crossed over her chest and a scowl on her face. Damn, she's gorgeous when she's mad.

"I, uh," I stutter, running a hand through my hair. "The smoke detector went off when Charlie was outside yelling at us and Eric ran in after her. I followed without thinking."

She stands on her toes and peers past me into the kitchen. "Looks like everything is under control. You can go now." She spins on her heel, but before she can step away, I grab her elbow.

"Wait. Don't go yet. Please." I drop my hand, plastering what I hope is a disarming smile on my face. "I'm sorry I was such an asshole last night. I got some...weird news and drank way too much before I even read your letter. I'm not actually an asshole. It's not an excuse, but I am sorry I freaked out and overreacted."

Her shoulders rise and fall, rise and fall, as she takes several deep breaths before turning to face me. "It's fine. You said what you needed to say. I meant what I wrote in the letter. I'll accept your decision, no matter what."

I huff. She's not getting it. Or maybe I'm not being very clear. Yeah, that's more likely. I'm probably still a little drunk, to tell the truth. Why did I drink *so much* last night? Why did Annabelle have to show up at the party like she did?

"It's not like that," I try to explain as she continues to walk away.

"It's fine," she says, her footsteps so quick I have to hurry to keep up.

She stops and opens a door, and then I hear the crying. *Did she hear that from out there?* I assumed babies cried loudly, but somehow Phoebe heard this when it barely even registered as sound for me. That's amazing. Is that one of those mom things people are always talking about? She steps over to a crib and bends to pick up a baby. No, not just *a* baby. Lincoln. Possibly my baby. He settles against her chest as she bounces him gently, making shushing noises and whispering things like "it's okay" and "I know". My heart beat races and I wonder if she can hear it pounding over Lincoln's crying.

"He didn't sleep very well last night, so he's having a rough day," she says without looking at me. "He's too tired to be awake and too tired to fall asleep."

"That seems counter-intuitive." My loud voice causes Lincoln to startle, and he cries harder. "Shit. Sorry," I whisper.

She waves off my apology.

"So, back to what I was saying—"

She cuts me off. "I said it's fine. You have all the information you need. For reasons I'd rather not get into right now, I know for a fact you're the father, but I understand if you can't take me at my word since you don't even know me. Do the test or don't. If you decide to do it, text me which lab you go with and I'll bring Lincoln in for his sample."

A shadow falls over us from the doorway as Gavin fills the space. He glares at me before crossing the room and lifting Lincoln from Phoebe's arms.

"Let me try," he says, already using the same bouncing step Phoebe used moments ago. "You two can *talk,* or whatever. Somewhere else."

She releases a long sigh. "Thanks, Gav."

I follow her out of the room and back to the living room, where she flops down onto a huge blue couch.

"Look," she says, lacing her fingers behind her head. "I don't want to deal with this today. When Lincoln doesn't sleep, I don't sleep. I'm exhausted, I have a ton of work to do, and—"

"Yes, of course. I'm sorry to have barged in like this," I interrupt. "I'll get out of your hair. We can talk about this later."

She turns her head to look at me with a smirk. "To be honest, I'd prefer not to talk again until we get the paternity test. I'm sure you understand why. You're the one who left that message, after all."

I nod. "Again, I am sorry about that."

"I get it, I really do." She looks away and takes a deep breath. "And I kind of admire your dedication to expressing yourself without cursing, even while you were obviously drunk." She smiles wanly and changes the subject. "We might as well get it all done at once, so make the appointment and text me the details. I work from home so I can be there anytime." She gets up, walks back into the room where Gavin is rocking Lincoln, and closes the door on me.

I nod to myself and step away. No sense pushing this when I've fucked up so phenomenally. At least now I'll have time to come up with a proper apology.

"Eric," I yell. "Let's go."

"Yup," he calls from the kitchen. "Coming."

I go to the door and step outside, waiting at the passenger side door of Eric's car. He joins me soon after.

We're halfway back to my place before he cracks a grin. "Well, I'd say that went well, wouldn't you?"

I snort a laugh that turns into a groan before lowering my head into my hands. "Yeah," I say, my voice dripping with sarcasm. "So well."

Chapter 12

It's Good To Have Friends

Archer

Eric and I have been sitting at our friend Mason's bar since we left Phoebe's house. He's drinking, but I'm not. I'll be sticking to plain water for the foreseeable future, especially after how much I drank last night. It's too bad, too, because I could use a drink right about now to help drown out the terrible Christmas pop music playing in the background.

"Do you really think she's trying to trap you with someone else's baby?"

"I mean, maybe? Her fiancé left her at the altar that same day. What if it's his baby?" That doesn't sit right with me, though. Something tells me Phoebe wouldn't lie about something like this.

Eric throws back the last of his scotch and signals the bartender for another. We came to see Mason, but he's unexpectedly off today. He never leaves this place unless we're meeting up to play basketball, making it extra weird that he's not here.

"I guess it's possible," Eric says. "But if that's the case, why would she leave contact information for every lab in the city that does DNA testing? I double checked her list. She didn't miss a single one. And she hasn't asked you for anything. The letter she gave you said nothing about child support. If she were trying to take advantage, you'd think that would be one of the first things she'd ask for."

He's probably right. I don't know her that well, but nothing about Phoebe strikes me as manipulative or conniving. Then again, I never thought that of Annabelle either, and look how that turned out.

"Unless the whole thing was an elaborate ruse. Maybe she spent her evenings wearing a wedding dress and sitting at different bars, waiting for an unsuspecting mark. You walked in and she knew she'd hit the jackpot."

I snort a laugh. "Oh yeah, because some asshole dressed like Santa Claus just screams money."

He holds his drink up in a toast. "Well, you did spring for the deluxe costume. It's not your average Santa that has the soft velvet suit and a luxurious, realistic-looking beard."

I shake my head with a laugh. "She took the jacket with her when she left in the morning. Didn't she say she still has it? You know, in the letter? I wonder if the costume shop still wants it?"

"See?" He laughs. "She knew you made enough money to rent the good costume. What more could a woman want in a baby daddy?"

I finish my glass of ice water and pour another from the pitcher the bartender left on the table. That move tells me he's seen enough hangovers to know how dehydrated I am. I have to remember to tell Mason to give him a raise.

"Okay, let's see what's next, shall we?" Eric pulls the packet of papers from Phoebe and spreads them on the table. "Which lab do you want to use?"

A thought occurs to me, and I pull out my phone. After a quick search, I find what I'm looking for. "CellSearch is on the list, right? Remember Mark Orosz? That's the lab he's running now." Mark went to the same college Eric and I went to. We didn't have any classes in common, considering he was a science major and we were business majors, but we all liked to play pick-up basketball to blow off steam when the course load became too much. He's a little odd, but he's a solid guy.

Eric scans the papers, settling on the third in the pile. "Here it is. You going to call him?"

I nod, already pressing the call button on my phone. "Maybe he can help speed it up? I'm not above owing him a favor for this."

"Good idea. You do that and I'll call the guys. They can meet us at the court and we can blow off some steam. This day has been hella stressful."

I roll my eyes as I listen to the phone ring. He thinks he's had a stressful day? I'm pretty sure my issues are a little more stressful than his at the moment.

"Fuck basketball," I groan with my head in a trashcan. "And fuck you, too. Why did you make me do this?"

Eric laughs and passes me a sports drink. "Here. Drink this. It'll help."

I sit up and take the cap off, chugging the cold blue liquid. I've spent more time puking today than I have playing basketball, but it's helped take my mind off the baby situation. Plus, as an added bonus, I'm finally feeling a little better. I guess throwing up all the remaining alcohol helped.

"Hey. Are we playing or what?" Mason yells from the court. "We didn't come here to watch Archer puke his guts out."

"Shut up, asshole," I say. "You're supposed to be distracting me, not shitting all over me."

"From what Eric says about the message you left this poor woman, you deserve to be shit all over." Lucas picks up the ball and comes over to where I'm hunched over on the bench. "You know how much I hate to say that Eric was right, but...Eric was right. You shouldn't have called her when you did."

"Yeah. Waiting until you were sober would have been so much better."

"Damn it, Eric. You've told me that eight hundred times today. I know I should have waited. You made your point."

He holds up his hands in surrender. "As long as you know." He laughs.

My phone rings as the guys start packing up, since it's apparent we won't be playing much basketball today. I can't seem to keep my head out of the trash can long enough to get down the court.

"Hello?"

"Archer? This is Mark Orosz from CellSearch."

"Mark. Thanks for getting back to me so quickly."

"My assistant mentioned this was a time-sensitive matter. I have to say, it surprised me to hear from you after all this time."

Shit.

"Yeah, sorry about that, Mark. I've been busy with the takeover at Fade Toys. It's been a long year." It's true, mostly. Honestly, the only time I've gone out in the last year were the times when Eric showed up and dragged me downstairs to play basketball in my building's gym. "And before that? Well, I don't have a reason, other than I've been a shitty friend. Why don't you join us next week to shoot some hoops? I'll text you my address."

He laughs. *"I'll take you up on that, even though I know you're only offering because you feel guilty for not keeping in touch. But about the paternity test."* He's all business now. *"I can get you in tomorrow at ten. We close for the holidays, so if you can't make it tomorrow, you'll have to wait until the new year."*

"No, thank you. That's perfect. I'll call the mother and we will be there."

"You and the mother of the child are coming in together? That's a little unorthodox."

I chuckle dryly. "It's an unorthodox situation. But I know she wants to get this sorted as much as I do. I'm sure she'll be okay with ten tomorrow. I'll see you then."

"Whatever you say, Archer." I can hear the disbelief in his voice. If Phoebe hadn't told me herself she wanted to get this over with, I'd be right there with him. "See you tomorrow."

I end the call and look at the guys. "Mark got us in tomorrow."

Eric grabs my shoulder and squeezes. "That's great. Now you have another chance to call Phoebe. How about you try not being an asshole this time?"

The guys all laugh and offer me words of encouragement as they finish packing up their stuff and leave me alone on the court to make my phone call. I take a few deep breaths to not only work up the courage but to calm my stomach enough that I can be sure I won't throw up while I'm on the phone with Phoebe. I'm feeling better, but I'm still not feeling great.

I'm pretty sure she hates me already, but there's no need for me to gross her out, too.

With one last deep breath, I press the icon to call her.

"Hello?"

"Um, hello. Phoebe? Hi. This is Archer Fade. We met earlier?" I slap my forehead and scrub my hand down my face. Smooth, Fade. Really smooth.

"Yes, Archer." Is that a hint of a laugh I hear in her voice? I like it, probably more than I should at this point. It makes the tension in my shoulders melt away and a small creep onto my face. *"Did you set up an appointment already? That was fast."*

Chapter 13

Have Yourself A Deoxyribonucleic Acid Christmas

Phoebe

"ALRIGHT MS. FOX, LET'S go over the procedure before we get Lincoln's sample. It's not painful, but he might be a little fussy for a few minutes." The lab technician describes the swab and how they get the sample before turning to her computer to prepare the labels.

When I arrived, Mark, the man who runs the lab, came in to introduce himself, and to reassure me that his involvement in the procedure stopped at fitting us in today and that the regular laboratory staff will handle the sample collection and the processing of the specimens. He wanted to assure me that even though Archer was an acquaintance of his from college—yes, that's the exact word he used. An acquaintance, not a friend.—our case would be held to the highest professional standards. He's a bit of a stuffy guy, but I like him. He seems like someone who's honest to a fault.

Truthfully, I breathed a sigh of relief when he told me that. I had been a little worried that they might tamper with the results with since the guy who runs the lab is also friends with Archer. Not that I have any doubt Archer is the father. He's the only option, after all.

"Please hold him facing out. Lincoln, I'm going to take this swab and wipe the insides of your cheeks. It doesn't hurt, but I know I'd be annoyed if someone stuck a swab in my mouth without warning." The lab technician smiles at me and whispers conspiratorially, "I always warn the patient, even when I don't think they understand me very well." I turn Lincoln to face her and she makes quick work of grabbing his little cheeks and getting the swab done before I've had the chance to blink. She's good at this. I didn't even need to distract him with the brightly colored sensory toy I brought for that purpose.

Lincoln lets out a squawk of annoyance but settles quickly. He's usually pretty relaxed, so I'm not surprised the swab didn't bother him much.

His father, on the other hand...

"How far back are you going to stick that thing? I have a, uh, a sensitive gag reflex these days."

More likely, he's hungover again like yesterday. I wonder if he has a drinking problem. Every time I've seen him, he's been drunk or hungover. Hmm, that's a bit concerning.

Not that it changes the way he looks much. He's still sexy as hell. The heat building between my thighs can attest to that. I need to get out of here before he causes me to leave a different kind of DNA sample on my chair.

"I only ask because I don't want to, uh, throw up on the sample. I'm sure that would be bad for it, wouldn't it?"

The lab tech simply nods and continues getting her supplies ready for Archer while Lincoln and I enjoy the show. He's wringing his hands and bouncing his feet. Why's he so nervous? And why is that so cute to me?

"Okay now, Mr. Fade. Hold still, this will only take a second." And to her credit, it does. She's swabbed, stored, and capped the sample in a flash. "That's it. We'll have the results for you soon. Mark asked for us to rush this, so I'm hoping we'll have the results today. Keep your phones on." She collects the samples and leaves me in the room with Archer.

"So," I say, gathering up the items I'd already taken out of the diaper bag. "You wasted no time making this happen."

He chuckles. "Yeah. It's good to have friends in the business of DNA testing."

"Don't you mean acquaintances?" I tease. "Mark made himself pretty clear on that."

The man in front of me lets out a loud laugh and a memory from our night together hits me full force. We were in the hotel bar, sitting at a table instead of at the bar where we first met, and we were talking over a plate of nachos so high we could barely see each other. We'd decided to overcome that obstacle by tunneling through the nacho tower using cocktail straws. It was surprisingly difficult, but strangely hilarious.

"You got me there. I haven't been as good a friend as I should have been and I intend to make up for that as soon as possible."

The sudden memory of our night together catches me off guard and I find myself distracted while I attempt to pack up. I'm trying to stuff everything into Lincoln's diaper bag one-handed and it's not going well. Every time I get something in, something else falls out.

"Can I help?" Archer is so close to me now I can smell his masculine scent. Soap and musky cologne. It makes me want to bury my face in his neck.

But that's not what I'm here for, so instead of making myself look like a creep, I pass Lincoln to Archer and finish packing the bag. The look of horror on Archer's face when I turn around forces a laugh from my throat. "Oh. My. God. You should see your face!" I howl. "It's...it's...it's like I handed you a basket of slugs or something." He's holding Lincoln at arm's length and staring at him with his mouth open in a half grimace-half grin. "You can hold him closer, you know. He won't bite. He doesn't even have any teeth yet."

Archer whispers roughly without taking his eyes off Lincoln, "I've never held a baby before. I have no idea what I'm doing."

Oh, that's too adorable. I snicker and help him bring Lincoln closer, showing him how to hold him close without smothering him. The two of them scope each other out, neither of them making a sound.

"His eyes are so huge and such a rich brown," Archer says. "Like chocolate, or really good coffee."

I huff a laugh. "If only they were coffee. Sometimes it feels like I haven't slept in the last year. He is pretty sweet, though, so chocolate is probably more accurate." His beautiful brown eyes are what people always notice about him because they are so large and striking. Just as large and striking as the man he gets them from.

It's been hard to forget my one-night Santa when I see him every time I look into my baby's eyes.

"You haven't slept? Why aren't you sleeping?" He asks, still staring at Lincoln, a smaller, less horrified, smile creeping onto his face.

This man is so good-looking it should be a crime. So good-looking that my lady parts tingle in his presence. But he didn't really just ask me why I haven't been sleeping, did he? No one could be that oblivious, could they?

"Are you serious?"

He tears his eyes away from Lincoln's. "Yeah. You shouldn't skip sleep, you know. It's not healthy."

I stare at him, blinking several times. He's joking, right?

"It's true," he continues. "Seven to eight hours is what experts say you should be getting."

I shake my head. "You..." I close my eyes and pinch the bridge of my nose. He *has* to be joking. It's the only thing that makes sense. "You're aware that babies wake up several times a night, right? Like, they wake up to eat or when they need their diaper changed? You know that, right?"

He chuckles. "Well, yeah. But he should have grown out of that by now, right? That only lasts a few days or something, I thought."

I bark out a laugh. This poor, clueless man. "I mean, some babies grow out of it quickly, but others don't. I met a woman in a baby yoga class who said her oldest, a five-year-old boy, still woke up once or twice a night. And before going back to sleep, this kid would march into his mom's room and wake her up only to tell her he was awake. Like, he'd walk in and stare at her until she opened her eyes, just to say 'I woke up'. Then she'd have to get out of bed to go tuck him back in."

He cringes. "And she still had another one?"

I laugh. "Yeah. And if that isn't irrefutable proof that sleep deprivation makes people stupid, I don't know what is."

Archer looks at me, seemingly mulling something over in his mind, before blurting, "Would you like to have an early lunch with me? Now? I'd like to hear more about babies, especially this one." He tips his head to where Lincoln snuggles in his arms. "If you have time, that is. I think it's pretty obvious that I know next to nothing about babies, and you clearly know a lot more than that."

I suck air in through my teeth. "I'd like to, but the thing about babies is they need regular naps. And it's getting dangerously close to this guy's nap time."

It really is time to get going. Lincoln doesn't do well when he misses his naps, and I'd like to get some sleep of my own while he snoozes. I reach out and lift him from Archer's arms, brushing my hands against a firm chest and getting a whiff of amazing cologne, both of which send a flash of heat racing down my body. If the snippets of memories I've had in the last year are to be believed, this man has all the muscles under that shirt he's wearing. Literally all of them.

"Oh." Archer's voice drops an octave, and he looks away. "I see. Another time, maybe?"

Shit. He looks genuinely disappointed. I suppose it wouldn't hurt to get to know him a little better. I don't need to wait for the test result to know that he is Lincoln's father, after all. There's no real reason to wait. Plus, being friends would make things easier for visitation schedules and stuff like that.

"Did you maybe want to come over? We can order some lunch and Lincoln can still have his nap on time." I won't get my nap, but I can drink coffee to make up for it later. It's not like I've never done that before.

The way Archer's face lights up makes my heart pound so loudly in my ears I'm sure he can hear it. He is so gorgeous when he smiles like that, I struggle to take a full breath.

Calm down, girl. He has a girlfriend. He's not interested in you. He wants to know more about Lincoln, that's all. I take a deep breath and blow it out slowly.

"That's perfect. I'll pick something up for lunch and I'll meet you there. Is there anything, in particular, you'd like to eat?"

"Surprise me," I say, hustling out of the office. "See you soon."

I'm in my car and on my way home before Archer makes it to the lobby, which had been exactly my intention. Between his solid chest giving me heart palpitations and his delicious scent making me drool, I am a mess of epic proportions. I need a few minutes alone to calm myself before he arrives at my place.

And I should probably warn my sister he's coming, so she doesn't freak out and try to burn the house down with another batch of cookies. That girl's stress baking is becoming a problem. She uses up all the ingredients and all we ever have to show for it is piles of ashes and headaches from the blaring of the smoke detector. Yeah, it's better for everyone if I warn her about Archer in advance.

Chapter 14

Let It Snow

Phoebe

"Charlie," I yell, as soon as I get the front door open. "Where are you?"

"Bathroom," she calls back. "I got called in to cover a shift, so I'm getting ready for work."

I release a huge breath. Thank god for small favors. She won't be here much longer. Maybe I'll get lucky and she'll be gone before Archer gets here. He has to wait for the food to cook, right? Yes, yes. He definitely has to wait for the food. There's plenty of time for Charlie to be on her way before he shows up. This is good.

Not that I'm looking forward to being alone with him. Of course that's not it. I just don't want Charlie to freak out and start yelling at him again when we're trying to get to know each other. That's all it is.

I love my sister, but sometimes this protector role she takes on can be a bit much.

Oh, who am I kidding? Of course I want to be alone with him. The guy's a smoke show and I want him all to myself, even if I know it's not going anywhere.

I drop the diaper bag on the couch and carry Lincoln back to the bathroom. "Give your nephew a kiss, Auntie Charlie. It's nap time."

She puts the cap back on the mascara her mascara and takes Lincoln from my arms, cuddling him close. “Sleep well for Mommy, okay, little guy?” She says before kissing him on the cheek and letting me take him back. “I’m closing tonight and afterward I’ll be heading out with Dax and Tanya from work.” She rushes to add, “Unless you need me to watch Lincoln?” I shake my head no. “Okay, cool. Hey, how did the test go?”

I step side to side, bouncing Lincoln a little. “Oh, yeah. Um, I think it went well. The guy who runs the lab assured me his friendship with Archer made no difference to the testing. Other than him getting us in so quickly, that is. The lab technician said there’s even a chance we could get the results back later today.”

“No shit? Geez, must be nice to have connections. What’d you say he did for work again?”

That’s a good question. He hasn’t told me much. “Something to do with toys, I think. A toy store? A toy maker?”

She snorts a laugh. “Wait a minute. Wait.” She holds up a finger and giggles. “You’re telling me that the Santa…who got you pregnant… is a toy maker?” She forces the last word out before uncontrollable laughter overtakes her. “Oh. My. God. I can—” a snort of laughter cuts her off. “You had sex with Santa Claus. You’re a Ho Ho Ho.” Her body shakes with laughter.

I roll my eyes and yell over the racket she’s making, “He’s not actually Santa, you ass.”

She tips her chin with a sarcastic nod, wiping tears from her cheeks. “Oh, yeah, sure. Tell me, Phoebe, how does the jolly old elf measure up in the downstairs department? What’s his candy cane like? Is it tiny? Striped? Ooh, ooh, ooh…” She pauses dramatically before whispering, “Does it have a big curve?” She crooks her finger and peals of hysterical laughter overtake her once again.

“Jesus. There’s something wrong with you.” I huff and spin on my heel. “I’m putting Lincoln down for his nap. Have fun tonight.”

"Oh, shit. Right," she says between bursts of laughter. "I need to go. I was already running late." She shudders after peeking into the mirror, and quickly sweeps her makeup off the bathroom counter and into her makeup bag. "I'll have to fix this mess and get pretty later," she says, wiping streaks of mascara from beneath her eyes.

I wave as she hurries past me. "See you later."

"Bye," she calls out, her keys jingling as she grabs them from the hook by the door. "Don't wait up. I might try to find my own candy cane tonight." Her laughter trails along behind her as she runs out and slams the door behind her.

Phew. I mentally wipe my brow. That was close. It's a good thing she got called into work today or she may have subjected Archer to another earful. My sister can be a little overprotective, but she usually means well. Her recent interest in his toy maker status, however, would no doubt supersede that. I foresee Charlie making many references to "candy canes" and "the real Santa" in Archer's future.

"Well, my darling? Should we get you down for your nap?" I've been working at feeding Lincoln as soon as he wakes up, instead of using his bottle to help him fall asleep, and it's been hit or miss. It's especially hard on those long nights when he doesn't want to settle to not slip back into feeding him to sleep.

I bring Lincoln to the bedroom, change his diaper, sing him a lullaby, then lay him in the crib. Another thing the parenting books say to do is to put the baby down to sleep while they're still awake. That's another tough one. Sometimes he cries when I lay him down, which obviously sucks even though it doesn't last long, but the thing I find really difficult is when he watches me leave. There's something gut wrenching about the sad look on his face that kills me every time. But I find he sleeps longer when I do it, so I keep at it. Longer sleeps for Lincoln equals more sanity and, if I'm really lucky, the occasional nap for me.

With a quick kiss and a brush of my hand over his fuzzy red hair, I turn on the white noise machine and the baby monitor and leave the room, closing the door softly behind me.

Archer will be here any second. Should I freshen up? Put on a little lip gloss or something? *No. That's stupid, Phoebe. He has a girlfriend. And you don't want anything to happen, anyway.* Remember Webster? Even your best friend didn't want you.

Ugh, no Phoebe. You know that's not true. It's got nothing to do with him not wanting me. We both got caught up in something that should never have started. He's been my friend almost as long as I can remember and he's apologized for the whole wedding and engagement thing every time we've spoken this last year. He loves me, but not romantically. And I'm not sure I ever loved him romantically, either. We were both to blame for the direction our relationship took.

None of that matters anyway, since this is about what's best for my son. No matter how amazing that night with Archer was, I need to focus on what this means for Lincoln. I already know what the results of the paternity test will be, but Archer has his doubts. Reasonable doubts, I suppose, at least from his point of view, but doubts all the same.

Fuck it.

I make a quick stop in the bathroom and brush my teeth. Okay, fine, I also add a little mascara and lip gloss. No one would judge me for not wanting to look like a swamp creature in front of Archer. The man's girlfriend looks like a supermodel fresh off the catwalk—I haven't figured out who she is yet, but I'm positive I've seen her somewhere—so it's not like he'll really be looking at me. It's for my comfort more than anything.

As I'm leaving the bathroom, a barely audible knock sounds at the front door.

"Hey," Archer grins when I get to the door and open it. "I hope I didn't wake Lincoln by knocking too loudly."

"Not at all." I motion for him to follow me to the kitchen. "Lincoln sleeps pretty deeply, so a little noise doesn't bother him. Plus, I have a white noise machine that helps block out any sound from out here."

He walks to the other side of the kitchen island, puts down two large paper bags from the Indian restaurant downtown, and starts pulling out takeout containers. "White noise machine? Like whale songs and stuff?"

I chuckle, leaning over and resting my elbows on the counter. "I think it has a setting for that, but I tend to stick with the regular white noise setting. It's more of a staticky sound. Like you'd hear on an untuned radio?"

He stops with a container halfway to the counter. "And that works? How did you figure that out?"

"I didn't figure it out," I say with a chuckle. "I read it in one of my many baby books. I must have bought out the entire pregnancy and parenting section of the bookstore when I found out I was pregnant."

A flash of sadness cross his face before he smiles and continues unpacking the bags like nothing happened. "You read a lot of books, then? You must be an expert on babies now."

"Ha! Not even close. I don't think a single one of those books agreed with what any of the others were saying. There are as many ways to care for a baby as there are babies on the earth. Other than the white noise machine, I'm not sure I learned anything from those books that my mother didn't teach me better. If you're looking for a baby expert, she's the one you want."

"So, you're close with your mom?" Archer opens a cupboard, getting lucky on his first attempt, and pulls out two plates, before moving on to pulling open drawers. He doesn't fare as well with the drawers, opening several in a row.

I suppose I could be a better host and help him find what he's looking for, but I'm frozen in place because of how right it feels having him in my kitchen like this. Like he fits. It doesn't hurt that his butt is nice to look at, either. Really nice to look at. A little whimper escapes my throat before I can rein it in.

"Phoebe?"

"Huh? Oh, yeah. My mom. We're super close. Having Lincoln would have been so much harder if she hadn't been there with me every step of the way. She came to all my prenatal appointments and everything. Although it took me a while to get used to the idea that she was going to be in the delivery room with me, I must admit." He hands me a plate and directs me to serve myself. "I wasn't ready for her to get up close and personal with my vagina, you know?" As soon as the words leave my mouth, my face heats. *What the hell, Phoebe? Why would you tell him that?*

Archer snorts a laugh and coughs. It takes a few tries of him banging on his chest with his fist before he gets himself under control.

"Ah, of course," he says with a chuckle. "I guess that would be weird. I know I wouldn't want my parents having front-row seats to my prostate exam or anything."

And it's my turn to choke on a laugh.

I calm myself and we both fill our plates before taking them to the table and sitting across from each other. The silence is so heavy after the laughter of the last few minutes that my shoulders sag under the weight.

"So, do you think your friend will really be able to get us the results today?"

Archer puts his fork down and wipes his mouth on a napkin, and I can't help but watch with rapt attention. His lips look as kissable as I remember. I wonder if he tastes as good as he did that night. *Nope. Don't go there, Phoebe. You don't get to wonder about that. He's here for Lincoln, not me.*

"I think Mark's team will do everything in their power to get the results to us as soon as they can." He leans forward, resting his elbows on the table and lacing his fingers together above his plate. "Can I ask you something?"

Shit. I think I know where he's going with this, and even though I can probably hold off until the test results confirm what I already know, I kind of want to tell him. I think. Maybe. I know I'll eventually have to tell him why I was so sure Lincoln was his, even without the test results.

I stutter and lose hold of my fork, sending it clattering to my plate. "Su-sure." I nod. "Yes, go ahead."

He drops his hands to his lap and drags in a ragged breath. He looks up at the ceiling and blows out a breath. "Canyouev-erforgivemeforthatbullshitmessage?" He blurts it so quickly I don't catch what he says. It sounds nothing like the question I thought he was going to ask, though.

"Pardon?"

He takes another deep breath and exhales slowly this time. "Can you ever forgive me for the message I left you? I was an ass. The hugest ass. A post-BBL Kardashian ass."

I chuckle, relief washing over me. Maybe I won't have to tell him after all. Thank god. I'm not ready to tell him why I know for a fact, without a test result, that the baby is his. Because telling him why I hadn't slept with my fiancé? Yeah, that's not a story I look forward to sharing.

"Yes, I forgive you. Truthfully? You were barely a medium-sized ass. You didn't even swear at me. But let's never talk about the Kardashians again. I'm not sure I enjoy knowing that you keep up with them."

He sags against the back of the chair. "Thank you. And I don't give a shit about the Kardashians. Eric does, though. Every time he's at my place, he puts their show on. I learned all of my Kardashian knowledge against my will."

I can't help but laugh. "Yeah, sure." He's so easy to talk to. I guess I'm going to be spending a lot of time reminding myself he has a girlfriend. I guess I have some pining to look forward to. Awesome.

"The information you gave me with the letter was...perfect," he says. "That was very thoughtful. I have to tell you, though. I haven't had the courage to read through the birth summary yet."

I snicker. "It's not very graphic, but I understand. I probably could have waited to give you that information until after we got the results of the paternity test."

He nods. "That's part of it. But it's mostly because it felt weird reading about it. I read the first few lines where it talked about your early labor and..." he shrugs. "I may have overreacted. I promise I'll try to read it."

Felt weird reading it? I wonder why.

"No, no. You don't have to read it," I tell him, shaking my head. "I can give you the rundown if you like."

He nods. "Yes. Sure. That would be good."

Over the next few minutes, as we eat our lunch, I tell him the basics about Lincoln's birth. I skip the more graphic parts because we're eating lunch, but he absorbs every word I say without comment. Until we get to the birthdate.

He drops his fork to his plate with a clatter. "Wait. Doesn't that mean he was born early?"

I nod. "A little over a month. But despite coming a little early, he was a healthy weight and didn't need any time in the NICU." He furrows his brows, so I add, "The neonatal intensive care unit. Where some premature babies spend time growing stronger before they can go home."

I can see the gears turning in his head and I prepare for him to ask again, given what he now knows about Lincoln being born early, if I'm sure the baby is his. But he surprises me.

"That must have been scary. Being alone and having to deal with that, I mean."

I release a huge breath. "It was. But when they said everything was fine, and I'd still get to take him home right away, I relaxed. And my family was there, so I wasn't alone."

He looks thoughtful. "I'm glad you had your family with you."

My eyes sting for some unknown reason because I can't possibly be crying about this after all this time. Can I? I came to terms with not having a partner a long time ago. Nothing has changed.

But maybe actually meeting Lincoln's father, and confirming he's not a bad guy, has me thinking again about what I missed out on.

I shake my head, open my eyes wide to dry the tears and say, "Let's change the subject. It's been way too long since I got to talk to anyone about grown-up stuff. What do you like to do for fun?"

Chapter 15

Passing Up Naps And Passing Tests

Phoebe

"Okay, wait. You're telling me you made that?" Archer points to the fruit hammock stuffed with bananas that I have hanging under the nearest cupboard. "With actual rope? Like the rope that you can buy at the hardware store?"

I laugh at the way Archer's mouth drops open. We were talking about hobbies we have and I told him about the textile art that I like to do and pointed out the fruit hammock as an example. "Not with rope, with macrame cord. It's softer and easier to work with than that scratchy yellow rope you can buy by the foot. That stuff hurts your hands so much. Plus, it's not as flexible as I like."

"Right, okay. But you made it?"

"Yes." I throw my hands up and laugh. "I made it. I make lots of things. Here look." I walk to the counter and pick up my phone. "I made this wall hanging for Lincoln's room at my parents' place."

His eyes widen as he looks at the wetland scene depicted on the woven tapestry in the photo. It's the first large piece I made when I started weaving with fiber, and I'm proud of it. It shows a small pond in the middle of a field with the setting sun in the background. I like the sense of peace that fills me when I look at it. The melding of greens, blues, reds, yellows, and oranges has a calming effect, which is why I have it in Lincoln's room at home. I like to think it helps him sleep.

"That's amazing, Phoebe." He zooms in on the picture and squints at it. "And that's made of rope? Or cord? Can I send this picture to myself?"

"Yeah, go ahead. Send away. That's a combination of different textured cords and yarn, and there's even a little packing string in there." What can I say? I'm not exactly a purist when it comes to my fiber art. You should see the cabinet full of art supplies at my parents' house. It's full of random bits of rope, string, and ribbons that I'm saving for when inspiration strikes. A professional artist, I am not. I'm more of a packrat who makes stuff with my collection of odds and ends. I do it because working with my hands is relaxing, and because I enjoy looking at the finished product. "I guess you could call me a rebel."

"A rebel with yarn. Who would have thought? You're a wild one, Phoebe." He wags his finger at me and grins. "You could get a man in serious trouble."

Get a man in trouble? What could he mean by that? That almost sounds like flirting. But that's not possible, is it? Nah. There's no way. I need to stop with the wishful thinking. I already got the number one thing on my Christmas list. Finding Lincoln's father is more than enough for me. I'm not looking for romance.

"Oh, yeah," I say with an exaggerated nod. "So wild. You know, on the nights that I'm not in bed by nine."

"Nine? That's late." He laughs. "If I'm not playing basketball with the guys, I'm lights out by eight at the latest."

Archer gets up and takes our plates to the dishwasher before focusing on cleaning up all the takeout boxes. I'm just now noticing how many there are. He must have bought a dozen different dishes.

"You want to keep the rest of this for dinner? Is your, uh, boyfriend coming home soon? I bet he needs a lot of fuel to maintain that giant body of his."

My face scrunches in confusion. "Boyfriend? Wait, what? Are you talking about Gavin? Ew, no. No, no, no. *Heurgh.*" I gag so hard my face hurts, the contents of my stomach clawing their way up my throat. "Gavin's my brother. Not only that, he's only eighteen." My eyes roll so hard I think I get a glimpse of my brain. "Did you really think he was my boyfriend? Gross."

He rolls his lips between his teeth, doing a poor job of hiding a grin. "I—wait. No, that's not—Shit. He was so protective of you when I was here with Eric yesterday that I assumed... Not to mention how good he was with Lincoln. Crap. That's embarrassing." He rolls his lips between his teeth, doing a poor job of hiding a grin.

I laugh. "What's embarrassing? Thinking I was a cradle-robbing cougar with my own brother? Yeah, I'd be embarrassed about that, too."

"No," he says with a chuckle. "I wouldn't say that's my finest moment, but that's not it. It's that an eighteen-year-old kid is so much better with babies than I am. You saw me earlier, right? I'm thirty-four years old and today was the first time I held a baby. And don't say I wasn't terrible at it."

I hold my hands up in protest. "No way I would even try to say that. You *were* terrible at it. Like, really, really terrible." I snicker, remembering the look on his face when I first put Lincoln in his arms.

He huffs a laugh. "Glad to hear we agree. Now, can we get back to my original question? Is your giant of a brother coming over today? I imagine he could use this food to fuel all his"—he gestures to his whole body with a waving hand —"huge muscles."

I gag again, making Archer laugh more. "Gross. I don't want to think about that ever again. But to answer your question, he should be here in the next couple of hours. And please don't mention his hugeness in front of him. He's had a very good growth year, but he likes to brag about how it was all hard work." Archer shoots me a pointed look. "Okay, fine. Maybe some of it was hard work. But you can't work your way into a ten-inch growth spurt. That's just dumb luck."

He nods, then returns to what he was doing. I watch while he packs the leftovers into my fridge without waiting for me to say I'll take them. I'm mesmerized by how his muscles flex and bunch under the snug t-shirt he's wearing, and heat is building between my legs. If this is the kind of reaction I get in my lady parts while watching him clean the kitchen, I might finally need to open up that new battery-operated boyfriend Charlie got me for my birthday a couple of months ago. I've had no interest in sex of any type, even solo sex, in such a long time that it's been sitting in my nightstand since I took it out of the wrapping paper. Hell, it's still in its original packaging.

It's probably not good manners to fantasize about him when I know he has a girlfriend, but he's too damn sexy to fight it any longer. Besides, there's no harm in thinking about it as long as I don't act on it, right? At least, that's what I'm going to tell myself if I work up the nerve to open that vibrator later.

For now, though, I need to focus on what's happening in the real world. Archer is right about Gavin. My brother eats like a horse. Two horses, actually. Clydesdales.

Archer turns back to me and I barely manage to drag my eyes up to his face before he catches me looking at his butt. He puts his fists on his hips and looks around the kitchen. "I think that's everything. What do you think?"

While I was busy ogling him, Archer cleaned the entire mess from lunch. There's nothing left for me to do. That in itself makes it the best meal I've had in months.

"Oh, yeah. It looks good." I must still be dazed because it takes too long for me to mumble, "Thank you. For everything."

He wipes his hands on the towel I keep hanging on the oven door and steps around the island. "I have to go to work for the rest of the day. Thanks for having lunch with me. It's been nice getting to know you a little better."

"Of course," I say, leading us out of the kitchen and back toward the door. "I guess we'll talk more after we get the test results?"

"Yes. Can I call you?" My breath catches in my throat. *He wants to call me?* "After we get the results?" And I'm back to reality.

"Please. We'll have some things to work out then, I imagine."

"Okay," he says, reaching out and patting my arm while half turning to the door. "I'll talk to you soon." He turns back to me and, without warning, leans in and kisses my cheek, leaving a trail of tingles dancing along my skin. "Bye, Phoebe."

I watch him open the door and step out without another word.

That was weird. Right?

The kiss, I mean.

I lift my hand to my face and touch the spot on my cheek where his kiss lingers. Funny. The skin beneath my fingers is normal. I guess all that tingling is under the surface.

I step away from the door and head back to the kitchen, where I left my phone. I don't want to miss the call from CellSearch, so I'm keeping this little piece of technology attached to me until I get it.

Turns out I don't have to wait long at all for that to happen. My phone rings the second I make it back to the couch to relax. Okay, fine. I was going to relax by taking a nap. Lincoln will most likely only sleep another twenty minutes or so and I could use that time to catch a few z's instead of relying on more coffee to get me through the day.

But sleep can wait. This phone call is more important. I press the answer call button and bring the phone to my ear.

"Hello?" I say, stifling a yawn.

"Hello. Is this Phoebe?"

"That's me." My heart is racing, which is stupid considering I already know what the result is. There's no chance Archer isn't Lincoln's father. Unless, of course, this is some sort of Christmas-miracle-immaculate-conception crap. Which, let's be serious, I'm the last person any deity would choose to impregnate with their one and only child. I post stuff about rock stars on the internet. That's not a solid foundation for any religion.

"Hello? Are you there still?"

Shit. I went off in my head for too long and must have missed something.

"Yes. Sorry. I'm here. Could you repeat that, please?"

"This is Mark from CellSearch. I wanted to call you myself to ensure you got your results. Is now a good time?"

"Yes, please. Thanks, Mark."

"You're welcome, Phoebe. Without preamble, Archer is Lincoln's father. There is a ninety-nine point nine percent probability of paternity, which is conclusive. I'm sure that doesn't surprise you, though."

I chuckle. "No, it doesn't surprise me. The test was for Archer's peace of mind. Thank you again for getting it done so quickly. I'm amazed at how fast you could do it, actually."

I hear a snicker on the other end of the line. *"I must admit, that was mostly for my own selfish reasons. I'm tired of playing basketball at my gym with all the prepubescent teens and old men that hang around there. Doing this test for Archer means I'm back in with him and the other guys, so I'll finally have some competition."*

I laugh. "Well, glad I could help, I guess. But seriously, thank you. I'm sure you didn't have to do it this quickly just to play basketball with them."

"No, you're probably right. But I figured it would be nice for both of you to get this sorted before Christmas. Now, if you'll excuse me, I'm going to call Archer and tell him the good news."

"Thanks again, Mark."

"Oh, and Phoebe?"

"Yeah?"

"Archer is a good guy. Give him a chance."

"Oh, it's not like that."

"I wouldn't be so sure about that. I saw how he was looking at you today. Anyway, I have some stuff to take care of before I get out of here. Have a merry Christmas, Phoebe. Bye."

"Wait, how was he looking at—" I pull my phone away from my ear and look at the screen. "He hung up on me. Unbelievable."

Oh well, at least it was a quick call. I should still have a few minutes for a little catnap. I stretch on the couch and snuggle my body into the cushions.

But, of course, as soon as I start to drift off, a little cry comes from the baby monitor on the end table beside my head.

"Shiiiiit," I groan as I force myself up and off the couch. "Looks like I'll be relying on coffee for another day after all."

Chapter 16

That Sneaky Santa

Phoebe

"My friend, Carol, told me it happened to her daughter's friend. The man took his child for a visit and then forgot him at the carnival. How do you know this Archer character won't do something like that? You know nothing about him. You didn't even know his name until a few days ago."

"Mom, you're being paranoid. I'm sure he's not like that." I honestly don't think anyone is like that, at least not without some warning that they're totally absentminded. Plus, Archer doesn't seem like the sort of man who would even go to a carnival, let alone forget his kid at one. "You know I want Lincoln to know his father."

I hear a heavy sigh through the phone. "*Honey. Promise me you're not letting your feelings about your father get in the way of making smart choices. Are you going to let this man take Lincoln for a visit? Alone? How do you know you can trust him?*"

Shit.

In a way, she's right. Not that I enjoy admitting that.

"I guess I wanted so badly for Lincoln to know his father that I didn't fully consider how this would all work. You're right, Mom. How do I know I can trust him? What do I do?"

"*Maybe you can ask him to get a criminal records check? If he's a decent man, he shouldn't object to that, right?*"

Wait a minute, what was that Devon was saying last time I was at Bump & Grind visiting Charlie? He was going to see what he could find out, and that was before he knew Archer's name. I wonder how much deeper he can dig with a name. Or maybe I can ask Xena to get me in touch with her brother? A cop would have access to the kinds of information I could only dream of.

"Yes! Mom, you're brilliant. I have to go. I need to go see Charlie at work. I love you. You're still coming for Christmas Eve for dinner, right?"

"Of course we're coming, sweetheart. We've already booked our hotel room. It's Lincoln's first Christmas. We wouldn't miss that."

"Right, okay. See you then. Bye, Mom." I hang up without waiting for her to say bye, too caught up in my idea to worry about it. I'll hear about it later, I'm sure, but I can't bring myself to care. Not after she got me all worried, then gave me the solution to my problems in the same breath.

I look down at the baby in my arms, his chubby little fingers gripping the now-empty bottle. "Well, baby? Should we go ask Auntie Charlie's new friend to do us a huge favor? I want you to know your dad, but I still need to know you'll be safe."

I get up and make quick work of getting us ready to leave, and soon I'm bundling Lincoln into his car seat for the short drive to Bump & Grind.

Let's hope Xena feels like prevailing upon her brother's kindness for us. Because having a cop tell me Archer is safe would go a long way in giving me some peace of mind when it comes to leaving Lincoln with him.

"I love that plan," Xena says as soon as I've laid it out for her. She's snuggling Lincoln to her chest right now, doing a little dance with him in her arms. "And you're in luck. Devon and

Kaden should be here for coffee any minute before Kaden heads in for his shift."

Like she summoned him, the bell over the door tinkles, and in walks Devon, the gigantic man momentarily blocking out the sun. He's followed by a man in a police uniform, who I'm guessing is Kaden. Even if he wasn't in uniform, it wouldn't be hard to guess he's a police officer. His short, dark hair and the mirrored aviator-style sunglasses he pushes to the top of his head scream cop.

"It's about time, dickhead. I need you to do something for me," she says to her brother as he walks up to where she's dancing with Lincoln. "We need you to look into a guy."

He puts his hands up and shakes his head. "No way, no. Not happening. I'm in enough shit at work because of you and your damn sword. I'm not using police resources for whatever illicit plan you've cooked up."

She turns Lincoln around to face Kaden. "*Please, mister,*" she says in a fake baby voice. *"Do it for me? It's really important."*

"Gah!" Kaden covers his eyes with the heels of his palms, his tattooed biceps testing the strength of his sleeves. He's attractive, in an authority figure way, but he doesn't make me weak in the knees like Archer. Too bad, because unlike Archer, I'm pretty sure Kaden is single. "Don't use a baby against me, you evil little witch. You know I'm powerless against adorable squishy babies."

Xena holds Lincoln up in front of her face, edging closer to Kaden. *"Please, mister? It's for my safety. Don't you want to be a good person and contribute to my safety and well-being?"*

Kaden peeks through his fingers. "What do you mean by safety? Explain."

Xena lowers Lincoln and snuggles him to her chest again. "Phoebe needs you to run a check on someone." She tips her chin at me. "Phoebe, this is my brother, Kaden. Kaden, this is Phoebe. She's Charlie's sister."

He lowers his hands completely and holds one out to me. "Hey. I've heard so much about you. I can't believe this is the first time we're meeting. I'm here all the time. Gotta support my little sister, you know?"

"Yeah, he's always here mooching free coffee from a small business owner," Xena says with an eye roll. "So supportive."

"Shut up and give me that baby so you can go make my coffee." He reaches out and Xena hands Lincoln over. It's a good thing I'm relaxed about letting people hold my baby because every time I come into this place, someone other than me ends up with him on their lap.

It wasn't always this way. Therapy and medication do wonders for postpartum anxiety. Without them, I probably wouldn't be here looking for Lincoln's dad at all, let alone contemplating what will happen when it comes time to leave Lincoln with him for visits. Even though the thought of it gives me heartburn, I know it's something I need to get comfortable with, hence speaking with Xena and Kaden.

Xena rolls her eyes at Kaden but walks over to the counter to make his coffee, anyway. Devon tips his head to me and tells us he needs to step outside and make a call, leaving me alone at the table with Kaden.

"Charlie mentioned you were here to find this little guy's father. How's that going?" Kaden isn't looking at me while he talks, instead, he's making funny faces at Lincoln. "Find him yet?"

"Actually, yes. I got the call with the paternity test results before I came here today. When I called my mom to tell her the news, she started putting all these *ideas* into my head. And she has a point because I don't actually know this guy."

Kaden looks up and nods sagely. "Ah, and she's worried he's a bad dude."

I snort at his use of the word dude. He sounds more like a surfer than a cop. "Actually, I believe she was most worried about him taking Lincoln to a carnival and forgetting him there.

I'm not sure she's made it to the 'bad dude' part of her worries yet."

"What do you think?" He cocks an eyebrow before going back to making Lincoln giggle with his funny faces. "Does he seem like the type to forget a baby at a carnival?"

I snort a laugh. "I don't know. Maybe? How would I be able to tell? Is there a registry for that sort of thing? Should I text him and ask him if he enjoys leaving babies at carnivals?"

Xena chooses that moment to drop Kaden's coffee off and steal Lincoln back from him. "Probably not the best idea. If he were into that, I doubt he'd come right out and say it. Good thing we have the very capable Officer Cross here to look into him for you. Isn't that right, Kaden?"

"This is really the favor you wanted?" He looks at me. "You want me to check him out? I thought Xena was messing around."

My cheeks heat and I nod. "It was a one-night thing. We had lunch earlier today after we met up at the lab, but aside from that, I know next to nothing about him. I don't want you to get in trouble or anything, though."

He laughs. "I get in more trouble because of Xena and her stupid sword. Quietly looking into one guy isn't a problem."

The tension that's been wracking my shoulders since I got off the phone with mom leaves me in a whoosh. "That would be amazing."

He looks down at his phone and stands. "I'm going to be late if I don't get going. Get my number from Xena and text me everything you know about this guy. The more details, the better. Middle name. Birthdate. Parents' names. All that stuff, okay?"

"Sure, yeah. Okay. Thank you so much."

He tips his chin to Xena, grabs his coffee, and heads out the door.

"See? Told you he would do it."

I laugh. "You didn't tell me you would use my son to guilt him into it."

She shrugs. "Meh. I know his weaknesses and exploit them at my leisure. You have siblings. I'm sure you know what it's like."

Speaking of siblings, didn't Charlie say she was coming to work? I haven't seen her since I came in.

"Where's Charlie?"

Xena looks puzzled for a moment before she forces a smile onto her face. "Oh, yeah. I, umm, I sent her out to run some errands for the store. Some days I hate doing the shopping, you know?"

I nod, a barely perceptible slow up and down of my chin. I know she's lying, but I don't know why. You can bet I'll figure it out, though, just as soon as this business with Lincoln's dad is finished. Because no matter how much I want to know why my sister is lying to me, Lincoln is more important. Always.

"Now. What are you going to do if he wants to get custody?"

I spin my head to where Devon is now standing, apparently having snuck up on me when he finished with his phone call. He puts his coffee down and turns a chair around to straddle it.

"What do you mean?" I'm imagining the sound of panic tinging my voice, right?

"Well, if he wants to be involved, it's not out of the question that he would want to have some sort of custody arrangement, right? If it were my kid, I'd want to have a formal agreement in place." He shrugs. "It's a litigious world, I'm afraid. Do you have a lawyer? Now that you're on the Sleeping Dogs payroll, I'm sure Denise wouldn't mind putting you in contact with one of ours."

I knew I'd need a lawyer, but I naively thought I had time before I'd need to talk to one. Surely Archer doesn't plan on trying for custody. That would be silly. I can't imagine a court granting custody to a seasonal Santa Claus impersonator and occasional toy store worker. So I'm safe. Especially now that I'm back to work doing the media management for Sleeping Dogs.

"That's probably a good idea, but I'm sure I can find a lawyer. I don't want to put Denise out."

Devon leans forward, crossing his arms on the back of the chair. "You need to get on it, then, darlin'. Because I'm sure this guy's already thought of it."

"Oh, okay." Shit. That doesn't sound good. My heart beats faster at the thought of having to share Lincoln. I'm not sure why I didn't consider the possibility that he may want an official custody agreement. Did I think he'd be happy with the occasional visit? I'm beginning to second-guess my decision to find Lincoln's father. At the very least, I should have been more prepared before I came here to track him down.

Stupid, Phoebe. So stupid.

"Oh, and Phoebe? I found out one more thing." Devon passes me a slip of paper with the words Fade Toys and an address written on it. "This Archer guy? He doesn't work at the toy factory. He owns it."

Fuck. I guess he's more than a seasonal Santa Claus and occasional toy store worker. He owns the damn factory. Maybe I should call Denise about a lawyer, after all.

Chapter 17

Special Delivery

Archer

"Okay, thanks, Mark. Bye."

I slump back into my chair and run my hands through my hair

Phoebe was right. Not that I thought she was lying to me, especially not after getting to know her a little better during lunch. Something told me she wasn't the type of person who would lie about this.

And the results from the paternity test have proved it.

I'm a dad.

I have a kid.

No.

I have a baby.

My face cracks into a grin so wide it almost hurts. "MaeLynn," I yell, as I shoot up out of my chair and run out of my office before sliding to a stop in front of my receptionist's desk. My heart is racing faster and expanding more than it ever has before. I need to share this news with someone I know will be as happy about it as I am.

I inherited MaeLynn when I took over the company last year, and one thing I'll never understand is how a woman so kindhearted put up with my father as long as she did. She would have retired last year, but that was before she learned I was taking over for my father. She was his assistant for over twenty years and during that time, MaeLynn had always acted like a grandmother to me. I guess that makes her like a great-grandmother to Lincoln. Not that you'd ever catch her looking grandmotherly, at least not in the traditional sense. The woman prides herself on her outrageous appearance and flawless, albeit incredibly colorful, makeup.

"MaeLynn. I need your help." I can't stop smiling and I'm sure I look a little wild-eyed due to the abundance of delirious excitement coursing through my veins.

I'm a dad. I can't fucking believe it.

When I first read the letter Phoebe gave me, I was afraid to admit, even to myself, that this is the outcome I wanted. But it really was. After all, I almost proposed to Annabelle, a woman I barely knew and hadn't been seeing very long, because I thought I was ready to start a family. And I guess I really was, considering I unknowingly fathered a child that very night with Phoebe.

Of course, now that I have that child, I have no idea what to do with him. I cringe at the memory of Phoebe laughing at me when she passed me Lincoln earlier at the lab, and I panicked. I may not have held him perfectly, but I think for my first time, it wasn't too bad. At least I didn't drop him. Plus, hearing Phoebe laugh again was worth the embarrassment I felt.

I shake my head and face MaeLynn, who looks up, her expertly made-up lips pursed in concern.

"Archer, honey. What's wrong? You look...unhinged."

The smile on my face grows impossibly larger. "Nothing is wrong, MaeLynn. Nothing at all. I have fantastic news. I have a baby."

She cocks a disapproving eyebrow. "That's not funny, Archer. You know how much I love babies." Her voice quavers. "Don't even joke about having a baby."

"I'm not joking, MaeLynn." I smile and hold my arms out, anticipating the hug that's sure to come. "I have a baby."

MaeLynn hops out of her chair and speed walks around her desk, only stopping when she has me wrapped in a tight hug. "Oh, honey. Congratulations. I didn't even know you were seeing anyone. When can I meet her? When is she due? Oh, lord. I need to get to work knitting a baby blanket." She pushes me away and reaches back across her desk for a notepad and pen. "Let's see. What colors should I use?" She taps the pen on her lower lip, getting bright pink lipstick on the cap.

I can't help but smile at her enthusiasm as I reach out and grab her hand. "MaeLynn, stop. I said I have a baby. As in, he's already born. That call you put through a minute ago? That was my friend at CellSearch calling with the results of the paternity test. The woman, Phoebe, tracked me down after the Christmas party this year. We, uh, we spent the night together after last year's party."

She blinks her dark, spidery eyelashes at me, once, twice, three times, and a final fourth time, before she opens her mouth. Even then, nothing comes out, not before she blinks a few more times.

"Oh. Well," she says before cracking a grin large enough to rival my own. "That makes things easier. What's his name? What colors do you think he would like?"

I chuckle and pull her in for another hug. When I release her, I press a kiss to her forehead. "MaeLynn, you're wonderful, you know that?"

She scoffs. "Pssh. Enough about me, kid. Tell me about this son of yours."

"Okay, okay," I say with a chuckle. "His name is Lincoln. He's five months old and ohmygodMaeLynnyougottahelpmeIknownothingaboutbabies." Despite my best intentions, sudden panic makes forces my words from my mouth in a high-pitched rush and has me grabbing MaeLynn by the shoulders. I clear my throat. "I mean, I know nothing about babies," I say in a normal voice. "What do I do now? Can you help me?"

She grabs my cheeks and drags me down to kiss my forehead. Her pink lipstick sticks in the wrinkles of my forehead when I grimace, and she laughs when I wipe it with the back of my hand. "Of course, you big dummy. Let me make some calls and we'll get it all sorted out." She hurries around the desk and has her phone in her hand before her ass hits the chair. "Call the boys," she says without looking up. "Tell them to meet you at your apartment in two hours. You go home now and wait."

"Two hours? What the heck do you think you can do in two hours? And you want me to wait? For what?"

"You'd be surprised what a person can do when they know the right people," she says, shooing me away with a wave of her hand. She presses the screen of her phone and lifts it to her ear. "Lana? It's MaeLynn. I need a huge favor."

I've been at my place for a little over an hour, waiting for some unknown surprise when security calls up from the lobby.

"Mr. Fade, I have a bunch of...people here who say they have a delivery for you. They said to tell you that MaeLynn sent them and that you'd know what that meant. Should I send them up?"

"Thank you, William. That would be great."

My penthouse has elevator access, but it opens into a private lobby instead of directly into my apartment. I like it because it seems a little more secure, even though nobody gets into the elevator without one of the security guards letting them in. I suppose I feel better knowing that if someone were to make it on, they'd be stuck in a small, windowless lobby instead of getting access to my home. I do think I look like a pretentious dick occasionally for living in the penthouse, though.

A secure lobby isn't protection against me carelessly letting a bunch of strangers into my home, however, a problem I only grasp when I open the door to an eclectic group of almost ten people. Men and women of all ages, shapes, and sizes have gathered in my lobby, a mountain of boxes and furniture stacked on the floor behind them.

An older woman steps forward and holds out her hand. "You must be Archer," she says warmly. "I'm Lana. MaeLynn is a dear friend of mine. She called and told me you recently found out you're a father. Congratulations. That's so exciting."

A murmur of congratulations comes from a few of the people behind her.

"Thanks?" I say, and she must read the confusion on my face.

"I run a baby boutique downtown. MaeLynn said you needed everything for a baby and asked if I would get everything together and have my team deliver."

I look past her again. Her team appears to comprise senior women, a few people with a bunch of tattoos, and a kid who looks to be about thirteen. I cock an eyebrow at Lana. "Kind of a ragtag crew you have, don't you think?"

She snorts a laugh. "Yes, well. The store is already closed for the holiday and my normal delivery guys are taking some much-deserved time off, so I called in reinforcements."

"Consider yourself lucky," a small elderly woman in a bright pink tracksuit yells from the back of the pack. "We're missing the holiday pudding-wrestling extravaganza at Peaceful Pines for this."

One man turns to look at her. "Gran, I told you that you didn't have to come. The guys and I could have taken care of this."

She scoffs. "You guys look like a bunch of criminals," she says, turning to address the most heavily tattooed man in the group. "We know nothing about this guy. He could be one of those stuck-up rich boys who thinks anyone with tattoos is a weirdo. And you and Becca have *a lot* of tattoos. And you certainly look weird. No offense."

He snickers and wraps an arm around the heavily tattooed woman next to him. "That's alright, Gran. We're used to the ridiculous shit that comes out of your mouth."

Another man, the most normal looking of the group despite his fiery red hair, reaches over and smacks the tattooed guy in the head. "Johnny," he snaps. "Braden's here." He jerks a thumb toward the teenager. "His mom is going to be so pissed at me if he comes home swearing a blue streak after this. I told her I was taking him to do a good deed for Christmas." He steps to the front and sticks his hand out. "I'm Travis." He points at each person and says their name. "The kid is my stepson, Braden. That's Connor, his wife Alex, Becca, and Johnny, Aiden, Rhea, Ryder, Gran, Gladys, and Cathy. And you already met Lana."

The woman he called Gladys sidles up to me in her neon green tracksuit.—what is with these older women and tracksuits, anyway? Even Lana is wearing one, only hers is a shiny purple—and looks me up and down, blatantly resting her gaze at the front of my pants.

"Well?" she asks, raising a sparse white eyebrow. "Are you married? Or can I get tickets to this ride?"

I choke on a laugh. Over her head, I can see the man Travis introduced as Ryder trying to mouth something at me, but the woman he called Gran slaps him on the arm before I can decipher what he wants me to say. I decide to answer honestly, because that's always the best policy, right?

"Um, no. I'm not married."

Gladys cracks a grin. "Perfect. All these idiots"—she gestures to the men—"got married before they showed me their dicks. You look like you might have something in there to make an old woman happy. What say you take me into that fancy penthouse and show me your ham candle, hot stuff?"

Travis pulls her back and puts a hand over her mouth. "Gladys," he hisses. "For the love of god, will you please shut up? Fin won't be too happy to hear you've moved on to propositioning strangers because all the men you know are married. Especially since you're doing it in front of your great-grandson."

She elbows him in the stomach and wrenches free. "Pssh. Braden's almost a man. I'm sure he's heard worse at school. Besides, what's wrong with ham candle? It's not like I'm swearing." Travis shakes his head while he massages his temples. "What? What do you expect me to do? Be happy with looking at the wrinkly pink pantserpillars the old coots at Peaceful Pines are carrying around? Gross. I'll pass, thanks." She turns back to me and flutters her eyelashes. "So what do you say, handsome? Grant an old lady her dying wish?"

I can't get any words out as I look around at the faces of the strangers gathered around me. I'm going to have to have a talk with MaeLynn about the kinds of people she hangs around with, if this woman is any sign. Although...Gladys seems to be enjoying herself. I guess there's nothing wrong with a little harmless fun. Besides, I run a sex toy factory. I'm pretty sure I can handle a little friendly sexual harassment from a feisty senior citizen. Lord knows I've experienced far worse when dealing with getting our products into new retailers.

I shake my head and smile at the group. "Why don't you all come in and I'll get to work on these boxes? Grab a drink and relax. I'm sure it won't take long for me to move this stuff in here."

"I don't think so," Braden, the kid, says. "We told my mom we were coming to deliver a bunch of baby stuff to some guy's apartment." He looks around the lobby with a smirk. "And if this is your apartment, I'd say you have bigger problems than not having any baby stuff." He steps back and grabs a box. "Now, where do you want this stuff?"

The rest of the group follows his lead, and after a few trips back to the lobby for more items, I soon have a mountain of boxes piled next to a bunch of new furniture in my living room. And that's not even taking into consideration all the shopping bags piled on my couch.

"Here," the woman named Alex says, passing me a slip of paper. "Connor and I host a family dinner for all our friends every Sunday when we're in town. You and your baby, and his mom, should come by some time."

I fold the paper and slip it into my pocket. These perfect strangers are giving me an open invitation for family dinner, and I didn't even get an invitation from my own parents for the holidays.

"That's nice of you, but I wouldn't want to impose."

A man steps up beside Alex and puts an arm around her. "Not an imposition, man. Alex loves to cook for a crowd, and she does it as often as she can. I have to warn you, though. That shit with Gladys? Yeah, that will probably happen again, several times over. We try to keep her under control, but nothing's worked yet."

"And nothing ever will!" Gladys yells from where she's rummaging through my fridge. "I'm too much woman. Silly men like you can only dream of suppressing my big vagina energy. That's right. I've got that B. V. E. And there's nothing you can do about it." She and the other women dressed in tracksuits make a squeezing motion in front of their breasts while nodding somberly. I don't even want to know what that's about.

A laugh breaks out, and a few people throw in head shakes.

"That sounds like something you should see a gynecologist for, Gladys. I wouldn't go saying that out loud just anywhere if you can help it," Alex calls back with a laugh. "You probably won't like the looks you get after."

"Well, well, well. Looks like you started the party without us. What's going on here?"

Eric, Mason, Lucas, and Damien walk into the apartment and take in my other guests.

"You said two hours, right? Looks like you needed us sooner." Eric says, looking at the diverse group of strangers gathered in my apartment. "Hey, Archer? Is there a reason all the guys from Sleeping Dogs are here in your apartment?"

Chapter 18

Doting Grandmothers With Donuts

Archer

"I STILL CAN'T BELIEVE you didn't know who they were." Eric is holding up the side of a crib while I screw it together with the end piece. He's been giving me shit since Lana and her "delivery crew" left because I didn't recognize any of them as members of the band, Sleeping Dogs. "We saw them perform live a couple of years ago," he says with a laugh. "I guess I should've sprung for the floor seats since it appears your old eyes couldn't make out their faces from the third row. Maybe you need bifocals?"

I grit my teeth and tighten the bolt I'm working on before reaching out and grabbing another from the pile of pieces next to me. Lana offered to have the guys stay and build it for me, but I told her I had my friends here to help with that. Eric is making me regret that choice now.

Like I could look any of those guys in the face after Eric informed me who they were, anyway. I'm still embarrassed that I had no idea who they were, not that any of them seemed to care. Hell, they have invited me for to Sunday dinner, so I can't have offended them too terribly.

But despite my embarrassment, I ought to have taken Lana up on her offer. It would undoubtedly be better than the grief I'm getting from Eric.

"And you let them carry all this stuff in here. Like they're regular delivery guys." He scoffs. "You know, sometimes you amaze me. And not in a good way."

I grunt and force myself to a standing position, my knees creaking in protest. *Maybe I am getting old.* "I have more important things to worry about than recognizing the members of a band that I rarely listen to." Okay, that last part isn't precisely true. I have all their albums downloaded, but it's not like I listen to them daily. "I don't have their poster on the wall above my bed like you, so I haven't memorized their faces."

"Hey, that poster is awesome," he says with mock offense. "The women I bring home seem to like it, anyway. I've never had any complaints."

I snort a laugh. I doubt he actually has a poster, but it wouldn't surprise me if he did. He's like an overgrown frat boy. He likes what he likes and is not afraid to show it. It's one of the things I like most about him. It's also one of the things I like least, but with Eric, the good outweighs the bad. It's why I've been friends with him for so long.

"Hey, Arch." Mason is standing in the doorway of the spare room that I've decided will be Lincoln's from now on. "You want this chair in here?" He points to the upholstered armchair with a matching ottoman he's dragged to the door. "It's one of those gliding rockers. Probably good for rocking the little guy to sleep."

I stand up and look around. This room has been a guest room since the day I moved in, and its neutral grays and blues have served that purpose well until now. Now that I look at it, though, it seems a little boring. Now that it's going to be my son's bedroom, I wonder if I shouldn't do something different with it. Hire an interior designer to make it more suitable for a little boy.

After we got the old bed out of the room, it became apparent how boring it is in here. But I suppose it will do for now. Lincoln is still a baby, after all. When he's older, we can redecorate with his favorite colors.

"Yeah, that's great. Put it in that corner over there," I say, pointing to the far side of the room next to the floor-to-ceiling bookcase. "What else needs to be in a baby's bedroom?"

Other than earlier today when I held Lincoln for Phoebe while she packed up to leave the lab, I've never been around a baby. I'm not sure what they need. But I trust MaeLynn got me everything I needed, so all that's left now is for us to figure out where to put it all. If I'd been smart, I'd have asked her to come here and tell me and the guys what to do. Sadly, I'm not that smart, so now I'm stuck here with my four best friends, trying to figure out where to put all this stuff.

As if summoned by my internal confession of ignorance, MaeLynn calls out from the entryway. "Yoo-hoo, boys. Where are you? Why is there still a pile of stuff on the couch? Have you done anything at all since Lana delivered these things? Or were you waiting for me to arrive and tell you all what to do?"

Lucas rolls his eyes from where he's standing at the bedroom door, his grin negating his display of irritation. He's not fooling anyone; I know he loves MaeLynn almost as much as I do.

Dusting my hands off, I walk out to greet her and find her piling bags onto my kitchen island. "I was just thinking that I needed your wise counsel. I'm sure you got everything I could ever need for a baby, but since I still know nothing about babies, I don't know where most of it goes. What will it take to convince you to stick around for a bit to tell us what to do?"

"Hmm, I don't know. I think five grown men should be able to handle this, don't you?"

I would never expect MaeLynn to stay. This is her personal time, after all. But I'm not above begging a little to get my way. I wiggle my eyebrows, shoot her a little pout, and she caves. "Oh, alright. I'll stay. I brought coffee and donuts from that little place downtown. The one near to the doll store I like?"

I nod. I know that one. I got myself a coffee there the last time I went to buy MaeLynn one of those horrifying dolls. I needed the fortification before going into that nightmare factory. I may never understand why she likes those things with their unnaturally white skin and creepy eyes, but they make her happy, so I keep buying them. Even if I don't sleep for a week after I shop there.

"It's got a funny name, right? Like Buzz and Brew, or something?"

"Bump and Grind," she says around a mouthful of donut. "And I'm lucky I made it in at all. They're closing early for a private party tonight."

"A private party? At a coffee shop?"

"That's what I said. But it seems some bride is having her bachelorette party there. I guess not everyone wants to go to a bar or a strip club."

I reach into the box and select a donut with bacon on top. *Interesting.* "I suppose so. I never would have considered asking a coffee shop to close for a private party. Seems a little entitled, if you ask me."

"You're not wrong." She licks her fingers, then wipes her hands on a napkin. "Boys!" she yells out. "Come get a donut before I put you to work."

She walks to the couch and looks through some bags while the guys gather around the counter and grab their donuts. "You'll need to wash these clothes before we put them away. Have you come across the baby detergent yet?"

I step up next to MaeLynn and pick up the bags. "I have detergent already."

She rolls her eyes at me. "Fragrance and dye free? The gentle stuff?"

I cringe. "Uh, no? Does that matter?" I'm barely started there's already too much to remember about babies and what they need. I thought this was supposed to be intuitive. Shouldn't people naturally know how to raise kids? With all the information Phoebe and MaeLynn keep throwing at me, how will I ever be able to keep it all straight?

She chuckles and keeps poking through the bags. "It matters. Babies have sensitive skin. Ah, here it is." She pulls out a white box and hands it to me. "There you go. Put a load in like I showed you, then come back." Of course she has to point out that she's the one who taught me to do my own laundry. This woman has done more for me than my parents ever have.

She turns her attention to the guys. "Hurry with those donuts, boys. This furniture won't move itself."

"Yes, Ma'am," Eric says, dusting his hands off before walking over to kiss MaeLynn's cheek. "We're at your mercy. Tell us what to do."

I leave them to it, take the bags of baby clothes and blankets and the laundry detergent, and head into the laundry room. After spending several minutes taking the tags off of everything, I finally start a load of laundry and go back to the guest room—I mean, Lincoln's room to see what else needs doing. With MaeLynn's guidance, the guys finished building the crib and placed the rest of the furniture. Books and toys have taken up residence on the shelves. A soft area rug has been rolled out under the chair and ottoman, and there's even a toy box in the corner. My guest bedroom has transformed into a nursery..

"What do you think?" MaeLynn asks, sliding an arm around my waist. The guys are already back in the kitchen; I can hear them laughing from here. "Once we get the mattress protector and sheet onto the crib mattress, you'll be ready for Lincoln to spend the night."

My heart flutters and I smile. I have a son and now he has a bedroom in my home. A small twinge of sadness pings in my chest when I realize he won't get to live with me full time, but it's overshadowed by the joy I feel at knowing he'll be in my life at all. He's an unexpected gift and I need to enjoy it. I'd almost written off ever being a dad, thanks to the Annabelle fiasco, and then Phoebe and Lincoln showed up to give me another shot at it.

"It's perfect, MaeLynn. I can't thank you enough." I wrap an arm around her and pull her into a hug. "I don't know what I would do without you."

"You would have figured it out, eventually. And your mom could have helped you, I'm sure."

I bark a laugh. "I doubt that, MaeLynn. You know my mother isn't concerned about this kind of stuff. She's probably going to shit when I tell her I had a baby with a stranger. I don't think this fits with her version of what's acceptable in the eyes of her so-called friends. She'd have been fine if it had been Annabelle who had a baby, but I don't think Phoebe is quite what she was hoping for in a daughter-in-law." I can picture the look on my mom's face the first time she takes in Phoebe's crazy copper curls and freckled skin. I somehow doubt my mother will think they're as adorable as I do.

MaeLynn pulls away and smiles up at me. "Oh? Daughter-in-law, is it?" She chuckles when my mouth drops open to protest. That's not what I meant to say. Of course I'm not marrying Phoebe. "I'm teasing you," she says, reading my panic on my face. "I know what you meant. I think you need to cut your mom some slack, though. She's doing the best she knows how in a situation she never wanted. Lord knows your dad hasn't made her life easy."

"Hasn't made it easy?" I scoff. "She spends her days gossiping with her country club friends and trying to force me to fit into some strange society ideal she's dreamed up. What could be easier?"

MaeLynn levels me with a look. "Did I ever tell you that your mom and I used to be best friends?"

That gives me pause. "You were?" For as long as I can remember, my mom has nothing but bad things to say about MaeLynn. She was forever making negative comments about her bright makeup and eccentric clothing choices. It's hard to believe they'd been friends at all, let alone best friends. "What happened?"

"Years ago, when I left my husband, she convinced your father to hire me as his assistant. As the company grew more successful, I gained a special insight into the kind of man he is. I thought she would want to know the way he was behaving, but I couldn't have been more wrong. She didn't believe me and she's never forgiven me for telling her what she considered to be lies about her husband." She shrugs. "She wasn't ready to uproot her entire life, so she severed our friendship. But I suspect this grandchild may be the catalyst she needs.The winds of change are blowing, Archer. Mark my words."

I shake my head. I know my dad has always been an asshole, but I thought it was because he was so focused on the business he didn't pay enough attention to his family. MaeLynn seems to be saying it was something else. "What did he do?"

"That's not for me to tell you." She reaches out and squeezes my hand. "But never mind all that. I only mentioned it because I don't want you to be too hard on your mother. She's made difficult choices in her life, and it hasn't always been sunshine and rainbows for her. Give her a chance."

My mother's been pushing me to fit in with her friends for so long that I don't know that I *can* give her a chance. But I suppose for MaeLynn, I can try. I nod.

"Good. Now let's go set up the living room items. Lana said this baby swing she set you up with is the best thing since sliced bread and I can't wait to see it in action. And after we're done, I expect you to tell me all about Phoebe and Lincoln." She turns and leaves the room. "You boys better have saved me a donut," she yells. "Or we're going to have a problem."

I can hear them laughing and arguing as I take a seat in the rocking chair. It glides smoothly, and I imagine soothing a fussy Lincoln as I slide back and forth while thinking about what MaeLynn said. Will my mom be willing to give up her idea of fitting in because she has a grandson now? And what was it my father did she was so willing to overlook that she lost a friendship with MaeLynn over?

Chapter 19

Visiting Santa's Toy Shop

Phoebe

The sheet of paper Devon gave me yesterday shakes in my hand as I read the address he's written, and then look back up at the building. The numbers match, so this must be it. Funny, it looks nothing like I expected a toy factory to look. Not that I'm sure what I expected it to look like, but this gray, windowless box isn't it.

Pulling my car into the lot, I drive around until I find the spots marked "guest parking" and pull into space. I look in the rearview mirror at Lincoln. "Well, buddy. This is it. Should we go in and see where your dad works?" And suss out where he is with his thoughts on a custody agreement under the pretense of inviting him to Christmas Eve dinner. But, you know, without letting him know that's what I'm doing.

Officer Kaden messaged me this morning with the information he found out about Archer Fade, which was nothing. Well, nothing worrisome. He's the thirty-four-year-old only son of Archibald and Vivian Fade. He's never been married, and he doesn't appear to have any kids. Besides Lincoln. He doesn't have a criminal record, and no one has ever heard of him forgetting a kid at a carnival. On paper, and according to the people Kaden spoke to, Archer's a decent guy. So it looks like as far as having him in Lincoln's life, everything will be fine.

Well, it *will* be fine as long as he doesn't have ideas about trying to get custody from me.

And that, of course, is why I'm even here right now. *I'm sure this visit will go well.* I roll my eyes at the sarcastic tone in my head before turning off the car and getting out. I'm not sure I can pull off sneaky, but I need to try. Ever since Devon brought up the custody thing, I haven't been able to get it out of my head. I need to figure out what Archer is planning to do.

Moving to the back door, I unbuckle Lincoln and get him out of his car seat. And with him and his diaper bag in my arms, I take a deep breath and stride toward the main doors.

Here goes nothing.

Stepping into the lobby, I notice that what looked like a windowless box on the outside is a nice, normal lobby on the inside. And it's not windowless at all. In fact, the entire wall facing the parking lot is one long bank of windows. There's some sort of privacy frosting on it that looked like gray concrete from the outside. That's pretty cool. Makes it look like they're hiding something, but that's ridiculous. What could a toy factory have to hide?

A young woman with expertly highlighted hair and ridiculously long eyelashes is sitting behind a high reception desk and speaking on the phone. She smiles and holds up a finger, letting me know she'll be with me in a second. Her desk is decorated with assorted sizes of modern-looking glass Christmas tree decorations in glittery red, green, and gold, making it look like a festive forest. Those would be perfect on the fireplace mantle at home. Christmas is in less than a week and my rental is woefully under-decorated..

"Hi, sorry about the wait. Can I help you?"

"Uh, yes. Thanks," I say, stepping closer to the desk. "Can you tell me where I can find Archer Fade?"

She looks me up and down and grins when her gaze lands on Lincoln. "He's probably in his office," she says. "It's down at the end of that hallway. His assistant, MaeLynn, will help you. She's dying to meet you." She points to a long hallway off to the right behind the reception desk.

MaeLynn is dying to meet me? Does that mean Archer told her about me? Oh god, what did he say? Wait. This girl knows who I am. What did he tell her?

"Thanks." I nod to the holiday display on her desk. "I love your Christmas trees. Where'd you get them?"

"Aren't they amazing?" She says with a chuckle. "We actually make them here at Fade Toys. It's our Christmas Cheer bundle. Can you believe Archer didn't want me to put up this display at first? He said they didn't look festive enough to be used as a Christmas display."

"You have a good eye. They look wonderful. I wouldn't mind a set for myself."

"Good for you," she says with an approving smile—and was that a wink?—as the phone rings. "Oh, I better get that. You go on back and talk to MaeLynn."

I give her a nod before hoisting Lincoln a little higher in my arms and going down the hallway. It opens onto a small reception area with a desk and two chairs off to the side, but I don't see the assistant who should be here. I can hear voices coming from the open door beyond the desk, though.

It's probably wrong of me to listen in, but...to hell with it. I'm sitting here. I can't exactly turn my ears off, can I?

"That's no problem at all, Roger."

"Oh, thank you so much, Mr. Fade. It would be fine if it weren't the holidays, but the wife and I went overboard on gifts for the kids. If I'd known I'd be replacing my kid's braces three days before Christmas, I wouldn't have spent so much on gifts." The man, Roger, if I heard correctly, scoffs. "Leave it to my son to bust his braces at the height of the holiday season."

"Don't worry about a thing. MaeLynn will make sure HR gets that into your account before the end of the day. Okay? Don't let this stress you out. We'll get it all sorted out. You focus on enjoying your time off. And be sure to say Merry Christmas to Mary and the kids for me."

"Thank you, thank you. I really appreciate it, Mr. Fade."

A deep rumbling chuckle sends a zing through me, and I know it's Archer. His laugh is as wonderful now as it was the night we met.

"No need to thank me, Roger. We take care of each other here. I am going to have to ask you to do one thing for me, though. Call me Archer, okay? I hate being called Mr. Fade. Makes me think my father is lurking around here somewhere."

It's the other man's turn to laugh, and it doesn't have nearly the same effect on me as Archer's did.

"You bet, Mr...I mean, Archer. And thanks again. Thanks, MaeLynn."

A moment later, a man walks out of the office with a smile on his face. He tips his head in greeting as he walks by me before going back down the hallway to the front lobby area.

"So you want me to call the orthodontist and have them put it on your credit card, don't you?" I can hear the smile in the woman's tone. "Instead of giving him the advance he requested?"

Archer laughs again, causing more of those infernal tingles to zip through my body. He has a girlfriend. He has a girlfriend. He has a girlfriend. Maybe if I tell myself enough times, it will finally sink in and I'll stop reacting to him this way.

"Close. Put it on my credit card but still put the money in his account only as a bonus instead of an advance. If he notices that we never ask for it back, we can say it's a computer error and there's no way to reverse it."

He's going to pay for the kid's braces? That's...that's so generous. My heart flutters in my chest. Lincoln's father is a nice guy. So far, he's sounding like the right kind of father to help my son grow into a good man.

"Archer, you know what your father would say about you handing out money like this, don't you?"

He laughs again. *Dammit, does the man have no consideration for the state of my panties?* "Oh, I don't know. Probably something rude about it serving a person right for not budgeting properly, or how people will never learn to be responsible if I give them handouts, blah, blah, blah. I don't really give a shit what he would say, to be honest, because I learned something better from this amazing woman I know. It's that if I can't afford to pay my employees a living wage, or pay for emergency orthodontia occasionally, then I don't deserve to be in business."

Oh geez. He's a really good guy. A really good guy that I'm eavesdropping on like a creep. My stomach drops into my feet.

I need to let these people know that I'm here. When they find out I've been sitting out here eavesdropping on their conversation, they won't be happy. But I can't stop. Listening to Archer talk to his staff is exactly the sort of insight I need into what kind of man he is. And so far it sounds like he's the best kind. Damn it.

Why does he have to be gorgeous and kind? Can't the man have some faults to make it easier to keep this friendly? Like, maybe he's a closet nose-picker? Or one of those guys who doesn't wash their butt? *Ugh. It's no use.* There's no way I believe Archer is anything other than a disciplined three-ply tissue-user with an immaculate ass crack.

Get it together, Phoebe. He has a girlfriend. A stupidly beautiful, ridiculously tall, gorgeously built girlfriend.

Ugh. I should have thought of that when I got dressed. My leggings and hoodie aren't exactly winning me any beauty contests, even if they are clean today.

The woman lets out a low chuckle. "She sounds like a brilliant woman. She's probably also incredibly wise, and beautiful, and kind, and a fabulous cook. Not to mention a superior assistant."

"Hmm. She is. She absolutely is." The woman laughs at Archer's assurances. "But you already know you're all those things, so stop fishing for compliments and get back to work." His voice takes on a stern edge and he pauses before adding, "How was that?"

"Meh. It needs work. But you're getting better. I almost believed you for a second. Keep practicing and you'll get it."

"Thanks, MaeLynn. You really are brilliant, you know."

"Yeah, I know."

"And so humble." He laughs again and I resign myself to the fact that I'm going to have to wash these panties as soon as I get home. Damn it. *I like this pair. They're cute and comfortable, which is difficult to find these days with my new mom bod. I should have bought more.* "Now we both really should get back to work. I want everyone out of here no later than three today. It's the last day before we close for Christmas, so no one works late today."

"Yes, sir. Mr. Fade," the woman says with a laugh.

I can practically hear Archer's eyes roll from here and can't stop the laugh before it jumps from my throat. *Shit.* I should've announced myself before that happened. The heels clicking in my direction tell me they heard me.

"Oh, hello there. How can I hel—Ahhh!" The woman interrupts her own greeting with a scream. "It's you! Oh, my god. I am *so* happy you're here. I was hoping I would get to meet you soon. Bring me that baby." She comes around the desk toward me and makes grabby motions with her hands. "Look at how handsome you are," she says in a sing-song voice, making Lincoln giggle. She raises her voice and calls over her shoulder, "You certainly don't get that from your daddy." She turns back to me. "You must be Phoebe. You're even more gorgeous than Archer said. I'm MaeLynn, Archer's assistant. May I?" She gestures to Lincoln, and he leans toward her.

Umm, hold up. Go back a minute. Did she say Archer told her I was gorgeous? Now I wish I'd made more of an effort when I got dressed to come here. Lincoln drags me from my internal monologue by attempting to jump headfirst into MaeLynn's arms.

"Looks like I don't have much say in the matter. He seems too interested in you for me to get in the way of you two." And with how colorful her makeup and clothes are, I can't blame him. She looks so fun I almost want to let her pick *me* up. "Watch your earrings," I warn as I pass her Lincoln. "He's starting to get grabby fingers."

MaeLynn cuddles Lincoln to her chest, pressing her cheek to his. "This adorable little muffin can rip my ears right off if he wants to."

"Looks like you met MaeLynn." Archer has come out of his office and is leaning against MaeLynn's desk, arms and legs crossed, looking like he doesn't have a care in the world. *How is it fair for a man to look that sexy in a suit?* "As you can see, she loves babies."

"I sort of figured," I say, standing up. "I think maybe it was the scream that gave it away. She played it totally cool otherwise." I wink.

Archer gives an exaggerated nod. "Oh, yeah. Totally cool."

"Lincoln and I don't need this negativity," MaeLynn says. "We're taking a walk." She stops and turns to me. "If that's okay with you, Phoebe?"

I look to Archer because no matter how nice this woman seems, we just met, and he's my best source of information.

"Don't go far," he tells her. "I want to be the one introducing my son to the staff."

"Don't worry. We'll only go out to the lobby and look out the windows."

MaeLynn holds Lincoln out so I can lean in and give him a kiss before she takes him on their walk. I watch until they're out of sight.

"He'll be fine. She has three grandkids that she watches all the time. They're a little older now, but I know she's been missing having a baby around to snuggle. You made her day by coming to visit. I'm sure this will be the highlight of her week."

I'm still staring down the hallway when I nod and mumble an answer. "Oh. Yeah, sure. I know."

And I do know, I'm not merely saying that. If I were here for any reason besides spying on Archer, then I'm sure MaeLynn's kindness would be more welcome. She seems wonderful. And her scream of delight when she spotted us, evidently knowing who we were before we officially met, was clearly genuine.

"So what brings you by? And how did you know where I work? I don't remember mentioning it. Not that I mind the surprise. I just wasn't expecting a visit."

Shit. He didn't tell me, did he? *Quick, Phoebe. Think of a plausible reason you know where he works when he didn't tell you. Whatever you don't tell him.* "I had a friend figure it out for me." *No, you weren't supposed to tell him that. That's too close to the truth.*

He chuckles. "Well, you found me."

I force a laugh. "Yeah, ha ha. I guess I did." I turn to look at him and I'm immediately struck by how good he looks today. Every time I'm next to him, he blinds me with how attractive he is. He's pushed his shirtsleeves up, showing off thick forearms with a smattering of dark hair. The pants he's wearing fit snugly across his thighs and the way they're stretched to capacity at the front hints at what I vaguely remember he's hiding behind his zipper. My tongue darts out to wet my lips as I wonder how I can get him to turn around. Maybe if I throw a pen on the floor, he'll do a "bend-and-snap" for me. I need to see if his ass fills out those pants like I think it does. *I recall he has a hockey player's ass. A big ol' bubble butt that would be perfect for sinking my tee—*

"Phoebe?"

"Huh?" I snap my head up, suddenly aware that I've been staring. "Sorry, what? Did you say something?"

"I asked if there was something you needed and that's why you came here?"

"Shit, that's right. Yeah. Well, you know, you know it's almost Christmas Eve, right?" *Damn it, Phoebe. He obviously knows when Christmas Eve is. Stop being stupid and try to string together a coherent sentence like the intelligent woman you are.* Thankfully, Archer doesn't acknowledge the stupidity of my question. He merely nods and waits for me to continue. "I was wondering if you wanted to come for dinner at my place? My parents will be coming to visit and they'd like to meet you."

The surprise on his face is quickly eclipsed by a huge grin. "Really?" He pauses and appears to think for a moment. "I'd love to. What can I bring?"

"Nothing." I breathe a sigh of relief. For a second I almost thought he would say no. "Just bring yourself. I'm cooking everything other than dessert. Charlie volunteered to be in charge of that, so be prepared to hear the smoke detector going off every five minutes. Also, don't be surprised when dessert is black on the bottom, like those cookies she made that first day you came by." I chuckle.

"I thought that was because Eric kept knocking on the door and distracting her."

"Nope. She is infamous for her baking disasters. Yet, for some reason, she insists on baking. All. The. Time. She says it helps relieve stress. I'm not sure how, though, with every baking session punctuated by the sounds of a smoke detector. Sometimes I wonder if she's hard of hearing from so many years of setting off fire alarms, but the way she responds when Lincoln cries in another room, even when I've forgotten to turn the baby monitor on, makes me doubt that."

"That does make your theory of hearing loss less plausible." He chuckles and hits me with that grin again. The ensuing flood of warmth reminds me of the situation in my pants. *Stupid panty-melting grin. He makes it impossible to not be attracted to him. No wonder his girlfriend was mad when she found us alone together. She knows the effect he has on women and assumed I was halfway in love with him already.*

"Well, I should get going," I hurry to say. "Don't want to keep you from work for too long. And I need to do some last-minute Christmas shopping. One great thing about babies that no one tells you? You can take them shopping with you to buy gifts for them and they'll never be the wiser. I've bought all of Lincoln's gifts while he was right there with me. He's even been next to me when I've wrapped some of them."

"That sounds convenient."

"Right? Makes things a lot easier." I take a step toward the hall to the front lobby.

"Let me walk you out," Archer says, lifting the diaper bag from my shoulder and draping it over his own. "We might have our work cut out for us with finding MaeLynn and Lincoln. I'm not at all confident she didn't find some people to introduce Lincoln to, despite telling her I wanted to do it myself."

"Another reason babies are great. I can pretty much guarantee he won't remember anyone he meets today, so you're free to introduce him all over again." I crack a grin and Archer chuckles.

"Well, I know that's not true." MaeLynn meets us as we enter the main lobby. "Lincoln and I have bonded. We're best friends now. Isn't that right, little man?" Strangely, Lincoln giggles and makes noises almost as though he agrees with her before tucking his head into her neck. "But I suppose it is time for you to go back to your mama." She gives him one last squeeze before putting him in my arms and running a gentle hand over his fluffy red hair. "Such a sweet baby."

Yeah, I know. The lucky kid got my ginger hair. Good thing he has his dad's beautiful chocolate brown eyes to balance it out.

"It was nice to meet you, MaeLynn."

"You too, sweetheart. Bring that baby around here anytime."

MaeLynn continues past us down the hallway, and Archer leads me to the entrance and outside. Lincoln kicks his little legs until we get to the car and I get him in his car seat, where he's suddenly intensely angry at being confined and makes it known by letting out a squawky little shriek. I shake my head and close the door. We'll be home in a few minutes. I'm sure he can handle his car seat for that long.

"Is he alright?" Archer asks, his voice thick with concern. "He sounds hurt."

I chuckle. "No, that's his angry cry. He's mad that he's being confined in his car seat after being carried around for the last half hour. The mirror I have on the headrest doesn't let him see as much as being held upright in someone's arms does."

"Oh, yeah. I guess that makes sense."

I open the driver's door and Archer passes me the diaper bag, which I throw into the passenger seat. "Okay, well. Thanks for taking the time to see me today. Dinner is at six on Christmas Eve, but come by anytime after four." Without waiting for his reply, I drop into the driver's seat and close the door. After pulling my keys out and starting the car, I open my window and wave.

He smiles, and with a wave of his own, turns and walks back to the building. He's almost back to the door when I realize I forgot to tell Archer that his girlfriend is welcome to join us for dinner, too. I back out of my spot and pull up alongside him. "Archer," I call out. "About dinner. I forgot to say you're welcome to bring your..." My stomach drops, and the word "girlfriend" gets stuck in my throat. The best I can do is squeak out, "friend." I stare at him for a moment before blurting, "Okay, bye."

I stomp on the gas and peel out of the parking lot without waiting for an answer, leaving a confused-looking Archer standing in front of his building. My eyes flick down from his face to Lincoln's reflection in the rearview mirror.

Is it possible for a baby to suffer second-hand embarrassment? Because the way he's looking at me right now leads me to believe they can.

At least one good thing came from the visit. Unless he's attempting to lull me into a false sense of security, nothing about Archer's behavior gave me the impression that he's going to fight for custody of Lincoln. Not yet, at least.

Chapter 20

Where's Krampus When You Need Him?

Archer

I STARE AFTER PHOEBE's car as she drives out of the parking lot, my heart longing to chase after her. I wish we were shopping together. At least I have Christmas dinner to look forward to.

What was that she said as she drove out of here fast enough to make even the most dedicated *Fast and Furious* fan proud? Bring my friend? Oh, she must mean Eric. That seems odd since she didn't seem to like him very much when we were at her place. Of course, she didn't seem to like me very much when we were there the first time, either, and she still invited me. But she said to bring him, so she must be okay with him after all.

I pull my phone from my pocket and message him while I walk to my office.

Archer

Dinner at Phoebe's on Christmas Eve. She told me to bring you if you're not busy.

Eric

I knew it. She wants me.

I snort a laugh despite the sudden twinge of jealousy in my chest, making the front desk receptionist, Amanda, shoot me a curious look. I shrug and walk past her to the back hallway. I'm not ready to explain these strange feelings to myself, let alone to my twenty-something receptionist.

Archer

You wish.

Eric

Whatever helps you sleep. What should I bring and what time is dinner?

Archer

Dinner's at 6. She said we don't need to bring anything.

Eric

Wine it is.

I was thinking of bringing that too, but now I'm not so sure. Maybe I should bring something a little more family-friendly? Or a little more festive? What do normal families do for Christmas, anyway?

I haven't had a normal Christmas since I was a kid. Before my grandparents died, we'd have Christmas at their house and it was okay, I guess. I got presents, and we ate food, but I wouldn't say it was fun. I'm an only child and my parents were both only children, so it's not like I had a lot of kids to play with. And they didn't even allow me to play with any of the gifts I received while I was at my grandparents' house. Both parents and grandparents were afraid I'd lose pieces, and they'd be stepping on them or tripping over them for the rest of the day.

I stop in front of MaeLynn's desk and wait for her to look up. If anyone can help me figure this out, it's my kind-hearted, motherly assistant.

"Yes?"

"She invited me to her place for Christmas Eve dinner with her family. What should I bring? My family hasn't had a normal Christmas in over twenty years, so I'm out of practice."

Her eyes turn soft. "Aww, honey. I'm sorry."

I force a smile and shake my head. "Nothing to be sorry for. My parents are my parents."

She leans forward and gives my arm a quick squeeze. "Okay, let's get this sorted. Do you know who else is going? That'll tell us what sort of celebration they're having."

"She said her parents would be there. And I'm sure her sister and brother will be, too. Lincoln, of course." We both smile. "Oh, and she told me to invite Eric."

"Eric?" She scrunches her face. "Why?"

I shrug. "She said to bring my friend, and the only one she's met so far is Eric."

MaeLynn taps her lower lip with a long fingernail. "That sounds like a decent-sized group. But not overly formal. Who's cooking?"

"Phoebe said she was. She can't let her sister help with the main meal because she sets off the smoke detector every time she touches the oven. She is letting her be in charge of dessert, though." I chuckle at the memory of the smoke detector blaring in the middle of her telling me off on their porch. Talk about bad timing.

MaeLynn snickers. "My daughter-in-law is like that. The girl has the best intentions but somehow burns everything she makes. It's almost like she tries too hard."

"Phoebe said her sister likes to bake when she's stressed, but that nothing ever turns out. I doubt the blaring of an alarm helps reduce her stress levels, either. She probably needs a new hobby."

"Hmmm," MaeLynn says, her face now in her phone, with her fingers flying over the screen. "What if you brought something like this?" She turns her phone and holds it up for me. "This bakery is offering a package of gourmet pies that you take home and bake yourself. They come in these gorgeous artisan made pie plates that you keep, then later you can recreate the pies using the recipes they give you." She shows me a picture of hand-painted ceramic pie plates followed by a picture of several beautiful, not to mention delicious-looking, and noticeably unburned, pies. "It's dessert and a gift."

"Sure, let's order that. But shouldn't I also bring something for Phoebe? I mean, she's the one who invited me." And she's the mother of my child, not to mention the most beautiful woman I've ever seen.

MaeLynn gives me an appraising look and I clear my throat, not ready to have that conversation out loud quite yet. "That's a fabulous idea. What does she like?"

I groan. "I hardly know her. We had lunch together once and aside from that, we haven't spent a lot of time together." She grins and cocks a knowing eyebrow. "Besides that," I say, rolling my eyes. "And neither she nor I remember that night very well, anyway."

"Okay, okay. Moving on, then. You don't have any ideas?"

Then I remember her fruit hammock and the picture she showed me of the tapestry she made for Lincoln. "Actually, I think I might."

By the time MaeLynn and I sort out what gifts I need to bring to Phoebe's, it's nearly three o'clock. I promised myself and the staff that we'd all get out of here at three today and it's a promise I plan to keep, so after sending MaeLynn home, I take myself to the production floor to make sure we all follow through.

I walk through the main doors and call out, "Alright, everyone. Dildos down. It's time to go celebrate the holidays with your families."

A cheer rings out and everyone packs up their materials before shutting down the equipment and filing past me out the doors.

"See you after the holidays," I say, shaking hands with everyone as they walk by. "Merry Christmas, and have a safe and happy New Year's celebration. And for the love of god, don't drink and drive. Call me if you need a ride and I'll find a ride for you." They all laugh and promise to call. "Good. I want to see you all in the new year."

Roger is the last to leave the room, and he stops me as we walk out the production floor door. "You sure you want to stop production for the week? That's a lot of products not being made. We've never closed the shop before. You could lose a lot of money."

"I'm positive, Roger," I say, putting a hand on his shoulder and steering him toward the staff room. "Now go home and enjoy the time with your family. And tell your son to lay off the sticky foods if he doesn't want his braces to break again."

He cracks a grin and nods. "Okay, Mr. Fa—I mean, Archer. Merry Christmas," he says, reaching out for a handshake. "And Happy New Year."

After Roger leaves, I take a quick walk around the production floor to ensure everything has been shut down safely before wandering out to the lobby.

The last person to leave for the day is Amanda. "Any fun plans for the holidays this year?" I ask as I hold the door for her.

"Nothing crazy," she says. "I'll be spending it at home with my brother, his wife, and their twins. They have some friends and their families coming, too, so it should be fun."

"Sounds perfect."

She waves as she walks to her car and I wait at the door to make sure she gets on her way alright. She's my youngest employee and I think of her as a little sister. I want to make sure she's good before I lock up.

This is what I've worked so hard for this past year, I think as I watch my staff exit the building with huge smiles on their faces and hugs for their coworkers. My plan to turn Fade Toys into an excellent place to work is taking hold now that the staff is trusting it. My father had run this place with an iron fist and when I first took over, the staff expected the same from me. Every meeting we had and every initiative I implemented was met with skepticism and mistrust. They thought I was going to turn around and snatch their higher wages, benefits, and perks away from them eventually, so they didn't want to let their guard down. I can't say I blame them, because that's exactly the kind of thing I could imagine my father doing.

But now, watching them head home to their families for a well-deserved break for the holidays? Yeah, that makes me think I might be okay at this job after all. It's taken over a year, but I might manage to make this the best sex toy factory to work at yet.

"Oh, before I forget." She yells from her open car window. "The woman who came to see you earlier? Yeah, she loved my display. I was totally right. The Christmas Cheer bundle is festive enough for the holiday marketing. She even said she wouldn't mind having a set for herself. So there, I win," she says with a laugh. "See you in the new year." She jumps in her car and speeds out of the lot like she didn't just drop a bomb on me.

Phoebe wants one of the Christmas Cheer butt plug training sets? It's probably too much to hope that I'd be the one lucky enough to use it with her, but I can't help the lust the thought inspires. My brain floods with images of Phoebe, bent over, hole slick and glistening with lube, as I tenderly slide in one of the glittery glass plugs while sinking my cock into her sweet pussy. The mere thought has me so fucking hard, it's like my dick is attempting to occupy the same physical space as my zipper.

Fuuuuck.

I lock the main doors and limp down the hallway back to my office after adjusting my dick in my pants. Images of Phoebe in various states of undress, in various positions, keep playing in my head. I'm excruciatingly hard, yet I can't stop the thoughts from coming. *Do I even want to stop them?* I'm debating between taking care of this hard-on right now and waiting until I get home when I discover I'm not as alone in the building as I thought.

"We'll need to rework the employee contracts once I come back, too. I can't make a decent profit if we keep paying out this much in wages. What was my idiot son thinking? Keeping wage costs low is the best way to maximize profits."

I'm walking past MaeLynn's desk when I hear my father's voice booming out of my office. *Well, that takes care of the boner issue.* What the hell is he doing here? And why's he going on about coming back? *He's retired.*

Needing to know what he's talking about, and who he's talking to, I stop short of my office door and stick close to the wall. My curiosity is the only thing keeping me from running in there and demanding an answer. I know I'll get better information if I can be patient and wait for him to slip up.

"I don't care what you have to do, Gerald. Figure it out. There's no way I can keep paying these ridiculous wages. Archer's going to put us in the poorhouse if he keeps this up."

First, the poorhouse? Gerald is his lawyer. Why the hell is he telling his lawyer I'm putting them in the poorhouse? My parents live in a mansion on the north side of Westborough. The worst they'd ever need to do is move back to a middle-class neighborhood and make do with a normal-sized bungalow. *Oh no, what a tragedy.* And second, I only lowered my salary and reallocated some of the company profits to pay the staff a thriving wage. My parents' company-paid pension was untouched. Besides, with the money he's made over the years, he can live off the interest from his investments, unlike the staff. Most of them are finally starting to dig themselves out of the financial holes they'd been forced into when my father was in charge. There's no way I'll let him go back to paying them as little as allowed by law.

"Okay, yes. That sounds good. He still has a chance. If he meets the conditions I've laid out, I'll let him keep playing boss. Production is up, so he must be doing something right. And now that I know the crew can work this hard, they damn well better keep it up, even when they're back to their old wages. Otherwise, they'll be out looking for a new job."

Rage fills me, my fists clenching so tightly they throb. My father is such an asshole. But I already knew that. What I still haven't figured out is why he's in my office. It's taking everything in me not to rush in there, but I know how my father operates. If I want to know why he's here, I'll have to overhear it from whatever conversation he's having on the phone.

"I know that Gerald, but I didn't think he would go all soft-hearted when I gifted him the company. I thought I'd raised him right. Yes, yes. We should have added the clause when we first wrote the contracts. Okay, I'll let you know when I find his copy of the paperwork. Goodbye."

Paperwork? I'm not sure what he thinks he's looking for, but he's crazy if he thinks I'll stand by and let him ruin all I've worked for.

"Hey Dad," I say, going for the element of surprise with the nonchalant lilt in my voice as I pop around the corner into my office. "What are you doing in my office?"

"Shit!" He yells, slamming a drawer on my desk as he jumps. "Where did you come from?" I watch him stand up taller and straighten his tie. He fixes me with a haughty expression that was far more intimidating when I was a kid. And would be a lot more intimidating now if he weren't trying to sneak out from behind my desk like he hadn't just been caught doing something underhanded. "Shouldn't you be working on making us more money?"

"Actually, *Dad,*" I sneer, knowing he's going to hate what I have to say next almost as much as I'm going to love saying it to him. "I was wishing the staff a Merry Christmas. We're closed until the new year."

"You're what?" He bellows, his eye twitching. "Why would you be closed? Our orders—the product—" he splutters, his face turning a brilliant shade of red. I can't say I don't love seeing him this way.

I walk around my desk and take a seat, leaning forward in my chair. "New orders are on hold until after the holidays. We fulfilled all the retail orders last week, and all the private orders already shipped. The team works hard. They deserve to spend the holidays with their families."

"I can't believe you, Archer. You're going to run this business into the ground."

I can't help the chuckle that escapes. "Profits are up. But I'm sure you already know that." I narrow my eyes at him. "Let me ask you again. Why are you here?"

He takes a deep breath, unbuttons his jacket, and lowers himself into a seat across from me. "I'm here to make sure you do the right thing. To make sure you do what it takes to keep this company looking respectable in the eyes of your mother's friends. You will marry Annabelle and make sure she's taken care of."

My fists slam down on my desk, and I launch out of my chair. "What aren't you understanding? Under no circumstances will I be marrying Annabelle."

My father stands up and buttons his jacket again. "That's where you're mistaken, son. If you want to remain at the helm of Fade Toys and continue with this ridiculous *healthy workplace, living wage, woke snowflake* bullshit, you'll marry Annabelle. And you'll do it soon. Because if you don't, I will take back control of Fade Toys and these employees you love so much? Well, they can get with my program, or they can be on their way."

All the bravado rushes from my system in a harsh breath as I watch him walk away, the silence of the building amplifying the sound of his footsteps echoing down the hall. When I can't hear them anymore, I lose it.

"FUCK!" With a sweep of my arms, everything on my desk goes flying before I sink into my chair.

Can he really take the company from me? Is that what he was talking to his lawyer about? How do I fix this? Can it even be fixed? Can they really force me to marry Annabelle?

Because as much as I don't want to marry her, I know there's no way I can subject my staff to working for my dad again.

And the first thing I need to do to prevent that is go home and read through that contract again.

And call my lawyer.

Chapter 21

Santa Claus Is Coming To Town

Phoebe

I REREAD THE TEXT for what has to be the hundredth time, my heart pounding in my ears with anticipation.

Archer

> Hey. This is Archer. Are you busy today? I was hoping I could come by and visit Lincoln.

The message came in this morning around eleven, right after I put Lincoln down for his morning nap, and I'd hesitated only a moment before answering.

Phoebe

Yes, Archer. I saved your number last time you called. I'm home today.

Come by around one, Lincoln should be up from his nap around then.

It's shortly after one o'clock, and Lincoln is still fast asleep. I've checked myself in the mirror about eighteen times, making sure I at least look better than I did the night of the party, and now I'm waiting for Archer to arrive. What? Just because he has a girlfriend doesn't mean I need to look like a bridge troll. Besides, it's not like I put in a *lot* of effort.

Okay, so maybe I stepped it up a tiny bit from yesterday when I went to see him at work in my usual leggings and hoodie, but not by much. A little more makeup and some light hairstyling. Plus, I'm wearing real pants. Well, jeans. Jeans that I recently bought in a larger size to accommodate all the baby weight that seems to want to stick around on my ass forever, but jeans nonetheless.

But that's it.

Oh, and a clean shirt.

But that's really all.

I'm not ready to admit that for a mom with a five-month-old who doesn't always sleep through the night, doing all that was like dressing up for a black-tie event. And I did it because Archer is coming over. At least when I had to get dolled up for the Christmas parties when I started looking for him, I had Charlie and Gavin here to help. Today it was me rushing through it by myself, trying not to breathe too hard in case Lincoln heard it and woke up before I was ready. Yes, I know that's crazy, but I didn't want to risk waking him.

Not that I actually needed to get ready. I mean, it's not like he's coming here for me. His message specifically stated he wanted to come over and visit Lincoln. So why was I driven to get spruced up?

It has to be because I'm still anxious over not knowing his thoughts on custody arrangements. I needed to burn off some of the extra energy caused by the stress. And shaving and moisturizing most of my body, then doing my hair and makeup all while breathing as shallowly as possible, was a way to do that. Yeah, that's it.

It's got nothing with wanting him to think I look good. I don't care if he likes the way I look. That has nothing to do with it. Right?

The doorbell rings, cutting off that line of thought before it goes down a road I'm not ready to explore.

He's here.

I rush to the door and fling it open with a little more force than necessary, catching it before it slams into the wall.

"Hey, come on in," I say, attempting to play it cool and failing miserably. Why does he make me so nervous? I mean, besides the obvious. Here he is on my porch again, looking good enough to eat. He looks amazing in suits, but there's something about the way those jeans are hugging his thighs that makes me want to throw my panties at him.

"Phoebe," he says, leaning forward and kissing my cheek. "Thanks for letting me come over. I brought these for you." He places a box in my hands. "Gourmet donuts. I wasn't sure what kind you liked, so I got an assortment to try."

I open the box and inhale the delicious scent of the sweet fried dough, using it to distract me from my lust-filled thoughts. Now that my libido is awake, I can't seem to keep it under wraps. I need to remember to open up that battery-operated boyfriend from Charlie so I can finally take the edge off.

"And Amanda from my office said you were, uh, admiring the Christmas Cheer set on her desk? So I brought you that, too." He hands me another box. "I hope that's not too weird?"

I grin. "What? Oh my god. That's amazing. Thank you so much. I haven't stopped thinking about these since I saw them. I can't wait to set them up and take pictures."

He chokes out a nervous-sounding laugh and looks to the side. That's weird. Maybe he doesn't take pictures of his Christmas decorations? Well, that's just too damn bad. It's Lincoln's first Christmas, so I plan on taking pictures of *everything*.

"Coffee?" I ask, smiling up at him. "Lincoln is still asleep."

"Should you wake him up? Won't he have a hard time sleeping later if he sleeps too long?"

I bark out a surprised laughed. "No. No, no, no. The first rule of babies is: don't wake a sleeping baby."

He chuckles and slips off his jacket, hanging it on a hook by the door. My breath catches at the sight of him in a t-shirt. If the jeans are unfair, the t-shirt is downright evil. It hugs his muscles, giving me a view of the spectacular chest I remember from my x-rated night with Santa.

If memory serves, I licked that chest a time or two that night. I kind of want to lick it again. Lick his chest, and all the other parts I licked that night, too.

"Phoebe?" Archer gets my attention, a knowing smile on his face. Can he read my mind? "You alright?"

"Huh, what? Yes, fine. I can't wait to get my mouth on these donuts." I spin on my heel to speed walk away. "How about that coffee?" I ask, dropping the box of donuts on the dining table as I walk by.

He chuckles and follows me to the kitchen. "I'd love one."

I pour two cups and bring them, along with cream and sugar, to the table. Archer adds a little cream to his cup and then offers it to me, pouring in a splash when I nod yes. He does the same with the sugar, adding a little for me before adding some to his cup.

"So, what was that you were saying about sleeping babies?" he asks before taking a sip of his coffee. I can hardly tear my eyes away as he licks his lips afterward..

"Oh, that? It's something my mom taught me. She said that babies sleep when they need it. When you wake them up from naps, they sleep worse at night. The only exception was when he was a newborn, I had to wake him up to feed him, because he was premature. The nurses in the hospital told me that sometimes newborns, especially those that are born a little early, forget to wake up to eat. Sometimes they sleep so long, when they wake up they're so hungry it hurts."

"Why do they need to eat at night?" He sounds genuinely perplexed, which makes sense. I didn't understand it at first either.

"Babies have tiny little stomachs."—I make a circle with my thumb and forefinger to illustrate how small they are—"They fill, and empty, quickly."

He nods and takes another drink. "Seems like I have a lot to learn about babies."

I chuckle. "They aren't that complicated. They mostly need the basics. Food, shelter, love, and lots and lots of clean diapers."

He chuckles. "That doesn't sound so bad."

"It's not." I shrug. "At least it's not too bad until you have to provide all that when the baby is screaming and covered in his own shit. That's when it gets a little trickier."

He lets out a bark of laughter and shakes his head. "That sounds terrible. I wonder if I can take lessons somewhere?"

You know those birthing and parenting classes they're always going to in the movies? The one where the couples practice breathing and then learn to put a diaper on a doll? A picture of Archer sitting next to me in one pops into my head and I can't stop the brief stab of sadness that settles in my gut.

Not for the first time, I find myself wishing I'd had a partner to go through it all with me. It was hard to do it alone, even with all the help from my family.

Especially when it came time to give birth. It would have been nice to have someone hold my hand. Or who I could yell at during childbirth, even if they weren't doing any of the work.

I clear my throat and reach into the box of donuts, pulling out the first one I touch. Chocolate covered with some sort of crunchy cereal, caramel drizzle, and flakes of sea salt. The noise I make when I bite into it is positively indecent, but I can't bring myself to care.

That's a damn good donut.

"I could teach you," I say around a mouthful of decadent dessert. "You know, if you want," I add, without looking up.

"Really? You would do that?" His voice takes on a husky quality and when I look up, there's a spark of...something in his eyes. As I'm about to ask if there's something on my face, Lincoln's babbles come through the baby monitor.

I stand up and dust my hands on my jeans. "I would. And it's time for your first lesson. Come on."

He gives me that panty-melting grin again, whatever was sparking in his eyes now gone, and stands. "Lead the way, professor."

Archer's gaze blazes hot on my back as he follows me to the bedroom I share with Lincoln. How amazing would it be if he were following me to my bedroom for another reason?

I huff a silent laugh. *Yeah, right, Phoebe. Like he'd want to take you to bed when he has that gorgeous blonde with the mile-long legs waiting for him when he gets home.* No, it's enough that he intends to be involved in Lincoln's life. I can't get greedy now. I wanted one thing when I moved back to Westborough and I got it. I found Lincoln's father.

And now I'm going to teach him how to be a dad. A great dad. Then he'll go off and have a baby with the blonde. *Would he forget Lincoln? No. There's no way.* A knot in my stomach has me rubbing my belly. Why does the thought of Archer having a baby with that woman hurt so much when he's not mine and never has been?

Damn it.

"Everything okay?" A hand on my shoulder drags me out of my reverie. "You've been staring at the door for a solid minute."

I shake my head and blink a few times. "Sorry. Guess I zoned out for a second there," I say, opening the bedroom door. "You ready?"

He nods and follows me into the room, stopping next to me at the side of the crib.

"Hi Linky, did you have a nice nap?" Lincoln kicks his little legs, a gummy grin on his face as I pick him up and carry him to the changing table. "So as soon as he wakes up, you want to change his diaper. If he sits in a dirty diaper too long, he'll get a rash and we like to avoid that. Make sense?"

"Can I try?"

"You want to change a diaper?" I cock an eyebrow. Starting with diapers is impressive. I thought he'd want to hang back and watch for a while before practicing on his own.

He shrugs. "Well, it's not exactly high on my list of fun things to do, but you said he can't stay in it long and I'm here to learn. Might as well start now."

I nod, a little stunned that he wants to jump right in with diapers first thing, but he said he wanted to learn. "Sure, uh, sure. Yeah. That's a phenomenal idea. That's what we're here for, right?"

"Put me in, Coach. I got this." Archer hops side to side like a boxer and feigns cracking his neck and I can't help but laugh.

"Okay, let's get to it. Grab a diaper and the package of wipes from that shelf," I say, pointing to the shelf above the changing table. "And whatever you do, don't let him go. He's started rolling, and he's already tried rolling off the table several times."

Archer looks at me with wide eyes. "Really? That's something that happens?"

I shrug. "I guess. They say babies are resilient, though, and it infrequently does much harm. But better safe than sorry, right? As long as you don't leave him unattended it will be fine."

I show him how to get Lincoln undressed and how to slide a fresh diaper under the old one before opening it. I explain how to properly clean the baby using wipes and show him where the trash goes. Then I step back.

And it's a good thing I do, too. Because there's one little thing I forgot to warn Archer about.

"Shit! What is happening right now? Dude, stop." Archer's arm is fully extended with a hand on Lincoln's belly as he turns away with his eyes squeezed tight, a grimace on his lips. He's holding his other hand away from his body, looking almost like he's leaning away from it, too.

A laugh rips from me when I see the arc of liquid reflecting the light and I realize what's happening. I rush forward to help, but I'm laughing too hard to do much more than flip the diaper back over Lincoln's front.

"I'm sorry," I force out in between laughs. "I forgot to say you need to be ready to cover him up quickly." I wheeze, my shoulders shaking with more laughter. "The cold air—hahaha—the cold air can make him pee!" I squeal the last few words before bursting into hysterical giggles. "Oh, my god. You should see your face!"

"Haha. So funny," he deadpans with a trace of laughter in his voice. "Are you all done, little man? Let's get you cleaned up then, okay?"

I continue to chuckle as I go to the dresser to grab a clean onesie and a pair of pants for Lincoln while Archer gets a fresh diaper on him. "Here." I stand next to Archer with the new clothes in my hand. "I'll get him dressed so you can go wash up."

"Oh, yeah. Good idea, thanks." He bends over Lincoln and tickles his tummy. "You were aiming for me, weren't you, buddy?" He laughs. "Aim a little higher next time, and you might hit more than my hand."

He walks to the bedroom door and stops. "Where's the bathroom?"

"Straight across the hall."

"Thanks."

I get Lincoln into his clothes and am picking him up as Archer comes back into the room. "That's better. I wasn't expecting to get peed on when I came over today. That was a fun surprise," he says with a chuckle as he comes to stand close enough that the heat from his chest warms my arm.

"A fun little bonus, hey?" My voice is breathy and my heart is pounding in my ears. I sway closer, pressing my hand against his chest when his palm comes to rest on my lower back. I turn to face him, one hand holding Lincoln and the other resting on his chest.

What is happening? My stomach is a riot of butterflies, and my breath comes faster and faster. I catch myself looking at his lips before darting my eyes back to his. Why's it so hot in here all of a sudden?

"Thank you," he says. His eyes search my face, his hand traveling up my arm as he inches closer.

"For what?" My voice comes out as barely a whisper, so muted I'm amazed I can hear it over the sound of my pounding heart.

"For everything." My pulse spikes as he leans even closer. What's he doing? The thumping of my heart is so loud there's no way he doesn't hear it. I'm pretty sure it's about to jump out of my chest and take a little stroll.

Is he kissing me? Holy shit, he is. Excitement, and relief, and euphoria rush through my system in equal measure. *Close your eyes, Phoebe. Don't be weird.*

I let my eyelids flutter closed and lick my lips, the thought of kissing Archer sending tingles all the way to my toes. I hope his lips are as soft as I remember.

"I'll take this." I sense the loss of heat from his body before it registers that he's stepped away. "Are you okay?"

My eyes fly open and he's standing in front of me holding Lincoln's rolled up dirty diaper ready for the trash.

He wasn't trying to kiss me; he was reaching past me to get the diaper from the changing table.

You're an idiot, Phoebe. Embarrassment floods my body, heating my face, and pissing me off. I'm glad he didn't kiss me. I guess I forgot for a moment that I don't mess around with other women's men. And I'm glad Lincoln pissed on him, too.

I clear my throat and force a laugh. "Oh, yeah. I'm fine. Just had something in my eye." I make a show of blinking hard. "I think it's out now." I step around him and walk to the door. "Should we move on to the next lesson? Let me show you how to make him a bottle."

Chapter 22

Meeting The Parents Part One

Archer

"And that's all there is to it. The instructions are right there on the formula container, if you forget. And promise you won't try to cheat and heat it in the microwave. The uneven heat distribution could leave hot spots that might burn him." She shows me how to test the temperature of the milk on the inside of my wrist. "I try not to heat his milk too much, anyway. I find it makes him sleepy and I'm trying this thing where he naps, then eats, then plays, before going down for another nap again. I read it in one of those millions of baby books I told you about."

Phoebe's been acting a little weird since we left the bedroom after getting Lincoln up. There was a moment while I was reaching for his diaper that I almost thought she wanted me to kiss her, but apparently she had something in her eye.

Too bad.

Honestly, the temptation to kiss her was almost too much to handle. When she closed her eyes as I was reaching past her, I nearly abandoned the diaper, turned my head, and pressed my lips to hers. Good thing I thought better of it at the last second and grabbed the trash before stepping back. I doubt she'd be happy to continue teaching me this baby stuff if she thought I was using it as an excuse to try to get into her pants again.

Not that I would *mind* getting into her pants. I haven't been able to focus on much else since I gave her the butt plug set and she said she wanted to take pictures, to be honest. But I'm sure she doesn't want me involved in that, so I push it out of my head. She has more than enough to worry about without thinking the father of her child brought her butt plugs, hoping to sleep with her again.

But damn if I'm not hoping. Hard.

And she didn't seem upset with me for bringing them, thankfully. I was worried about it the whole way here. It could have gone so much worse.

"That makes sense. I can't tell you how many times I've tried to reheat Thanksgiving leftovers, only to have them be ice cold in some places and scorching hot in others."

She chuckles. "Exactly. Come on." She gestures for me to follow her to the living room.

I've got Lincoln in my arms, practicing holding him, and he's so soft I want to nuzzle into his squishy little neck. Babies must be magic if he has me wanting to do that a mere ten minutes after he pissed on me. "You ready to eat, little man?" He reaches up and smacks me in the face. "Hmm, that sounds like a yes to me."

"Sit there," she says, pointing to the end of the couch. "He likes to snuggle while he eats, and it's easier if you have somewhere to rest your arm."

She positions me with Lincoln resting in the crook of my arm and gives me the bottle. "He likes to put his hands on it, but he's not great at holding it yet, so you need to keep it in position."

As soon as I raise the bottle to his lips, Lincoln sucks at it like he's starving. I guess what Phoebe was saying about babies having small stomachs is true even now that he's a little older. He's drinking like he's never had a drop of milk in his life. My heart melts a bit more with each of the little grunting noises he makes every time he sucks the bottle.

It's so weird staring into his huge brown eyes. They're so much like my own, it's like looking in a mirror to the past. I need to go dig up some baby pictures at my parents' house to confirm, but I suspect Lincoln looks almost identical to the way I looked as a baby. Other than the crazy red hair he gets from his mother, that is.

"So I have a confession to make." Phoebe hands me a cup of coffee and sits next to me on the couch. I hadn't even noticed she'd left the room because I was too busy staring at Lincoln. I can't help it. The kid is so mesmerizing I almost miss what she's saying. "I checked you out."

My head snaps up. She certainly has my attention now. "You checked me out?" I ask, wiggling my eyebrows. "Do tell."

Her mouth opens to protest when she realizes what she said. "No, shit. No. That's not what I meant."

Pity.

"I meant I had you checked out. By a private investigator. And the police."

I snort a laugh. "Yeah. Right." She looks at me, her face devoid of expression but for a little redness on her cheeks. "Wait. You're serious? Why?"

She cocks an eyebrow. "Do you really need to ask that? You may be Lincoln's father, but it's not like I know you. I needed to make sure he would be safe with you."

I suppose that makes sense. Still, it's a little disconcerting to know she had someone looking into me. Does she not trust in her own ability to keep him safe? Should I be worried about her bringing him around strangers if she isn't confident she can keep him safe around me?

"Do you have self-defense training?" I blurt. "My buddy Lucas goes to a gym in town that teaches a lot of self-defense classes for women. Maybe we should get you registered for one."

It's her turn to snort a laugh. "What? Where did that come from?"

I look down at Lincoln and notice he's sucked back almost the entire bottle. The little guy eats fast.

"If you can't keep Lincoln safe around people, maybe you should get some self-defense training. You can't have a private investigator look into every person who might come in contact with our son."

She stands with a huff. "First off, I can keep Lincoln safe just fine, thank you very much. I didn't have a check run on you because I can't keep him safe. It's because you're his father, idiot, and I needed to know that you'll keep him safe when I'm not around." She stomps into the kitchen and yells back, "And I had to get a private investigator to find out your name because you didn't give it to me in your long-winded, asshole-ish message."

Ahh, fuck. *There you go, being an asshole again, Archer. You need to cut that shit out.* Of course she'd want to have me checked out. I should have thought of that and gotten a criminal records check done for her peace of mind.

"And another thing," she says, storming back into the living room. "I've already talked to a lawyer. So don't think you'll be getting full custody."

"What?" I splutter. Holy shit. When did the wheels fall off this thing? "I have no intention of taking a child from his mother. Do you think I would do something like that?"

"I don't even know you!" she yells, throwing her hands up and running them through her hair. "For all I know, you could be dressing up in your Santa costume every weekend and impregnating women all over town to breed your own baseball team."

I can't help the grin that takes over my face. She's adorable when she's freaking out like this. Her hair is sticking up at odd angles from when she ran her fingers through it and her eyes are more than a little wild.

"Actually, I'm more partial to basketball," I tease. "So if I were breeding any kind of sports team, it would have to be a basketball team."

She rolls her eyes. "Don't mock me. You don't know what it's like being a mom. All I do is worry about Lincoln. So I was worried about what kind of person you are and had some friends look into you. And then someone mentioned the custody thing and I've been freaking the fuck out. You can hardly blame me for that." She comes over and flops back on the couch, a little farther from me this time. "I wanted my baby to have the chance to know his father. I guess I didn't think about what would happen if his father also wanted to know him." She heaves an enormous sigh.

"Phoebe," I start, infusing my voice with as much sincerity as I can. I need her to believe what I'm about to say. "I don't want to take Lincoln from you."

She sniffles and refuses to look at me. "You don't?"

I shake my head. "It never even crossed my mind. Why would I take my son away from a mother who clearly loves him?"

"I don't know," she whispers, her shoulders slumping as she draws in on herself. "I didn't think that far into it."

I slide closer to her, taking the full weight of Lincoln in my arm when I leave the comfort of the armrest behind. He doesn't feel that heavy, but I imagine he would if I sat here and held him long enough. And damn, do I ever want to do that.

I reach over and take Phoebe's chin in my hand, turning her to face me. "I didn't either," I admit. "But I promise we'll figure it out. Whatever we come up with, it will be fair to both of us. And I will be paying child support."

Her letter mentioned something about not wanting money from me, but I'll be damned if I don't support them both in every way possible.

"No," she says, shaking her head before turning to face me. "That's not why I tracked you down. I want Lincoln to know his father."

"And he will." I bump her with my shoulder. "He'll just get to do it with some of my money helping to pay for his necessities."

She shakes her head and sighs. "Did anyone ever tell you that you're stubborn?"

I shrug. "Only every person I've ever met."

"Yeah, I can believe that about you." Phoebe leans over and looks at Lincoln. "He looks like he's done." She takes the empty bottle from his mouth and places it on the table before standing. "Pick him up and hold him against your chest so he's facing behind you. Let me grab a burp cloth from the bedroom and then you can burp him."

Burp him? Oh, I've heard of this. I need to pat him on the back to help the gas bubbles move up. Easy. I can handle this.

"We can do this, can't we, buddy?" I say to Lincoln while I gently pat his back with one hand. "I bet we'll have you burping before your mom even gets—"

He lets out an enormous belch just as Phoebe yells, "Don't start until I get there. He sometimes spits up, so you'll want to put a cloth over your shoulder to protect your clothes."

The wetness hits my shoulder and drenches my t-shirt before she's done speaking. Instinctively, I lean forward to stop the liquid from dripping off me onto the couch.

"Oh. Oh no," Phoebe comes around the front of the couch and takes Lincoln from my arms. She wipes his mouth with a cloth before gesturing for me to turn around. "I am so sorry," she says, her voice straining with her attempt to hold back her laughter while she dabs at my shirt. "First you get peed on and now this."

I grimace. Getting covered in bodily fluids repeatedly isn't exactly the best way to instill Phoebe with confidence in my ability to take care of Lincoln.

"I'm sorry," I say, grabbing the cloth from her and taking over the cleanup of my shirt. "I came over to learn how to take care of a baby, and it seems like I need someone to take care of me instead."

She laughs. "Because you got pissed on? And then puked on? No, that's pretty normal with babies. It happens." A grumbling noise comes from Lincoln and Phoebe's eyes widen. "To be on the safe side, though, I'll take care of this diaper change. Wouldn't want you to run screaming when you discover the sort of mess Lincoln's truly capable of making." Another rumble from Lincoln's rear end punctuates her statement. "Be back in a minute."

She carries Lincoln back to the bedroom, her ass looking even better in her jeans than the last time I allowed myself to look. I didn't know who she was that night at the company party, and Annabelle's appearance had made me too angry to pay attention, but there's no denying that Phoebe's ass is the stuff my dirty fantasies are made of. Especially after learning of her interest in the Christmas Cheer butt plug collection.

I picked up a set for her when I left work the other day, refusing to let my dad's threats distract me from the mission I'd set for myself. When Amanda told me Phoebe had complimented the Christmas display she'd insisted on setting up on her desk, I knew I had to get it for her. It's probably wildly inappropriate, but I'm hoping the excuse of being able to gift products because I own the company will be enough that she won't think I'm some kind of creep.

Although, I do feel a little like a creep. Not that it stopped me from giving her the set. I've thought about using it with her at least a hundred times since I brought it home, and every single time it's made me disturbingly hard. My dick can't handle that kind of punishment for much longer. If I'm not careful, it will have an imprint of my zipper on it until the day I die.

With a sigh, I push that thought from my mind and finish cleaning my shirt as best I can before taking the burp cloth to the kitchen sink to rinse it out. It's amazing to me how sour the milk smells after Lincoln just finished drinking it, but what do I know? Babies are a mystery.

The smell of sour milk doesn't dissipate when the cloth is clean and I'm embarrassed to admit how long I take to figure out it's me that smells. Or more accurately, it's my shirt that smells. *Well, that's disgusting.* Reaching back, I grab the neck of my t-shirt, pull it over my head, and drop it in the sink with a wet splat. No wonder it still smells. I missed most of the mess when I wiped it. I'll give it a quick wash with dish soap, then run out to my car to grab the spare I keep around for workplace emergencies. It would shock you to know how much lube gets on you at a sex toy factory if you're not careful.

When I look up, Phoebe is standing in the doorway with her mouth open wide as she stares at my naked torso. Blood rushes to my dick at the heat I imagine in her eyes. "I should have gone out and grabbed my fresh shirt before taking this one off, I guess, hey?" I release a nervous chuckle and rub the back of my neck. I'm doing an excellent job of convincing her I'm a creep. First the butt plugs and now this.

Well done, Archer. You're such a dickhead.

"Well, *hello there,* handsome. Are you going to introduce me to your friend, Phoebe?" An older, dark-haired woman squeezes around Phoebe and joins me at the sink. "I'm Sheila. I'm Phoebe's mom. You must be Archer." She wraps her arms around my waist and squeezes. "It's so nice to finally meet you."

"Jesus, Mom. Get off of him." Gavin comes along behind Sheila, taking Lincoln from Phoebe and leaving her standing in the doorway. He sniffs the air like a dog might. "From the smell in here, I'm guessing he got puked on."

Sheila lets me go and I reach out to shake the hand I'm surprised to see Gavin holding out to me. "Nice to see you again, Gavin," I say. "And you're absolutely right about the puke. I got too cocky and didn't wait for Phoebe to grab the burp cloth. I was just about to go to my car and grab a shirt."

"Now, don't rush off to grab it on my account. I don't mind one bit." Phoebe's mom looks me up and down, a teasing grin on her face as she flutters her eyelashes with exaggerated precision. "You can leave that shirt in the car forever for all I care."

"That's enough now, Sheila. You don't want to scare the man away." A man is squeezing past Phoebe. "Warren," he says, holding his hand out. "Don't mind my wife here. Her sense of humor can be...bawdy at times."

I shake his hand. "Archer." I jerk my thumb toward the front door. "I'm going to run out and get my shirt before we can continue this conversation. I'm suddenly very aware of my nakedness."

The sound of laughter follows me all the way to my car. It should embarrass me to meet Phoebe and Lincoln's family while I'm only half dressed, but for some strange reason, I'm not. I wonder if it has anything to do with the warmth of their welcome? It's been a long time since anyone hugged me and greeted me like they were glad to see me. I absently rub an aching spot in my chest. Nah. That can't be it.

Chapter 23

Stripper Cops And The Coffee Shop Bachelorette Party

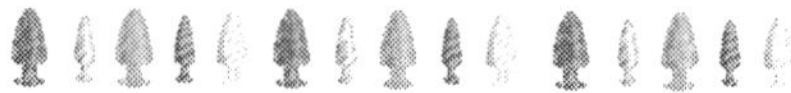

Phoebe

"So, you're here earlier than planned," I say, setting up the coffeemaker to brew a fresh pot. "I wasn't expecting you two until the day after tomorrow. What gives?"

My mom shrugs and starts unpacking a container of homemade treats onto a tray. "I was going through Lincoln withdrawal and thought if we came out a couple of days early I'd get more snuggle time. Gavin said he was coming today, so we followed him here." She rolls her eyes and shoots Gavin a pointed look. "I didn't think I'd have to worry about fighting my own son for snuggle time, though."

"You snooze you lose, Mom." Gavin grins and holds Lincoln up in front of his face. "I love my Uncle Gavin so much," he says in the baby voice he reserves for when he's pretending Lincoln is talking. "He's my favorite person ever. Way better than my old Grandma."

My family arrived right as I'd finished changing Lincoln and had come into the kitchen to find Archer shirtless at the sink. Perhaps it's a good thing they got here when they did because I'd also just confirmed that those V-line abs I remembered weren't a dream. I was perilously close to walking over and licking them to find out if they tasted as good as they looked, which would have been difficult to explain to all those involved. When he went outside to grab a shirt and came back in covered up, I could have wept at the loss. Okay, so maybe I wouldn't have literally cried, but it was disappointing.

Maybe I can get Lincoln to puke on him again next time?

I'm still sorting through my disappointment over him leaving so soon after that, too. He came back in with a shirt on, stayed for around ten minutes, and then left, stating he wanted to give me a chance to visit with my family. I'm not proud of the stab of jealousy that went through me when I realized that was most likely an excuse he made to go spent time with his gorgeous girlfriend.

I'm pathetic.

"So, Phoebe. You didn't tell me Archer was so handsome. Hubba hubba." Mom wiggles her eyebrows at me and fans herself with her hand. "I couldn't tell if I was having a hot flash or if he's really that sexy."

"Hey!" Warren yells with a laugh. "What am I? Chopped liver?"

Mom places a hand on his arm. "Oh, you have nothing to worry about, honey. Only you know how to do that thing with your tongue that I like so much."

"Ew, ew, ew. Gross, Mom." Gavin passes Lincoln over to her. "I'm leaving before you can do any more damage to my virgin ears."

"You say that like I haven't seen where you keep your condom stash. I know darn well you don't have virgin ears," she says to his back as he walks out of the room.

He groans as he spins around. "I meant they're virgin ears in that they're not used to hearing about my parents' sex life, not that they're virgin because I am a virgin who has ears." He smiles and walks backward. "But I'm sure you know that already, since you're keeping track of my condom stash," he calls as soon as he's out of sight.

Mom chuckles and nuzzles Lincoln's neck, making him giggle. "Works every time," she says with a sly grin. "You're all Grandma's now, aren't you, Linky? Yes, you are."

Warren shakes his head and smiles at my Mom indulgently, love shining in his eyes. "You're something else, Sheila," he says, leaning in to kiss her cheek. "Scarring our children for life so you can steal some cuddle time with the baby."

She scoffs. "He's not scarred at all. If he didn't want me to find his condom stash, he'd hide it better."

Warren shakes his head. "You see what I have to put up with?" he asks me. "This woman has no boundaries."

Mom continues to make funny faces at Lincoln but uses a baby voice to tell Warren, "If he would put his own laundry away, I wouldn't have a reason to be in his sock drawer."

It's adorable that Mom thinks Gavin's only condom stash is in his sock drawer. After his glow-up this last year, he's been having plenty of fun. He came to me a few months ago worried what our parents will think when they find out he's attracted to girls and guys and I told him as long as he wraps it up and gets enthusiastic consent, no one should care where he put his dick, but I don't think he's told Mom and Warren yet. I know they won't care, but Gavin isn't sure. Sometimes I wonder if the reason he visits me so often is so that he doesn't have to talk to them about it.

"I think we've waited long enough," Mom says, interrupting my thoughts. "Tell us about Archer. He seems alright. But that could be a ruse to distract you from his evil plan to leave Lincoln at a carnival."

My eyes roll before I can stop them and Mom shoots me a dirty look.

With an exasperated huff, she adds, "I saw it on the news, Phoebe. It has happened before."

"You're right, Mom. I'm sorry I ever doubted you. But you don't have to worry about Archer. I had a police officer friend look into him. He's safe."

"Hmmm. I don't know."

"Mom..." I pinch the bridge of my nose. "He came here today to learn how to take care of Lincoln. I don't think he'll do anything dumb with him."

"You don't know for sure, though."

"What doesn't Phoebe know?" It appears Gavin is already over his previous discomfort, no doubt due to his need for food. He's made his way back to the kitchen and is already rummaging around in the fridge. My brother is a bottomless pit, and I can't help but smile. No wonder he keeps building muscle. With the amount he eats, and how much he works out, he almost has to.

Mom lifts her head to look at him. "She doesn't know that Archer won't do anything dumb with Lincoln. Like abandon him at a carnival."

Gavin stands up straight, balancing a pile of fruit and a container of yogurt in his arms. "I don't know. He's an idiot for not waiting for the burp cloth, but I don't think he'd do anything to hurt Lincoln. From what I've seen, he's an okay guy." He drops his fruit and yogurt on the counter before pulling the blender out of the cupboard. "He only left that one stupid message for Phoebe, but besides that, he's been cool about it all. And really, that message wasn't all that bad. He didn't even swear at her." He walks to the pantry and grabs his giant tub of protein powder. "What was it he said, Fee? Oh, that's right. He called her a "not-very-nice-lady". That's literally the worst thing he said."

I look at him, shocked. Out of everyone, Gavin is the last person I would expect to defend Archer. He was pretty pissed when Archer first showed up at the house, after all.

But also... "You heard the message?" I thought Charlie was the only one who listened to it.

"Oh, yeah. Charlie sent it to herself and then let me listen to it. It was pretty hilarious."

I huff. "Not that funny."

Gavin chops fruit and drops it into the blender. "Oh, it really was."

"What was funny about it?" Warren asks.

"Well, when he said Phoebe found an innocent Santa and got him pregnant, that part was pretty funny."

I chuckle. "I guess it was kind of funny when he said how cute Lincoln was and explained that all babies look like weird little old men or something like that."

"See," Gavin points to me with his knife before going back to chopping. "Honestly, he sounded a little overwhelmed. And a lot drunk."

"Oh, yeah. Hearing someone in the background telling him to shut up was hilarious, too."

Warren laughs and puts his arm around Mom. "It sounds like he should have listened to the friend."

"Definitely," I agree. "I'm sure it was a shock to hear from me after all this time. And really, he was *mostly* respectful in the message. As Gavin said, he didn't swear once."

Mom shakes her head and purses her lips. "I'm still not sure. So, when will we get to see him again? I think he needs some intense questioning from Detective Mom before I'll be comfortable."

I love my mom, really I do. But sometimes she acts like I'm still a teenager like Gavin, instead of a woman in my thirties who's been on my own for over ten years. If I've done my due diligence and I'm comfortable with Archer spending time with Lincoln, that should be enough for her. But if it will help her feel better, I suppose I could let her grill him a little.

"Sure, Mom. He's coming to Christmas Eve dinner, but he'll be bringing his girlfriend, and I don't want you to embarrass me in front of her. You can grill him then. As long as you get him alone first."

"Oh, honey. He has a girlfriend?" Mom frowns and hands Lincoln to Warren, who's more than happy to take over entertaining duties. "Are you sure? The electricity between you two when we came in was off the charts. And I don't think it was only because he was shirtless. Although, again, hubba hubba." She fans herself with her hand.

I laugh. "Yeah. I'm sure. She was with him the night I found him and gave him the letter. And believe me, I can't compete with her. She's gorgeous. I'm pretty sure I heard angels sing when she walked in."

"There's no way she's that pretty," Gavin says, pressing the button on the blender and filling the kitchen with noise.

"She was beautiful, Gav," I say after the blending stops. "Easily in the top ten most beautiful women I've ever seen. Hell, maybe even top ten most beautiful in the world."

"Oh, I doubt that very much. I'm sure you're just as pretty as she is." Leave it to a mom to think her kid is on par with the most beautiful women on earth. Mom takes the blender from Gavin after he pours the thick liquid into a cup and begins washing it in the sink. She can't resist taking care of us. "And that doesn't matter. I'm serious about the electricity I felt. You can't fake that."

I roll my eyes. "I was staring at an attractive shirtless man in my kitchen. That wasn't electricity you felt. It was the heat from me spontaneously combusting."

"Mark my words, Phoebe. There's something there."

"Sure, Mom. Whatever you say."

In the background, the front door slams shut and Charlie stage-whispers, "Shit. Sorry."

"It's fine," I call out. "Lincoln's awake. We're all in the kitchen."

"You're never going to believe what happened," she says as she storms into the room and heads straight to the coffeemaker. "Remember how I said I was working late last night because someone booked the coffee shop for a private party?" She climbs up on the counter and grabs a coffee mug from the cupboard before hopping down and pouring herself a cup.

"Charlie, use a stool for crying out loud," Mom says, attempting to talk some sense into my petite and utterly reckless sister. "You're going to fall and break your neck."

Charlie waves her off. "Yeah, yeah. You keep saying that, but thirty-one years of climbing on counters without incident says otherwise."

Mom finishes washing the blender and grabs a towel to dry it. "You haven't been climbing counters for as long as you've been alive, Charlie," she says with a roll of her eyes.

"Pretty damn close," I say. "She can't have been much older than two when she started climbing to the top of the fridge to get us the cookies that you always tried to hide from us, Mom."

Gavin laughs.

"When I first met your mom, she told me all about your love of climbing to the top of tall furniture," Warren says. "It's not surprising that you were a flyer in high school." His face falls at his screw up.

Charlie freezes at the mention of her old cheerleading days. She only lasted a season and a half and she hates talking about it. We never found out what made her quit. But we usually know better than to talk about it.

"So you were telling us something that happened?" I hurry to distract her. "Was it at work? Did Xena pull out her sword?"

That works, and she rushes to continue into her story. "Okay, so did I already say I worked late for the private party?" I nod and she continues, "Turns out it was for a bachelorette party."

"A bachelorette party? At a coffee shop?" That sounds bizarre. I need coffee to live and not even I love it that much.

She shrugs. "I guess the bride is trying to quit drinking and wanted an alcohol-free venue, so her mother booked Bump & Grind for a private party. Too bad her soon-to-be mother-in-law didn't get the memo. She brought champagne and then she and the bridesmaids all got shitfaced."

"No," Mom gasps. "That poor girl. She relapsed?"

Charlie shakes her head. "I don't know, but she looked like she was having a terrible time at the beginning. I think she might have had a drink when no one was looking because she's the one who started the obnoxious chant demanding their entertainment. They were stomping so hard the floor was shaking."

Gavin stops chugging his protein shake and looks up. "Entertainment? What kind of entertainment can a coffee shop offer? Do you invite some performers from open mic night? A local high school marching band?"

"Nope," Charlie says with a pop. "But we found out why Xena calls Devon *Tiny Dancer.*"

I turn to her, my eyes wide. "Wait. You're not saying—"

"Oh, that is exactly what I'm saying. Check this out." She pulls her phone out of her pocket and cues up a video. "This is from when he first arrived."

I take the phone from her and press play. Sure enough, there on the tiny screen is Devon in all his gyrating, hip-thrusting glory. He's dancing to *Pony* by Ginuwine, the mainstay of male strippers all over the world, not that I can hear it well over the chorus of screams in the background. Who knew the guy had such slick moves?

"That's only his first dance. I left after a neighbor came by to complain and say they were calling the cops." Charlie is sitting at the table next to Warren now, drinking her coffee with a grin on her face.

"Someone called the cops? How rowdy were these women?"

"I wouldn't say they were rowdy, but they were pretty loud. I can't be sure what they did after I left, though."

"What happened with the cops, do you know?"

"That's the thing. Xena was sure Kaden would take care of it, like he always does when she gets reported for her rubber sword, but something happened when he got there and now everyone is in shit. I went to the shop this morning to help Xena dispose of all the perishable foods because Bump & Grind is closed pending the investigation. Shit. That reminds me, there's a bunch of boxes full of cookies and stuff in my car. Gavin?"

"On it." Gavin abandons his protein shake and heads out to the driveway.

Mom stands next to me and looks over my shoulder. "That man is enormous," she says with a voice full of wonder. "How does he move like that?" She tries to imitate the hip roll Devon does in the video, but her hips make a loud popping noise and she grimaces in pain. "That cannot be real. Bodies can't really move like that, can they?"

"I'm not sure. But it makes me wonder if private investigating is the right way for him to go? With moves like that, he could make a killing stripping."

Warren looks up. "That's your P.I.? You hired a stripper to look into Lincoln's father? That seems a little irresponsible, don't you think?"

I snort a laugh. "No, he's not a stripper. He's the head of security for the band that I do media management for. But he also trained to be on the police force with Xena's brother, Kaden." Warren squints in confusion. "The police officer friend who also looked into Archer for me," I clarify.

Charlie gets up and takes her phone. "I have a feeling that's not all they trained for together. Look at this other video Dax sent me. He took this last night after I left."

She hands the phone back and I press play, only to be greeted by a stripper in a traditional cop costume. Only it's not a stripper, and it's not a costume. It's Kaden, stripping out of the same uniform I saw him wearing the other day, to the song *Closer* by Nine Inch Nails, and, if anything, his moves are even filthier than Devon's.

"Hold on," I say, shaking my head, trying to make sense of this. "Are you telling me that instead of reputable members of law enforcement, I had my baby daddy investigated by strippers?"

"To be fair, I still think Kaden's a solid cop. Plus, he loves kids, so I doubt he would have told you Archer was okay if he wasn't. And Devon takes his side job private investigating seriously. The stripping has nothing to do with the quality of their investigations, nor the information you got from it."

I nod absentmindedly at Charlie's reassurances and walk myself into the living room before dropping onto the couch. This is going to take me a few minutes to work through.

I had Lincoln's dad investigated by strippers. That should give me pause, but I think Charlie is right. Kaden and Devon are reliable men. The information they discovered is still valid despite both of the investigators being good at shaking their junk for strangers. Remarkably good at it.

Besides, if worse comes to worst, and Archer isn't who he says he is, I'm sure the stripper cops will have my back.

Chapter 24

Meeting the Ex

Archer

My reflection in the window beside Phoebe's door is faint, but it's enough to fix my hair and straighten my monstrosity of a sweater. Whose terrible idea was it to wear ugly Christmas sweaters today, anyway? *Oh, yeah. Mine.*

I can't do anything now about how stupid the sweater looks, but I can pat down my hair one last time before knocking. The door flies open a moment later, revealing Phoebe looking as sexy as ever with her bright red hair tied in a knot on top of her head. She was sexy as a brunette, but this copper color takes her to the next level. Top that off with tight, dark jeans that show off her short but shapely legs and a hideous Christmas sweater that does nothing to hide the sweet curves underneath, and I'm left standing here with my tongue hanging out.

Figuratively, of course. I'm not an animal.

"Hey, come in. I need to get Lincoln dressed. Gavin just finished giving him a bath after he made a mess of himself." She rolls her eyes and turns to walk back inside. I shake my head and step in behind her.

"Here you go, little guy. Go to your mommy." Gavin passes a towel-clad Lincoln to Phoebe, and she carries him back to his bedroom.

"Hi Gavin, how's it going?" I reach my hand out and shake his hand. With how much Phoebe cares for her brother, I've decided it would be good to get him on my side. One day, when I get it together enough to ask Phoebe out, it can only help if Gavin already likes me.

"Not bad, Archer. How's the Daddy life treating you?"

I bark a laugh. "I'm still learning. I'm taking Phoebe and Lincoln out to visit Santa today so fingers crossed I can handle it."

He looks me up and down, then looks like he comes to a decision. "Give me your phone," he says, holding his hand out. The question on my face prompts his reply. "I'll give you my number. If you ever need a hand with Lincoln, and you don't want to call Phoebe and, you know, have her think less of you or something, call me."

Yes! I'm one step closer to winning over the little brother. I hand my phone over. "Thanks. I'll take all the help I can get. But how is that going to work when you go back home?"

He looks side to side before leaning in to whisper, "I graduated early. I'm looking for my own place here in town. If everything works out, I'll be moving here right after the Christmas holiday."

"Gavin that's...wow. Graduated early? That's impressive. Good for you." I'll be the first to admit, looking at Gavin, I wouldn't have thought he'd be the type of guy to finish high school early.

Which obviously makes me a judgmental prick. I sigh. So much for being nice to Phoebe's brother.

He smiles. "It's not that impressive. But don't tell Phoebe yet, okay? I want to surprise everyone after I've found somewhere to live."

"I won't say a word."

"Say a word about what?" Phoebe appears beside us like she popped up out of nowhere.

"Gah!" Gavin and I both jump.

Phoebe squints between us. "That wasn't suspicious at all."

"I was telling Archer about a, uh, Christmas surprise I'm planning. I needed another man's input."

She tips her chin with a sarcastic nod. "Sure, sure. I believe you." She holds Lincoln out to Gavin. "Say bye to Uncle Gavin."

"Bye Linky." Gavin kisses Lincoln on the head, then tousles his fluffy red hair. "Be good for Santa."

"Well?" Phoebe turns Lincoln to face me. "What do you think?"

He's wearing a tiny ugly Christmas sweater with a picture of a dinosaur in a Santa hat.

"Does that say Merry Rex-mas?" I chuckle. "Adorable. How's mine?"

I stretch out the front of my shirt so she can see the image of a man's buff chest and abs under an unbuttoned festive cardigan that adorns my ugly sweater.

She laughs. "I love it. It would probably be funnier if you didn't actually look like that underneath, though." I watch as her cheeks redden before my eyes. "I mean...Here, take Lincoln." She thrusts the baby into my arms and he promptly smacks my face, forcing a surprised laugh from me.

"Hello to you too, little man. Is it just me, or did your mom tell me she's been thinking about me shirtless? Yeah, I thought so."

"Oh my god," Phoebe says, scrubbing a hand down her face. "Forget I said that, please. Here, take the diaper bag for a minute." She passes me a bag, then grabs a set of keys from a hook on the wall. "Let me grab the car seat from my car and then I'm all set."

"Oh, no need," I tell her. "I already have one in my vehicle."

She turns back and studies me. "You do?" She hangs the keys back on the wall. "Is it installed?" She bites her lip and looks away.

I wonder if she knows I didn't know how to install a car seat and she's worried about Lincoln's safety? Or worried she'll have to tell me I'm an idiot and did it all wrong? I bet she wants to inspect it.

"Yes. I put it in yesterday." I step out onto the porch and wait for her to join me. "Let me show you."

I lead her out to my car and open up the back door. "Does it look alright?"

She climbs in and kneels in the seat, pulling straps and wiggling around. Her butt is right in my face and I'm so fucking mesmerized I can't think straight. What I wouldn't do to grab that juicy ass in both hands and grind her down on my dick while she straddles me. *Jesus, Archer. Get it together.* It will be hell to spend the day with a hard-on and no way to deal with it. Especially since we're trying to have a nice day as a co-parenting family.

"It looks perfect. You did a great job installing it. I know how much of a pain in the ass they are. I was a little worried you wouldn't know how to do it and it wouldn't be secure enough."

"Oh, I know how to do it," I mumble, thoughts of Phoebe straddling me still front and center in my mind.

"Excuse me?" She climbs out and smiles at me with her eyebrows drawn. "What was that? I couldn't hear you properly from inside the car."

Shit. Did I say that out loud?

"Oh, I said that I know how to do it now. Did you know you can go to the fire department and they'll show you how to safely install a car seat? MaeLynn made the appointment for me when she helped get my apartment set up." I step around her to put the diaper bag into the car. "I might need you to show me how to tighten the straps properly, though. I practiced with a doll they had at the station, but I'm sure it's a lot harder with a real baby."

She chuckles. "Well, they do tend to move more than dolls." The smile she gives me is everything, and my heart trips over itself. "Why don't you strap him in and I'll double-check?"

She puts a hand on my arm and guides me to the door. Maybe I imagine it, but I swear tingles erupt where she touches me. Weird.

"Alright, Lincoln. Help me out here. Can you try not to wiggle too much while I buckle you in so I can try to impress your mom with my car seat skills?" Lincoln makes a gurgling noise and laughs, which I take for his agreement. "Thanks, kiddo."

I get Lincoln buckled in and Phoebe checks it out, telling me I need to tighten the straps a little. "I know it seems too tight, but it needs to be secure enough to keep him safe if anything happens." She steps back and looks at the back headrest. "Hold on, I want to grab something."

I watch as she runs back into the house, admiring the view the whole time. Her ass in those jeans is spectacular.

"Your mom is something else, kid." Lincoln kicks his legs and makes some baby babbles, which I'm choosing to understand as him encouraging me to get to know her better. "I know, I really should. But knocking her up and then not seeing her for a year probably didn't leave her with the best impression of me. And that fucki—I mean, that fudging message I left her doesn't help either."

"Got it." Phoebe is jogging out the front door, waving something in the air. "This makes life so much easier when you're driving with a baby." She comes around and climbs back into the vehicle for a moment before hopping down. "There. Check it out."

She's installed a mirror on the headrest so it's facing Lincoln. "That's so smart," I say, opening the driver's side door and leaning inside. "I can see him in the rearview mirror."

"Yeah. I was so scared when I first learned he had to face the back of the vehicle and I wouldn't be able to see him. A mom from baby yoga told me about these mirrors. Total sanity saver.

And time saver, too. Before I had one, I'd pull over every couple of minutes to check and make sure he was still breathing. I was late for everything."

"I bet that drove all your friends crazy."

"You know it," she says with a grin. "Should we get going? I'd like to keep Lincoln on his sleep schedule, if possible."

"Probably a good idea." I walk around the vehicle and open her door, holding a hand out to help her in. When she places her fingers in mine, those tingles flare to life again. *That can't be my imagination. Not this time.* "You ready to go to the North Pole?"

She snorts a laugh. "As long as Santa doesn't get me pregnant this time, I'm ready for anything."

My stomach drops as I force a chuckle and close the door. "He better not get you pregnant," I mutter. "I'm the only Santa who gets to do that." Not that I'm trying to get her pregnant. But I'd prefer no one else got the chance yet. *Or ever.*

When I get into the driver's seat, I sneak a glance and notice Phoebe is once again blushing, which I'm taking as a positive sign. Maybe she's thinking about the Santa who knocked her up in the first place, and if she's thinking about it now, maybe I can get her to think about it again.

I like that plan.

Because no matter how much I know I should stay away from her, I desperately want to get to know her better, like Lincoln said. Well, like I imagined Lincoln said when he was babbling to me earlier.

"I can't get over you going to the fire department. That's..." Shit. She thinks I'm a terrible provider for getting someone else to do something that I should have done on my own. I guess I could have, but it seemed like a better idea to have one of the trained car seat technicians at the fire house teach me how to do it properly. I'll do whatever I have to do to keep Lincoln safe.

"Genius," she finishes. "Do you know how many video tutorials I watched before I was confident enough to install my seat? And that was *after* reading the manual at least fifty times. The fire department? I wish I'd thought of that."

I chuckle, releasing a nervous breath. She doesn't think less of me for outsourcing the car seat install. It's almost too bad she put my mind at ease because now that I'm not worried about that, thoughts of being the Santa who gets her pregnant come flooding in again. Does Lincoln need a little brother or sister? *Get it together, Archer. Now's not the time for ridiculous daydreams.*

"I can't take credit," I say, starting the car and maneuvering out of the driveway before turning us toward the local farmer's market. "MaeLynn made the appointment and forced me to go. She deserves all the accolades."

I can see Phoebe's smile out of the corner of my eye. "I like her," she says. "She seems nice."

I nod. "She's the best. I couldn't make it without her." I could leave that statement as it is, without further explanation, but I think the mother of my child deserves to know a little more about me. "MaeLynn worked for my father as his assistant before I took over the company. She's always been like a mother to me, probably more than my own." I blow out a breath. "My mother isn't exactly what I would call maternal. I'm sure you noticed MaeLynn is, though."

"You can say that again." She chuckles. "I still can't believe I let her walk off with Lincoln not two minutes after I met her." She blows out a noisy breath. "Wanna know something? For the longest time, I was too nervous to have anyone but my immediate family watch him. Even that was hard. It's been a lot better since I talked to my doctor about postpartum anxiety. It's amazing what some time spent talking with a counselor and taking anti-anxiety medication can do."

I do a double-take. "Really? At the lab, you passed him off to me like it was nothing."

She laughs. "That's got to be one of the top five funniest things I've ever seen," she says, shaking her head. "It's right up there with Lincoln peeing on you and then throwing up all over you not five minutes later." She snorts out another laugh. "It's a good thing he didn't really have it in for you, though, or you'd have gotten pooped on that day, too."

I force a nervous laugh. That has to be a joke, right? There's no way poop travels fast enough to make it out of a diaper and clothing. Nah. I'm sure I've seen the worst of it when it comes to being covered in the bodily fluids of babies.

She snorts a giggle, and I grin. Even though it's usually at my expense because of my lack of baby knowledge, I love hearing her laugh.

Chapter 25

Kris Kringle Is Kranky

Phoebe

"This is so pretty." The Santa set-up in the Westborough farmer's market is like a woodland fairytale come to life. There's a spot for Santa to sit on a wooden bench surrounded by trees draped in twinkle lights and the effect is much more in tune with nature than your standard North Pole display at a mall. I smile up at Archer, who's holding Lincoln close. "I love it."

"I wish I could take credit," he says with a grin. "But this was MaeLynn's suggestion. She brings her grandkids here because she thinks it doesn't encourage as much blatant consumerism as a regular mall Santa experience."

I look around the display and notice the distinct lack of packaged gifts or references to a toy shop of any kind and realize he's right. This place is pure magic.

"Yeah, she definitely gives the impression that she's a smart woman."

"Really smart," he says, turning to address Lincoln. "She's the reason we're here early enough to be first in line. We'll keep you on your nap schedule yet."

Lincoln giggles and grabs Archer's mouth, and then Archer pretends to eat his hand. He may not have known how to hold him the first time, but he seems so natural with Lincoln now it's hard to imagine he doesn't already have a houseful of kids at home. It's like he was made to be an honest-to-goodness family man.

That tightening in my chest can't be jealousy, though, right? Oh, who am I kidding? Of course it is. I'm so jealous I could look in a mirror right now and it wouldn't surprise me to see I was turning green. His girlfriend is a lucky woman.

I don't have long to linger over my jealousy, though, because I hear someone calling my name from nearby.

"Phoebe? Is that you?"

I haven't heard that voice other than on the phone in a long while, but for most of my life, until around this time last year, I heard it every single day. I could never forget it. I spin to see Webster Day smiling down at me with his perfect smile. We've spoken often since our ill-fated non-wedding day, but I haven't seen him in person since then. He looks as perfect as always. He's styled his bright blond hair with the perfect amount of tousling, and even his jeans look like they've been freshly pressed. Amazingly, it doesn't hurt to see him as much as I thought it would. It's like coming home, and I can't stop the smile from crossing my face at the sight of him.

"Hi, Webster."

"Oh my god, it *is* you. I can't believe it." He pulls me into a tight hug and rocks me side to side. "I can't tell you how *much* I've missed you." He puts a hand on each shoulder and holds me away from him, studying me. "You've gone back to your natural color, I see," he says with the tiniest hint of disappointment. He never was a big fan of my red hair. "I always thought you looked more elegant with dark hair, but I can see why you like the copper. You look so youthful and vibrant. And your tits look fantastic with the extra weight. Turn around and show me that ass, girl. I bet it's phenomenal."

I choke out a laugh at his mention of my tits and ass, but not before an irritated look crosses Archer's face. What's that about?

He interrupts Webster's diatribe when he sees I'm not even trying to defend myself. "I don't believe we've met," he says, shuffling Lincoln to one arm so he can reach out for a handshake. "Archer Fade. And you are?"

Webster does a double take between me, Archer, and Lincoln before his face splits into a huge grin. "Oh, you're cute," he says to Archer before leaning close and whispering to me, "He's cute. Is this him?" I pull my lips between my teeth and nod, not sure how this is going to go. "It is? Oh, that's so exciting. Hi, I'm Webster Day." He shakes Archer's hand and offers no further explanation.

"Webster is my ex-fiancé," I tell Archer, giving him a little context when I read the confusion on his features.

"And current and forever best friend." Webster wraps his arms around me for another hug. "Oh, I'm so happy to finally see you again, babe. I can understand why you wanted space, but I've been a wreck without you."

"We're working our way back up to BFFs, Webster." I chide. "I need a little time."

He lets me go and smooths his shirt. "Yes, well. I know we'll get back there eventually. I can be patient." He smiles at me. "We were friends before we were anything else, remember?"

I roll my eyes. "Of course I remember. You marched up to me in my front yard the summer after third grade and forced me to let you style my Barbie dolls before you would play dolly dog wash with me." I laugh at the memory. "I should have probably known then that we were destined for friendship only."

"Hey. It's not my fault you had terrible taste in fashion even then. Your dolls would have never gotten any customers if I hadn't stepped in to help." He gives my ugly Christmas sweater a sidelong glance, then smiles wistfully. "I am sorry for everything, though, Phoebe. I never meant for it to go as far as it did."

"I know, Webster. You've told me approximately thirty-nine thousand times. I'm sorry, too. We both could have stopped it before it got that far. You weren't the only one who knew we weren't the right fit for each other."

Archer looks between us, his brow furrowed in confusion. Just as he opens his mouth to ask the question I'm sure is on his mind, another man arrives, interrupting him before he has the chance.

"Second in line. You were right, babe. It was smart to come this early." An attractive man joins our group, and he's every bit as stylishly coiffed as Webster, but with darker hair that's more slicked back and to the side than tousled.

"Frederick, there's someone you need to meet." Webster reaches out and wraps his hand around the newcomer's fingers. "This ginger goddess is Phoebe Fox."

Frederick's eyes light up as a huge grin overtakes his face. "Phoebe! It's so wonderful to finally meet you face to face. It's like I know you already." He drops Webster's hand and wraps his arms around me. "This day keeps getting better and better."

"It's nice to meet you, too," I force out. Frederick's hug is so tight it's constricting my airflow. "And here I was thinking we'd only ever get to talk on the phone."

"Speaking of the phone, I was actually going to call you later, because I wanted you to be the first to know," Webster says, taking my hand and forcing Frederick to release me from his hug. "Frederick proposed to me last night, and I said yes." He holds up his left hand and flashes a gold band with a single ruby embedded in the center.

My eyes widen as shock floods my system. He's engaged again so soon? Though I suppose our engagement didn't really count since he never actually wanted to marry a woman. And with how much he's talked about Frederick over the last six months, I was pretty sure this was coming.

So what's causing this ached in my chest?

I glance at Archer to see what he thinks of this revelation, only to see him staring back at me with sympathy in his eyes.

"Wow...I...Wow." I struggle to find the right thing to say, but plaster a supportive smile on my face. Despite everything, I want Webster to be happy. "That's amazing. Congratulations."

"I know it's fast," Webster says. "Especially since it's only been a year since you and I...well, you know."

Concern colors Archer's face and he mouths, "Are you okay?" All I can do is nod.

But am I okay?

I know I'm not in love with Webster. And I don't begrudge him his happiness. In fact, I'm thrilled he's found someone to love. And if I really think about it, he is my best friend. So what's my issue?

I swallow a groan, disappointed in myself when it hits me: I'm jealous. I wanted to be the one to find someone first. I may have been having second thoughts of my own, but there was a small part of me that wanted to rub his face in my happiness because of how much it hurt when he left me at the altar. Now he's gotten engaged first and robbed me of my chance to be petty, and it's so damn...annoying. It should devastate me that the man I was going to marry is marrying someone else, but all I can manage is a little minor irritation.

But, despite how irritated it makes me, I'm not about to act like an asshole who can't be happy for my best friend.

"Congratulations, you two. I'm so happy for you." It's my turn to wrap my arms around Webster. "Thank you for telling me before the gossip line got hold of it. You know they're going to love having another reason to drag up their favorite story about how I turned you gay."

Webster holds me tighter and laughs. "You and I both know you didn't turn me gay, babe. I was always gay. I was just so platonically in love with you, not to mention more than a little afraid of what my family would say, that I wished I could be straight. I got carried away when I allowed it to go on for so long, and that was so, so wrong. I should have told you the truth."

"Yeah, I know. But you know how the people back home love their gossip."

He rolls his eyes. "Believe me, I know. Why do you think I tried so hard to be straight? Now that I'm out, even my own parents would rather talk *about* me than talk *to* me. I don't think they have said more than ten words to me since we canceled the wedding."

"Jesus, and here I thought my parents were bad." Archer holds a hand out to Frederick. "I'm Archer. Thought I should introduce myself since these two are busy getting reacquainted. And this is Lincoln." He shakes Frederick's hand, then picks up Lincoln's and holds it out to do the same. The relief from seeing Archer accepting my ex-fiancé and our strange relationship leaves me giddy.

"Lincoln. Say hello to your Uncle Frederick," I blurt with a grin before turning to Webster, "and your Uncle Webster."

Webster's eyes get shiny and he fans his face with his hands while Frederick coos to Lincoln and makes goofy faces, and I know I made the right decision. Before Webster and I were ever together, I knew he'd be great with kids. For a while I thought he'd be the father of my future children, but having him act as an uncle to Lincoln is better somehow.

"Are you serious, Phoebe? Do I really get to be an uncle?" He eyes me hopefully while sneaking glances at Lincoln. "Are you sure?"

Until today, I'd been afraid to see Webster in person, scared it would dredge up too many thoughts of hurt and abandonment. I didn't want to have him act as an uncle to my child when I wasn't sure I could be around him without it being weird. But it's not weird. Well, not *that* weird, and I'm sure it will get easier. He's been my best friend for nearly twenty-five years, after all.

"Of course I'm sure, Webster. You're family."

He chokes out a sob and wraps his arms around me, squeezing for all he's worth. "Thank you, Phoebe. You don't know how much this means to me. I thought I'd lost you forever. That you'd never forgive me."

I bury my face in his shoulder. "Of course I forgive you. You're my best friend. I can't stay mad at you. Even if you *did* leave me at the altar." I wrap my arms around him and squeeze before pulling back with a smile. "Seriously though, does Frederick know that you're a runner?" I tease in a stage whisper.

"Ahh, so rude," he gasps, then chuckles. "I missed you so much," he says again.

"Oh, here comes Santa." Frederick pulls Webster to his side. "This is going to be so cute for our socials." The two of them tilt their heads together and start whispering excitedly, so I turn to face Archer to give them some privacy.

"Ready, Phoebe?" Archer asks. "Time for Lincoln's first Santa Claus pictures."

A quick look behind us tells me that while we were talking, several more groups of people joined the line-up to visit Santa Claus. It looks like we were right to get here early. If we'd waited any longer to come, there's no way we'd have gotten out of here in time for Lincoln's nap.

A kind-looking older woman dressed like a pretty fairy version of Mrs. Claus comes over to where we're standing in line. Instead of the dress, apron, and bonnet you normally see on the wife of the big guy, she's wearing a flowing dress made of multiple layers of gauzy material, with a sweater over top that almost hints at wings with the way it folds over her back. Her face has a youthful blush about it, and the smile she gives us is welcoming.

"Good morning. Welcome to Kris Kringle's Holiday Wonderland. And who do we have here?" She bends to get close to Lincoln's face. "Looks like we have a first-timer. Is this your first Christmas, young man?"

"It sure is," I say. "We're here for our first Santa pictures."

"Oh, no, sweetheart. This is Kris Kringle, not Santa." Fairy Mrs. Claus—Mrs. Kringle, actually, I guess—says, her voice suddenly serious. "But we will take pictures. And I'll let you in on a little secret. It's Kris's first time, too. Isn't that a wonderful coincidence?"

"Oh, uh. Yeah. Sorry."

"Oh, that's okay." Her voice takes on its former sing-song quality. "Not everyone knows there's a difference."

"There's a difference?" Archer asks. "I thought it was only a different name?"

"Oh, well, yes. Essentially. But it's still quite interesting."

Archer turns to me to widen his eyes in a *can you believe this chick?* sort of look. I fight to contain the chuckle that threatens to burble up. Luckily, I'm saved by the jolly laugh of Kris Kringle as he makes his entrance through a wall of fairy lights and greenery.

"Who's ready to see Kris Kringle?"

My heart swells with anticipation. The setting is so beautiful, and Kris Kringle looks so magical, that I know we're going to have amazing pictures. I take a moment to straighten Lincoln's ugly Christmas sweater before Archer places Lincoln on Kris's lap. Lincoln is alright for a moment, but that's before he turns and catches sight of Kris Kringle smiling down at him...and he immediately bursts into hysterical ear-splitting screams. And he doesn't. stop. screaming. For five straight minutes. We try everything we can think of to distract him, using toys, bottles, keys, phones, and our own faces, but nothing works.

"That's it. I can't work like this." Kris passes Lincoln back to me. "Cancel the photo shoot. The mood is ruined."

"I am so sorry." Archer is trying to console Kris while I shush Lincoln and bounce him in my arms. "I don't think you need to cancel the rest of the day, though. That's not fair to the rest of the people who came to visit you."

"Fine. Fine. But I need a break before I can see the rest of these people." Kris turns to his fairy helper. "I'll be back in thirty minutes. Please let the people in line know. And please tell the parents and friends of that *baby* that I won't be seeing them at all."

A twin gasp behind me tells me exactly which friends he's talking about.

"No, Kris. Come back. Please. We wanted this photo for a Christmas engagement announcement. It will only take a minute. We'll wait." Webster tries to follow the man back behind the curtain of lights and greenery, but the fairy helper puts an arm out and stops him.

"I'm sorry, sir. You heard him. May I suggest a mall Santa? I'm sure the Santa at the Westborough mall will be there until the end of the day." She pats Webster's hand and reaches over to touch Frederick's arm before following Kris Kringle behind the curtain of lights.

"Well, that's perfect. Now what will do? There's no way we're not waiting in line for at least five hours if we try to go to the mall Santa now." Frederick's eyes get misty, and Webster wraps him in a tight hug. "I just wanted a cute way to tell our friends that we finally got it right, you know?"

"Shh, shh. I know, honey. It's okay. We'll make it work."

The four of us, plus Lincoln, walk past all the booths of winter vegetables and Christmas crafts to the exit of the farmer's market, Kris Kringle's rejection weighing heavily on our shoulders. Christmas carols play over the tinny speakers, but I'm not in the mood for holiday cheer right now. I don't care that much about getting a picture of Lincoln and Santa, not after my son's epic freak out, but Webster and Frederick seem pretty bummed about not being able to see him. It sucks that we're the reason they won't get the Santa photo they wanted for their announcement.

It should have been simple enough to get Santa Claus to hold Lincoln. We could have taken a few pictures and been on our way. And it would have been, if Lincoln hadn't screamed his little head off the second good old Kris got ahold of him. Poor Lincoln. Poor Kris.

"What are you guys doing tomorrow?" Archer stops outside the main doors, pulling Webster and Frederick aside. "Can you wait one more day to get your picture? I think I have an idea."

Chapter 26

SANTA SAVES CHRISTMAS

Archer

"WE CAN GET LINCOLN's first Santa picture tomorrow, too. If you want to try again, that is."

Phoebe chuckles at my offer. "I don't know if we should. It's been twenty minutes, and he's only now settling down."

"Well, I'm not a first-timer, so hopefully I can handle it better than our buddy Kris back there."

After bursting Kris Kringle's eardrums and ruining his first day on the job, we walked out of the farmer's market with plans in place for Webster and Frederick to come to Phoebe's house tomorrow for an impromptu Santa photo shoot. Phoebe and I stayed to walk around downtown for a little while to take in the various storefronts' holiday displays, while the guys left to continue celebrating. They said they were meeting up with some members from the singles group where they first met. But I'm glad Webster and Frederick have each other now. I know too well what it's like when you're forced to conform to your parents' unrealistic expectations.

Not to mention, there's no way Phoebe would ever consider me if Webster was still an option for her. The guy is pretty much perfect.

"That's true. That poor man. Do you think he ever came back out? There were so many people waiting in line. I hope Lincoln's little crying jag didn't scare him off the Kris Kringle act for good."

"Tough to say. I didn't notice any other babies in the line, though, so maybe he did."

"I hope so. I'd hate to think Lincoln's crying scared him away for good. Maybe Lincoln isn't made for Santa visits? I'm not sure we should attempt pictures tomorrow."

"Well, if you change your mind, let me know. We'll have everything we need for it."

"That sounds good."

The streets are busy with people out doing their last-minute shopping. Phoebe and I each hold one of Lincoln's stroller handles, both to keep him close and, at least for me, to keep us from getting separated. The forced proximity is nice, even if Phoebe's nearness threatens to overwhelm me.

"So...yeah. I understand now why you knew Webster wasn't even in the running for Lincoln's father." I scrub a hand over the back of my neck. "I know you two were joking around, but you know you had nothing to do with him being gay, right? Please tell me you're not hanging on to some old-fashioned, misguided notion it was something you could have caused. Or that it's something that needs to be blamed on anyone, for that matter."

She chuckles. "Well, the few times we tried to do anything beyond kissing were a blow to the self-esteem, I won't lie. He'd seriously freak out every time he tried to touch my breasts. I should have guessed it was more than wanting to wait until after we were married. It was easy to convince myself that's all it was, though. Because he's never been afraid to vocalize his appreciation for my body, as you heard earlier."

"He freaked out?" I'm cringing so hard it hurts. How could he freak out from touching her breasts? "That's...wow. That's horrible. I'm so sorry that happened. But that has nothing to do with you. From what I recall from our night together, which isn't much, by the way, your...uh, your breasts were quite nice." Spectacular, actually. But that might take this conversation too far for Phoebe's comfort.

She barks a laugh. "Thanks. I don't remember much either, but I do recall feeling somewhat vindicated that someone as attractive as you are was interested in me. Even if it was only for one night." She takes a deep breath and continues. "When he came out to me, it made prefect sense. I'm only sorry he felt he had to go to such lengths to hide himself. And it took him many a long phone conversation for him to convince me that I'm not the worst friend on earth for not immediately turning him down when he proposed."

"Why *did* you say yes?"

She shrugs. "He's my best friend. I couldn't think of anything more comfortable than marrying my best friend. Of course, that was before I spent the night with you and realized what I'd be giving up."

Now's your chance, stupid. Tell her you'd like to get to know her better. Tell her you'd like to date her for real. "Listen, Phoebe. I was thinking maybe—"

"It was nice of you to offer to help Webster and Frederick," she cuts me off without looking away from the window display. "I suppose it makes sense, since we ruined their photo op, after all."

I chuckle ruefully at her abrupt change of subject. Point taken. Now's not the time to ask her out. Maybe I'll try again later.

"Who knew Lincoln had such a set of pipes on him? Poor woodland Kris Kringle will probably have a ringing in his ears for the rest of the day."

"Not exactly a promising start to his first day of playing the character." She laughs. "Is it just me or did it seem to you they were playing up the Lord of Rings style of elves with their costumes and props? That looked more like Rivendell than the North Pole to me."

I tip my chin in an eager nod. "Yes! It was more... ethereal magic than Christmas magic. It would have made for a cool picture, though."

Phoebe nods and looks into the stroller. "Uh oh. Someone is playing with his ears. Time for us to be heading home, I think."

I'm sure the confusion shows on my face because she then says, "He's getting tired. He always grabs his ears when he's tired."

"Really? That's what that means?" There's yet another thing that I didn't know about babies. "I think I'm going to need a manual for him," I joke. "I can't keep up with all this new information."

Phoebe laughs. "I'll lend you some of my baby books. You'll be an expert in no time."

"Nice try. You already told me those books can't agree on a single thing. I'll end up more confused than I am already. No, I need to rely on my powers of observation and my listening skills."

She shakes her head and laughs. "I did say that, didn't I? I'm sure between MaeLynn and I, we can set you straight anytime you need help. She seems like she knows what she's doing." Phoebe gets the stroller turned and heads back toward my car. "It's too bad we didn't last longer at the farmer's market today. I saw a few things there that my mom would absolutely love. She's a huge fan of that cottage core type of design but with a snarky twist. A few booths there looked like they had her brand of kitsch."

An idea forms in my head, and before I can stop myself, I blurt it out. "What if Lincoln comes to nap at my place so you can shop while I watch him? I live not too far from here. You can even take my car if you want to go somewhere farther away."

She jerks the stroller to a stop and her eyebrows meet in the middle as she stares at me as if I've lost it.

"I mean, only if you want. I need the practice, and I'm sure I can look after him for a short while during his nap." She starts walking again without answering. "I have everything I need," I continue. "You can come and inspect it all before you decide. Or you could stay at my place while he naps, if that would make you more comfortable. It's up to you."

We walk in silence all the way back to my car, and I'm sure I've blown it. She doesn't trust me enough yet to leave Lincoln with me, and my suggesting it now has forced her into the position that she has to *tell* me she doesn't trust me. I've made her uncomfortable twice today. *I'm such an asshole.*

She gets me to buckle Lincoln in and then checks the straps again. When we get into the vehicle, she puts a hand on my arm to stop me from starting it. My heart races, and a hundred horrible scenarios rush through my head. *She's telling me she doesn't want me around Lincoln. She's regretting ever finding me at all. I'm going to have to go to court just to visit my son on alternating weekends.*

"I think we should go to your place," she says. "I don't know if I'll leave him with you yet, but I should at least look at the space. To ease my mind. I'm sure everything is fine but...Sorry."

I blow out a relieved breath before looking over at her and smiling. "I get it. There's nothing to be sorry for. You're his mom. It makes sense that you'd want to make sure I have a safe space for him. I'd be more surprised if you didn't want to check it out first."

She gives me a tentative smile. "Yeah?"

I nod. "Definitely."

Her smile grows. "Okay." She nods. "Okay, then. Let's go to your place."

I start the car and grin the entire three-block drive to my building.

"You live here?" She's looking up at the building as I pull into the parking garage. "It's so tall."

I open my window and scan my parking card at the security gate, nodding to the guard who waves me through. "It's forty-three stories. Only about half of those are residences, though. The rest are offices."

I park in my private space and get out. Phoebe joins me beside Lincoln's door, his diaper bag already in her hand.

"You can go ahead and get him out," she says distractedly.

Her head swivels as she takes in the other vehicles. Most are high-end luxury vehicles, hinting at the pretentiousness of my neighbors. Even my vehicle is on the pretentious side, but I bought it mostly to keep my mother off my back. If it were up to me, I'd still be driving the old Jeep I had in college. I used to love driving it out to local hiking spots and going off grid for a few days. My mother always thought it looked low-class. But I have to admit, the SUV is proving to be useful now that I have Lincoln to think of. It has high safety ratings and tons of space for a car seat in the back.

And I could still drive to hiking spots and take it off-grid if I wanted to. I just haven't had the time yet.

I unbuckle Lincoln and snuggle him to my chest. I'm still a little nervous holding him, but I'm much more comfortable than I was that day in the lab. With a little more practice, I should be an expert. Or at least somewhat competent.

"Elevator's over here," I say, turning and leading her to the silver doors at the end of the lot. "It's a secure building. You need a card to get into the lot, and a card to get into the elevator from the parking garage. There are security guards at the main entrance, and nobody gets in unless they're approved."

Her shoulders relax. "That's great. Sounds very safe."

The doors open and I let her get in first, then I follow. I swipe my keycard and press the button for the penthouse, a pang of worry hitting me out of nowhere. What if she hates my place? It is a little extravagant, and not something I would buy now. Couple the penthouse with my vehicle and I look like a rich asshole, which is the farthest thing from who I am. I've spent so long doing things my parents' way, to keep them off my back, that I'm living a life I don't even recognize. Maybe I need to buy a house with a yard for when Lincoln gets older? I smile as the thought of us playing catch together crosses my mind. Yeah, I think I'd like that.

"If you decide to leave Lincoln with me when you go shopping, I'll give you my keycard so you can access the elevator and parking garage. Oh, I'll call security when we get up to my place so I can have you added to the list of approved visitors, too." I turn to see her looking at me with her mouth hanging open. "You know what? You're right. I'll have them make you a keycard. You'll probably have to go to the security office so they can get your picture, but it will be a lot easier for you in the long run to have your own entry card."

She shakes her head and looks pointedly at the elevator's control panel. "I'm sorry. I didn't hear a single thing you said. Did you hit the button *for the penthouse?*" Her voice takes on a high-pitched tone. "You live in the penthouse?"

I incline my head and am about to say yes when she interrupts me.

"But not like *the penthouse*, penthouse, right? It's one of many upper-level apartments all called the penthouse? Just to make everyone feel special? Like the participation ribbon penthouse?"

Shit. She hates even the idea of the penthouse. What do I do now? We're almost on my floor. My realtor is great, but I doubt he could find me a new place before we reach my floor. As if to confirm my thoughts, the elevator glides to a gentle stop and the doors slide open with a chime. My personal lobby greets us from the open doors and I gesture for Phoebe go first again, trying to gather my thoughts.

Stepping around her, I open my door and guide her inside, not missing the wide-eyed stare she casts around my apartment.

"This place is three times the size of my house." She wheels around to face me. With a grin, she says, "Tell me the truth. Do you ever get lost in here?"

A relieved breath escapes me, and I grin back at her. "Only at night, when it's dark. I keep a flashlight by the bed for midnight trips to the kitchen."

She laughs and takes a few more steps into my space. The sight of her in my home triggers a flood of warmth in my chest. *She fits here.*

"Oh, look at him," she nods to where Lincoln sits in my arm, his head resting against my chest while his hand pulls on his ear. "He's so tired. We better get him changed and ready for bed." She looks left and right. "Where are we going?"

I lead her down the hallway and open the door to Lincoln's room. She steps in ahead of me and stops dead in her tracks.

"You made him an entire bedroom?"

Chapter 27

Visits With B.O.B. And The Not-Quite-Good-Enough Orgasm

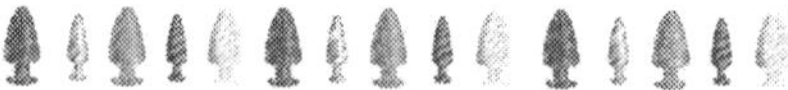

Phoebe

"You made him an entire bedroom?" My eyes scan the pristine furnishings and toys arranged throughout the room. "His own bedroom?"

There are two dressers against one wall, and upon inspecting them, I discover they're full of clothes for Lincoln. I walk over to the plush armchair and sit, delighted to realize it's a glider rocker. My feet find their way onto the matching ottoman, and I snuggle into the soft fabric. I need this chair. It's amazing. Now I understand Gavin's unnatural obsession with the couch at my rental. I could easily marry this chair.

Archer carries Lincoln to the changing table on the other side of the room and starts undressing him. He looks more confident than last time, like he knows what he's doing now. "Uh, yeah.

MaeLynn helped me figure out what I needed, which turned out to be the entire inventory from a baby store owned by her friend."

I sit forward and drop my feet to the ground. "No," I gasp. "She took advantage of you for her friend's benefit? I don't know her very well, but that doesn't really seem like something she'd do."

He chuckles and shakes his head. "No. Nothing like that. She took advantage of her relationship with her friend to get everything I needed delivered to me after the store was already closed for the holidays. Besides"—he gestures to the room with the diaper he removed from Lincoln—"I can afford it. I'd rather help a local business than a huge corporation, anyway. Especially if it belongs to someone who's important to MaeLynn."

"Hmm." I lean back and put my feet up again. How is he for real? Everything he says tells me he's a terrific guy. "That makes sense, I guess. She didn't make you buy any non-essentials, did she? You don't have a wipes warmer over there, do you?"

He laughs outright. "Guilty."

"Archer," I chide.

"What?" He grins over his shoulder. "I don't want him to suffer with a cold butt. Is that so wrong?"

An abrupt laugh burst from me. "The wipes aren't that cold, Archer. It's not like they're kept in the fridge."

He shrugs. "I want him to be as comfortable as possible. Remind me to show you the instant formula bottle-making machine after this."

"That sounds...excessive. And super convenient." It would be awesome to let a machine do the measuring, mixing, and heating for me sometimes.

"I'm excited to try it. Maybe after his nap?"

"Sure." I force myself out of the chair as Archer finishes with the diaper change. He then zips him into a special sleep sack blanket, picks him up, and passes him to me.

"What's next?"

"We lay him down, tell him to have a good nap, then sneak out of the room while he's still awake." I swivel my head. "Do you have a baby monitor?"

Archer walks to the table beside the chair I'd been sitting in and points to the camera mounted in the room's corner. "The display unit is in the living room."

"Perfect." I put Lincoln in the crib, pleased when I see it's outfitted with only a sheet, and slide a hand over his head. "Have a nice nap, Linky."

Archer steps up beside me and ruffles Lincoln's hair. "Have a good sleep, little man." When he kisses his fingers and touches them to Lincoln's forehead, I swoon.

Together, we sneak out of the room and close the door.

"Come check out the display for the monitor," Archer whispers before leading me to the living room. "I didn't get one of these wi-fi enabled ones you read about. Not because I think a stranger would try to hack in and talk to Lincoln, but because I think Eric would. It wouldn't surprise me in the slightest if Eric hacked my baby monitor to teach my son to say stupid shit."

I can't stop the laugh that bubbles up. "He seems like that kind of guy. I guess we know who we need to keep an eye on when Lincoln starts talking. I've ruled out my brother. Gavin already knows I'll have his balls for earrings if he tries."

"I think Eric needs to be warned of that, too. MaeLynn would kill me if I let Lincoln swear like a sailor before his third birthday." He laughs. "Or ever, probably."

He picks up a device from a side table in the living. "So this is the display." He turns it on and hands it to me, a picture of Lincoln filling the screen. He's not asleep yet, but he's not crying, so that's a good sign.

"That's perfect," I say, handing it back to him. "You have quite the setup. I'm a little surprised, actually." Turning my back to him, I take a few steps into the living room, looking around. "This is a really nice place."

"Thanks, I guess. I've been thinking it's about time to sell, actually. But never mind that. What about the setup makes you surprised?"

I walk a little further, taking everything in. Funny. There's no sign of a woman living here. No decorative cushions, no throw blankets, no feminine decorative touches of any kind. My heart beats double time when I realize his girlfriend must not live with him. Maybe they're not that serious?

Never mind, Phoebe. Serious or not, he's taken.

Aside from his oversized furniture, enormous television, full bookshelves, interesting art, and a few tastefully arranged plants, all that's in this room is baby stuff. Tons and tons of baby stuff. There's a swing, another rocking chair, a playpen, a basket of toys, tummy time mats, and a bouncy chair all in my line of sight. If he has all this in the living room, I wonder what he has in all the other spaces?

I wonder what his personal space looks like? His bed?

I wonder what *he* looks like in his bed?

I wonder what he would look like in his bed, naked, looking down on me from above as he drives into me, his back flexing, his hips thrusting—

"Phoebe? Are you okay?"

Archer's voice cuts into my thoughts right as they take a turn for the dirty. My face heat because he's caught me, but even the thought of that does nothing to curb the desire that's run roughshod over me. I need to get out of here. And luckily for me, Archer has proven he's ready to look after Lincoln for a short time. The way he got him ready for his nap was perfect. He didn't even get peed on this time.

I know where he lives, where he works, and what he drives. Not only that, I have the stripper cops in my corner. Everything will be fine if I leave Lincoln with his dad for a couple of hours.

"Uh, yeah. Sorry. I was thinking maybe I'll take you up on your offer after all." A plan takes shape in my head. "You said I could use your car? Is that still okay?"

Archer's face splits into a wide grin, and he nods vigorously. "Yes. Definitely." He digs his keys and a plastic card out of his pocket and passes them to me. "Here. Take these."

His fingers graze my palm and the heat building in my belly cranks up another notch. Am I really doing this? The answering throb and rush of wetness in my underwear says yes. Yes, I am. And the sooner, the better.

"Okay, perfect. I'll get out of here." I jerk a thumb to the door as I ramble. "Call me if he wakes up, or if you have questions. He has extra diapers, bottles, and formula in his bag if you need. I noticed you have tons of clothes already, but he has a couple of extra outfits if he needs one."

As I turn to walk to the door, Archer steps up and places his hand on my lower back. The heat from his fingers is scorching my already too warm skin, but I love it.

"Take as long as you need. I'll have my phone on me at all times so you can call and check on him whenever you like. Or video call and I can show you the monitor, too." His hand sneaks around to the side of my waist and my breath catches. "I almost wish I'd gotten the wi-fi camera now, so you could log in from wherever you want. Maybe I'll ask if MaeLynn can have her friend send one over?"

I know he's talking about cameras, but I can't concentrate with his hand nestled in the curve of my waist.

"Great. Yup. Sounds good." I throw open the door and rush out. "I'll call you if I'm going to be longer than a couple of hours."

Archer smiles again. "Lincoln and I will be fine. Have fun shopping." Before it can register, he leans forward and kisses my cheek. "Thank you. For trusting me. I know this isn't easy."

I can only nod, stunned at the tingling his kiss leaves in its wake. What is happening? Oh yeah, I'm leaving. I walk across the small lobby and press the button for the elevator. When the doors open behind me, I walk backwards and swipe the card on the security panel, pushing the button for the parking garage level. Archer watches me the whole time, a crooked grin on his lips. I manage an awkward wave as the doors close, before sagging back against the elevator wall in relief.

Could I have been weirder? I don't think so. But at least I'm out of there now and I can follow through on my plan.

I'm not going shopping. I'm going home to tear open that battery operated boyfriend and put it to some use, finally. Because if I don't give my lady parts some sweet loving, I'll never be able to stop fantasizing about Archer every time I lay eyes on him.

I just need to get home and take care of myself, then everything will go back to normal and I can stop having filthy thoughts about my baby's father.

I hope.

After a quick drive, during which I thought only of Archer doing delicious things to my naked body, I'm throwing open the door at my house and kicking off my shoes.

"That was fast. Hey. Where's Lincoln? Isn't it nap time?" Shit. Gavin is lounging on the blue couch, his phone in his hand and a shaker cup full of yellow liquid in front of him on the coffee table. I thought he'd be gone by now. How can I get acquainted with my battery operated boyfriend when my brother's sitting in the other room?

"Oh, hey. Yeah, he's at Archer's place having a nap. I figured I'd give him a chance to look after Lincoln alone for a couple of hours. How hard can it be when he'll be asleep the whole time, right?"

Gavin chuckles and sits up. "Well, he already had an off morning, remember? What are the chances he sleeps as long as he normally does?"

Shit. He's right. Lincoln has been a little off all day, starting with a fussy morning. Gavin had to bathe him before we left because he spit up more than usual after his morning bottle. And then there was his crying jag when seeing that Santa—sorry, Kris Kringle—at the farmer's market. What if he gets cranky with Archer? Maybe I'll skip the shopping and go straight back to Archer's place after I'm done here, instead. Because there's no way I can skip what I'm about to do.

At the very least, I need to change my underwear.

"I'm sure it will be fine. I won't be away for long." I walk as calmly as I can manage down the hall to my bedroom.

"Okay. If you say so," Gavin says to my back. "I'm heading to the gym now. Mom and Dad said to tell you they went out shopping, but they'll be by later, and Charlie's out with friends."

Yes! He's leaving after all. Sexual satisfaction, here I come.

"Alright, thanks. Bye," I say as I slide into my room and lock the door behind me. With a deep breath, I turn and stalk to my nightstand.

The toy Charlie bought me hasn't seen the light of day since I unwrapped it and stuffed it into my nightstand. Other than the little field trip it took when I moved into this house, it's been inside its original packaging and in a drawer the entire time.

Until today.

I open the drawer, pull out the shiny purple box, and rip it open, dropping the package straight into the trash can. I'm left with a purple wand vibrator and a cord. Wait a minute. I grab the box out of the trash and check the back. Thank god. The sigh of relief I breathe is enormous. It comes charged already.

Thank god for that. I don't have the patience to wait for it to charge. This is a quick, self-care, jilling-off session. I just need a couple minutes of buzzy-time and I'll be good to go.

I take the vibe over to my bed and drop it on the blanket before undoing my jeans and pushing them down. Next, I take off my soaking wet underwear and lay down on the bed, my legs flopping open.

It's been a while since I've done this, but with how I'm already throbbing, I don't think it's going to take long to get into the swing of things. A push of a button sets the toy to vibrating at a nice steady speed that seems about right for my needs, and I lower it to my thigh.

As I push the vibe closer to my clit, I replay my earlier fantasies of Archer climbing over me, both of us naked in his bed. I imagine his hands roaming my skin as I bring the toy closer and closer, allowing it to finally touch me where I need it most. Less than ten seconds of maneuvering it around my slick clit and my orgasm shoots through my body. I arch up off the bed, a low moan escaping my throat as the pulsing slows and the orgasm ends too soon.

I turn off the vibrator and drop it beside me on the bed.

Well. That was...adequate, I suppose.

I doubt it will be enough to stop my Archer fantasies, though.

Damn it.

Now what?

Chapter 28

Feeling Down In The Dumps

Archer

PHOEBE HAD BEEN GONE for all of five minutes before Lincoln started fussing in his crib. He wasn't crying, exactly. Mostly he was making angry squawking sounds. Per Phoebe's instructions, I didn't rush in to see if he was alright. I let him try to work it out.

When he let out an actual cry, though, I couldn't take it anymore. I ran straight in and got him.

Since then, I've done everything I could think of to help him calm down, but none of it worked. I changed his diaper, rocked him in the glider chair, walked around and around my apartment with him while bouncing him gently in my arms, and still nothing. I even used my fancy formula machine to make him a bottle in case he was still hungry, but he wanted nothing to do with it.

It was a last-ditch attempt at comforting him that led us to where we are now. I'm laying on the couch with Lincoln on my chest and I've been rubbing his back for the last fifteen minutes. I guess he likes that and the slight movement from my breathing because the last I looked, his eyes were finally closing.

Thank god for minor miracles. I never knew how much it would hurt me to see my child in pain, but let me tell you, I understand those movies where fathers take hostages to get their kids proper medical care much better now.

I thought I was going to have to call Phoebe to come back early from her shopping trip, and I *really* didn't want to do that. I know she's had a lot of help from her family, but I wanted to be the one to step up this time. I wanted to be the one to spend time with my son while his mother took care of herself.

I wanted to be a parent to him.

And damn, is it ever good to finally get that chance.

So good, in fact, that I'm still silently congratulating myself on my fine parenting skills when I hear the first rumblings of discontent from Lincoln's lower half.

The first *pfft* gets past me almost without notice. *Aww. He's so relaxed he let out a cute little toot. Adorable.* It's the *thpptpht-phphhph* that comes next isn't nearly so cute.

And the smell that accompanies it is downright *foul.*

"Geez, dude. How do you smell this bad? You only eat milk." Lincoln answers with another *pfft.* "Is that why you've been so unhappy? You had to fart? Well, better out than in, right? Fart away, if that's what helps."

I look at him, only to see his eyes are still closed, a serene smile on his face. He's so cute. *MaeLynn needs to see this.*

I maneuver my phone from my pocket and snap a picture of the two of us, texting it to MaeLynn immediately. I take a few more pictures for good measure, and as I'm about to put my phone back in my pocket, Lincoln unleashes another long, smelly fart. And then another. And another.

And then another. The trouble with this last one, though, is that I don't just hear it and smell it, I *feel it* seeping through my shirt. Liquid pools on my stomach. I roll up, trying to see it, hoping it's not what I think it is, but Lincoln lets out a whimper, so I plaster my back to the couch again. Now what? I can't see from this angle. A stroke of genius occurs to me and I grab my phone again. I open the camera and snap a picture, horrified at what I see.

A greenish brown sludge seeps from Lincoln's lower half and onto me, soaking through my shirt, drenching my ugly Christmas sweater, making it even uglier. It drips down my side, pooling where my back hits the couch. *"Heurgh." Oh. My. God. "Heeuurgh."* The contents of my stomach are attempting to claw their way up my throat, and I'm stuck on the couch while baby shit drips down my stomach. Every time I try to move, Lincoln squawks and whimpers unhappily. I can't move without disturbing him, and besides, I wouldn't know what to do with him after that, anyway. This requires more than a simple diaper change.

What do I do?

I think for a moment, and realize I have the answer in my phone. Pulling up my contacts, I call the only person who can help me. Gavin.

"Hello?"

"Gavin, you've got to help me."

"Archer? What's wrong? Is Lincoln okay?" The panic in his voice is palpable. If I weren't doused in baby crap, I'd feel guilty for worrying him.

"He's sleeping right now—*heurgh*—But I need—*heuurgh*—your help." The more I talk, the more of the noxious odor seeps into my mouth. Oh, god. I think I can taste it. *Heurgh.* "Come to the Westborough Business Tower. I'll get security to bring you up to my place. *Heurgh.* Please. Hurry."

"Shit. Yeah. Okay. I'm nearby. Maybe five minutes."

I hang up without saying goodbye and dial the security desk. I don't know how much longer I can keep my breakfast on the inside. How do babies smell this bad? It's like the leaky dumpster behind a fast-food restaurant on a scorching summer day.

"Good afternoon, Mr. Fade. How can I help you?"

"William! I'm so happy to hear your voice. I'm incapac-it—*heurgh*—ated at the moment and I have a guest coming shortly. Can you bring him to my apartment? I'll need you to open my door and bring him all the way inside." I gag and choke out a cough. "His name is Gavin...Gavin... Shit. Hold on." I pull the phone away from my ear and navigate back to my contacts. "Gavin St. James. He's my son's uncle."

"Are you alright, Mr. Fade? Should I call an ambulance?"

"No, no, William. I'm—*heurgh*—fine. I just need some help with my son. Nothing serious. Gavin can handle it."

"Yes, sir. Mr. Fade. If you're sure. I'll bring him up as soon as he arrives."

"Thank you, William. And call me Archer, would you?" The request to use my first name falls from my mouth habitually despite the situation.

I hang up and drop the phone on the coffee table, where it's still within reach.

Pfft. Thpptphtphphhph. THPPTHPHTPPPHTHPPFT.

"Not again," I groan as another rush of liquid cascades down my side and drips onto the couch. "Lincoln, buddy. That's not cool, man. Not cool." He lets out a tiny whine in response before stretching his little arms up with an enormous yawn. Aside from the poop soaking through his diaper and clothes, he doesn't seem any worse for wear. His forehead is cool to the touch, and he doesn't appear to be in pain.

I'm the only one here who's in obvious distress. My head is swimming and my stomach is roiling, threatening to empty itself with every whiff of poop that hits my nostrils. *Deep breaths, Archer. Deep breaths through your mouth. You can't throw up just because it smells bad.* I'm so lost in my misery that I don't even hear my door open ten minutes later.

"Archer? Where are you?" Gavin's voice cuts through the stench and helps me focus.

"Over here," I call out. "In the living room."

"Is everything alright?" William's voice sounds like he's still standing by the door.

"Oh, shit. And I mean that literally." Gavin barges into the room, gets one look at me, and bursts out laughing. "William. Get in here. You gotta see this."

William steps into the room behind Gavin, a snicker escaping before he schools his features. "Oh. Mr. Fade, I mean, Archer. You're looking...uh, well?"

Gavin laughs harder, doubling over and holding his stomach. He wrestles his phone from his pocket and snaps some pictures. "I'm keeping these for future blackmail opportunities. You never know when something like this could come in handy."

"You assholes. Someone come help me, please. I need a towel or something. It's dripping onto the couch." My stomach rolls. "And if I don't get a bucket soon, I'll be adding to this mess."

"Where are your towels?"

"There's a linen closet in the hallway. There should be some in there."

William takes off at a jog.

"And where can I find a bucket?" Gavin asks, still catching his breath after laughing so hard at my misfortune.

"Get a trashcan from any bathroom. I don't have a dedicated bucket." I've never been sick enough to require one. Who knew babies, along with being messy little creatures all on their own, could make adults physically ill with only their stink?

Gavin takes off down the hallway as William returns with towels.

"Here you are, Mr. Fa—I mean, Archer," he says as he hands me one. "I brought a few."

"Thank you, William." I take the towel he offers and carefully bundle it around Lincoln, holding him in one arm. "I don't suppose you know of a good upholstery and leather cleaner who's open for business over the holidays?" I sit up and reach for another towel.

He scrunches his nose in disgust and looks at the spot on the couch where I was laying. "With all due respect, it might be best to burn it."

I use the second towel to soak up the mess on my shirt and wipe my stomach as best I can. When I look at the couch cushion beside me, there's an hourglass shape where my body protected the cushion from Lincoln's explosion.

"Here you go, man." Gavin drops a bucket on the floor beside me. "Oh, shit. Look at your couch!" He chuckles. "I knew he wasn't feeling well. Do you have a baby bathtub around here somewhere?"

I nod. "It's in Lincoln's bathroom."

"He has his own room? That's awesome." He looks around. "This place is nice. You looking for a roommate?"

I chuckle, the worst of the nausea behind me. "Not on your life, kid. I like you, but there's no way I'm letting you move in."

Gavin shrugs. "It was worth a shot. I think I have a place lined up already, anyway."

"I need to get back to the security desk. Will that be all?"

"Yeah, William. Thank you for everything."

I turn to Gavin while William lets himself out.

"Want me to take care of Lincoln's bath?"

"Nah. But can you show me how to do it? I'm at a disadvantage with all this baby stuff. I could use all the help I could get."

He gives me a strange look, then shrugs again. "Sure, come on."

Together, we move into Lincoln's room and make our way to the bathroom. He pulls the baby bathtub out of the linen closet and brings it to the shower stall.

"I need to have a full tub installed for him. I doubt he'll fit in a baby bathtub for much longer."

"You don't have a tub in one of your many other bathrooms? He'll need supervision for years still. Probably no need for you to remodel your bathrooms yet."

He has a point. It's not like I can let Lincoln sit in the tub alone for any amount of time.

And besides that, who's saying I'll still be living in this penthouse when he's old enough to bathe without supervision? The more I think about it, the more I like the idea of a house with a yard for Lincoln to play in. Maybe we'll even get a dog.

"Okay, so now that I'm thinking about this, it might be easier if you take him into the shower with you." Gavin's voice drags me from my daydream. "You're not exactly smelling very fresh either."

I shoot him an incredulous look. "How would that work?"

He shrugs. I'm beginning to think it's the only gesture he knows. "Hold him in your arms and wash him. I know it seems like he'll be slippery, but it won't be that bad. I've done it a few times after taking him swimming. It shouldn't be much different for this."

I look down at Lincoln, then past him to my shirt. Gavin's right. I could use a shower too.

"Yeah. Yeah, okay. That's probably a good idea. Here." I pass Lincoln to Gavin before going to the linen closet and pull out some towels.

Back at the shower, I turn the water on, warming it up so it's not as much of a shock to Lincoln. Unbuttoning my jeans, I push them to the floor and then strip off my ugly Christmas sweater, dropping it on my pants, leaving me in only my black boxer briefs.

"Wow. Someone works out." Gavin gives me an appraising look. "I can see why my sister likes you."

I shake my head and chuckle. "Your sister doesn't like me."

Gavin shrugs again. Yup, it's definitely his signature move. I wonder why he's trying to convince me he doesn't care. "Agree to disagree. Here." He passes Lincoln back to me. "I'll leave you to it." He turns and leaves the bathroom. "I have to get to the gym to meet my date."

"Thanks for your help." I yell.

"Anytime."

I strip Lincoln out of his soiled clothes and the dirty diaper that I'm now noticing I didn't fasten tightly enough, and get into the shower.

"Well, little guy? We sure made a mess of us, didn't we? Looks like I need more practice with getting those diapers onto you properly." Lincoln smiles up at me and smacks my chest with his chubby little fist. "I hear you, kid. We'll get cleaned up real quick, then we'll try the nap again. How's that?"

His only reply is another gummy smile.

I chuckle as I wash us both with the baby soap that Mae-Lynn insisted I needed. Now that the smell of rancid baby poop has dissipated, this situation is a little easier to laugh at. And Gavin was right. It's not as hard showering with Lincoln in my arms as I thought it would be. The kid's a little slippery, but it's not that bad as long as I move carefully. After we're clean and smelling fresh, I turn off the shower and open the door.

"Wow." A voice startles me, and I jerk my head up to see Phoebe standing in the doorway. Her mouth is open wide, and she's devouring my body with her eyes. I could get used to this. "Wow," she whispers again.

Huh. Maybe Gavin was right.

Maybe she does like me.

"Hey, you're back early." I step out of the shower and grab a towel, wrapping it around Lincoln. "Not as ready to leave Lincoln with me as you thought?"

She blinks several times, then shakes herself. I flex for good measure, loving that she's enjoying looking at me. I know if the situations were reversed, I'd be staring at her the same way.

"Oh. Yeah," she says, forcing a smile onto her face. "I guess I missed him?" She shrugs, leading me to believe it might be a family trait. "I went home and I—" her eyes widen and she stops short. "Well, I had something to do, then I decided to come right back here."

I nod and grab a towel before stepping around her into the bedroom. I put Lincoln is his crib so I can dry myself, then fasten the towel around my waist, Phoebe's hot gaze on me the entire time. I wish I had more time to explore what that means, but there are other things going on right now.

Lincoln needs to get dressed, so I get new clothes and bring him to the changing table. This time, when I put his diaper on, I make extra sure that I fasten it properly.

"So, what's with the shower?"

Shit.

I forgot that she'd want to know why Lincoln isn't napping. But I don't want her to know how close I was to puking all over our son.

"Oh, he was a little fussy, and when I checked on him, I realized I hadn't put the diaper on properly. I figured a shower would be easiest to clean him up, and it might help settle him down. I'm about to lay him back down, actually."

I can see her nod from the corner of my eye. "I think I'll stick around this time, if that's okay?"

My heart beats a little faster, and I can't stop the grin from taking over my face. "I'd like nothing more," I blurt, without thinking.

And I'm not even a little surprised when I realize it's true.

Chapter 29

Butt Plug What Now?

Phoebe

"Where do you want this stuff?" Eric juggles an armful of fresh greenery. "Is there even any room left?"

Archer and Eric showed up bright and early to decorate my front porch for an impromptu Santa Claus photo shoot. They've been fastening evergreen boughs, twinkle lights, and various ribbons and baubles to the support beams for the last three hours.

"That's the last of them?" Archer asks from the top of a ladder. "Is the backdrop covered? No holes?"

Eric looks to the end of the porch where they've made a solid wall of greenery and lights. It's even prettier than the enchanted forest at Kris Kringle's.

"Webster and Frederick are going to love this." I grin up at Archer. "Thank you."

He smiles. "No thanks necessary. I wanted to do this. After all, what kind of Santa would I be if I let them miss out on their engagement announcement when I have the suit at my disposal?"

I chuckle. "True." I'd be lying if I said I wasn't interested in seeing him in the Santa suit again, too. Will it bring back any more memories of that night? Or are they lost forever, washed away with that morning's hangover, never to be seen again. "It's still nice of you to go to this much trouble."

He climbs down the ladder and dusts his hands on his jeans, drawing my attention to the way his thighs test the seams. Why does he have to be so sexy? It's unfair for him to look so good all the time.

"I didn't go to that much trouble, actually. I delegated most of this to Eric. He gathered all these decorations together for me."

I look at Eric where he's fastening the last of the boughs to a section of railing. "That's impressive. Where'd you find all this stuff at the last minute like this?"

Eric darts a glance in my direction, a smirk on his lips. "Let's just say it wasn't easy, and leave it at that."

"Okay," I drawl. "That sounds...suspicious."

Archer laughs. "We won't need to hide you from the cops later, will we?"

"Nah," Eric says with a chuckle. "My feet are way too fast for that. Damien, though? His slow ass might need bail money."

He tells us a story about Damien getting caught by the owner when they were raiding the Christmas tree lot for scrap branches that's so hilarious we're still chuckling when Webster and Frederick pull into my driveway. The look on their faces when they get out of the car is one of complete and utter delighted shock. They look like...well, they look like kids on Christmas.

"Phoebe. I can't believe you did all this." Webster comes up the stairs and pulls me into a hug. "It's so beautiful." His eyes are shining and I know we're seconds away from tears.

"I didn't do it," I say quickly, to circumvent any crying. "Archer and Eric did everything. I've been in the kitchen all morning."

Webster turns his shiny eyes to Archer. "You did all this? For us?"

Archer scrubs a hand over his neck. "Well, yeah? I hope it's okay."

Webster pulls Archer into an even tighter hug than he gave me. "Yes, you silly man. Of course it's okay. This is even better than that farmer's market set up. It's gorgeous."

Frederick, the more sedate of the two, joins us on the porch and reaches a hand out to Eric. "Hi. I'm Frederick. You must be Eric. Thank you for this. It looks amazing."

Eric grins. "You're welcome. It was nothing." He looks between Webster and Frederick. "I hear congratulations are in order? I brought champagne. You should go in and pop it to celebrate."

I smack my head. "Yes, of course. Come inside. Mom and Warren are dying to see you, Webster." He cringes. He hasn't seen my parents since our fateful non-wedding day, and I think he's worried about what they'll say.

"I didn't know they would be here. Should I have worn a bulletproof vest? Or brought an offering of some sort?"

A booming laugh comes from the open doorway. "Get your butt over here, Web. And stop being ridiculous. We stopped being upset with you when Phoebe told us why you stood her up." Warren is standing inside the open door, wiping his hands on a towel. "Bring your fella, too. We can't wait to meet him." He turns and walks back inside. "Sheila. They're here."

"Well, tell them to get in here. I've got my hands in a turkey's asshole, so I can't very well go out to see them on the porch." Mom insisted on taking care of the turkey today, and no matter how many times I tell her how much better it is when cooked in a dish, she insists on cooking the stuffing inside the turkey.

"I did. He looks scared."

"Pssh. There's nothing to be afraid of. He's family."

Webster's eyes widen at the overheard conversation and the tears that were merely threatening moments ago finally spill over. "I'm family?"

I shake my head and give him a sad smile. "That's what I told you, didn't I?"

He takes my hands in his. "Thank you." Frederick looks on with a small smile. "Thank you."

I squeeze his hands and steer him to the door. "Don't thank me. Go in there and hug my parents. They've been waiting impatiently all morning."

He snorts a laugh and nods before reaching back for Frederick's hand.

"I'll be right behind you."

Eric leaves too, saying he has to get ready for dinner, leaving me alone on the porch with Archer.

Crap.

It would be best if I could avoid being alone with him. It's what needs to happen if I ever want to get over this little crush I seem to have, anyway. Being alone with him leaves too many opportunities for him to show me his sweet side. It's bad news for my heart.

Yet here we are. Alone again.

"Are you coming to the kitchen for a toast before you change?" He's standing next to me, so close the heat of his body seeps through my clothes, and I can't seem to concentrate on anything but his scent. The smell of the pine boughs he's been handling all morning makes the scent of him that much more delicious. He smells like a sexy lumberjack.

He steps even closer, his hand reaching out for my hip as his eyes dip to my mouth. My heartbeat pounds in my ears and heat floods my chest. What is happening here? Is he kissing me?

No. That can't be right. This is like last time. I'll close my eyes and pucker up, only to find him reaching for something behind me. Again.

Not this time, buddy. Fool me once and all that.

"Okay. I'll see you in there," I blurt before spinning out of his grasp and marching into the house. I don't even look back to see what he was actually looking for when I crazily thought he was trying to kiss me.

I don't stop until I'm in the kitchen, surrounded by other people. There. That's better. It's hard to misinterpret his intentions when I'm this far away from him. It's hard enough to guard my heart when I watch him come alive when he's with Lincoln. I don't need him being sweet to me and giving me the wrong impression, too.

"And when he sat up, there was an hourglass shaped void where his body had been. It was hilarious." Gavin barks a loud laugh. "Poor guy looked like he'd rolled in shit."

I spin around at the sound of a groan. Archer has an embarrassed grimace on his face, his cheeks reddened. "Did you have to tell everyone?" he asks. "I was hoping we could keep that between you and me."

Gavin laughs again. "When I get a frantic, gag-filled call to go help with a shit emergency, I tell. That's how it works. Besides, telling this story to everyone I know is my payment for cleaning your couch before I left."

"*That's* why you were in the shower when I got back to your place? I thought you said Lincoln made a mess. You didn't say he made a mess all over *you*." My face screws up in confusion, then I snap my fingers. "And that's why we sat on your patio for coffee? Because your couch was wet?"

Archer scrubs a hand down his face. "I didn't want to tell you I had to call Gavin for help. It was bad enough that I was gagging at being covered in baby crap without having to tell you all about it. I'm trying to prove to you I can handle things. Telling you I needed your little brother's help didn't seem like it would instill confidence, you know what I mean?" He blurts it all in a rush, then stares at me anxiously while waiting for an answer. Why is his nervousness so cute?

I snort. "Do you think I knew what to do the first time Lincoln had a blowout diaper? No. I called my mom for help. I don't think less of you because you needed help. Babies are hard." I touch his arm, ignoring the tingles in my fingers. "Especially when they crap all over you."

He chokes out a laugh, then shakes his head. "Thanks," he says before walking over to Gavin. "And thanks again for helping me. I'm pretty sure I was one baby shart away from puking all over myself."

"You were not," Gavin says with a chuckle. "You would have been fine if you'd taken a minute to think about the problem. I get it, though. It's hard to think when he's stinking up the place. For a kid who only drinks milk, he sure has a nasty rear end."

Webster catches my eye and jerks his head for me to come over. Archer and Gavin are chatting, and my mom, Charlie, and Eric are arguing about the turkey, and everyone else is otherwise occupied.

"What's going on there?" he asks without preamble. "I see that look in your eye. Tell me."

Damn it. He always did know me better than I know myself. I drag him to the far side of the kitchen, away from the others.

"It's nothing. A harmless little crush. He's attractive, and he's a good guy. You, of all people, should know how I feel about guys like that." I attempt to distract him with flattery, but the knowing look on Webster's face tells me it didn't work.

He cocks an eyebrow. "You mean he's sexy as hell and he's sweeter than sugar, right? Because if you're saying that man is merely *attractive,* then we need to get you a dictionary. Because you don't know the meaning of the word."

I roll my eyes and smile. Of course he's calling me out. He knows me better than anyone, and if he didn't sense that something was up, I'd have been stunned.

"Fine. I have a giant crush on my baby's dad, and I don't know what the hell I'm doing."

He nudges me with his elbow when Archer looks at me and smiles before going back to talking to my brother. "See? He can't go more than a minute without knowing where you are. I think he likes you."

I scoff. "You won't think that later when you meet his girlfriend. She's beautiful. Way more of a catch than I am." My shoulders sag and I sigh. "She's got to be a model. Or a dancer. It's the only explanation. You'll see. Her legs are eighteen miles long and she has the face of an angel."

"Oh, honey," he says with a pout before wrapping his arms around me. "You are better than any dancer or model. In fact, if you had a penis, you'd be perfect."

I snort a laugh. "Too soon."

He puts a hand on my head and pulls me to his chest. "I know, honey. But at least you laughed."

I chuckle and shake my head against his chest. "Fine. You got me there."

He pats my head, then lets me go, turning to take Frederick's hand. Warren pours champagne for everyone while mom and Charlie distribute the flutes. When we all have a glass, Warren makes a short toast to the happy couple. Webster's tears finally flow when Warren officially invites Frederick to the family. I swallow a lump in my throat. Knowing my family will be there for Webster when his own family won't makes me love them even more.

We chat a little longer while Mom gets the turkey into the oven, before Archer excuses himself to get changed into his costume.

"Phoebe?" he calls from the living room after several minutes. "Can you come here for a minute?"

I nod to everyone, then head to the living where I freeze in my tracks at the sight before me. I'm stunned speechless like I was yesterday when I saw Archer stepping out of the shower in his sopping wet boxer shorts. I think I may have even short-circuited yesterday when I watched the water dripping down over his abs. Either that or I imagined myself standing there unable to say anything but "wow".

It's so much worse now. He's standing in my living room, Santa costume hanging perfectly on his hard frame, but there's one issue. The jacket is hanging open, and he's naked underneath. Nude. Naked. Shirtless. Pecs popping and on full display. Nipples. Out. The suspenders extending over his naked chest make it more scandalous than if he were merely shirtless. I swallow hard against the desert my mouth has become. He's left off the beard, showing his own sexy scruff instead, and he looks like every naughty Santa fantasy come to life.

I'm definitely going to need some private time with my vibrator after this.

"Phoebe?" His face sports a knowing grin, and I groan inwardly. How does he keep catching me staring? Why can't he let me ogle him in peace? It's not fair. "I was most of the way dressed when I realized I forgot the shirt. Then I had this idea," he says, gesturing to his open jacket, "but now that I see it, I'm not sure. What do you think? Is this okay? Is it too risqué for a social media engagement announcement?"

The words don't come, and I nod mindlessly.

"It's too much?"

I shake my head.

"It's not too much?"

I shake my head again, and he laughs. "You're going to need to use some words because I don't understand what you mean."

Before I can get my thoughts in any semblance of order, a hand on my shoulder stops me, and I hear a rough intake of breath followed by a squeal of excitement.

"Oh my god, this is perfect," Webster claps his hands together. "Frederick, come in here and look at Santa Hottie. He's way better than that Kris Kringle at the farmer's market, isn't he?"

It's true. Kris Kringle was a skinny twerp compared to the glory that is Archer Fade half-naked in a Santa suit. I wonder if he'll let me sit on his lap?

Or maybe his face?

I scrub that thought from my mind in time to see everyone filing into the living room behind Frederick.

"I love it. Our friends are going to die."

Gavin lets out a long wolf whistle, and a frisson of jealousy hits me in the gut when Archer laughs.

"And we *must* add those butt plug Christmas trees to the decorations in the background." Webster's voice grabs my attention right before I hear the sounds of squeaking brakes as my brain screeches to a halt.

I cock my head to the side in confusion. "I'm sorry. Butt plug what now?" My eyes are blinking too rapidly and I wet my lips awkwardly. *He didn't he actually say butt plug just now, did he?*

He gestures to the new Christmas tree decorations Archer gave me. I've set them up on the fireplace mantle and draped them in twinkle lights so they sparkle, and yeah, so maybe their modern shape looks a little like...No. That can't be.

I force a laugh. "Oh no, that's silly. Those aren't butt plugs. They're Christmas decorations. Archer gave them to me." I look at Archer for confirmation, only to see his face turning as red as his suit. Suddenly feeling unsure, I add with a stutter, "They...they make them at his toy factory."

Gavin chokes on a laugh and someone else snickers.

"Right?" I look at Archer for confirmation, my confusion growing.

Archer clears his throat and drops his head, looking up at me through his lashes, the barest hint of a smile on his lips. I step closer to the mantle to inspect the trees. "Look at how pretty they are." I pick one up to inspect it, noticing the way the glitter swirls through the cone shaped glass, the slightly rounded conical shape of the tree before it narrows then expands again in a...flared... base.

No! I spin on my heel after shoving the tree back on the mantle, then sprint to the kitchen and drop to my knees in front of the recycling bin. Packaging goes flying as I throw cardboard and paper over my back until I finally find what I'm looking for.

No, no, no!

Christmas Cheer Training Set. *Training set.* Not *tree set.* Training set.

"Holy shit. They'*re* butt plugs." How did I not see that? Why did I think it said Christmas Cheer Tree Set?

I stare into nothing for a moment before flipping the packaging over. *What? No!*

I'm hit with a mental image, a flash of purple packaging sparking in my memory.

My face drops and bile rises in my throat.

"No," I whisper before taking off down the hallway and into my room, leaving a tornado of cardboard in my wake. "No."

I ease into my room, creep up to my garbage can like it's a dangerous animal that could bite my arm off at any second, and peer inside. There, right on top where I left it, is the shiny purple packaging from the vibrator I ripped open yesterday. I pinch it between two fingers and pull it out for a closer look.

There, right on the bottom in plain white lettering, it says "manufactured by Fade Toys" with the address of Archer's toy factory directly beneath that.

Exactly like the one on the box from the Christmas Cheer Training Set.

No.

"No, no, no, no, no."

I groan and slide to the floor, the purple package tumbling from my fingers. I decorated my mantle with festive butt plugs, that I told him I wanted to use, *and photograph.* He thought I wanted to take pictures of his Christmas trees in my butthole. I masturbated to thoughts of him with a toy made by his company. The mortification eats its way through my stomach as acid crawls up my throat, and I wrap my arms around myself to contain my embarrassment.

That's it. It's official. I can never look him in the eye again. The humiliation will kill me as soon as I do. I know it. The man runs a sex toy company, and I mistook their butt plugs for Christmas decorations. I told his receptionist I wanted a set of my own. I'm surprised I'm not dead already.

I slide further down the side of my bed and curl into the fetal position replaying the moment over and over in my mind, cringing every time I hear Webster say he wants to use the butt plugs in the background of their photos, then cringing even harder when I hear myself tell everyone that Archer gave them to me.

Ugh.

But one good thing has come of this. I won't need to worry about my little crush anymore. Because even if he *were* single, I'm way too embarrassed to ever act on it now.

Chapter 30

Santa Picture Retakes

Archer

"Okay, so…why don't we go ahead and get these pictures taken while we wait for Phoebe?" I take in the stunned faces of Phoebe's family. Evidently, Phoebe isn't the only one surprised by what I do for a living.

I'm still a little shocked that no one knew. It's readily accessible information. And it's not like I hide it. The company is called Fade Toys and my last name is Fade.

She visited the factory. What did she think we made there? I know the name Fade Toys isn't very suggestive, but come on. Did she see any regular toys around anywhere?

Webster is the first to shake out of his stupor. He answers me with a grin. "Yes. Let's take these pictures. Frederick, babe. Are you ready?"

Frederick stares, eyes wide, nodding absently before finally turning to Webster. "Yes. Pictures. Of course."

Charlie burst into laughter, breaking the tension in the room. "You own a sex toy factory. Oh. my. god. Hahahaha. That's freaking awesome. Do I get the family discount?"

Gavin presses his fist against his mouth and chuckles.

Sheila and Warren shake their heads, but I can see small smiles on both of their faces.

Everyone thinks this is hilarious.

Except Phoebe.

She's embarrassed. I get it. She thought they were Christmas trees instead of butt plugs, and she put them on her mantle. Then she got called out for it in front of her whole family.

Oh...so that's what she meant by setting them up and taking pictures. Now I understand why she would tell me about wanting to do that. I suppose when I think about it, I never *really* believed she wanted to use them for their intended purpose and then take pictures. I may have had a couple of dirty fantasies, but I didn't believe she was actually going to do it. At best, I'd hoped she was flirting with me a little.

"Okay, how about this? I know this is funny. But it's Christmas. What if we hold off on the teasing for the day and pretend like this"—I jerk my thumb to the butt plug display on the mantle, which garners a chuckle from the gathered crowd—"never happened?"

Charlie barks a laugh. "Why would we pretend that? This is the funniest shit ever."

Webster snickers, and I see Frederick elbow him from the corner of my eye.

"Archer's right," he says. "It's an honest mistake, really." He grabs a plug from the mantle, testing the weight of it, turning it in his hands so the glitter sparkles in the light. "They're really quite beautiful. Excellent craftsmanship." He smiles at me. "But it's probably safe to assume that Phoebe's not well-versed in butt plugs."

Warren chokes on a laugh.

"Okay, that's enough." Webster says, trying to hide a smile. "Frederick is right. They are gorgeous. Why do you think I wanted them in the background of our photos? I mean, besides the fact that it would be hilarious, obviously."

Everyone bursts into laughter again, and irritation hardens my jaw. I have a burning need to help Phoebe and getting her family to stop laughing at her mistake is the best way I know how to do that right now.

"That's not helping, Webster," I whisper harshly. "Shut up."

"Sorry," he whispers back, before the giggles overtake him.

"Alright." I clap my hands together, cutting through the laughter permeating the room. "Let's all go outside and get these pictures taken, shall we?"

Webster grabs the training bundle from the mantle as I herd everyone out the door, leaving Phoebe's mom and stepdad in the house to take care of dinner. Charlie volunteered to be on camera duty for the photo shoot and after almost an hour of progressively more risqué posing at her direction, Webster and Frederick have several daring choices for their engagement announcement.

"These really are festive," Frederick says while placing the butt plug trees back on Phoebe's mantle. "It's completely reasonable to want to use them to decorate."

I nod. "My front desk receptionist said the same thing. She had them set up as a display on the desk in the lobby at work. That's where Phoebe saw them." I should have realized she thought they were decorations. I let my dick get the best of me, though, and I hoped she wanted to use them. With me. Which is stupid. Why would she want me? I'm just the guy who knocked her up.

"Well, if you have any more sets available, I would love to send one to Webster's parents. Anonymously, of course. I think it would serve them right to display a set of these bad boys for all their homophobic friends to admire." He winks at me. "I'll even craft new packaging, so it looks like a legitimate Christmas decoration. It could be years before anyone catches on."

I bark a laugh. "Yeah, I think that could be arranged. If we don't have any, I'll repackage the display and you can have that."

"Thank you. That would be wonderful."

"Hello boys," Phoebe's mom comes out of the kitchen and heads straight to me. "Archer, would you mind trying to talk to Phoebe? She hasn't come out of her room yet and she won't talk to any of the rest of us. I think she's embarrassed."

Yeah, no kidding. If the color of her face was anything to go by, she's beyond embarrassed. Not that she has any reason to be. As Frederick was saying, it's an easy mistake to make with a set like this. It was designed to be festive. And if you're not expecting anything other than decorations, then the Christmas Cheer Training Set could easily be mistaken for that. That's why Amanda asked if she could use them to decorate her desk, after all.

"Sure, I'll give it a shot. I doubt she'll want to talk to me any more than the rest of you, though."

Sheila pats me on the shoulder. "Please try. And tell her we're all sorry for laughing. If Webster hadn't said anything, I wouldn't have known what they were, anyway."

I nod and take off down the hallway, stopping and tapping my fingers on Phoebe's door.

"Go away," she mumbles pitifully.

I smile sadly. I hate that I caused this. We could have avoided this if I'd told her it surprised me she was interested in the set. If I wasn't thinking with my dick when she said she wanted to set them up and take pictures, I would have realized something was up.

"Phoebe. It's Archer. Can I come in for a minute?"

"No," comes her immediate reply.

"Please, Phoebe."

"Leave me alone. Christmas is canceled. Tell everyone to go home."

I chuckle at that. There's no way she would cancel Christmas. Not with it being Lincoln's first. But for her to say it without hesitation, well, that means she's still incredibly upset. My stomach is burning with a need to fix it, but I don't want to talk to her through the door. I'm sure she'd be even more embarrassed if I did that.

"I know you don't mean that, Phoebe."

"Oh, I do."

"But you were so excited about Lincoln's first Christmas. Christmas Eve dinner is part of that experience, isn't it?"

I hear her muttering to herself. "No. Today will forever be known as the day we celebrate stuffing butts instead of stockings. It's too dirty for Lincoln now."

I stifle a laugh. Stuff butts, not stockings would make a decent holiday slogan. Or maybe stuff butts and stockings would be better. I shake my head. That doesn't matter now. I need to get to Phoebe and explain that it's not as bad as she's imagining.

And I have just the thing.

"Okay, fine. You don't have to come out. But can I at least come in and get my clothes? I changed in there earlier and but now that we're done with the Santa photo shoot, I'd like to get out of this suit. You'd be shocked at how warm velvet is, even without a shirt on."

I hear more grumbling through the closed door before she answers. "Fine. Come in."

I grin when I turn the knob. She didn't even lock the door.

"Hey," I say, closing the door behind me. "Mind if I sit for a second?"

She shrugs. She's sitting on the floor beside the bed, elbows resting on her knees, and she won't even look at me. I lower myself to the floor beside her, close, but not touching.

"So, about what happened earlier..."

She turns further away from me, but not before I see her face redden. "I said I didn't want to talk about it."

"I'm not talking about it, not really. I owe you an apology. I wasn't clear when I told you what I did for a living, and I think that contributed to the misunderstanding." She angles her body marginally in my direction, but she's still not looking at me. "And I always forget that there's nothing about my factory that really says what we make there. Amanda putting out the Christmas Cheer Training Bundle as a Christmas decoration probably didn't help, either."

Phoebe huffs a laugh. "Making them that pretty wasn't such a good idea, either."

"No, I suppose maybe it wasn't."

She turns to face me and I see her face is still red, but at least she's smiling now. "They really are pretty, though. All that glitter swirled through them looks really magical."

"Yeah, it does."

She heaves an enormous sigh and flops back against the side of the bed.

"So...how did the photoshoot go?"

I chuckle. "Quick, and mostly painless."

"Mostly?"

"Someone kept pinching my ass, but neither Frederick nor Webster would admit to it. It's still a little sore."

She snorts. "That seems like a strange move for an engagement photo."

It's my turn to shrug. "They were arguing about whether I have butt implants. I wouldn't say yes or no, so they were trying to figure it out on their own."

"Butt implants?" Her smile takes over her face as she tries to suppress a giggle. "Well? Do you?"

I look at the ceiling and roll my lips between my teeth.

"Oh my god. You do not," she gasps, slapping me on the arm.

I laugh. "No, I don't. But Webster and Frederick were really invested in finding out. They were pretty thorough."

She sways and bumps me with her shoulder, the contact making my heart beat faster. "You could have saved yourself some bruising if you'd told them."

"Meh." I shrug again. "They were having fun, and I didn't mind. A little harmless butt pinching now and again is good for the soul. Plus, it made for some fun pictures."

"I'll bet." She heaves a sigh. "Thanks for doing that for them. I hated thinking Lincoln ruined their chance at a cute engagement photo."

"That had nothing to do with Lincoln, and everything to do with it being that Santa's first time. I hope for everyone's sake that he gets over it. If there's one thing you can count on with being Santa, it's that some kids are going to cry when they see you."

She nods and looks down at her lap.

"So how bad is it going to be when I get back out there?"

I hate that she's feeling this way because of something I could have prevented. I could have told her explicitly what I do for a living. Or I could have refrained from gifting a butt plug set to a woman I barely know. Either option would have saved her the embarrassment.

"I told them they weren't allowed to mention it to you," I confess. "But who knows how long that's going to last."

She snickers and drops her face into her hands. "Oh my god," she says, her voice rising until she yells the last word, placing extra emphasis on the *d*. "I can't believe I put a set of butt plugs on my mantle like they were nothing more than a festive tree scene."

"Well, if it makes you feel any better, they did make an appearance in the engagement photos, too. Webster and Frederick loved the addition." Hesitantly, I wrap an arm around her and pull her to my side. She stiffens at first, then softens against me. I gotta say, I love the way she melts in my arms. "And your mom confessed she wouldn't have known what they were if Webster hadn't said it out loud. She thought they were decorative glass Christmas trees, the same as you."

She lifts her head and looks at me through splayed fingers. "They are pretty, right?"

I nod. All the glass toys we make are beautiful and these are especially so. "Yes, they are. That's why Amanda set them up on the reception desk in the first place. She thought it would look festive but still on brand for us."

At that, Phoebe's eyes widen, and she pushes away from me. "You own a sex toy factory and you didn't even tell me," she accuses, her face an angry mask. "I thought you made kids' toys."

I choke on a laugh, torn between taking her anger seriously and laughing at the ridiculous notion that my factory makes kids' toys. I mean, she's never been on the production floor, but the logo...

Luckily, she can't maintain her anger. The mad look on her face drops and she lets loose a huge, braying laugh.

I snort. "I'm sorry I wasn't clear," I say, forcing the laughter down. "But how could you see our logo and not realize what we make?"

"Your logo?" Her eyes cut to the side before she turns to face me. "What's wrong with your logo?"

I scoff. "You don't think it's a little...I don't know, phallic?"

Her eyes cut to the side again, then widen. She drops her head into her hands and laughs.

Yup. She sees it now.

Chapter 31

Happy Family Christmas

Phoebe

"Alright." I slap my thighs and lurch to my feet. "Let's get out there."

I leave Archer sitting on the floor beside my bed and head to the door. I throw my shoulders back and plaster a confident, but fake, smile on my face.

Okay. This is no big deal. So I thought butt plugs were Christmas ornaments. Who could blame me? They're too pretty for anyone's first guess at what they are to be their intended use. Yeah. That's it. Why are they so cute if they're not meant to be shown off?

Oh, who are you kidding? Now that you know, it's impossible not to see it. As pretty as they are, they are definitively, one hundred percent no doubt about it, butt plugs. And that doesn't mean the right person wouldn't want to show them off. A blush creeps up as I recall that's exactly what Archer thought I was going to do with them. You know, since I said I was taking pictures after setting them up.

I groan and drop my head to the door frame, my bravery leaving me in a breath.

"You got this." Archer's hands grip my shoulders, and he massages my tense muscles, causing my blush to deepen. *God, that's good.* "I made them promise not to say anything." I snort and laugh and he chuckles. "Yeah, I doubt they'll keep their word. But hopefully, they'll try."

I shake my head, take a deep breath, then open the door. "Let's get this over with."

Strong hands spin me in place. "Hold on." Archer wraps his arms around me and my breath catches.

His biceps bunch as he pulls me close, and I instinctively wrap my arms around his waist under the velvet jacket of his Santa costume, breathing in his masculine scent like I have a right to. Like he's mine to touch like this. He smells delicious. I want to bathe in whatever cologne he's wearing, but only if it also smells like his warm body. I spread my fingers on his back, loving the feel of his bare skin beneath my hands.

I wonder what his abs would feel like? Taste like?

"Wha...what are you doing?" I stutter when I finally pull myself out of the stupor his nearness puts me in.

"A hug for luck," he says, giving me a squeeze, pulling me tightly against his bare chest. "They won't be cruel, but...yeah. They're in the mood to tease you a little, I'm afraid." He chuckles again. "I'll take as much attention away from you as I can. I'm a gentleman like that."

I laugh and push him away. Just in time, too. My thoughts were taking a side for the naughty, like they often do when I let myself get too close to Archer. I was about to bury my face in his chest and inhale deeply enough to embed his scent in my nose to stash it away for later. And that was only the start of the fantasy.

"Yeah. 'A gentleman' says the guy who crushed me to his bare chest with no warning."

"Shit. Right. Sorry about that. I guess. I should..." He jerks a thumb behind him. "I'll get dressed and meet you out there? Or do you want to wait for me?"

YES! I'll watch. Go ahead and strip that Santa suit off nice and slow. I want to get reacquainted with what you've got going on under it.

"Oh, uh..." My face is burning at the turn of my thoughts.

"No, never mind. Wait for me in the hall? I'll be quick."

I nod and step into the hallway. "Sure. Yeah. That sounds good."

Does it sound good? Or do I only want to spend a little more time with him alone?

I groan internally when I remember I shouldn't want to spend time alone with him. And I won't get to, anyway. I told him to invite his girlfriend for dinner. I imagine she'll be here soon, if she's not out there already.

"Ready?" Archer steps up beside me and puts a hand on my shoulder.

I nod. "Best get this over with, I guess."

He drops his hand and we walk down the hallway side by side, our shoulders brushing with every step. He gives me a slight nod before we step into the living room. We're only a few steps in before Webster calls out.

"Archer. I'm going to need more than the one set Frederick asked you for." He gestures to the Christmas trees that started this whole mess. "I can't get over how pretty they are. We would love a set to decorate with too."

"Yes, me too," my mom says, nodding her head in agreement. "I have the perfect spot for them next to the nativity set."

I choke on a laugh. "Mom. I'm pretty sure the church would consider it sacrilege to put butt plugs near the nativity."

"Pssh," she scoffs, waving a hand. "I'm sure none of our friends will even know what they are." She gives me a small smile. "And they're too pretty for *that*, anyway."

Gavin snickers. "I don't know, Mom. Some people like *those things* to be pretty, you know." He laughs harder when she blushes.

"Alright, Gavin," Warren warns. "That's enough. Quit teasing your mother if you don't want her telling you more personal detail than you're ready for."

"Sorry, Mom."

She nods and waves him off without looking right at him. I imagine learning about your son's interest in butt stuff can make for an awkward conversation, so I don't blame her. It makes me wonder how she'll fare when she figures out he's bisexual, though. Knowing her, she'll take that in stride. It did not phase her in the slightest when I told her I'd gotten pregnant by a random Santa on my wedding night, after all.

Even so, I don't want her embarrassed on Christmas, so I clap my hands together to get everyone's attention. "Okay, now that we've embarrassed all the moms in the house, why don't we move on to the games part of the afternoon?"

Every Christmas Eve, my family spends the day playing board games while waiting for dinner to cook. Throughout the years, we've had some epic Christmas Eve cribbage tournaments and games of Scrabble. It's one of my favorite traditions. It might be a little more complicated this year with extra people in attendance, not to mention a baby to look after, but I'm sure we can figure it out.

Charlie and Gavin both chuckle, but get up and go to the bookshelf to a selection of board games, followed closely by Frederick and Webster. I'm about to join them when I hear a squawking giggle from the baby monitor announcing Lincoln's finally awake from his nap.

"I'll get him," Archer says, raising an eyebrow in question. "If that's okay?"

Gavin laughs. "He's had a long nap today. I'd be prepared to find that whatever should be inside his diaper is actually outside of it."

Archer looks at me for an answer, his eyes widening in response to Gavin's statement.

"Sure," I say with a shrug. "You could use the practice. Give me a yell if you need me to run a bath for him, though. If he did have a blowout, it will be easier to bathe him than to use wipes to clean him. Unless you want to hop in the shower again, that is."

He turns a little greenish, but I have to hand it to him. He gives me a nod and marches to Lincoln's room without another word. I almost feel bad for tricking him into thinking he'll find a colossal mess when the giggling sounds from the monitor hint at Lincoln being fine. He usually cries more when he's covered himself in shit. It's like an early warning system.

"So, what are we playing?" Charlie asks. "One game for all of us? A couple of different games and we can swap out?"

"Why not *Uno*?" Frederick says. "You can play up to ten people and it's usually good for a laugh."

"Perfect," I say, reaching around them to grab the deck from the shelf. "We can play in the kitchen and keep an eye on dinner at the same time."

The four of them head to the kitchen where my mom and Warren are setting out snacks, and I sneak back down the hallway to check on Archer and Lincoln. I know he can handle it, but I need a visual confirmation. Hearing about how he called Gavin to help him with a blowout helped with my confidence, strangely enough. It's reassuring to know that even if he doesn't know how to do everything, he does know when to call for help. It doesn't hurt that it's my brother he called for help, either. I know Gavin is great with Lincoln, and Archer couldn't have asked a better person for help.

MaeLynn would likely be a suitable choice, too, even if I hardly know her.

I peek in the door of Lincoln's room. I gave up on room sharing soon after we moved in since Gavin likes the blue couch so much he prefers to sleep on it when he visits.

"What do you think, little man? Comfy?" Archer's back is to me, but it looks like he's testing Lincoln's diaper. "Too tight?

Nah. That's perfect. We don't want a repeat of last time, do we? Not that I begrudge you the mess. Other than almost puking up my lunch a few times and having to call your Uncle Gavin to come rescue us, I was fine. Plus, I'll wash you up as many times as you need. I'm here for you now." His shoulders tense as he takes a breath. "I know I wasn't there when you were born, but now that I'm here, you're stuck with me."

My heart swells hearing him promise Lincoln that he'll always be around. What more could I ask for? Not much. It's the outcome I was hoping for when I moved here to find him, after all.

So why am I wishing he was saying those things to me, too?

I shake my head to get rid of that thought. *Get it together, Phoebe. He's your kid's dad, nothing more. At least not to you, he's not.*

"Well, now. Don't you look handsome?" Archer's voice grabs my attention again. "Who knew you had more than one ugly Christmas sweater? I wish I'd worn mine today, then we could match. We could have taken family photos with your mom in hers, too."

Family photos? He can't mean the three of us, can he? No. Of course not. He means some with him and Lincoln, and some with me and Lincoln. We're not a family together.

"Okay, that's it. We can go see everyone else now." He picks Lincoln up and snuggles him to his chest. "Should we give your mom a head start on getting back there so she can pretend she wasn't spying? Or should we turn around and show her how cute you look right now?"

Gah! He knows I'm here. *Act cool.* I spin around, then spin around again, only to see him looking straight at me, a huge grin plastered on his face. "Uh. Hey?" I say with an awkward wave. *So much for acting cool, Phoebe.* "I wasn't spying, I was just...checking everything was okay."

He nods, his mouth turning down at the corners. "Oh, yes, of course."

"So is it? Okay, I mean?"

He turns Lincoln to face me. "Yep. Totally okay. No mess this time. He didn't even try to pee on me."

"Great. Perfect. Way to go, Lincoln. You'll be wiping your own ass before you know it." I groan, burying my face in hands. I'm babbling again. What is it about this man that turns me into a bumbling idiot? No, scratch that. I'm a mom. I'm allowed to celebrate my son waking up not covered in poop. That's something worth celebrating. Telling a five-month-old he'll soon be wiping his own ass might be taking it too far, though.

"First step, wake up clean, next step, wipe your own butt. You'll be there in no time." He gives Lincoln a little fist bump. "You're nailing this growing up thing, kid."

I force a snicker and change the subject. "Uh, so we're playing *Uno* in the kitchen when you're ready."

He narrows his eyes at me. "Perfect. I'm fantastic at *Uno*."

I laugh again, not needing to force it this time. His confidence strikes me as funny. "Well, bring it on then, champ. Let's see what you're made of."

His eyes darken, his eyes raking over me. "I can't wait to show you what I'm made of, sweetheart," he rumbles, the heat in his voice turning me liquid. Arousal blasts through me unexpectedly.

Well, that took a turn, didn't it?

Chapter 32

He's Available?

Archer

"THANK YOU SO MUCH for dinner, Sheila. Everything was amazing." I sent Phoebe to the living room to relax while I clean up after dinner so she can visit with her family. After that moment in Lincoln's room, the one when she looked at me like she wanted me for dinner, she's been a little off. When Eric came back for dinner, she seemed surprised to see him, but I swear she told me to invite him. It shouldn't have been a shock to see him here. Besides, he fits in perfectly with everyone. One benefit of being an overgrown kid, I guess. People love it until you're their responsibility.

"You're so welcome, Archer, but I only handled the turkey. Phoebe took care of everything else. I have to say, though, I am a little disappointed you had your shirt on during this visit. I'll have to remember to spill something on you next time."

"Whoa, whoa, whoa. What's this? You've seen him shirtless?" Charlie joins us in the kitchen while I help Phoebe's mom clear up the plates after dinner. "How about you strip down now? Give me something to look at while I'm making dessert."

"Oh, that reminds me." I dry my hands on a towel and turn to the fridge. "I got you a small gift," I call back over my shoulder as I reach in to grab the tray with the pies I brought. "My assistant and I found this amazing bakery that was doing a package of pies and handcrafted pie plates, and I thought of you as soon as I saw them." I put the tray down on the counter and pass the information card to Charlie. "I got four different varieties: apple, pumpkin, peach, and, for something a little different, chocolate bourbon pecan."

Charlie's eyes narrow as she looks between the card and the pies and I worry I made the wrong decision. Maybe she wanted to use her own recipes and try to burn down the kitchen again. She has to realize she still could burn the kitchen down, right? Starting with prepared pies won't make a difference. After a moment, she puts the card down and goes to the oven, turning it on.

"I can't wait to taste that chocolate bourbon pecan," she says. "Thank you."

I blink several times. That was almost too easy. I wasn't expecting her to give in without a little more convincing. But it's not like I'm going to argue. I can't afford to be on Charlie's bad side. Not if I want to take this thing with Phoebe further.

And the more time I spend with her, the more I realize I really, *really* want to take this further.

"You're welcome." I step around Phoebe's mom and run the hot water into the sink. "Now, why don't you let me finish up with the dishes? You go sit in the living room with everyone else while I wash up."

She cocks an eyebrow in question, and I nod. "Well, you'll forgive me for not trying to talk you out of it." She squeezes my shoulder, smiles, and opens her mouth, but instead of saying something, she closes her mouth, shakes her head, then turns and leaves the room.

Weird.

Charlie and I work around each other in silence, with me washing dishes, and her setting up cooling racks and getting the pies ready to go into the oven. Finally, the oven dings that it's preheated to the right temperature, and she puts the pies in before going to join everyone else in the living room.

I continue washing dishes alone for a few minutes before Phoebe joins me in the kitchen.

"How are you doing in here? Can I help clean up?" She asks with a glance at the nearly empty sink.

"Nope. I've got it covered, thanks. I wouldn't say no to some company, though."

She leans back against the counter, crosses her arms over her chest, squinting at me and taking my measure. It takes everything in me to keep my gaze on her face instead of the swells of her breasts over her arms. Even without looking, my dick stirs in my pants.

"So, uh..." she twirls a strand of bright copper hair between her fingers. "Sex toys. That sounds...interesting."

I snort a laugh. "It's alright." Hearing the words *sex toys* coming from her gorgeous lips sends a surge of lust to my dick, taking it from slight stirrings of interest to a more insistent hardening. *Pay attention, idiot. She's willing to talk about your work now. Don't waste this opportunity.*

"How'd you get into that?"

I scrub at a tough spot on the roasting pan while I think. Should I tell her? Does it matter? Will she care I was given my job rather than earning it? I don't want to lie to her though, so I throw caution to the wind and tell her. What's the worst that can happen? She thinks I'm basically a nepo baby and that I don't deserve my position? She wouldn't be the first to think that.

"Family business," I say. "My father gifted it to me when he retired early, a little over a year ago."

A look of surprise takes over her face. "He gave it to you? That's generous." There's no judgement in her tone, only surprise, much to my relief. She wouldn't have been the first to think I didn't deserve my position, but it would have bothered me more if she had.

I scoff. "Not that generous. He still takes a salary, but I do all the work."

She laughs. "Okay, that's a little less generous."

I nod and finish scrubbing the pan before rinsing and placing it in the dish drying rack. "I've enjoyed it. He was a terrible boss, so I've spent the last year fixing all the mistakes he made. The best part is seeing how happy all the staff are."

"Oh, yeah? People like working there?"

"They do now," I say with a smile.

Transforming Fade Toys from just another factory job to one of the best places to work in Westborough is something I'm damn proud of. It's more than I ever hoped I'd be able to do when I thought I'd be working *for* my dad for the rest of my life. That's part of the reason I'm so worried about my dad being in my office the other day. I still haven't figured out what he thinks he's doing threatening to take the company back. I suppose I'll need to figure that out soon.

"You're not at all like I expected you'd be after that first message." Phoebe shakes her head. "You're alright, Archer."

I shake my head. "I don't think I'll ever be able to apologize enough for that."

"It's fine," she says with a shrug. "I'm over it. You turned out to be pretty great, anyway."

My body immediately reacts to her declaration, the blood rushing south as one thought goes through my brain: kiss her. I take a calming breath, pull the plug from the sink and watch the water swirl down the drain before rinsing the washcloth, squeezing the water out of it and placing it over the faucet to dry. I dry my hands on another towel and turn to face Phoebe.

Her face takes on a red tinge, and she looks down at the floor instead of at me. Like she's embarrassed she told me I'm great. But I'm not. I'm glad she said it. I take a step closer, take her chin in my fingers, and tilt her face toward me. She tucks the strand of hair she was playing with behind her ear and licks her lips. *Fuck.* I *need* to kiss her. Now. I don't know how I've been able to hold off this long, to tell the truth. Phoebe is temptation incarnate.

I cup her cheek in one hand, slide the other to her waist, lean in...

Only to hear Phoebe's sharp intake of breath as she pushes me away when the oven timer goes off a moment before my lips meet hers.

Damn it. I step back and look away, taking a moment to calm myself. I can't believe I almost kissed her. The heat from her lips warmed mine, I was that close.

"Phoebe, I'm sorr—"

Charlie comes jogging into the kitchen, interrupting my apology, and grabs the oven mitts from the counter. She peeks in the oven door before turning the timer off. "Huh. Would you look at that? The smoke detector didn't even go off once. I wonder if that's because I followed the directions?"

I choke on a laugh, thankful for the distraction. Is that why she sets off the smoke alarm all the time? Because she doesn't follow the instructions? That would make sense.

She takes the pies out one at a time and places them on cooling racks to rest before going back to the living room.

"I'm sorry, Archer," Phoebe says, cutting off the apology that was on the tip of my tongue.

She's sorry? What?

"I got caught up in the moment. Trying to kiss you was inappropriate. I won't let it happen again."

I swivel my head. Are we in the same room? She tried to kiss me? No, no. I don't think that's what happened. And even if it did, I wanted to kiss. I *still* want to.

"No, I'm sorry, Phoebe. I know that's not what you're looking for."

She blinks at me several times in a row. "What are you talking about?"

I huff out a breath. "I shouldn't be complicating your life this way. You've had a hard enough year with the pregnancy and having Lincoln on your own. The last thing you need from me is unwanted advances."

She throws her arms up. "Well, yeah," she says, her exasperation clear. "Of course I don't want that. I don't want your advances at all."

Ouch.

"Yeah, I get it. I'm sorry. I'm the one who got carried away. It's like the second I get close to you, I want to wrap you up in my arms and kiss you silly. You're damn near irresistible, Phoebe."

"Well...fuck. Try harder to resist. I'm not that kind of woman."

I rear back like she slapped me. Not that kind of woman? *What* kind of woman? The kind of woman who felt a connection with a strange man the night she was supposed to be married? The kind of woman who could be attracted to the father of her baby? The kind of woman who could see herself with a man who's doing everything he can to be a proper dad to the kid he recently found out about? Because she is that kind of woman. I know she is. I feel it.

So what's holding her back? What is keeping her from taking that one extra step and seeing where this could go?

What am I missing?

"Despite what happened that first night, I don't normally sleep with someone I just met, especially when I don't know their situation."

I nod, even though I'm more confused than ever. What is she talking about?

"Phoebe, I'm not sure what you're getting at, but I assure you, I only think good things about you."

She splutters. "Obviously."

I screw my eyebrows down. I'm getting more mixed up the longer she talks. "Phoebe. I don't understand."

"I will not be the other woman, Archer. I deserve better than that."

I can't stop the laugh that escapes me, which garners me a dirty look from Phoebe. Oh, shit. She's serious?

"Is this why you didn't bring your girlfriend today?" she asks. "You wanted to see if you could get into my pants? I have news for you, buddy. I. Don't. Sleep. With. Unavailable. Men."

I open my mouth, but no words come out.

Speechless.

This is what it's like to be completely, unequivocally speechless.

"Nothing to say to that, huh? Unbelievable." She throws a hand up.

I shake my head to gather my wits. Phoebe has me more off balance than I've ever experienced. It's like we're having two separate conversations. "Phoebe. No one thinks you're the other woman." There'd have to be a first woman for there to be an other woman.

"Ha." She spits a laugh. "I bet your girlfriend would beg to differ."

My what?

"My girlfriend?"

She does that excessive blinking thing again. "Yes. Your gorgeous supermodel, ballerina, blonde bombshell girlfriend. She was with you at the Christmas party when I gave you the letter, remember? Or did you get so drunk afterward that you forgot?"

I choke on the sensation of my dinner making its way back up my throat. "Her? Why would you think she's my girlfriend?"

Phoebe widens her eyes at me. "Uh, because she called you babe and almost set me on fire with her death glare when she caught me talking to you? What do you think?"

I step closer, desire growing deep in my belly. "I think you're mistaken."

She scoffs and rolls her eyes. "Mistaken? Yeah, okay."

"I don't have a girlfriend, Phoebe." I reach out and grab her waist with one hand before cupping her cheek with the other. "You weren't the other woman that first night, and you're not the other woman now."

She takes a shuddering breath and looks up at me through her lashes. "I'm not?"

I shake my head and lean in close, running my nose up the column of her neck, inhaling her sweet scent, barely holding back a groan. "No. You're not. And since we've got that settled, I trust you have no objections to my kissing you now?"

She inclines her head slightly, which is all the permission I need. I take her mouth, thrusting my tongue inside, and inhale the soft moan she releases. When her fingers creep around my waist and she pulls me close, I exhale a relieved breath, and she melts against me. I had no idea how *badly* I wanted this until this very moment.

How have you gone an entire year without kissing this woman?

I wrap her in my arms, turn our bodies and lean her against the wall, pressing myself as close as is humanly possible while she pants hotly against my mouth. My dick is straining against my zipper and I can't stop my groan when Phoebe's hands slide to my ass and she grinds herself against me.

Oh, fuck.

Her legs wrap around my waist, and I'm pinning her against the wall before I realize I'm doing it. Phoebe's hands are gripping my hair and it hurts so fucking good I thrust into the cradle of her legs, her heat reaching me clear through the thickness of both of our pants.

This. This is what's been missing from my life.

"More," she whispers. "More, Archer."

I slide my hands to her ass and squeeze, grinding my dick into her heat, and I kiss across her cheek and down her neck, sucking her sweet skin into my mouth, grazing her with my teeth before laving the mark with my tongue. Phoebe's resultant panting breath in my ear is the sweetest sound I've ever heard.

"Are you guys almost done? Everyone wants pie." Phoebe scrambles out of my grip when Charlie's voice cuts through the fog of lust, her face adorably red.

With my back to Charlie, I adjust myself in pants and Phoebe's eyes darken, her breath catching in her throat. I bend low and whisper in her ear. "We'll talk more about that later."

"It's about time, Santa. I've been waiting patiently for ten minutes while you tied to suck my sister's soul out through her mouth. Help me serve this pie, Phoebe."

I smirk and walk from the kitchen straight to the bathroom to get myself under control. Phoebe's kisses are even hotter than I remember, and my dick is going to need more than a few minutes to calm down.

And I'm going to need a little time to figure out why on earth Phoebe would believe that Annabelle was my girlfriend. Because that ship sailed long ago.

Chapter 33

Oh. My. Santa.

Phoebe

"What the hell was that?" Charlie hisses as soon as Archer is out of earshot. "I thought he had a girlfriend?"

I can't stop the grin from taking over my face. "Turns out he doesn't," I say, my voice teetering on the edge of hysteria. "I was yelling at him about how I refuse to be the other woman when he told me there wasn't anyone else. Then all of a sudden, he was kissing me."

And boy, did he ever kiss me. I think I destroyed yet another pair of panties if the wetness between my legs is any sign. As soon as I can sneak away, I'm changing them. And taking a minute to calm the tingling in my belly before I float away from sheer giddiness.

Charlie snickers. "From where I was standing, it looked like a little more than just kissing," she says while putting slices of pie onto plates. "He was grinding you into the wall. I know it's been a while for you, but you must recall simple kissing rarely requires that much contact in the downstairs region?"

Remembering the way Archer pressed himself against me sends another flood of heat to my core, and if I didn't need to get these panties off before, I absolutely do now. How hot was it when he scooped me up like that? I wouldn't mind a lot more downstairs contact after that.

"Shut up." I grab a tray from the cabinet and start loading it with the plates of pie. "We're not talking about that."

She snickers. "Oh? We'll see about that."

"Charlie. Please. Not now. I've had enough embarrassment for one day, don't you think?"

The belly laugh that erupts from her sounds like it should have come from an enormous man instead of a tiny woman. The snort she makes in the silence following several deep-breathed guffaws sends me into my own fit of giggles.

"How could you not know?" she finally chokes out. "We've been to the adult store together. You know damn well what butt plugs look like."

I wipe tears from underneath my eyes, forcing my giggles into submission. "I don't know," I huff. "When I look at them now, it's all I can see. It's like one of those optical illusions where once you figure it out, you can't *not* see it. My brain refuses to see the innocent Christmas trees it once did."

Charlie snickers. "Yeah. I don't suppose you'll be using them as decorations next Christmas."

I frown. After all the fuss today, I probably *shouldn't* use them to decorate again, but what a shame that would be. They're just so darn pretty. I almost wish Webster had kept his mouth shut about them. Ignorance is supposed to be bliss, right? I would have been fine decorating with them every year if I'd never realized their true, naughtier, purpose.

But then I'd have gone on thinking Archer was some sort of real-life Santa Claus, with his own toy factory and everything. An image of him climbing down the chimney with a sack full of Christmas tree butt plugs, candy cane vibrators, and twinkle light nipple clamps flashes through my mind unbidden, and a hysterical giggle escapes my lips. I drop my head into my hands, my shoulders shaking with uncontrolled laughter. How is this my life?

"Okay, okay, okay." Charlie pats the air with her palms down in a stopping motion. "Everybody calm down. I have an important question."

From the way she's biting her lips between her teeth, it's clear that she's fighting off another laugh. Whatever she's asking is going to set her off again, I can tell.

"Do you think this revelation makes it more or less likely that he has a curved candy cane penis?" She splutters a laugh on the word penis and doubles over, holding her stomach. "Oh my god, it hurts." She sucks in a stuttering breath. "I can't...I can't...haaaa... I can't breathe."

I snicker. I know for a fact his penis isn't striped or curved, at least not as curved as a candy cane, but Charlie's laugh is infectious and I can't help but laugh right alongside her.

"He's a sex toy Santa," Charlie squeals, sending us both reeling into peals of laughter again.

We're still laughing when Gavin walks in several minutes later. "Hey, we're wasting away out here. I thought you were bringing the pie to the living room. Should we all come in here?"

Charlie shakes her head while wiping tears from her cheeks. "No. No. I got it. Take that tray and pass out the plates." She points to the tray we've already loaded with pieces of pie. "I'll cut a few more pieces and bring them out in a minute. Make sure sex toy Santa gets a piece."

Gavin screws his eyebrows down and shakes his head at us. "You guys are nuts," he says when we both start giggling again. "Don't forget to bring more pie. It's my cheat day and you can bet your ass I'm having a piece of each."

Gavin takes the tray and leaves the room.

I force myself to stop laughing and turn to Charlie. "What am I going to do, Charlie?"

She shrugs, pushing a slice of pie off the lifter and onto a plate. "What do you want to do? I say you jump his bones and ride him right into next year."

I snort a laugh. "I don't think that's a very sensible idea. That's asking for some really uncomfortable chafing."

She tilts her head. "Yeah, you're probably right. How about you ride him until, say, tomorrow? Minimal chafing, maximum enjoyment."

"What if it isn't worth it, though? What if it messes up the relationship we're creating as co-parents of Lincoln?"

Charlie picks up two plates and gestures for me to take the others. "Well, then you'll be like any set of divorced parents who dislike each other but are civil for the sake of the kids. But do you really want to throw in the towel before you give it a chance? You might be giving up on something amazing before it even starts." She walks out of the kitchen without waiting for an answer.

Is she right? Should I throw caution to the wind and give it a shot? Is there even something to give a shot to? All we've established so far is a mutual attraction. He hasn't come out and said he wants a relationship. I need to stop getting ahead of myself.

With a sigh, I pick up the plates and follow Charlie to the living room. That's a mystery for another day.

"Alright, I've got a peach and an apple," I say when I walk in.

"I'll take some of your peach." Archer raises a hand and I snort a laugh. He drops his hand, realizing what he's said, and cringes. "I mean, I'll take the peach pie."

Charlie barks a laugh. "Yeah, right. That's not what it looked like in the kitchen a few minutes ago."

My mom widens her eyes in question, but before Charlie can open her mouth, I jump in. "Everyone, shut up. Now's your chance to let your pie hole do what it does best and eat the damn pie. It's getting close to Lincoln's bedtime so I'm implementing quiet time. If you can't keep quiet, you can leave now."

Later, when the pies are all put away, Lincoln is asleep, and a few more games of *UNO* have been played, I realize my ungrateful guests didn't keep their mouths shut after all. Somehow, they all conspired to leave early without my noticing.

Eric leaves first. Webster and Frederick follow shortly after, with promises to talk soon. Mom and Warren are next to leave, which isn't a surprise. They're staying at a hotel while they visit because they like to watch TV at full volume while they fall asleep. It *is* a surprise, though, when Charlie and Gavin leave, considering Charlie lives here and Gavin always stays here when he visits. He didn't even care when I moved Lincoln into the third bedroom, because of his unnatural love for the big blue couch in my living room. He loves sleeping on it.

But that doesn't stop him from leaving with Charlie at the end of the evening. My mouth drops when he shoots me a wink after telling me they're letting me get back to *whatever* we were doing in the kitchen.

Somewhere between too many pieces of delicious pie and several games of *UNO* so vicious they nearly came to blows, the rest of my family conspired to leave me alone with Archer. I can't decide whether I love them or hate them for that.

"About that '*whatever*' Gavin mentioned," Archer says, slipping in behind me when Gavin closes the front door. He turns me by the shoulders until I'm facing him. "Are you okay?"

Am I okay? Heat floods my belly as I remember the way he pushed himself against me. *Heck yeah, I'm okay.*

I answer by pressing my lips to his, smiling at his quick intake of breath before he wraps his arms around me and pulls me close.

"Thank god," he whispers against my mouth. "I was worried you'd changed your mind."

I shake my head while chasing his kiss, not wanting to stop long enough to say the words. My hands find their way under his shirt without my express permission, but when I touch the smooth expanse of skin covering his hard abs, I'm forced to forgive them. *God, it's good to finally touch him.*

I whimper when his hands squeeze my ass, and he presses his hard length against my stomach. The answering throb of my clit is achingly familiar, and it prompts me to slide my hands down to his belt. I'm so feverish with the desire to get into his pants that I'm confused when Archer wraps his hands around my wrists and stops me from lowering his zipper.

"Phoebe?" Archer says, his harsh breaths and strained voice telling me he's just as turned on as I am. "I'm trying really hard to be good right now." A disbelieving chuckle escapes his throat. "But if you keep doing that, I'm not sure I'll be able to stop myself from stripping you naked and burying myself as deeply inside you as I've been dreaming of doing since the night we first met."

Yes! That. Do that! I want to yell. My voice won't come out, though, so instead of words, I let my hands do the talking. I stare into his eyes, lower his zipper, reach into his boxers, and grasp his shaft in my fist.

He hesitates a moment before slamming his mouth to mine, his tongue tasting me as he groans from my touch.

Our kisses are sloppy as we back away from the door, navigating through the living room, down the hall, and into my bedroom.

"Jesus, Phoebe. You're killing me." Archer closes the door and pushes me against it, thrusting his hard length into my fist. "Don't blame me when I come all over your hand like an eager teenager."

I snort a surprised chuckle. "Noted."

Archer buries his face in my neck, licking and sucking the sensitive spot behind my ear, making my knees weak. "Not fair," I gasp. "You said you hardly remembered anything from that night."

He smiles against my throat. "Oh, I remember a few things. Like how much you loved having this spot of your neck kissed."

He thrusts into my hand again, pushing me against the door. "I also recall a little something about this spot right here." He slides a hand down and cups one breast, his thumb brushing the nipple through my shirt and bra.

My head drops back and hits the door behind me.

"And I know another spot you like even better." He thrusts into my hand once more before pulling back, forcing me to release him. "But I think you're going to need a few less clothes if we're going to find that spot." He traces my collarbone with a finger, and a shiver races through me. "Can I undress you, Phoebe?"

I nod three, four, fives times. *Geez, Phoebe. Calm down. That's way too much nodding.* "Yes. Undress me. Excellent idea."

He chuckles and slides his hands under the hem of my shirt, making quick work of dragging it over my head, throwing it onto the floor behind him before moving on to my pants. When I'm left standing in only my bra and underwear, he devours me with his gaze, top to bottom, before settling on my face.

"Fuck, Phoebe. You're more beautiful than I remember."

I can't help the disbelieving snort that escapes me. "I'm kind of glad you were drunk that night. If you remembered how I really looked then, there's no way you'd be saying I look beautiful now, not with all these stretch marks. Never mind the extra weight that won't budge."

He frowns and takes my face in his hands. "Listen to me, Phoebe. You are fucking beautiful. I don't give a shit about stretch marks or any extra weight. I look at you and there isn't a part of your body that I don't want to kiss. That I don't want to lick. That I don't want to fuck." He takes my lips in a punishing kiss. "And I won't hear any different from you."

"But..."

"Nope. Not having it. You're fucking gorgeous and I'm dying to touch you." He punctuates his statement by sliding his hands down to my waist and grinding against me. "Can you feel that? I'm so fucking turned on by you I'm about to come in my pants like a pubescent teen seeing his first pair of boobs."

I choke out a surprised chuckle. "You can't even see my boobs. I'm still wearing a bra." *Brilliant, Phoebe. You're awesome at this dirty talk thing.*

Archer lets out a low groan. "Well, then. We should fix that." He trails a hand up my back, sparks igniting everywhere his fingers touch, and flicks open the clasp on my bra. With a finger hooked between the cups, Archer drags the bra down my arms and drops it to the floor. "There. That's better."

He palms my breasts, the rightness of it making me weak. Heaviness builds in my belly and wetness floods my underwear. A pinch to my nipples sends a shock straight to my clit and I'm transported to that hotel room a year ago, where a sexy Santa Claus was the one taking me to bed.

Oh. My. Santa.

Chapter 34

Freaking Finally and Freaking Out

Archer

I'M THANKFUL FOR THE anger that swells in me at Phoebe thinking she's not the most fucking beautiful woman in the world all because of a few silly stretch marks. I know, I know. That's stupid. But if it weren't for being mad, I'd have come in my jeans as soon as I got her out of her clothes and got a look at her matching black bra and panties.

There's nothing particularly fancy about them. The fabric looks to be plain cotton, and the panties are perilously close to being granny panties. But the swells of her breasts over the cups of the bra leave me breathless. And the way the panties hug her hips and skim along the narrowing of her waist is sexier than any thong I've ever seen. *Ugh.*

Yeah. I'm pissed that she doesn't know how gorgeous she is.

I grab her by the hips and grind my erection into her belly, loving the gasp that slips from her lips. "Can you feel that? I'm so fucking turned on by you I'm about to come in my pants like a teenage boy seeing his first pair of boobs."

She chuckles. "You can't see my boobs. I'm still wearing a bra."

"Well, we can't have that." I drag my fingers up her back, making her shiver beneath my touch, and open the clasp on her bra. I hook a finger at the fabric between her breasts, where the cups of her bra meet, and pull down, exposing her to me. "There. That's better."

I swallow roughly as I drag my gaze over her breasts. Her dusky pink nipples stiffen under my scrutiny, her chest flushing beneath my gaze. She looks like my every fantasy come to life. And she is, since I've just now realized every fantasy I've had over the last year has been about her. I may not have remembered exactly what she looked like, and she may look a little different now, but there's no denying that every dream I had was about her.

My hands trace the line of her waist, skimming up her ribcage before testing the weight of her breasts in my hands. I could do this all fucking day. Her pink nipples beg me to pinch them, so I do.

Her gasp makes my dick swell impossibly, painfully, harder.

"God, Phoebe. You're fucking perfect." My voice is gravelly and I'm tenuously holding on to my control. I barely have my hands on her soft skin and I'm about to lose it.

She reaches for me. "I get to touch you, too, right?" Before I can react she has her hands up my shirt attempting to peel it over my head. I bend over to make it easier to drag it off of me. "Might need a stepladder for that next time," she says with a chuckle after she drops my shirt on the floor.

I dive in for a kiss, taking her plump lips in mine, her answering moan flooding me with need. She shoves her hands into my pants and takes my dick in her hand, squeezing me with the perfect amount of tightness.

"Fuck, Phoebe. That's too good." She gives me a solid stroke and my knees weaken. I brace myself on the door frame above her head, all thought of touching her driven out of my mind by the maddeningly erotic sensation of her hand stroking my shaft.

My body focuses all its attention on the softness of her hand gripping me and the orgasm building in my balls. Each pump of her fist brings me that much closer to coming all over her stomach.

No. No, no, no. You can't let it happen like this.

"Stop," I say through gritted teeth, thinking unsexy thoughts to push off the impending orgasm. "Phoebe. Stop." I force myself to grab her wrist and reluctantly remove her hand from my dick, dragging a ragged breath into my lungs.

"What? Why?" Phoebe looks up at me, her breath coming short little pants, making her breasts bounce with the effort. "You seemed to be enjoying that."

I let out a humorless laugh. "I was. Too much. But I don't want to come until I'm buried deep inside you."

"Oh." Her eyes turn liquid, the pupils blowing up until all I see is lust, and how much she wants me. "Yes. That. Let's do that."

She ducks under my arm, grabs my dick with a firm grip, and drags me to the bed. It's weird, but so fucking hot.

"Whoa, slow down."

"Can't. Need you inside me." She shoves my pants and boxers to the floor and throws me down on the bed. She stops next to the bed to shove her own panties down before straddling me. "I got an IUD after I had Lincoln," she whispers while hovering over me. "And I haven't been with anyone since you."

She kisses me with a fervent energy, her tongue tangling with mine as she presses her hot centre against me, trapping my dick between our bodies.

Her panting breaths and wild eyes nearly push me over the edge. I stop myself from flipping her onto her back, burying myself balls deep, and driving her into the mattress, but just barely.

"Jesus, Phoebe. Are you sure? I'm clean, I promise."

She licks her lips and nods before pressing herself harder against me, sliding her wet center over the length of my shaft, coating me in her desire. I'm not sure who groans louder, me or her.

Unable to take it any longer, I reach down and notch myself at her opening. When she slides herself down my length, I swear I can feel my eyes roll right to the back of my head. A groan escapes my throat, sounding something like, "Oh, fuck yes. Phoebe...Yes."

Her hand presses into my chest for leverage as she rocks her hips, dragging her clit against me every time she slides to the bottom of my shaft, her needy moan making me throb.

With her wild red hair, flushed skin, and parted lips, she looks like a fucking goddess as she rides me. My balls are tightening already.

No. I'm still not ready.

"Phoebe, stop." I grip her hips and force her to stop rocking. "I'm going to come."

She grins and rocks her hips again, forcing another groan from my throat. "That's kind of the point, Archer." She bends over, pressing her breasts against me as she takes me in a brutal kiss. "If all goes well, I'll be coming too."

I drive up into her, her grip on me driving me closer to the edge. "Jesus, babe. You feel so fucking good." I can't hold back much longer. With a surge of energy, I flip us, covering her body with mine. She looks up at me with eyes wide. "And there's no *if* about it. You're coming. Several times, if I have anything to say about it."

I thrust into her, bottoming out, and her nails scrabble against my back, scratching me as she attempts to pull me closer. I swallow her moans with another kiss.

So damn good.

"Archer," she pants against my lips. "I'm so close."

"I got you, baby." I slide a hand between us and press her clit with my thumb, making small, soft circles, and she whimpers, clenching around my dick. "Oh fuck. You like that, don't you?"

She nods, dragging me down for another kiss before burying her face in my neck. Her teeth clamp down as she spasms around me, muffling her cries into my throat. "Oh, god. Archer. Yes. Like that." Phoebe releases her grip on my neck, still panting. She continues to clench around me, the sensation drawing out my orgasm. My dick throbs in response and I pump into her, loving the sensation of sliding through her slick heat.

I follow her over the edge, driving deep until I release into her, gritting my teeth against the yell attempting to claw its way out. "Oh my god, Phoebe. How do you feel this good?"

She grinds against me, moaning her agreement. "How do *you* feel so good? Ugh." She rolls her hips. "Yes. Fuck." Her head drops back against the pillow. "That was amazing."

I thrust lazily, enjoying the pulsing of her aftershocks squeezing my dick. "It really was, wasn't it?" I pump my hips one more time before slipping out of her and rolling to the side, pulling her with me until her head rests on my chest. "And this time, I didn't have to spend twenty minutes getting you out of a wedding dress first. Although, I remember even that being kind of fun. Like unwrapping the best gift on Christmas morning."

She laughs and waggles her eyebrows at me. "Well, it is after midnight now, you know."

I nod sagely. "Yes. And here my present is, already unwrapped." I tickle her ribs. "That must mean I get to enjoy it sooner."

She shoves my hand away with a laugh. "Was I somewhere else just now? Because I'm pretty sure you enjoyed all this"—she gestured down the length of her body—"mere moments ago."

"Mmmm," I hum, pulling her closer. "Give me a few minutes and I'll be ready to enjoy you all over again."

She places a soft kiss on my chest, then pushes herself away and gets to her feet, her stomach growling. "While you recover, I'm going to check if there's some of that pie left. I'm starving."

Her ass disappears under the hem of my shirt, and she turns to give me a shy smile before leaving the bedroom. I settle back into the pillows with my arm under my head, smug satisfaction making itself at home in my grin. This feels so natural. I can't remember the last time I felt this comfortable with a woman.

That's a lie. You remember. It was with Phoebe. Last Christmas.

That only makes sense, since I haven't been with anyone since then. Even before that, though, it had been a while. Annabelle had never been one for goofing around after sex, or any time for that matter. Not that we'd been together much in the months leading up the ill-fated proposal attempt. She'd been too busy traveling for work, and I'd been too busy turning Fade Toys into the kind of place anyone would be thrilled to work. We were never compatible.

I can't believe Phoebe saw Annabelle that first night and thought she was my girlfriend.

I haven't been able to keep Phoebe out of my head for more than a second or two since I saw her crazy red hair and messy, oversized sweatshirt that night. I could hardly be bothered to even acknowledge Annabelle's presence when she arrived. How Phoebe could have seen me with her and thought we were anything more than acquaintances is beyond me.

But that's nothing to worry about now. Not after what Phoebe and I just did. And what we'll do again very soon, if I have anything to say about it.

Phoebe walks back into the room, two small plates balanced in her hands. "I brought you a piece," she says. "Thought you might need a snack." She passes me the plate and sits next to me on the bed.

"Thanks," I say, grabbing the plate and picking up the fork. *I could use a snack, alright,* I think to myself. *But this isn't the pie I'm actually hungry for.* Still, I take a bite of the peach pie and sigh escapes my mouth. God, that's good.

"I know, right? It's so good." Phoebe shoves a bite into her mouth. "Good call bringing the pies for Charlie to cook. This is the first time she hasn't set off the smoke detector while baking a dessert." She laughs. "I had no idea she never properly followed the directions before. No wonder she set everything on fire."

I chuckle, scraping the last of the pie into my mouth. "I hear following the directions is crucial in baking. That, and following the measurements. It's pretty much chemistry, but with tastier results."

She nods, licking the last of the pie filling from her fork. The sight of her tongue poking out does something to me, and all the blood in my body starts rushing to my dick.

I look down at my lap. "Well, would you look at that? Looks like that snack was exactly what I needed." I grab her plate and place it with mine on the nightstand. "Now, what should we do with the rest of our night?"

She looks at me through her lashes. "I might have a few ideas." She inches down the bed as she slides a hand down my chest. She teases the edge of the sheet where it covers me, and my dick bobs in anticipation.

I think I like where this is going.

"Waaaahhhh!"

There's a shrill cry from the baby monitor, immediately followed by several loud coughs.

Phoebe's eyes widen. "What the hell?"

Several more loud coughs have Phoebe jumping from the bed and running to Lincoln. I follow, my chest tight, stopping only to pull on my boxers before running from the room.

Phoebe is in Lincoln's room, already cuddling him to her chest. "Shhh, shh, shh. It's okay, Linky. Shh." Her voice has a hint of panic when she says, "I don't like this. He sounds weird. What should we do?"

She's right. He does sound weird. My heart-rate ratchets up a few notches. His coughs seem louder than what should come from a baby. I don't like it. And if Phoebe is asking *me* what we should do, then something is really wrong.

"Change him. I'll pack a bag. I'm sure it's nothing." I push down my worry and keep my voice light despite my heart trying to pound its way out of my chest. "But let's get him checked out just to be sure."

I grab Lincoln's diaper bag from near the door and begin throwing in everything I think we'll need for a night away. I wasn't lying when I said I thought everything was fine, but I wasn't exactly telling the truth either.

Truthfully, I don't know what's wrong. But I do know the doctors at Westborough General Hospital are better equipped to help Lincoln than we are if it turns out to be serious, so that's where we're going.

I only hope I can calm my racing heart before we get there, or I might need a doctor to examine me, too..

Chapter 35

Falling For My Baby's Father

Phoebe

Gavin looks Archer up and down, a smirk on his face.

"Stop looking at him. I already explained."

"Okay, but did you *really*?" Gavin asks, a laugh teasing the edges of his voice. "Because I still don't understand why you both walked in here wearing ill-fitting hospital scrubs. Archer has disposable flip-flops on, for crying out loud."

When we rushed out of the house earlier tonight, neither of us thought to get dressed. We grabbed Lincoln and the diaper bag and ran out of my house like our butts were on fire with Archer wearing only his boxers and me wearing only a t-shirt and my winter boots. After checking in to triage at the emergency department, a nurse took pity on us. She called down to the hospital's laundry and had one of the staff dig up some scrubs for us to wear. A drag queen waiting to see a doctor for a wig-related injury felt sorry for Archer, who was standing there with bare feet, and gave him the disposable flip-flops she kept in her purse for impromptu pedicures. After getting a better look at his unpolished toes, she also insisted he promise to visit her nail lady for a proper pedicure.

I'm sure we're both still quite the sight.

While we waited to see a doctor, Archer called Gavin, Charlie, and my parents to update them on the situation. When we got back home six hours later, with a diagnosis of a simple cold and instructions for helping Lincoln get better, my entire family was waiting in the living for us.

"We were in a hurry."

"I can see that," Gavin says. "That must be why you're wearing Archer's shirt, huh?"

"Shut up."

He shows me his palm. "Alright. I'll shut up. For now."

Presently, Lincoln is sleeping in a playpen in the living room instead of the crib in his bedroom. Archer set it up the playpen the minute we walked in the door, somehow sensing I didn't want my baby to sleep in a separate room after the ordeal we went through. Truthfully, he seems as shaken by the trip to the emergency room as I am. As embarrassing as it was taking Lincoln to the emergency room for what turned out to be a cold, I'm so glad it wasn't something more serious.

Sitting in the waiting room rocking Lincoln in my arms, I could barely drag in a full breath before we saw the doctor. My heartbeat is only now resuming a normal pace instead of the frantic, off-beat staccato rhythm from earlier. The adrenaline is gradually leaving my body, and I release a long, shuddering breath.

My mom comes to my side and pulls me into a hug. "Oh, honey. That must have been so scary. I remember the first time I heard you cough seriously. I threw you in the car half-dressed and broke every traffic law on the way to the emergency room. When we got to the hospital, the nurses had to give us a blanket from the warmer because your little legs were freezing."

I choke on a combination of sob and laugh. "So you're saying this isn't the first time I've gone to the hospital sans pants?"

Gavin barks a laugh that makes Lincoln jump. He cringes and puts a finger in front of his mouth, shushing the rest of us as though he's not the one being loud.

"Phew," he says when Lincoln settles back to sleep on his own, wiping his brow. "That was close."

I shoot Gavin a dirty look. "You better not wake him up. He's had a long night." The nap schedule is out the window for today. That goes without saying. "He needs to sleep."

"He's not the only one who needs to sleep," Archer chimes in. "I'll make some coffee for anyone who wants to hang out, but Phoebe is going to sleep. And I'm sure she wants to stay next to Lincoln right now, so she'll be taking the couch. The rest of you can come have coffee with me in the kitchen, silently, or come back in a few hours when Phoebe and Lincoln have rested. It's up to you."

Charlie smirks and gets out of her seat. "I think we'll all take the opportunity to nap, too."

"Definitely," Warren agrees. "It's been at least thirty years since I've been able to pull an all-nighter, let alone one followed by an all-dayer. This old man needs his beauty sleep." He comes over and kisses my cheek, placing a big hand over mine and giving it a reassuring squeeze. "Everything is going to be fine, Phoebe."

Mom gives me a hug. "We'll be back later. Call me if you need anything."

With relief, I drop face first onto the couch while Archer lets everyone out. My nerves are shot and I'm crashing fast. Thank goodness Archer suggested sleeping, because I desperately need it. I would have forced myself to stay awake to play hostess if everyone had stayed, but it's nice being taken care of for a change.

Some time later, I'm roused from sleep when I feel Archer slipping behind me.

"Shhh. Go to back to sleep," he whispers as he wraps an arm around my waist. "It's been a long night."

A huge yawn escapes me. "Sleep sounds perfect. Just a quick little nap," I mumble while tucking myself more firmly under his arm. "'Night."

"Shhh, shh. Let's let Mommy sleep a little longer. What do you say, bud? Yeah. That's right. Hmm, smells like someone needs a diaper change. Great work not getting it all over, though. You're getting better."

I'm alone on the couch now, tucked under a fuzzy blanket, and I can hear Archer talking to Lincoln. My heart swells hearing their conversation, one-sided though it may seem. Lincoln makes some cooing noises and Archer laughs.

"You bet, kiddo. We'll get you something to eat after we change your stinky butt. Don't you worry. I know exactly what to do."

I can't stop the grin from taking over my face. I love hearing Archer talk to Lincoln. He's so good with him. Not everyone can carry on a conversation with a baby. Not that I blame them, since babies don't hold up their end of the conversation most of the time. That just makes it more special when someone can do it.

And Archer does it so well.

Just like he does other things so well. I stretch my arms over my head and there's a pull low in my belly. I'm sore from last night. Deliciously sore.

I can't believe I was so...*forward.* I practically forced myself on him. Butterflies run riot in my stomach and a throb of awareness hits my center as I remember dragging him to the bed and climbing on him. I press my legs together against the frisson of desire building between my legs.

Go to sleep, Phoebe. You can revisit that later.

I screw my eyes shut and try to calm down. The yawn that tears through me confirms my need for more sleep. But the knock on the door signals the end of my nap time.

I shoot up off the couch, yelling out to Archer, "I got it."

The light in the house tells me it's late afternoon now. Somehow, I slept the entire morning away.

No, not somehow. Archer must've let me sleep. He woke up and took care of Lincoln while I was dead to the world? He took it upon himself to let me get the sleep I so desperately needed?

I didn't think I could like him any more, but I was mistaken. And thanks to Archer stepping up, I know I can't blame whatever is happening with my emotions on sleep deprivation anymore.

"Hey Mom," I say when I get the door open and see her and Warren on the front step. "Come on in." I turn around and let them follow me in. "I just woke up. I'll go into the kitchen and see what I can get started for something to eat."

When I turn into the kitchen, my mouth drops open. Every surface is covered with trays of food. Every. Surface.

"What is all this?"

"Oh, hey guys. Welcome back." Archer is standing by the sink holding Lincoln while he gets a bottle ready. "I called a buddy of mine and had him bring over some stuff from his bar. I hope that's okay?"

"You did all this while I was asleep?"

He shrugs. "I wanted to make sure we'd have stuff to feed everyone when they came back. It's a good thing I checked the fridge because it looks like *someone* raided the leftovers while we were at the hospital with Lincoln last night."

Gavin coughs, hiding a guilty look with his fist. "Oh, man. I wonder who that could have been," he deadpans.

Mom rolls her eyes at him. "I told you not to eat all the leftovers." She reaches over and pinches his arm. "You were supposed to bring food."

"Do you know how many places are open on Christmas day? None. None of the places are open on Christmas day."

Warren screws up his eyebrows and looks at Archer. "Then how did you get food here?"

Archer chuckles. He shakes the bottle he's holding, pops the lid off, then squeezes some of the formula onto his wrist and a flush of heat creeps across my face. *Who knew watching him test the temperature of my son's bottle would be so sexy?*

"Like I said, my buddy Mason owns a bar. He owed me a favor."

"Must be some favor if he's making and delivering food to you on Christmas day." Gavin has already lifted the lid off a tray and he's examining the selection of sandwiches. "These look amazing."

"I'll tell him you said so. Everyone dig in. Lincoln's sucking this down like he hasn't eaten in days."

As I watch my family circulate the kitchen with Archer in the middle of everything, I can't help feeling the rightness of it all. He fits in. He's feeding Lincoln while joking with my parents and siblings like he's done it a thousand times.

And I love it.

I love how easily he teases Gavin about eating all the leftovers. I love how he brought pies for Charlie to bake and effortlessly solved her problem of setting the kitchen on fire every time she tried to make a treat. I love how it's already second nature for him to take care of Lincoln while he's doing all these other things.

Shit.

I think I might love *him*.

I look over at Archer and, like he read my mind, he shoots me a smirk, making my heart flip-flop.

Oh yeah. I'm in deep.

Well, I suppose it could be worse. I could be falling in love with someone who wasn't already the father of my child.

Or I could be falling in love with someone who was already involved with another woman.

Thank god that's not the case.

Chapter 36

He's Doing What?

Archer

"I'm no expert, but I'm not sure it's safe to play basketball with a kid strapped to you." Eric steps off the court first, followed by the rest of the guys, and gives Lincoln a little fist bump, eliciting a giggle from the bundle currently strapped to my chest.

It's our usual weekend game, but I've sent Phoebe and Charlie out to the textile arts festival for the day while I spend some quality time with Lincoln. From the sounds of the squeals Phoebe made when I finally gave her the tickets late on Christmas day, this is earning me major bonus points. I'll have to let MaeLynn know that my gift was a hit.

"No, it probably wouldn't be very safe. That's why we'll be hanging on the sidelines today."

"Skipping out on us? Why doesn't the kid play too? We can take it easy on him."

My eyebrows inch into my hairline. "He's five months old, Lucas. He's still working on sitting up unassisted. It's going to be a while before he can play basketball with us."

"No way. You're serious? Well, what do I know? This is the closest I've ever been to a baby." Lucas gives Lincoln an appraising look. "You're lucky you're cute, kid. Or else you'd be in trouble for disrupting our game."

Lincoln giggles and kicks his legs, causing Lucas to break out into a grin. Lucas might not know much about babies, but they seem to like him fine. At least, Lincoln's not holding his ignorance against him.

"We'll sit over here and watch you guys play for a bit. We can't stay too long, though. It's almost his nap time."

"Alright, Linky. Watch and learn, little man. Uncle Damien is going to show you how basketball is supposed to be done. You know, I'm basically the Michael Jordan of this little group." Damien wiggles his eyebrows and makes a face at the baby attached to my front. "They don't call me M.J. for nothing."

Lincoln giggles, and I choke on a laugh. "We call you M.J. because you squeal like Michael Jackson when you get excited about something. *Hee-hee.*" I mimic the prince of Pop's famous falsetto call. "You don't even come close to Michael Jordan's skill level with basketball. You might be comparable to his baseball career, though."

"Fuck yeah. You hear that Link? I'm as good at basketball as Michael Jordan was at baseball. That's pretty damn good."

I cover Lincoln's ears before Damien can finish his little speech. "Dude, don't swear so much around my kid. Phoebe will kill me if his first word is"—I lower my voice to a whisper and cover Lincoln's ears—"fuck."

Eric laughs. "Come on, man. That would be hilarious. Imagine the look on your mother's face when her grandson starts dropping F-bombs in front of all the stuck-up bitches she keeps trying to impress."

"Don't go there. I haven't even told my parents about Lincoln yet. I'm not sure I want them being involved." My parents aren't exactly what one thinks of when the subject of loving grandparents comes to mind. I shudder as I imagine my mother trying to use him to impress her friends somehow. "And besides, one of those stuck-up bitches is your mom, remember? I doubt she'd appreciate it, either."

Eric shrugs. "Meh. She knows she's a bitch. She's been trying to use it for good lately, though. It's been a nice change of pace. Plus, her face would be just as hilarious as your mom's. If I ever have a kid, I'm teaching it to swear right away so I can see it."

"Hey guys, sorry I'm late." Mark, my paternity testing fairy godfather, comes jogging into the gym. "The lab has been crazy today. I had to spend a couple of hours answering phones. It seems like many people were surprised with pregnancies and babies over the holiday." He stops and drops his bag on the bench next to where I'm standing. "Hey man, good to see you. Thanks again for letting me join your game."

Eric clears his throat. "It's not Archer's game. It's all of ours. And we're all happy to have you."

Mark nods and turns back to me. "So, how's fatherhood treating you? Looks like you're a natural." He gestures to Lincoln. "Baby-wearing is an excellent way to encourage a bond."

"It's also an excellent way to prevent him from attempting to jump out of my arms when he sees someone he wants to get to know. This kid has no fear of strangers yet."

The guys laugh.

"That's not necessarily a bad thing. That means he's a happy baby with a secure attachment to his family. It's nice that you get to be involved in that now, too."

"Blah, blah, blah. Are we going to sit around talking about babies, or are we going to play basketball?" Mason yells from center court. "If I'm not back before the lunch rush, Brooke said she's going to drop my nuts in the deep fryer."

"I thought it was your bar?" Eric runs up to join him. "You're going to let your bartender tell you what to do?"

"When she can run circles around me and the rest of the staff? Yeah, I'll let her tell me what to do any day of the week."

"Don't limit yourself to daytime." Eric steals the ball from Mason and dribbles down the hoop. "I've seen the way you look at her. I bet you'd let her tell you what to do any night, too." He takes a shot and sinks the ball into the hoop before turning and waggling his eyebrows.

"Shut up, Eric. You don't know what you're talking about."

Just as the guys begin the game, and their trash-talking, in earnest, my phone rings.

"Ah fuck," I mutter at the sight of my father's name coming up on the screen. I haven't heard from him since the day I found him snooping around my office and I was hoping without really believing that was the end of the matter. I had my lawyer look over all the paperwork from when I took over the company and she could find nothing that would allow my father to take over again unless I specifically invited him to come back. I'm still worried about what he has planned, though. My father is never one to let a little thing like a contract get in the way of his ambitions. He's just an asshole like that.

"Archer Fade here." I answer the phone like I don't know who's calling. It's always best to throw my father off as soon as possible in a conversation. Letting him think I don't have him saved in my phone, or even recognize his number, is enough to irritate him at least a little.

"Archer? Where are you? I'm at the factory and it's all locked up and the parking lot is empty. Is this any way to run a business?"

"Dad? Is that you?"

"Yes, it's me. Who else would it be? Now answer the question. Why is my factory closed today?"

I chuckle, making Lincoln giggle when he bounces. "Don't you mean my factory? At least, I think that's what the paperwork says, anyway."

My father doesn't respond for a moment, and I know he's thinking over what I've said. If I can make him think I don't have my paperwork anymore, he might slip and tell me what his plan is. That snippet of conversation I overheard when he was snooping around my office makes me curious. It's like he thinks he's can force me to marry Annabelle by threatening to take over the company. It's impossible, but I'd like to know what the hell he thinks he can do.

"I think if you have a look at the paperwork again, you'll see that it tells a very different story. I'll have my lawyer send you a copy."

Hmm. That's suspicious. Why would his lawyer need to send a copy when he knows I have my own? Something isn't adding up.

"Sure. I look forward to reading what I already know: the factory is mine, and there's nothing you can do about it."

"Now, now, Archer. There's no need to be like that." I want to punch the smugness out of my father's voice. "You know how to keep everything going as it is. Marry Annabelle and all of this goes away."

"Jesus, Dad." Lincoln cries out in protest at the anger in my voice and the guys all stop their game, turning to face me. "Shit. I have to go. The baby is crying, and it's time for his nap. Email the contract and I'll look it over."

I don't wait for his response before stabbing my finger at the end call button and shoving my phone into my pocket.

"Shh, shh," I whisper as I kiss the top of Lincoln's head, rocking side to side like I've seen Phoebe do when he's upset. "It's okay, buddy. Everything's alright. Daddy's not upset with you. Shh, shh."

Eric walks over and grabs a drink from his bag. "Everything good?"

I shake my head. "Not sure. My father is sending over a copy of the paperwork from when I took over the factory that he seems to think shows how he's going to be able to take it back from me. I've read over my copy and there's nothing in there that I can see. But he's still saying I need to marry Annabelle if I want to keep the company."

"No. Absolutely not. That's not good for either of you." Eric paces. "You have a copy?"

I nod. "Yeah. I have one in the safe in my home office and my lawyer still has one on file. I don't know why my dad still thinks he needs to email me a copy."

Eric looks off into the distance. "That seems odd. Let me ask my mother and see what I can find out. If my mom is good for one thing, it's knowing everyone else's business."

I chuckle. "My mother is the same way, but I doubt it would be wise to ask her about this."

"You're probably right." He digs his phone out of his bag. "I'll message my mom now. Want me to come up to your place when I find out more?"

I nod, looking down at Lincoln. He's rubbing his ears in his trademark "I'm tired" maneuver. "Yeah. I better get this guy down for his nap before I throw him completely off schedule. Phoebe would never forgive me if he didn't sleep tonight."

I give the other guys a wave and take Lincoln to the elevator and up to my apartment. That's one great thing about playing basketball at the gym in my building. I'm always less than three minutes from a hot shower, and now, a crib for Lincoln to nap in.

After getting Lincoln settled into his crib, I take the handheld for the monitor and go straight to the safe in my office. I need to see what my copy of the contract says, then compare it to the one I'm sure is already sitting in my inbox.

I'm behind my desk comparing the contracts line by line when Eric lets himself into the apartment.

"Arch? Where are you?" He whisper yells from down the hall. "I have some interesting news."

Interesting news? Yeah, I have some interesting news too. I find it interesting that these two contracts are different in a few crucial areas.

It's almost laughable, really. How did my father think he was going to get away with this? And why?

"Oh, there you are. You better sit down for this. You'll never believe what my mom said."

Chapter 37

Santa's Side Chick

Phoebe

"Oh my god. Look at that one." Charlie smacks me excitedly in the arm and points to another giant tapestry hanging from the ceiling of the convention centre. "Where would you even make something that size? The artist must have their own warehouse studio to accommodate something on that scale."

Charlie and I are spending the day at the textile arts festival, thanks to the tickets Archer gave me for Christmas. He said after seeing the picture of the tapestry I made for Lincoln, he knew I'd love something like this. And I do. I so do.

We've seen only a fraction of the artists' booths and I already have so many ideas for new creations, I've started a fresh note on my phone with lists of materials I'll need. I can't wait to get started.

"Whoa, that's impressive. I can't believe the variety in scale of projects we've seen here today." Some people make medium to large size items like me, but there is such a vast difference in the size of projects I can hardly believe it. "That one is astronomical compared to the one we saw that was so small it needed to be looked at a through a microscope. I can't imagine working at either scale. I work in the size I do because it's a size my hands can handle."

Charlie waggles her brows. "So you're telling me Archer's candy cane is on the small side?" She throws her head back and laughs. "I would have thought you'd need something girthier than a strand of yarn to make those noises you were making last night."

My hand shoots out and I backhand her shoulder before I know what I'm doing. "Shhh," I whisper harshly while scanning our surroundings to see if anyone heard her. "Will you shut up?"

Since Christmas Day, after we took Lincoln to the hospital together, Archer has spent most of every night with me at my house. Let's just say neither of us has been sleeping much, and it has nothing to do with the baby in the other room. No, the ways Archer has been keeping me awake have been way more enjoyable than your average sleep deprivation.

She laughs harder. "Why? You don't want anyone to know how much you *really* love yarn?"

My cheeks burn as the people surrounding us turn to look in our direction. I stare at the floor with a hand on my head, hoping I'll escape notice.

"Oh yeah, yarn. Oooh." Charlie wraps her arms around herself and pretends like she's making out with someone, tongue sloppily bathing her own face as she makes kissing noises, forcing a chuckle from me. I can't help but laugh at how stupid she looks. "You know how I like 'em skinny and floppy."

I yank her arm and drag her away, the sound of laughter drifting after us from the few people who'd been standing nearby.

"Jesus, Charlie. Do you need to draw so much attention to us?"

She shrugs and says with a laugh, "Why does it matter? We don't know these people. And besides, no one cares anyway. There were *maybe* three people who saw me and heard what I said. Fuck 'em."

I can't help but chuckle at her laissez-faire attitude. She truthfully doesn't give a shit what people think of her. Sometimes I wish I could be more like that, but I'm not there yet. The memory of people staring at us mere moments ago makes me flush again with an uncomfortable heat.

Charlie shakes her head and links her arm through mine. "Come on, then. The yarn-bombing demonstration starts in ten minutes, and I want to get a drink before we head over there." She pats her purse with her other hand and whispers, "I brought a flask of the good tequila to keep things interesting."

I roll my eyes and let her lead me to the concession area. I'm not surprised she brought alcohol. The textile arts festival is more my scene than hers. Still, I'm glad she came with me today. While she scans the offerings from the many booths serving food and drink, I pull out the paper program I grabbed on the way in to the convention center. Other than the yarn-bombing demonstration, I want to check out the felting section, take in a presentation on modern spinning wheels and spinning practices, and get a closer look at, oh, I don't know, every exhibit in the place. With over six hundred booths, that could take a while.

"I'm going to run to the washroom. Can you grab me a drink, too? A water would be great."

"Sure thing. Want to meet at the yarn-bombing demo? First one there saves the seat."

I agree, then make my way to the closest set of restrooms. When I'm done with the bathroom, I wash up and head back out to the main area of the convention center.

I still can't believe Archer got me tickets to this. Not only got me tickets, but knew about it in the first place. I didn't even know about it, and I'm the one who does the weaving. A flood of happiness fills me when I imagine him researching this event and deciding to get the tickets. He was nervous when he gave them to me, like he wasn't sure if I would like it or not. It was a risk, considering I never really said how much I loved making my projects, but he must've sensed something, because this gift hit it out of the park. I have so many ideas for new things I want to try and I've only seen a few of the booths so far. I can't wait until I get through the rest of them to see what else I'm inspired to create.

The walk to the yarn-bombing demo takes me through the lace maker's section. There have to be at least ten different women running around with giant wedding binders, each of them looking for the perfect handmade lace for their special day.

Must be nice. Before today, I wasn't even aware people still made lace by hand. I thought it was all machine cut these days. The glimpses I spy as I walk by intrigue me. I need to bring Charlie back to see these after the demonstration. I wonder if she knows that lace can be handmade?

Finally, I make it to the presentation room, and after a minute of scouring the sizable crowd, I spy Charlie sitting up near the front. I excuse myself and slide by several people already seated in the row before taking my spot next to Charlie.

"How'd you get seats this close? This place is packed."

She shrugs. "I bribed an old lady."

"You bribed an old lady?"

"Yeah. I gave her and her friend some of my tequila and they were happy to give up their seats. They didn't even stay for the demonstration after that. Said something about going to look for some young guys to help with their own booth. I almost offered to go with them before I remembered I was waiting for you. They seemed like they know how to have a good time if their matching shiny track suits and fanny packs are anything to go by. We should find them after this. Something tells me their booth won't be your standard knitting or crochet."

I glance at her sideways. "Matching track suits *and* fanny packs? That seems a little over the top, don't you think? Whatever they have in their booth is something I think I need to see."

Another shrug. "They also had matching white high-top sneakers and one of them was wearing a trucker that read 'fuck bitches, get money' so...I wasn't going to question it. They seemed cool."

I open my mouth to answer when a man and woman walk out to the center of the stage at the front of the room. The man taps the microphone, causing a squeal of feedback to blare through the speakers, sending the room into a chorus of pained groans followed by uncomfortable silence.

"Welcome to Yarn-Bombing: Time to Take a *Strand*. In this demonstration, we will explain our theory of yarn-bombing as a form of peaceful protest and then share ways to take your yarn-bombing to the next level."

"Well, that was...informative?" I snicker. "I mean, I liked the beginning and the middle, but the end was a little suspect."

Charlie snorts and takes a full swig of her tequila before I take it and do the same. "Yeah. I was not expecting the *next level* to be...to be...yarn *bumming*." Charlie bursts into hysterical laughter and I follow suit. The thought of butt knitting is too disturbing and ridiculous to be taken seriously.

"The way he opened the flap on the back of his overalls and bent over—" My voice cracks with laughter.

"—and then she reached between his cheeks, grabbed a strand and started pulling. I can't...I don't understand why. WHY?" Charlie wails dramatically, shaking her hands to the sky.

We stumble our way to the wall and slide down to sitting, our legs tucked close so we don't get trampled by the crowd passing by.

"And then she started knitting with it. And he sat there, hands on his knees, ass out, smiling at the crowd like this was a totally normal thing."

I twitch my shoulders in the barest of shrugs, laughter still rolling through me. "Maybe it is to him? This is just another day where he stands around while his wife knits with his butt yarn."

"It had to be in something, though, didn't it?" Charlie asks. "Like, it's not *in there, in there?*"

Is it? No. That wouldn't be safe. "I'd think it would have to be in something. Like one of those yarn bowls we saw earlier? It can't be loose in there. That could cause way too much damage if it got loose and tangled up internally, wouldn't it? Imagine the damage to his intestines."

Her sneaky grin tips me off that she's about to say something she finds hilarious, that I'll no doubt find completely mortifying. It's the look she always gets when she tries to make me uncomfortable.

"You know, you could ask Archer. As the owner of a sex toy factory, I'm sure he knows all about what should and what should not be inserted into the butt. He gave you those gorgeous trees, after all."

I groan and drop my head back against the wall. "You're never going to let me live that down, are you?"

She shakes her head and takes her flask back. "Never. It is officially my favorite holiday story. Someday, when Lincoln is old enough, I'm going to tell him the story of how his dad made his mom fall in love with him with an offering of butt plugs. It will humiliate both of you, making it doubly hilarious for me." She lets a laugh out before taking a drink from her flask. "Actually, it might be more than doubly hilarious. I'm not sure we can adequately measure the level of hilarity yet. I might need a few years to determine how much distance I'm going to get out of this story. I'll talk to Gavin, too. I know he thinks it's as hilarious as I do. I'm sure together we'll be able to parse out an adequate measure of the hilarity we can reliably expect this story to produce."

"Awesome," I deadpan. "I can't wait to hear how much laughter my humiliation can garner."

She nods sagely. "I'll be sure to add it to the family newsletter." Charlie gets to her feet and holds out a hand for me. "Now come on. Let's go find the ladies I shared my tequila with. I want to know what they're up to."

A few booths down from the conference room is the booth hosted by the Yarn Bumming couple. The man has already returned to his station, thankfully with a refastened butt flap. He's sitting on a stool, knitting from a multicolored skein of yarn that is in a bowl, not coming out of his rear-end. Evidently he's no worse for wear for having been shitting out yarn on stage mere moments ago. Good for him, I guess. Whatever makes you happy.

I'm working hard to avoid making eye contact with him when someone calls me.

"Phoebe? Oh man, what a coincidence. What are you doing here?"

I spin toward the voice and spot Ryder sitting on the ground in the booth across from me. Am I drunk off Charlie's tequila, or is he wrapped in a pink rope tied in intricate knots?

"Hey, it's you." Charlie makes her way through the crowd, stopping in the booth where Ryder is, for lack of a better term, resting. "This is what you do? Shibari? So cool."

I wrench my eyes away from Ryder and the pink rope he's tied with, to see two grinning old ladies in matching track suits. They look exactly as I pictured when Charlie described them to me.

"Oh, hello girlie. Glad you could come by. What'd you think of that demonstration? I bet you were real glad you had that tequila with you when they started talking about taking yarn bombing up a notch. We have some whiskey here if you need more fortification."

"I see you've met my grandmother," Ryder says from his spot on the ground. "Gran, this is Phoebe"—he points as best he can with his nose—"and I see you already know her friend. Ladies, this is my Gran, Delores, and her friend Gladys."

"Oh, yes, now I remember. I recognize you ladies from the media coverage after the incident with Denise's ex." I cringe, realizing too late that Ryder probably doesn't want to talk about Denise's crazy ex-boyfriend. "Sorry, Ryder. This is my sister, Charlie. She was at work the day you and Denise came over with Cole."

"But I heard all about your daughter's excellent head butting skills, so kudos for that," Charlie says with a laugh. "I still catch Gavin rubbing his nose when he thinks no one is watching. It's hilarious."

Ryder laughs. "Glad we could be of service."

"So, uh…why are you tied up on the floor?"

"Oh, that's easy," the woman Ryder introduced as Gladys answers. "He's our hunk of man-meat for demonstration purposes. You know what they say: sex sells. Ryder is our sex. We couldn't find any volunteers for some strange reason."

I choke on a laugh when I see Ryder roll his eyes. "Gladys, I'm not your sex. I'm here to help you demonstrate some Shibari techniques and that's it. I won't be taking my clothes off, no matter how many times you say sex sells."

Gladys puts her fists on her hips and sticks her bottom lip out. "Oh, pooh. You're no fun. I told you I'd buy you a banana hammock from the lingerie booth two rows over." She leans toward me and whispers behind her hand, "It's made of Angora, so it's sure to be soft on the man-bits."

Ryder shakes his head, having heard every word she said. "No banana hammock, Gladys. Not a chance." He shakes his head and purposely changes the subject. "So, what are you two doing here?"

"Oh, my…Lincoln's dad gave me tickets to check out the festival because I like macrame and weaving. He thought I'd like to see all the different textile arts."

"He must not have known about the yarn bumming." Ryder's Gran chuckles. "That's probably not the kind of art he was thinking of when he sent you here."

I laugh. "No, probably not."

"Well, it was nice to meet you all, but we should get back to the festival." Charlie segues into our departure with all the finesse of a stampeding goat. "I don't think Phoebe is going to last much longer without checking on Lincoln."

I nod in agreement. "She's right. It's a miracle that I haven't texted his dad a hundred times by now. Time's running out."

We say our goodbyes, but no sooner do I let Charlie pull me into the aisle than she's pulling me to the side of a booth and pointing out two women arguing near one of the lace maker's booths I'd wanted to look at earlier.

"Look," she hisses in my ear. "That's the future mother-in-law of the bride from the stripper cop bachelorette party. The one who brought champagne for her alcoholic daughter-in-law who was trying to quit drinking. Oh, and the mother is there, too."

I surreptitiously sneak a look, taking in the two well-dressed women arguing in front of the booth. They appear to be in a heated discussion over which lace is better. One is holding a traditional looking, cream-colored swatch, and the other has a shimmery, modern-looking piece.

"I don't know what they're arguing for," I whisper to Charlie. "They're both pretty, but the traditional one is clearly the better choice for a bride."

"Are you insane?" She whispers back. "The other one is way more magical. If I ever get married, I want to look like an otherworldly goddess, and that shimmery lace has ethereal fairy princess written all over it."

The women look off to the side and call someone over, saying something about letting her decide since she's the one getting married.

"Let's make a bet." I say. "If the bride picks the traditional lace, I'll buy lunch. If she picks the modern one, you buy. Deal?" I stick my hand out and Charlie grabs it in a firm handshake.

"You're on."

As the bride steps into view, my stomach drops to my feet and I'm struck with the sudden surety that I won't need lunch today at all. Because I've seen that gorgeous face, beautiful blonde hair, and supple dancer's body before.

That's the woman who interrupted me that night I found Archer. The one who called him babe while I was working up the courage to tell him about his son.

The one he said wasn't his girlfriend.

That lying fucker.

Wait. I guess he didn't technically lie. She isn't his girlfriend. She's his fiancé.

And I guess that makes me Santa's side chick.

Chapter 38

I'M LOSING HIM

Archer

"THAT'S EXACTLY WHAT I'M saying, Miranda. Yes. That's what he just sent me. And you're sure you've never seen this document?"

"*I absolutely have never seen this before. I would never have let you sign a contract that was so easy for your father to revoke. I'm too familiar with men like him to have let that slide. Leave it with me, Archer. I'll make some calls and get back to you. Don't worry about a thing. I'm going to enjoy every minute of this.*" My lawyer, Miranda James, laughs like the cutthroat legal shark she is. "*One more thing. Are you comfortable pressing charges against your father and his lawyer? Because that's where I'm going with this.*"

"More than comfortable. That's not my signature on the contract he sent me. It hardly even looks like my handwriting. I don't know how he thought this would work."

Miranda's hearty chuckle rumbles through the phone. "*It sounds like he was desperate. Desperate men aren't known for thinking clearly.*"

"Yeah, you're right about that." It's my turn to chuckle. "He must have been pretty surprised when I refused to bend to his ultimatum. I'm not sure Annabelle's father will be interested in forgiving my parents' debt once he realizes I won't marry her."

"I suppose he won't. Too bad for your father. Okay, let me make those calls now, and I'll get back to you tomorrow at the latest."

She hangs up without saying goodbye, which is fine by me. Every minute we spend on the phone counts as billable hours for her, and she's not cheap. That's not an issue for me either, since I know she's worth every penny. And now that her name is in question because of the falsified document my father has in his possession? Well, let's just say I'm glad I'm not the one on the receiving end of Miranda James' ire.

Still, there's a small part of me that worries she won't be able to figure this out. After everything I've accomplished this past year, the mere thought of letting my father take over Fade Toys again is enough to set my insides to burning. I can't let him ruin all my hard work like that. More importantly, I can't let him destroy what I've built for the staff. If he has his way, they'll all be out of a job or back to working for as little as he can legally pay them. Within the law or not, it's not right.

"So, how much do you think your dad owes the Meyers? It must be a lot if he's willing to forge signatures on fake contracts and get his lawyer involved. What do you think? Five million? Ten? Twenty?"

I release a slow breath and slump back in my desk chair, stretching my neck to work out some of the tension of the last hour. It's a relief to know my lawyer has this handled, but it's still frustrating to see the full scope of what my father had planned for me. Imagine promising my hand in marriage for the forgiveness of his debts. It's positively medieval.

"However much it is, it's up there," I tell Eric. "What I'd like to know is how he got into so much debt in the first place. The pension my parents get from Fade Toys is nearly six figures. Add that to the income from their investments and they should have more than enough to get by."

"Wow, sex toys really are good business." Eric laughs. "But you should know your parents better than that. The elder Fades have no interest in getting by. They want what all Westborough society folks want; to lord their wealth over everyone and to make other people feel less than by comparison."

He's right, of course. I do know my parents better than that. All they've ever wanted is to prove that they're better than everyone else. Well, since Fade Toys started making real money, that is.

"At least I know my virtue is worth a small fortune. Not that I would consider marrying Annabelle. I dodged that bullet once, and I have no intention of putting myself in the line of fire again."

Eric looks out the window for a moment before looking back at me. "Do you think she knows? That her father and yours are trying to arrange a marriage?"

I shrug. "I don't really know. I don't know that I ever really knew Annabelle, not the way I should have. For all I was planning to propose to her, we were virtually strangers. The months we were together, we were rarely actually in each other's presence, you know? She was modeling a lot then and always flying off to another fashion show or photo shoot. And when she wasn't away, I was busy rebuilding Fade Toys. Revamping all the means of production, sourcing new materials, and changing the entire company culture took a lot of late nights and early mornings."

Eric nods. "It wasn't really fair to either of you."

"No, it wasn't. But I'm so much better off now. Phoebe is amazing." I can't stop the grin from spreading across my face. "And Lincoln is the best."

Eric smiles. "He's a pretty cool kid. You're a lucky guy. Who would've thought you could score such a cool little family after a one-night stand dressed as Santa? I bet that wasn't on your wish list."

I chuckle and shake my head. "No, it wasn't. This family is all I ever wanted, but after Annabelle I was sure I'd never get it. I mean, being crapped on wasn't the greatest thing to ever happen to me, but still...I wouldn't change much."

Truthfully, the only thing I would change about the whole situation is, I would have liked to have been involved much sooner, well before Lincoln was actually born. If Phoebe and I had met under normal circumstances, I know I would still have been interested. Even without the wedding dress, fancy hairdo, and full makeup, she's the most beautiful woman I've ever seen. I love the way her freckles give her an outdoorsy glow, and how her hair never seems to behave. And when she blushes? It makes indecent thoughts run rampant through my head.

Eric's sudden gagging noises break through the near silence and I can't help but laugh at the thought that he's inside my head and seeing the filthy things I'm imaging doing with Phoebe the next chance I get. It doesn't strike me until speaks up that he's still thinking about babies.

"I can't believe you were covered in shit and you didn't immediately go to the hospital. What about that disease, Ecology? Ebola? Esophagus? I don't know exactly what it is, but I know there's something in poop that can make you sick."

I bark a laugh and shake my head. "I think you mean E. Coli. It's bacteria. And It's not like I sat there in filth for hours, Eric. I got up and showered right away."

He shakes his head in disbelief. "I don't know, man. I'm not sure regular soap is up to the task when there's that much crap on you. At that point, you should call the hazmat team to hose you down with a medical grade disinfectant just to be safe."

"You're an idiot."

"Maybe, but at least I can say I've never been covered in shit."

"Touché"

The sound of Lincoln's babbling comes through the monitor and a look at the screen tells me he's awake and playing with his feet. It's so adorable I can almost feel my heart growing inside my chest as I sit here. That's not possible though, is it? I'm pretty sure that would qualify as more of a medical emergency than being covered in poop would be.

"Sounds like the big man's waking up. If you're afraid of poop, I'd advise you to stay away until I get him cleaned up. He has a penchant for filling his entire sleeper with the stuff when he's had an excellent nap."

He leans back in his chair and throws his hands up in a hands off motion. "Noted. I'll stay out of your way. You got anything to eat in the kitchen? I skipped lunch to call my mother for you."

"Yeah. Eat whatever you want."

I leave Eric to his own devices and go to Lincoln's bedroom. My son's bedroom in my apartment. God, I love that. I grin to myself as I open the door.

"Hey, Link. How'd you sleep, buddy?" I look over the side of the crib and am greeted with a huge gummy grin. "Oh, yeah? You must feel well rested. Got any surprises for me?" I pick him up and bring him to the change table. I make quick work of changing him, and bring him out to the kitchen to make him a bottle.

"Hey, dude." Eric takes a break from eating a sandwich to fist bump Lincoln. "I would have made you one, but I figured the lack of teeth would hold you back."

Lincoln giggles and buries his face in my neck.

"He's on bottles only right now, but I'm sure he'll take you up on that sandwich in a couple of years."

I busy myself making Lincoln's bottle while Eric finishes up his sandwich. We head to the living so I can sit while I feed Lincoln.

"So, are you going to talk to your dad? Tell him you know the contract is fake?"

"I probably should. That would be the responsible thing to do, but I think I'll let Miranda take care of it. I don't want him to think there's any way he's getting the company back from me, and if I give him any leeway in this matter, I'm sure he'll start scheming up a new way to get what he wants. It's best to let the professionals take care of it."

"And you don't think he'll try to force the Annabelle issue?"

"I don't see how he can. I know he can't take the company from me, and that was the only thing that he was holding over my head. He has nothing to scare me with now."

Eric's mouth opens to say something, but instead of words, all I hear is the crash of my door banging open.

"You dirty son of a bitch. I can't believe I admired your adonis lines that day I saw you in your boxers. I feel so dirty." Gavin storms into the room, followed closely by Charlie, but Phoebe is nowhere in sight.

"Hey, Gav. Hey, Charlie. How was the textile arts festival? Did Phoebe love it? Where is she, anyway?" I stand up and pass Lincoln into Gavin's waiting arms, looking to the entranceway for Phoebe. "Did she find some inspiration?" I hope she did, because I plan to take her to the craft store to load up on supplies as soon as possible. I can't wait to see what she comes up with after seeing the other artists at the festival.

At Charlie's cruel laugh, I snap my head in her direction. "Oh, she found some inspiration all right. Some inspiration to cry herself to sleep, you sadistic son of a bitch."

My stomach drops. Phoebe is crying? I can't stand the thought of her crying and not being there for her. My body surges with the need to go comfort her.

"What do you mean? Where is she? I need to see her."

"You should have thought of that before you lied to her about your little girlfriend. Oh, excuse me. I mean, your little *fiancée.*" She spit the last word, like it tasted bitter on her tongue.

"My what?" I splutter, the words still tumbling from my mouth as I look to Gavin for an explanation. "What is she talking about, Gavin?"

He shrugs, taking the empty bottle from Lincoln's mouth and dropping it onto the couch. "I don't know for sure, man. I wasn't there. It sounds to me like they met your fiancée, though."

Eric's eyes are wide as he looks between the three of us. Charlie's mouth is set in a severe line, her grasp on her temper tenuous. Gavin looks calmer, but I'm not sure I'm imagining the heat from the rage bubbling under his skin. They're both pissed the fuck off.

And here I stand, with my mouth hanging open, confused as shit. *Girlfriend?* I don't have a girlfriend, though I was hoping after all that had happened between us, Phoebe would fill that position, and I certainly don't have a fiancée.

Unless...

I look at Eric as he comes to the same conclusion.

"Annabelle," I growl through gritted teeth to his answering nod. "Looks like I don't have the luxury of letting my lawyer deal with my father, after all."

Chapter 39

Give Santa A Chance

Phoebe

Phoebe

After somehow convincing Charlie not to confront the gorgeous woman at the textile arts festival, the one who I now know is Archer's fiancée, I insisted she take me home and go pick up Lincoln for me. I've been sitting on the couch, staring at a bottle of tequila on the coffee table ever since, debating whether I should crack it open and start drinking.

My stomach has been practicing its trampoline act since I realized what Charlie was saying to me about the beautiful woman, and what that meant for me, so I'm still not sure if tequila is the best idea. On the one hand, it would numb the pain a little. On the other, it would likely make this churning in my guts even worse. It's a toss up.

I'm also trying to figure out what I'm going to say to the cheating scumbag when I work up the courage to see him again. Thankfully, Charlie offered to pick Lincoln up and keep him for a couple of hours to let me relax. Plenty of time to come up with the best way to tear a strip off the cheating bastard. Because I have to say something. I can't let him get away with this.

I flat out asked him if she was his girlfriend and he said no. Did I honestly need to specify the word "fiancée"? Is that how he can sleep at night? Who knew I'd have to be on the lookout for an equivocating asshole when I was first tracking down Lincoln's dad?

I wish I could say I can't believe he would lie to me about having a girlfriend when I flat out asked him, but I guess I can. I thought he was too good to be true, and it looks like I was right. When will I learn to trust my instincts? I knew he wasn't for me when I found him again that first night. If the discrepancy between his immaculate three-piece-suit and my leggings and dirty-hoodie combo didn't tip me off, the stupid message he left me the next day should have.

Who doesn't swear when they're drunk and pissed off? That's just weird. You can bet your ass I won't be making that same mistake. Whatever I end up saying to him, it's going to be chock full of profanity. So much profanity. *All* the profanity. He's going to need to flush his ears with holy water by the time I'm done with him.

That's it. I've decided. Tequila it is. But only a reasonable amount. I have a baby to take care of later, after all.

I get a glass from the kitchen, fill it with ice, and head back to the couch, where I crack open the tequila and fill the glass to the brim. I toss it back, relishing the burn as it slides down my throat, and am about to pour another when the door flies open, slamming into the wall with a bang.

"Phoebe. Please say you're here. I'm so sorry, baby. It's not what you think. And I can prove it. I need you to come with me." Archer stands in the doorway, eyes frantically searching as he calls out for me. "I can't explain exactly what you saw, but we're going to go find out together. Right now."

The tiniest spark of hope flares to life in my chest before I remember that I'm mad at him. No, not mad. I'm fucking pissed.

"What the hell makes you think I'd go anywhere with you?"

He snaps his head in my direction, and his tense shoulders relax when he takes me in. His long strides eat up the floor until he's kneeling in front of me, taking my hands in his. "I promise you, Phoebe. I did not lie. That woman, Annabelle, is not my girlfriend, or my fiancée, or whatever other nonsense you might have overheard at the convention center. She's my ex. I found out she cheated on me the night that I met you, and I had broken it off with her before I ever set foot in that bar. Until that night you found me again, I hadn't had any contact with her at all. I recently discovered she's been scheming with my parents, and why. I want you to come with me when I put an end to their stupid plan once and for all."

I scoff, pulling my hands away. Did he think I would fall for this? What an arrogant ass. How could he think I'm that gullible? "Scheming with your parents? That doesn't even make any sense. Scheming with your parents, how?"

He sets his mouth in a line and shakes his head. "Believe me, I know. I thought I'd be fine to let my lawyer deal with it, but I'm realizing that won't be enough. I need to put a stop to this. Say you'll come with me. Please, Phoebe. Once you see what my parents are like, you'll understand."

The tequila must already be affecting me, because I almost believe him. Something about the sincerity in his eyes and the panic in his voice is tugging at me, telling me to trust him.

I'll go, but first I'll need to steel myself against his charms.

"Fine. I'll come with you. But you're driving," I say, filling my glass with the tequila and drinking it in one gulp, "because I've had too much to drink."

He reads the label on the bottle and, wincing, puts the cap back on for me. "Yes, okay. I'll drive. No problem." He stands and holds a hand out for me. Instead of letting him help me, I smack it away.

"I haven't forgiven you, yet. I'm interested to see how this plays out, but that doesn't mean I believe everything you're saying. It's too...weird."

He smiles sadly. "Fair enough. Hopefully, this trip to my parents' house clears things up. I can't lose you again, Phoebe. These last few weeks with you and Lincoln have been the best of my life. I'm not ready to give that up."

What he's saying sounds insane, but I'm so curious to see for myself that I'm nearly bursting with the anticipation. What could it hurt? If I meet his parents and decide that Archer is still a scumbag liar, I'll call for a ride and leave. It's as simple as that.

I hoist myself off the couch, grabbing my phone and shoving it into my pocket on the way up. "Okay, let's get this over with."

He stands aside and allows me to lead the way to the door, where I grab a jacket before stepping out into the late December air. I look around at the decorations that are still up from the engagement photo shoot Archer did with Webster and Frederick, and my heart flutters. That really was sweet of him. Especially after they started with the ass pinching. He could have stopped as soon as the groping started, but he didn't. And he did it all because he wanted my ex-fiancé and his boyfriend to have a fabulous engagement photo. A guy who would do that couldn't be all bad, could he?

Maybe not. But a guy who would cheat on his girlfriend, fiancée, whatever, is pretty bad in my books. Especially when he makes me an unwilling accomplice in said cheating. I never would have slept with him if I'd known he was involved with someone else. That's not who I am.

"Ready?" Archer gets my attention by tapping my elbow.

I nod, reaching around him to the lock the door. "As I'll ever be."

When we're on the road, I send a text to the group chat I have with Gavin and Charlie.

Phoebe

You guys still good with Lincoln? Archer showed up to apologize. He's taking me to his parents' house to explain the situation.

Gavin

You went?

Charlie

I don't work today so I can hang out with Lincoln as long as you need. Don't let him get away with anything. Say the word and I'll be there to rip his nuts off and shove them down his throat.

I let out a snort of laughter, causing Archer to glance in my direction. I wave him off and look back at my phone.

Gavin

OUCH! That hurts me just thinking about it. I doubt that will be necessary.

Charlie

Phoebe will tell us what is necessary. You and your sensitive little boy parts can mind your own business, Gav.

Phoebe

I'll let you guys know when I know more.

I close out of the messaging app and put my phone back in my pocket, making a point not to look at Archer again. If I look at him too long, I might do something stupid like beg him to marry me instead of the blonde bombshell who's currently planning her wedding to him. And I refuse to stoop that low. I'm not that desperate. If he'd cheat on her with me, he'd cheat on me with someone else.

Before long, we're pulling through a hideous golden gate into the circular drive of an obscenely large house on the north side of Westborough. This neighborhood is known for being one of the richest, and therefore best, in the city, but I can't for the life of me figure out why. One look at this place and all I see is someone who's trying to compensate for something.

"Ho-ly shit! Is that a gold fountain in the middle of the driveway?" I scoff in disbelief.

Archer's grimace tells me everything. He's embarrassed. If this were my parents' house, I'd be embarrassed too.

"It's gold-plated," he says, "much to my mother's chagrin. A recent addition to the property. Apparently, she wanted solid gold."

I take in the monstrosity of a house, momentarily blinded by the sunlight glinting off what appears to be hundreds of gleaming windows. "The sex toy business must be *amazing.*"

"We do alright." He shrugs and focuses his gaze on the hideous fountain. "From everything I've seen with our accounts, the business is doing better than it ever has since I took over last year. It's funny, though. The pension my parents get is generous, but I never thought it was gold-plated-fountain-in-the-front-drive generous."

"I'd say the evidence speaks for itself."

"*Hmmm.*" Archer gives me a nod. "Shall we?"

Instead of answering, I open my door and get out of the vehicle. "If I'd known we were visiting Buckingham Palace, I'd have dressed a little nicer." I pull my phone out and send a pin of my location to Gavin and Charlie, in case something happens. Rich people are weird and I want someone to come looking for me if I go missing in some *hunting-the-poor-for-sport* scenario. "So what do you expect will happen here?"

I'm walking behind him, his broad back blocking my view of the house while I take in the flowerbeds lining the driveway. I wonder how often their gardener tends them? Because they're so lush, there's no way they aren't professionally maintained. I wonder how much something like that costs?

If this was the kind of money Archer comes from, it's no wonder he was worried that's what I was after. If a woman were so inclined, she could really cash in having a baby in this family.

He shrugs. "I expect to get some answers from my parents once and for all. I thought I'd have time to let my lawyer handle things, but it turns out we need answers sooner than that. I'm not losing you, Phoebe. Not again."

"Archer. There you are. I've been calling you all afternoon."

"Mother."

I don't even notice Archer has stopped walking until I slam right into his back and crumple awkwardly to the ground. "Ouch," I yelp when my butt absorbs the impact. It's a good thing I'm fortified with tequila, or that would have been way more painful.

"Shit, Phoebe. Are you alright?" He reaches a hand out to help me up from my new position on the ground, and the touch of his fingers sends a surprising riot of tingles up my arm. So surprising, in fact, I pull away and lose my balance, landing myself flat on my butt. Again.

I roll to my side and rub my hip where it connected with the cement of the driveway. "Whoops. Guess I had a little more tequila than I thought. Who knew I'd become such a lightweight in the last year, huh?"

"Archer, who is that unkempt woman and why does she keep falling down in my driveway? What will the neighbors think?" The woman rocks forward on her toes, her eyes scanning the surrounding area.

Archer helps me to my feet and dusts me off. "You sure you're alright?" His grip on my upper arms is the steadying force I need to help me stop swaying. *Did I drink more than I thought?* No,

I only had the two glasses. Guess I really *can't* hold my liquor anymore.

"Yeah," I nod, the lie slipping easily from my lips. "I'm good. Barely even tipsy."

He nods once before turning to face the woman standing on the steps of the mansion. She's wringing her hands and darting glances to either side, as though she'll see the neighbors spying on us past the vast expanse of property on either side. Her skirt suit is impeccable, and her hair is one of those sleek bobs that you know cost hundreds, maybe even thousands, of dollars a month to maintain. It looks so soft I want to nuzzle my face in it.

"Archer, why is that woman looking at me like that?" His mother curls her lip in disgust and Archer heaves an audible sigh.

"This is Phoebe, Mom. She's the mother of my son. And once you clear up some misinformation for us, I'm hoping she'll be more than that, too."

Chapter 40

Meet The Parents Part Two

Archer

"What are you talking about, Archer? You don't have a son."

Rather than attempt to argue, I take out my phone and pull up my photo album, choosing a picture of myself wearing Lincoln in his baby carrier from earlier today. I pass the phone to my mother. "This is Lincoln. Phoebe recently found me to tell me about him. And before you ask, yes, we did a paternity test, and yes, he is actually my son."

"Hmm." She holds the phone out from her face. "Are you sure he's yours? I mean, he's certainly this woman's son"—she gestures to Phoebe with a flick of her wrist—"the red hair really gives it away."

I smile because my mother has unintentionally hit on one of the many things I love about Lincoln. "Yeah, he looks just like her, doesn't he? Except for the eyes. Those are all me. But to answer your question, yes, I'm sure."

My mother narrows her eyes. "How do you know she didn't fake the test results? Someone with your social standing should know this sort of thing happens all the time to men with the amount of money we have. That's why you're marrying Annabelle, after all. Her family is as well off as we are. You can rest assured she's not in it for the money."

My mouth opens to tell my mother to drop the act, that I know she and my father are the one's in it for the money when Phoebe stiffens next to me, calling my attention to her growing discomfort and away from my mom's misplaced faith in my family's wealth. I'll have to deal with that later. For now, I grab my phone back from my mother and shove it in my pocket. We're here to dispel the idea that I'm marrying Annabelle and here my mother is declaring that is exactly what I'm doing. How can I get it through to her?

"I need you to listen to me carefully, Mother. Do you understand?" She nods, a look of uncertainty flashing across her features. "I. Am. Not. Marrying Annabelle. Ever. Stop your preparations. Cancel any bookings you've made. It's not happening,"

Phoebe snickers at my back and my mother splutters.

"Well..."

"No. That's not good enough. I've already told you this, and I assumed you understood. I'm sure you can understand my surprise today when I learned you were out shopping at the textile arts festival with Annabelle and her mother, and for what? Shit for a wedding dress for a wedding that isn't happening. How is this possible?"

My mother wrings her hands some more, a habit I'm only now noticing corresponds to her feelings of guilt. The more guilt she feels, the more she wrings her hands. "Well, your father told me he'd spoken to you and you'd seen how advantageous it would be to marry Annabelle. He told us to go ahead with planning the wedding. Her mother even hosted a bachelorette party for her." She laughs cruelly. "That turned into a nightmare in itself. Can you believe Annabelle wanted an alcohol-free venue? They booked out some ridiculous little coffee shop downtown."

An alcohol free venue? That doesn't sound like the Annabelle I know. That Annabelle would never be caught dead without a drink in her hand at a social event. Come to think of it, that Annabelle had a drink in her hand more often than not.

Phoebe steps around me, drawing my attention to her instead of the mystery of an alcohol free party and Annabelle. "That was you? My friend could lose his job because he danced at that party. Not to mention the owner of the coffee shop nearly had to shut down entirely. Luckily, she had video footage that proved it was the out-of-control party guests who brought alcohol into an unlicensed establishment."

My mother taps a finger against her lower lip, humming as she thinks. "Which one? The large burly man, or the smaller man covered in tattoos? They were both a little rough around the edges for my tastes. And what does it matter if they lose their jobs? It's not like taking their clothes off for money is anything to be proud of. The money they make from something so indecent is dirty. They should look to obtain a more respectable career. Something with longevity. Something they won't need to be ashamed of."

"Neither of them are strippers," Phoebe yells, her hands gripping her hair in exasperation. "One is head of security for a famous rock band who was there doing the store owner a favor. The other is an actual police officer who was called to deal with the unruly partygoers when someone pulled out bottles of champagne. One of the woman snatched his gun out of his holster and now he's suspended pending an investigation."

My mother's face pales, and she fidgets with her fingers. "Well," she sputters, "it's not my fault. You can't have a bachelorette party without champagne."

"Oh my god, Mom. *You* brought the alcohol? When someone says they want an alcohol free party, you don't bring champagne. Tell me. Where does a police officer rank on your scale of respectability? Is it above a stripper? How does it fare against sex toy maker? Surely a police officer is a more respectable than the owner of a sex toy factory and yet you've never had any qualms about taking the money earned from that, have you?"

She splutters and won't look me in the eye.

"You had no issue with using the money we earned by making dildos, butt plugs, and vibrators to buy that monstrosity of a fountain." I jerk my thumb behind me toward the golden monument in question. "It doesn't bother you that the money people have spent chasing orgasms buys you all those fancy clothes you wear? That nice jewelry? You're such a hypocrite, Mom. Now, where's Dad? I need to talk to him."

My mother doesn't look up from the careful inspection she's suddenly conducting of her feet when she answers. "He's in his study. He got an important phone call as you came through the gate."

"Thanks. And allow me to suggest that you have your own conversation with him when I'm done. I came here thinking you already knew what was going on, but it seems like you've been misguided as to the extent of the Fade fortune." I turn away, dismissing my mother. "Phoebe? Will you come in?"

She looks up at me, dumbfounded. "I... uh... yeah. Totally. I'm right behind you." I take her hand and lead her past my mother. "That was..."

I chuckle. "Yeah. It was. And I'm sorry, but it's going to get worse before it gets better. My father won't fold so easily. Do you believe me now when I tell you I'm not engaged to Annabelle?"

She nods, her eyes wide and her steps quick as she struggles to keep up with me. "I can't wait to tell Charlie about your mother bringing the alcohol to that party. That's crazy."

Hot guilt slices through my gut. "Is that guy really suspended? The cop?"

"Kaden? Umm, yeah. He really is. It's partly his fault, though. He started getting into the dancing and one of the party guests got too close. He should have been paying better attention.

He's just lucky it wasn't a criminal who lifted his gun, or he'd probably be dead by now."

I shake my head, sure I heard wrong. "Wait. Did you say he was getting into the dancing? Like, he started stripping of his own volition?"

Phoebe laughs. From what I saw in the video, he wasn't stripping, but he was shaking his ass and getting his *Magic Mike* groove on. Apparently the two of them, the cop and the security guy, used to work at a men's dance revue when they were in college. He must've missed the feeling of being objectified by women so much that he couldn't resist a little rolling of his hips for old time's sake."

I try to imagine what it would sound like to have a bunch of women screaming at me to take my clothes off, and all I get is a sense of dread. That's not for me. On the other hand, Phoebe demanding I take my clothes off? That's something I can get behind. And under. And on top of. Actually, any position will do. I'm not picky.

But first, we need to get this situation with my father cleared up. I grab her hand, lacing our fingers together, and continue down the hall. "Come on. Let's get this over with so we can get back to Lincoln. And if you believe me after all this, maybe you can convince Charlie not to castrate me? She was pretty adamant that if I didn't present you with irrefutable evidence, she would take kitchen shears to my junk."

Phoebe snickers, then fixes me with a sorry excuse for an angry glare. "Your mom had some interesting things to say, but let's wait to see what your dad says before I to step in on your behalf. There's a chance you'll still need castrating at the end of this."

I stifle the sigh of relief that threatens to make its way out of my lungs. I'm not out of the woods yet, but I can tell Phoebe is doubting her initial assessment of the situation. Hopefully, after talking to my father, she'll realize I'm not involved with anyone else, and that I didn't lie to her. Because after spending all this time with her these last few weeks, I know she's the only one I want to be involved with.

"ARCHER!" My father's voice carries down the long hallway, a testament to his anger. He doesn't normally yell, preferring to intimidate others with a calm voice, something he always told me was the best way to put fear into people. It's hard to defend yourself against someone who comes across as a robot, after all. "Where is that boy?"

My father comes storming out of his office, his face red, his shirt askew, as though he's been tugging on his tie, looking unusually disheveled. His face grows angrier when he spots me, his fists clenching and unclenching with barely contained rage. Satisfaction floods my system. He's angrier than I've ever seen him, and I know this has something to do with what my lawyer cooked up for him.

"Archer," he says as he comes to a stop in front of me and Phoebe. Instinctively, I block Phoebe with my body, not wanting to risk my father lashing out at her. "Do you care to tell me what this is all about?"

I shrug, and his face contorts with a snarl at my nonchalance. "I'm not sure what you're talking about, Father. Can you elaborate for me?"

"Your bitch of a lawyer is pressing charges against me. She can't get away with this. Does she have any idea who I am?"

I barely suppress a chuckle. "I think she does, Dad. At least, I'm sure she needed your name in order to press charges." Phoebe snickers beside me and my father's head snaps in her direction. "But that's good, right? At least she's not taking you to court for impersonating an officer of the court."

"What do you mean? I've done nothing to her."

I let the chuckle loose this time, which only enrages him further. "Oh, come on, Dad. You know you can't go around falsifying contracts and forging signatures and expect there to be no consequences, especially not when there are lawyers involved. I'm surprised she's not suing you for everything you have."

The mask of anger drops from his face, and he folds his hands together. "Well, yes. I suppose there is that." Huh, that's weird. "I'm sure you can get that all cleared up after the wedding, though."

And there it is. My eyes drift skyward. Not him, too. "That's why I'm here, actually. To clear this up once and for all."

"Clear what up?"

"Dad, this is Phoebe." I step aside while pulling out my phone. "And this is Lincoln." I show him the same picture I showed my mother moments ago. "He's my son with Phoebe. I'm not marrying Annabelle."

Dad barely looks at the picture before laughing. "That doesn't matter, son. You can keep your little tart if you want after you're married. It's what all men with money do. I can't tell you how many mistresses I've had over the years. Your mother turns a blind eye because she enjoys the life I've afforded her." He shrugs. "I'm sure Annabelle won't care if you keep banging Phyllis here, as long as you're making enough money to keep her in the lifestyle she's become accustomed. Believe me, you don't want to be stuck borrowing from friends because the things they want in return are more trouble than they're worth."

Dread settles heavily in my belly. This is my chance to get him to admit to what he's done. "Her name is Phoebe, Dad. But what do you mean? Who did you borrow from? And what do they want in return?"

My father laughs heartily, as though his panic from moments ago has completely dissipated. "Come on, Archer. I thought you would have figured that out by now. Peter Meyers got me out of the hole I found myself in, and in exchange, you will marry Annabelle."

"Oh shit," Phoebe whispers, and I nod along.

"Oh shit, is right."

Chapter 41

Not Such A Ho Ho Ho After All

Phoebe

We left Archer's parents' house with less fanfare than when we'd arrived, his father having taken his leave from us as we stood there stunned by his revelation. The man confessed to selling Archer into an arranged marriage to clear his debts and he walked away without so much as a goodbye after dropping that bomb. His mother was conspicuously absent when we took our leave as well.

God, I'm not sure whether I hope she heard what her husband said about having had so many mistresses or whether I hope she missed that part. She seemed remorseful when she realized Archer sincerely had no interest in marrying Annabelle, and I could see the sparkle in her eyes when she was looking at the picture of Lincoln. Other than her rather unflattering assessment of me, she didn't seem like an *entirely* terrible person. Is she still pretty awful? Yes. But she's not wholly unredeemable.

Archer hasn't said a word since we got back into the vehicle. He simply started driving in the opposite direction of either of our homes. If memory serves, he's driving toward the lake where many of the more affluent families in Westborough have summer homes, or in my friends Denise and Ryder's case, their year-round home away from the bustle of the city. I wonder who Archer knows out this way.

"So..." I drawl, letting the word hang in the air. I was expecting this to be an uncomfortable excursion, but not for this reason. I was worried he wouldn't convince me of his innocence and I'd have to forget about any romantic future with him because of that. I never thought I'd be forced to let him go for anything like this, though. The weight on my chest hurts makes it hard to breathe. Watching him marry someone else to get his family out of trouble is going to hurt more than if he'd been a lying scumbag. I can hate a scumbag. I *can't* hate a man for wanting to help his family. "That was... interesting."

He snorts but continues looking straight ahead, showing no other sign he heard me.

"Your mom seemed to like Lincoln's hair," I lie. "It is pretty impressive, if I do say so myself. At least I've had a lot of experience with taming mine, so when he's a teenager I'll have lots of tips if he wants to make it do anything other than sit in a puff on top of his head. These curls are no joke."

He laughs a little louder this time, the corner of his lip turning up ever so slightly. I take it as a hint to continue.

"I think she likes me," I say, plastering a huge grin on my face, ignoring the tears welling in my eyes. "At least, I think she could like me if she gave me a shot. She seemed like she wanted to see more of Lincoln, anyway."

Archer sighs. "My mom's never been the best at expressing herself. When I was really little, she was a decent mom, but when the company started making money, she changed. She started focusing on what other people would think at the expense of everything else. But when she was looking at this picture of Lincoln, for one quick moment, I thought I could see a little of that old spark in her eyes." He shrugs. "But maybe that's wishful thinking on my part. I want her to love Lincoln.

I want her to light up when she sees him. I want her to be more like... more like MaeLynn."

I nod even though he's looking at the road ahead, because I don't want to interrupt his train of thought.

"Did I tell you that my mom and MaeLynn used to be best friends? But my mom broke it off shortly after MaeLynn started working as my dad's assistant. I always thought it was because she got so full of herself that she could no longer stand to associate with 'the help'. It was like she thought MaeLynn wasn't good enough for her anymore, but I'm beginning to think it was something else."

He sinks back into himself and we're silent until he turns into the lake community about twenty minutes later. He takes the road to the private residence section of the lake and soon he's turning into a brick driveway blocked by a huge black gate. Whoever this is has better taste than Archer's parents. That golden gate back at their house rivaled the golden fountain for the title of most garish yard decor.

"Let's hope this still works," he mumbles as he leans out of the window and punches a series of numbers into a box beside the gate. The doors swing open as he sits back in his seat. "Well, looks like it's my lucky day. They haven't bothered to change it."

"Where are we?" I ask, finally giving in to my curiosity.

He opens his mouth to answer, but before he can, I see a somewhat familiar blonde standing next to a man struggling to load a giant suitcase into the back of a tiny little sports car and I have my answer. "This is where Annabelle lives."

Archer pulls the car up behind her and jumps out, walking around to my side and opening the door. He reaches his hand out and I take it. I don't know what we're here for, but the way he's acting toward me doesn't make me think of a clandestine affair. It's like he's claiming me right in front of her. Not that I would have agreed to be a mistress, but it's nice to know that even though he's stuck in this crappy situation, he's still considerate of my feelings.

My chest hurts thinking about how much I'll miss him.

"Mason?"

Archer's voice drags me from my private pity party. I look up to see him staring at the dark-haired man holding the end of the enormous trunk that's resting on the back end of the sports car. Annabelle looks between the two men, the appreciation obvious on her face as she watches when Mason sets the trunk on the ground. He clears the distance to Archer and reaches out for a handshake.

"Hey, man. What...what are you doing out here?" He doesn't look guilty, exactly, but he looks a little uncomfortable.

Archer's mouth is hanging open as his head swivels between Mason and Annabelle before his face settles into a bemused expression. "I was coming to introduce Phoebe to Annabelle and explain why I can't marry her like our fathers have arranged. This is Phoebe. Phoebe, this is my friend, Mason." Mason nods, like he's heard all about this before. "What are you doing here?"

"Oh, about that. I'm helping Annabelle with something before her parents get home."

I peek at Annabelle and find her looking at me with curiosity. She gives me a small, sad smile before joining Archer and Mason.

"Mason is driving me to rehab, Archer."

My breath leaves me in a rush. If she's going to rehab, then does that mean... does that mean Archer will want her back after all?

"You don't even like Annabelle," Archer spits at Mason, the anger plain on his face. "Why would you be driving her anywhere?"

Mason scrubs a hand over the back of his neck. "Yeah, about that."

Annabelle stomps her foot and huffs. "That's not important, Archer. I assume you're here because of the wedding? Well, I'm calling it off. I don't care what my father says, I'm not marrying you." I'd be lying if I said I wasn't relieved to hear it from her mouth and not just Archer's.

Archer throws his hands up. "*I* know that," he yells. "That's what *I'm* here to tell *you*. I had no idea you were planning a wedding until I heard you were out shopping for wedding crap today. You have no idea how much trouble that's caused me."

"What do you mean? My mother and yours dragged me all over that textile arts festival today looking for what they called 'the perfect lace' because you apparently decided we were getting married after all. You're telling me that's not true?"

Archer scoffs, a confused chuckle escaping his throat. "No. I don't want to marry you, Annabelle. Looking back, I don't think I ever wanted to. I just thought it was what I should do at my age."

I swivel my head back to Annabelle in time to see her nod, a rueful smile on her lips. "My father told me I would marry you or he would cut me off, and well..." she shrugs, her smile widening as she nods to Mason "I have enough in my own accounts to pay for this stint at rehab, and then I'll be looking for a different job, I guess. I don't care what it is, as long as it's anything but modeling. I can't keep living this way. I'm miserable."

"Oh my god! That's why you look so familiar. I've watched you in your underwear," I blurt before I can stop myself. "I'm sorry, that was weird. I meant I've seen video of you on the runway. I don't blame you for wanting a new job. It must be exhausting having people stare at you all the time."

Annabelle nods. "It really is. And the rigs that hold those wings on are so much heavier than you'd think. If I never see another feathery appendage again, it will be too soon." We share a chuckle. "And I won't be sad that I won't have to parade around in my underwear anymore."

I can see the relief as it rolls off Archer's shoulders in a wave, and this time when he smiles, it's genuine. "For what it's worth, Annabelle, I'm proud of you."

She laughs and I can't stop myself from smiling too. "Thanks. It's not worth a lot, but I'll take it. Lord knows very few other people will be proud of me when they find out."

Mason clears his throat. "About that, Annabelle. We should be leaving. Eric's parents will only be able to keep yours distracted for so long before they get suspicious. We need to get out of here before they get back."

"Wait. One more thing. Annabelle, I want you to meet Phoebe, officially. She's the mother of my child." He already has his phone out and a picture of Lincoln pulled up for Annabelle to see. "Isn't he amazing?"

Annabelle cocks an eyebrow before smiling. "Congratulations, Archer. I'm happy for you. And it's nice to meet you, Phoebe. I'm sorry we can't extend this little meeting, but we really should get going. Apparently, they're pretty strict about check-in time at rehab. Mason? Are we all set? Did you get my bags?" She doesn't wait for an answer before walking back around to the passenger side door of the car. Mason rolls his eyes and jogs over to open her door.

"I'll call you when I get back," he says to Archer as he opens his own door. "I imagine you have questions."

"So many questions." Archer nods once and watches as Mason gets in the car. "So. many. questions."

I watch Archer, not knowing what else we should be doing. It's clear to me now that he was telling the truth. It appears both he and Annabelle weren't involved in the wedding planning; rather, it was something their parents had cooked up between them as some sort of debt repayment scheme.

"So..."

"Yeah. That's not what I was expecting to happen. I was sure Annabelle had her heart set on marrying me. At least, the last time I saw her, she seemed pretty interested. She was three sheets to the wind that day, though. I wonder if that had something to do with it?"

I shrug. I don't know Annabelle enough to make any kind of guess but if what I heard from Charlie about the bachelorette party is any indication, I'd say Annabelle has, at the very least, a problem with binge drinking, which could explain some things. It's all too much for me to think about. I'm glad she's getting help, but at the end of the day, she's not my concern. That spot belongs to Lincoln. And maybe a little to Archer. If that's still what he wants, anyway.

A knot of nervous energy builds in my stomach as I work up the courage to ask him. If he says no, I'm not sure what I'll do.

Archer must sense my nervousness because he breaks the silence first. "So, how many goats do you think I was going for? How much livestock did my father get for my hand in marriage? I'm thinking it was a lot. At least fifty, for sure."

I snort a laugh, the tension broken. "Fifty? Don't sell yourself short. You're worth at least a hundred goats. Hell, he probably could have negotiated to get a few cows thrown in, too."

Laughter fills the air as Archer pulls me to him, wrapping his arms around me in a crushing hug. "Fuck, Phoebe. Thank you for sticking with me today. That was not at all how I thought it would go."

I nod against his chest, the giggles settling as I wrap my arms around his waist and squeeze. I fill my lungs with the scent of him before blowing out a breath and releasing the tension from my shoulders. "Yeah," I agree, nodding. "That was… rough."

Gripping my chin, he tilts my face up so he can look me in the eye. "I'm so sorry, Phoebe. I know that had to be hard to go through. But I hope now you understand I was never going to marry her. And it turns out she never wanted to marry me, either. Our parents fabricated the whole thing in their minds, as though there weren't messing around in the lives of two grown ass adults. I've been able to think of nothing but you since you found me again after my company party."

I nod again, my chest warming at the sincerity in his eyes, but I can't help get one more dig in. "Even with that super long rant of a voicemail?"

He groans and drops his head back, still not releasing me from his arms. "I can't believe I did that. I will do anything to make it up to you. Name it, it's yours."

I pretend to think for a moment before whispering, "Kiss me." The shock on his face gives way to a sneaky smile.

"Done." He lowers his face and brushes his lips against mine in the softest kiss, and everything clicks into place.

I thought I was simply looking for Lincoln's father, but what I was really looking for was this. The connection I felt that night with a stranger in a Santa suit. The kind of connection that I could easily fall into for the rest of my life.

Maybe I wasn't such a Ho Ho Ho, after all.

Chapter 42

Christmas Party Do-Over Again

Archer

"You've done it again, Archer. And I have to say, I think this suit is even better than last year's." MaeLynn fusses with the lapels on the velvet Santa suit I'm about to slip into as I prepare for handing out gifts at the third annual Fade Toys Family Christmas Extravaganza, pulling off stray bits of fluff that don't belong. "And think how adorable it will be for Lincoln to have his picture taken with his Santa Daddy."

I roll my eyes and take a sip of fortifying Scotch. "Haven't I told you a hundred times not to call me that? It's too weird."

"Pshh," she says, flapping a hand at me. "It's cute and you know it. Now, put this on and let me get a look at you." She holds out the jacket, sliding it up my arms before spinning me. She straightens the lapels before patting my cheek and smiling indulgently. "There. Such a handsome Santa Claus. I've done my duty. I'll see you down there."

MaeLynn has been a godsend this past year. It's hard to believe that last year around this time, I was still having trouble with my parents and their attempts to force me to marry Annabelle with threats of taking over Fade Toys. All it took was my lawyer threatening to sue my father's lawyer for the entire plan to fall apart. It all boiled down to money. My parents had been living far above their means for far too long, and when Annabelle's father bailed my father out of his poor investments, he demanded I marry his daughter to take her off his hands while keeping her accustomed to her life of leisure. My father and his lawyer came up with the plan to falsify the documents involving the transfer of the business in order to force my hand. Now they're both suffering the consequences and spending a few years in a minimum security prison. Not the most arduous of punishments, but it's enough.

"Hey, man. You almost ready? The crowd's getting rowdy." Eric walks into the hotel room and looks me up and down. "Looking good, fat man. I like this suit better than the last one. It's very Kris Kringle."

Okay, so I may have leaned into the Elvish style of Santa Claus like the young man we tried to visit last year for Lincoln's first Christmas. In my defense, it was too magical to resist. I even hired a designer to recreate the magical forest theme for the banquet room downstairs. I have Damien and his wife to thank for that. If she hadn't caught him stealing from her tree farm last year, I don't know where we would have found the number of trees and branches the designer needed to pull this off.

"Thanks, I'm a pretty big fan of this look myself." I look past him to where Mason is waiting at the door. "Hey. Glad you made it. Did Annabelle come with you?"

Mason's mouth forms a line. "She said it was too weird, but thanks anyway. I think your company Christmas party in particular holds some bad memories for her she's not ready to deal with. These things take time."

I never would have guessed Annabelle would take matters into her own hands after the arranged marriage debacle by cutting ties with her family and taking herself to rehab. She's no longer the spoiled model she once was, and she's proven to be a decent friend to Phoebe after everything. And best of all, she's still sober.

"Yeah, I thought that might be the case, but I wanted to extend the invitation just in case. She's always welcome."

Mason nods. "Thanks, Archer. That means a lot. She hasn't forgiven herself for the trouble she caused while she was drinking, and there are too many memories tied up with you and this party for her to deal with right now. She said she'd still be at your place for Christmas Eve dinner, though."

"I get it. It's a hard road she's on. I'm sure my opinion's still not worth a damn, but I am proud of her. So is Phoebe." After Annabelle's stint in rehab last year, she's turned over a completely new leaf. She quit modeling, moved out of her parents' house and into a tiny apartment, and took a job at Mason's bar. I didn't think working in a bar would be an appropriate choice for someone with a drinking problem, but Mason's made it work all these years, so I'd say she's in good hands.

Mason clears his throat and looks away after giving me a tight nod. I know he's proud of Annabelle, too, because he never shuts up about how amazing he thinks she is. I'm about to tell him how glad I am she has him in her life when he interrupts. "Anyway, Annabelle wanted me to stop by to tell you she couldn't make it. I need to get back to the bar. She's covering for me for a little while, but I still don't like leaving her alone too long in there." He gives me a wave before heading back out the door.

Eric claps his hands together. "We need to get going, too. Unsurprisingly, the employees of your sex toy factory have a shit ton of kids, and they're all eager to see Santa Claus. I suppose it only makes sense that people who work with sex toys all day enjoy fucking so much." He shoots me a sly look and taps a finger against his chin. "Hey, that reminds me. Doesn't your mom work on the factory floor now?"

I choke on air while Eric laughs his ass off because he's right. She does work on the factory floor now, in the quality control department. There's not a dildo that leaves Fade Toys that my mother hasn't touched, a fact I try to forget every day. But that doesn't mean she needs to be lumped in with Eric's incorrect assessment of my employees' fondness for sex. At least, I don't want to hear about it.

When my father's illegal dealings came to light, and she'd heard his confession of his many infidelities, my mother finally left him. After a brief adjustment period, she's been living contentedly within her means ever since. The best part is, now that she relies on the paycheck and benefits supplied by Fade Toys, she better understands what a living wage means to a person. When you're responsible for all your own expenses, you really appreciate working for a company that takes care of its employees.

Hell, she's made a complete turnaround from the person she used to be. She's even taken steps to be a better mother to me, while being a grandmother to Lincoln, something MaeLynn has been helping her with since they rekindled their friendship. MaeLynn was quick to forgive when my mother apologized for destroying their friendship so many years ago. She explained she wasn't ready to face my father's infidelity at that time, and her only option was to cut MaeLynn out of her life so she could pretend it had never happened.

I snort a laugh when he waggles his brows at me. Choosing to ignore the comment about my mother, lest he continue down that line of thinking, I focus on the other comment about my employees' large families. "People who have secure jobs where they're supported and taken care of have a lot of love to share. Fade Toys has given them the ability to support families if that's what they choose to do. It has nothing to do with liking sex."

Eric rolls his eyes. "Sure it doesn't," he drawls.

I'm still shaking my head as we leave the hotel room and head down to the party. All that's left is to distribute the gifts. Once again, I've gone way overboard for all the kids, but only with the permission of their parents, of course. I still don't want to step on anyone's toes.

"I'll go out and let them know you're here," Eric says, stepping through the curtain to the front of the makeshift stage. He pokes his head back through the curtain. "Don't take too long. I wasn't kidding when I said they're getting rowdy." He goes back out front and yells, "Get ready, kids. Here comes Santa Claus."

I can't help but smile when the sound of kids cheering meets my ears. This is the cherry on the top of the sundae that is my job with Fade Toys. Making the Christmas party something that all the staff and their families can attend is one of the first things I did when I took over, and it's still one of my favorites. Other than the living wage, benefits, and more supportive direction I took the company in over all, anyway. This party is pure fun for everyone, but I don't think there's anyone who loves it more than I do.

With a quick tug on my fake beard and an adjustment of the small belly I have strapped under my costume, I step through the curtain to see the shining, cheerful faces of hundreds of kids smiling up at me. Okay, it's not hundreds, but it's at least fifty. Fifty-seven, to be exact. I know, because I bought all the gifts myself. And now I get to give them all away. I can't wait.

"Well, would you look at that? This makes three times I've found a handsome man in a red suit at this hotel. This place must have Christmas magic flowing on tap."

Phoebe wanders up to me as I finish tidying up the banquet room, still in most of my Santa gear after another successful holiday party. Even Lincoln visited with me three times while I was in costume, and I'm happy to say he didn't cry once. That might have had something to do with MaeLynn keeping him distracted with sugary Christmas treats, but I'm still going to take it as a win. At least he didn't scream when he saw me like he did when he saw that other Santa. And he won't get the chance to this year, either, since MaeLynn insisted on taking him for a sleepover with her other grandkids tonight. She packed them all up a little over an hour ago and brought them back to her house for the night. She even brought my mother with her for moral support. Two grandmas are better than one, I guess.

Which is extra lucky for me, because I have plans for the redheaded beauty in front of me. Big plans.

"Hmmm," I say, pulling her in close, running my nose up the column of her neck, and dropping a soft kiss in the hollow behind her ear. "I'd say I'm the lucky one. The first time you found me, I got to have what was, until that point, the best night of my life. The second time you found me, it began the series of events that brought you back into my life. Not to mention I got Lincoln along with you. And now, the third time you find me, well... let's just say I'm hoping to relive that first night with a lot more sobriety. I plan to remember every second this time around." She responds by wrapping her arms around my neck and pressing her body close to mine, her soft curves leaving me breathless.

"Good thing I'm not in that wedding dress, then," she teases, running her hands through the hair at the back of my neck. "Leggings might not be the most fashionable attire, but there are at least a hundred fewer buttons to undo before getting to the goods. I'm a little sad the beard is gone, though. I was curious what it would be like to kiss a man with a long beard."

I chuckle nervously, my stomach turning itself into a knot. She doesn't know, but the beard she's talking about is currently in my pocket with the moss agate engagement ring I had my mother's former jeweler design for me.

My mom might not be living a life of luxury any longer, but she still has a few of the friends she made along the way. Funny how the only people who stuck around those who were the furthest from the society types she was always trying to impress. Regardless, I'm happy she was still in touch with the jeweler because the ring I envisioned for Phoebe wasn't something that could be found in just any jewelry store. Not that I need it to stab her if she tries to take it off, or anything. I'm not nuts. But I had a particular vision in mind, and the jeweler executed it perfectly. Now I need to wait for the perfect moment to drop to my knees and pledge my life to her. No big deal.

I inhale deeply, the scent of Phoebe working to calm me as it always does. "I'll put it back on when we get upstairs, if it's important to you," I tease. "If I'd known you had a beard kink, I'd have grown a real one long ago."

She laughs, extricating herself from my arms. "Nah, don't do that. I'm not sure I want to know what a beard burn is like, you know"—she drags her eyes from one end of the banquet room to the other, ensuring we're alone, before settling on my eyes and whispering dramatically—"between my thighs."

I'm instantaneously hard, the blood rushing to my dick at dizzying speed. Thank god we're the last ones here. I don't need my employees and their families seeing me tenting my pants because my sexy as hell girlfriend merely mentioned that sweet spot at the apex of her thighs.

Phoebe presses herself against me briefly before stepping out of my arms. "I guess I'll leave you to it," she says, dancing out of my reach. "I'll head upstairs and you can join me when you're ready."

Chapter 43

Santa Makes An Honest Woman Out Of Me

Phoebe

I BARELY MADE IT to the banquet room doors before Archer ran up behind me and swept me off my feet. Literally. One second I stood on my own two feet and the next Archer carried me in his arms as he ran to the elevator.

"That wasn't very nice," he says with a hint of a growl in his voice. "I can't believe you would tease me and run off like that."

"Who me?" I try to suppress a giggle, but Archer isn't falling for it.

"You knew exactly what you were doing. Tell me. How do you think I should I punish you for that?"

A shiver of anticipation runs through me. Archer's punishments usually result in many orgasms for me, so I'm not complaining. And he's right. I knew what I was doing when I was deliberately goading him like that.

What can I say? It's the first night we've had alone in ages. Who could blame me for wanting to start the night off with a bang?

"I'm sure you can figure something out."

"Hmm." The elevator doors open and Archer carries me inside. "I'm sure I can."

He lowers me to feet before pressing the button to our floor, not taking his eyes off me the entire time. Heat builds in my belly even while another shiver runs through me.

I step to the back of the elevator, and watch as he stalks toward me, all lithe muscle and naughty intent.

If you'd asked me a year ago what I'd be doing this Christmas, I would have told you I'd be at my parents' house in Fallbridge getting ready for our normal Christmas celebration. I definitely wouldn't have thought I'd be eagerly anticipating a night with my son's father, now my partner, while two of his loving grandmothers—yes, I consider MaeLynn his grandmother—spoil him rotten at a sleepover with a bunch of their other grandkids.

Every day since I found Archer is almost too good to be true. I'm so happy I…I—oh, shit. Not again. Not now.

"What's this?" He cups my cheek with the palm of his hand, his thumb softly swiping under my eye and coming away wet. "Why are you crying?"

I shrug. "I'm so—" I choke on a sob. "I'm so happy." I gulp a breath, trying to calm myself, but I break down instead. Huge, shuddering sobs tear through me as fat, salty tears roll down my face.

Archer wraps his arms around me and holds me close. "Yeah, I can tell." He chuckles. "Uncontrollable weeping in elevators is one of the better known symptoms of happiness in a person."

I laugh through a sniffle and poke him in the side. "Shut up. I am happy. I was thinking how—" I sniffle loudly "—lucky it was that I found you. And then the tears started coming and I couldn't stop them. But they're happy tears, I swear."

A soothing hand rubs circles on my back. “I know, baby. I know. Why don’t we go back to the room and get something to eat?” His voice is laced with concern. “Did you have any food at the party?”

I shake my head. “No. My stomach felt a little queasy. I didn’t want to risk being the one puking at your party. I figured I should leave that up to the kids who’ve been stuffing their faces with all the Christmas goodies you have out.”

He pulls back to look at me, concern written all over his face. “Well, that’s it then. We’ll get something to eat, then you’ll feel better. Then you can smile when you’re happy, like normal. Instead of crying and making me think there’s something seriously wrong.”

“Yeah.” I nod half-heartedly. “That sounds good.” But it doesn’t sound good at all. This is not what I wanted to happen when we first came back to our room tonight. We have a limited amount of time and I’m planning to make the most of it.

The elevator stops moving, and the doors open up on our floor. Archer laces his fingers with mine and leads me into our room.

“I’m going to get out of this suit,” he says, leaving me next to the bed while he walks toward the bathroom. “Then we can kick back, order some room service, and watch a Christmas movie.”

“But...but...we can’t waste this night. MaeLynn and your mom are watching Lincoln. We have the entire night to ourselves. We can’t sit around, eating food and watching movies. We have to take advantage of this time while we have it.” I close the distance between us, stopping in front of him. “So why don’t you let me help you out of this suit?” I slide a finger under his suspender strap and slip it down over his shoulder. “And then you can help me out of my clothes and we can see what happens after that. How does that sound?” I slide the other suspender strap down and pull his shirt from his pants. “Hmm?”

His Adam's apple bobs as he swallows, a muted groan filling this space between us. I slip my hands inside his shirt, reaching around the back to unbuckle the fake stomach he wore as Santa. I drop it to the floor.

"That's better. Now I can touch your skin." I drag my nails up his belly, loving the shiver that runs through him at my touch. "Isn't this so much better than watching TV?"

I palm his length through his pants, making his head drop back against the bathroom door in a moan. "Fuck, Phoebe."

"That's the plan, Archer. Now, are you going to get me out of these clothes, or do I have to do everything myself?"

He snaps his head up, his eyes black with desire, and my stomach alights with a riot of butterflies. "Oh, honey. I'll be taking care of everything for you tonight. I know what you like."

His hands slip under my shirt and he rips it up over my head, forcing a laugh from me. He does the same with my leggings and underwear, sliding them down and off before I can react. He slides his arms around me and unfastens my bra, dropping it to the floor. He uses his grip on me to spin us, then presses me against the door.

He grabs a handful of hair at the back of my neck and tilts my head up. "Get on your knees," he whispers as he runs his nose up the column of my throat.

My eyes widen at his harsh words, but a punch of lust hits me in the gut and my core throbs with need.

"My knees?"

He nods and a wicked grin creeps onto his face. "It's time for you to apologize for teasing me the way you did. Now, get on your knees, Phoebe. Don't make me ask you again."

I waste no time dropping to my knees and reaching for his pants again. He pulls back.

"Ah ah. I'll do that. Put your hands on the door behind you." My stomach tightens deliciously and I flatten my hands to the door. "Good girl."

Oh god. A rush of heat floods my panties, and I clench around nothing. *Why do I like this so much?*

Archer takes another step back, unzipping his pants and shoving them and his boxers down to rest at the top of his thighs. He grips himself and gives a firm stroke. A groan crawls up my throat at the sight.

His dick is as beautiful this time as it is every time. Hard, long, and thick, and sprouting from a nest of neatly trimmed dark curls. Moisture beads on the engorged head, and my mouth waters, anticipating the taste.

"Open your mouth, Phoebe." Archer leans over me, one hand on the door frame above my head, the other stroking his dick with long, slow, measured strokes. My mouth drops open so fast I surprise myself. "That's it. Tongue out, sweetheart."

I let my tongue fall to the front of my mouth and Archer pushes his hips until he's touching the tip with the crown of his dick. His salty, musky taste explodes on my tongue and I can't stop my mouth from watering.

"You're going to stay very still for me, aren't you, Phoebe?" He looks down at me, his eyes black with lust as he wraps my hair around his fist. He must see my answer on my face. "That's my good girl. Open up."

The moan he makes as he slides into my mouth, right to the back of my throat, is so beautifully obscene I nearly come from the sound of it alone. The wetness between my thighs coats my legs as I press them together in search of relief.

"Ah-ah." He pulls out until he's barely touching my lips, leaving me straining to reach him. "Legs apart, baby. This is your punishment, remember?" I rush to spread my knees, adjusting my position so I don't lose contact with him for a moment. "That's better. Keep your legs spread and your hands against the door."

I nod and hum my assent. The throbbing in my clit is so strong, my orgasm threatens to crest every time I clench around nothing. Without warning, Archer slides himself to the back of my throat, and I swallow hard against the intrusion, his answering groan causing me to clench and throb even harder.

"Fuck, Phoebe. You look so beautiful like this. You take my cock so well, don't you, sweetheart?" I hum around his length, loving the way he twitches in response. He pulls back before thrusting back into my throat, his grip on my hair holding me still while he fucks into me. "Oh... Jesus, babe. Your mouth feels so damn good."

I suck him back as deeply as I can without being able to use my hands, encouraging him with my moans to get in deeper. He obliges by fisting his other hand into my hair and fucking into my face hard enough for it to be just this side of painful. *Yes, that's what I want.* Holding me tightly, he pumps into my mouth, pressing my face against his body with each thrust.

"Oh god, Phoebe. You love this as much as I do, don't you? I can smell your arousal. Look at me, sweetheart. Give me your eyes." He slows, pressing himself into my mouth, then dragging himself out with aching precision as I look up at him. "When I'm finished with your mouth, I'm going to pick you up off your knees"—he makes another slow pump in and takes a deep, shuddering breath—"carry you to the bed"—he drags his dick out slowly, and exhales while staring directly into my eyes—"and feast on your pussy until your legs shake and you can't stop screaming my name."

He buries himself in the back of my throat, coming with a groan as I swallow reflexively around him until he's completely spent. His grip on my hair loosens, and he slides himself from my mouth.

"You have no idea how much I love that," he whispers before pulling me to my feet. "I accept your apology. Now get up here."

He bends low and throws me over his shoulder, forcing a laugh from me. "I'm not all that sorry, you know."

He shrugs, hoisting me higher. "And we both know that wasn't really a punishment." He drops me on the bed and crawls over me, trailing kisses as he goes. When he reaches my neck, he drops a long, sucking kiss below my ear, setting a pulse throbbing between my legs and leaving me clenching around nothing again. "And we also know that this is my favorite place to be." Archer slides his hand down my body, igniting tingles as he goes, before sliding his fingers into me, touching that spot inside that only he's ever reached. He covers my lips with his and licks into my mouth with a featherlight touch. "Now, let's move on to the second part of my plan, shall we? Because if I have to wait any longer to taste you, I think I might explode."

He dives down my body, throws my legs over his shoulders, and buries his face in me, sucking my clit into his mouth, hard. I arch off the bed, the spike of pleasure nearly instantaneous, and he only has to circle my clit with his tongue once before sparks are shooting behind my eyelids and I'm screaming his name.

"Archer. Oh my god, please don't stop."

Epilogue

Archer

"You know what would be amazing right about now? Some of that pie we had last year. Remember? It was that pie you brought Charlie for Christmas." Phoebe is looking over the room service menu, trying to decide what to order. "Oooh, or some of that curry you brought over for lunch that one day. Remember that?"

After fulfilling my promise to make her scream my name, and her laying on the bed near-comatose for a good half hour after that, she jumped up, slipped on my shirt, and dug the room service menu out the drawer. For the last twenty minutes, she has been asking my opinion on the menu and reminiscing about the food we've shared in the past. If she doesn't decide soon, the kitchen will close. And given her current interest in foods that aren't listed on the menu, I think that's likely to happen.

And I know for a fact if I don't get some food in her soon, she won't be in any shape to hear the speech I've been planning almost since the moment she walked back into my life after last year's Fade Toys Christmas party. Her stomach growls loudly, forcing me into action.

With a sigh, I roll out of bed. Phoebe quirks an eyebrow and licks her lips, clearly appreciating my nakedness, which my dick likes a little too much. I don't have time to explore that right now, not if I'm going to get her any of the dishes she's craving.

"Eyes to yourself, sweetheart." I grab my boxers from the floor and slip them on. "I'll go out and get us something to eat. Why don't you relax for a bit until I get back?" I pull on my Santa pants and the shirt I was wearing before I changed into my costume. "It's been a long day."

I take her into my arms and kiss her neck, inhaling the salty scent of her skin. God, I don't think I could love this woman any more than I do right now. My heart has never felt this full.

"Yeah. That sounds good. Maybe I'll take advantage of that jacuzzi tub I saw in the bathroom. It might be nice to have a bath without Lincoln and Cooper busting in to drop their toys in the water."

A few months ago, we finally moved into our house at the lake. We took a page from one of the Sleeping Dogs guys and had our realtor knock on doors until we found someone willing to sell. The first weekend after we moved in, we adopted Cooper from the animal shelter and it's been nothing but chaos ever since.

"Not to mention, there's zero risk of Cooper deciding to share your bath with you. Who knew golden retrievers loved water that much? The videos online make it seem like dirty puddles are more their thing."

Phoebe laughs. "Don't underestimate Cooper's love for dirty puddles. The last time he jumped in my bath was after he'd been rolling around in that hole he keeps digging in the yard. I needed an extra long shower to get all the mud off me after that one."

"No matter what I do to fill that darn thing, he's right back out there digging it up again the next time it rains." I shake my head. "I think it might be time to bust out the concrete. Okay, it's settled. You have a relaxing bath while I track down something for us to eat."

Eric

Well. Did you ask her?

Archer

Not yet. I'm out on a food run. She wanted a variety of very specific food items that the hotel didn't have.

Eric

Interesting. You must be terrible in bed if she's thinking about food right now. Didn't you pack any toys? You own a sex toy factory. That's pretty much an unlimited arsenal.

You should have brought the Christmas trees from your mantle.

Too soon? LOL

After the Christmas tree butt plug fiasco of last Christmas, I wasn't sure what Phoebe would want to do with the toys this year. I wasn't even sure she had kept them, to be honest. I thought maybe she'd been too embarrassed to want them around and had thrown them out instead of packing them up at the end of the holiday season. I'm sure you can imagine my surprise when she unpacked them and placed them on the mantle in our new house when we were decorating this year.

But that doesn't mean I want my asshole best friend teasing her about it.

Archer

Shut up. Asshole.

Eric

LOL

Let me know when you finally ask. I don't want to send a congratulations text until we know she's said yes. There's a still a chance she'll come to her senses.

Archer

Why are you my best friend again?

Eric

Because you love me.

And none of the other guys will put up with your shit like I do.

I chuckle and grab the food bags from the seat of my car. There's a chance I called in a few favors to get everything Phoebe wanted. There's also a chance that the three bags I'm carrying into the hotel cost way more than this amount of food has any right to. But that doesn't matter. The woman I love wants certain foods, so I get them, even if I have to pay a late night holiday premium for them.

Eric's texts are running through my brain the entire trip back up to the hotel room. The ring is still burning a hole in my pocket, and I'm not sure how I'm going to ask the question. The only thing I'm sure about is that I need to do it tonight. I can't wait much longer without asking Phoebe Fox, the love of my life, the mother of my son, to be my wife.

First things first, though. I need to get her fed before the hangry *really* kicks in.

"Phoebe?" I call out as I enter the hotel room and set the bags on a table. "Food's here."

"I'm still in the bath," she yells back. "No kids' toys and no muddy dogs. It's pretty much heaven. I've added hot water three times since you left. I'll be right out, though. I'm starving."

It does sound like heaven, but not for the reasons she thinks. No. The reason that bathtub is heaven is that right now it's occupied by the most amazing woman to ever walk the earth.

And I'm getting carried away. I need to ask Phoebe to marry me before I revert to a pimply faced teenager and start writing her awful love poems. My heart rate increases and my mouth goes dry. I'm nervous. *Now. I have to do it now.*

"Hey. You alright?" Phoebe steps out of the bathroom wearing a fluffy hotel robe, her hair in a loose pile on top of her head. She is so beautiful. She runs a hand up my arm and into my hair as she looks back and forth between my eyes. "Is everything okay?"

I wrap her tightly in my arms, ducking to bury my face in her neck. "Everything is perfect. You're perfect."

She chuckles and runs her hand through my hair. "I mean, I am pretty impressive. But I wouldn't say I'm perfect."

This is it. I'm doing this. I inhale deeply, Phoebe's scent filling my nose, then step back and take her hands in mine.

"You're better than pretty impressive, Phoebe. You're everything I've ever wanted. You're gorgeous, that's obvious, but you're so much more than that. You're loving. You're kind. You're a wonderful mom to Lincoln. You're the best partner for me. And you're hilarious. When we met that night at the hotel bar, I didn't know it, but my life was about to change for the better. I laughed harder that night than I had in years. Years,

Phoebe. The stress of my life washed away that night because of you. No matter how hard everything was, you made it better for those blissful hours we spent together."

Her eyes search mine, and I smile. "And then you disappeared. While you were gone, I felt something was missing, but I couldn't figure out what. So I buried myself in work. Spent all my time making Fade Toys something to be proud of. And I am. I'm so proud of what I've done with Fade Toys. But it doesn't hold a candle to how proud I am that I get to love you. Or how proud I am of being Lincoln's dad. I know it's not what either of us expected that night, but I am so thankful that we got Lincoln from it. And that having Lincoln led you to find me again."

"I'm so glad I found you, too. What's this all about, Archer? You're freaking me out."

I bring her hands up and place a kiss on each palm before sliding down to one knee. "Phoebe Fox, everything in my life is better because you're in it. You showed me what being part of a family should feel like. You gave me a son. Phoebe, I wake up every day knowing I'm the luckiest man on earth because I have you next to me. And I want you to be next to me always. Phoebe Fox, will you marry me?"

I slide the ring out of my pocket and offer it to her with a shaky hand. Her face is blank, and I can't tell if she's stunned in a good way, or a bad way. My stomach clenches with a stab of fear. Maybe Phoebe isn't ready for this. But when her face splits in a brilliant grin, and all my worries disappear.

"Yes, of course I'll marry you." She drags me to my feet and throws her arms around my neck. "I love you, Archer."

"I love you, Phoebe. I love you so fucking much." I smash my lips against hers in a fierce kiss, letting our tongues dance. A moment later, her stomach growls. I break away with a chuckle. "Now, will you put this ring on so I can get some food into you?"

She holds her hand out and I slide the ring on. "Oh wow, Archer. This is so beautiful." Phoebe holds her hand up to admire the ring before a sad smile crosses her face. "It's a shame I'll only be able to wear it for a few months before I'll have to take it off."

My thoughts screech to a halt, and it's suddenly hard to drag in a breath. "Take it off? Wha...what do you mean?"

Her smile becomes radiant. "Relax, it won't be forever. It will only be until the swelling goes down."

I shake my head. Nothing she's saying makes sense. "Swelling? What swelling? What are you talking about?"

She rolls her eyes and laughs. "Do I need to spell it out for you? Here. I have a visual aid. One sec."

She goes into the bathroom, then returns a moment later with a white pen-like object. "So, I'm not sure if you've noticed, but I've been a little off lately. Extra hungry, extra tired, extra cranky?" I hold her gaze, forcing my head to remain still rather than nodding in agreement like I want to. She's been a little strange the last few weeks, but she said she wasn't feeling well, so I put it down to that. "Anyway. I had my suspicions, so I brought this with me and took it while you were out getting food. Here."

I take the object and look at the screen. One word is written there: pregnant.

Every thought flies out of my head, leaving that one word.

Pregnant.

Phoebe smiles expectantly, her eyebrows raised. "Well?"

I look down at the stick again, then back at Phoebe. "You're serious? You're really pregnant?"

She nods, the grin never leaving her face. "You kind of stole my thunder with the proposal. I should have guessed what you were up to and told you sooner."

My face breaks into a smile so huge it's about to split wide open. "No. No, no. This is too amazing. Oh my god, Phoebe. We need to tell everyone. Now. Right now." I pat my pockets again and again before finally finding my phone and pulling it out.

Phoebe tries to take it from me, but before she can, I've pressed the button to call Eric.

"So? Did you do it yet?"

"I did. She said yes. But that's not the best part. She's pregnant, dude. We're having another kid."

"I knew it! Called it. Damien owes me twenty bucks."

"You bet on Phoebe being pregnant?"

Eric's laugh comes through the phone. *"We bet on whether you'd manage to propose before she got pregnant again. And since you only asked her to marry your dumb ass tonight, well, that means she was pregnant before."*

I snort a laugh. "You know what? I don't even care that you made a bet. I'm going to be a dad again. I have to go. More people to call."

I hang up with Eric laughing in the background and dial Webster and Frederick next.

"Archer! Merry Christmas. How was the party? Did you ask her? Tell me how much she loved the ring."

"Webster, put me on speaker. Frederick needs to hear this, too."

"Okay. You're on speaker. Go ahead."

"She said yes, but it gets better. She's pregnant. We're having another baby."

"I knew her boobs looked bigger," Webster says with a laugh. *"I can't believe she hid it from me."*

"Tell me, Archer," Frederick interjects, his voice serious. *"If you're newly engaged,* and you *just found out your new fiancée is pregnant, why are you on the phone with us?"*

"Oh, shit." I spin around and spot Phoebe dishing food out of a takeout container, her mouth already full of something as she grins at me.

"Don't worry about me. You go ahead with your phone calls." She shoves another bite of food into her mouth. "This is so good."

"She's fine. She's stuffing her face with Butter Chicken at the moment."

"Hey. She's growing your child. She deserves to stuff her face if she wants to." Webster laughs through his defense of Phoebe's eating habits. *"You better keep her well fed."*

"Archer. Listen carefully. I'm going to hang up this call and when I do, you will go back to Phoebe. Do not call anyone else. Do you understand me? This is a special night for the two of you. Don't ruin it by being even more of an idiot."

Oh, shit. I am an idiot. Frederick is right. I should be spending this time with Phoebe.

Damn it. Leave it to Frederick to be the voice of reason, as usual.

"Gotta go, guys. Talk later." I stab the end call button and drop my phone on the dresser. "Hey, sweetheart. How's the food?"

Phoebe nods and gives me a thumbs up. "Better than I remembered." She swallows and wipes her mouth with a napkin. "So, which one gave you shit? Was it Frederick? It was Frederick, wasn't it? He's always so sensible."

I cringe. "Yeah. Sorry about all that." I pull up a chair and sit next to her. "I got a little carried away."

She shrugs, taking my hand in hers. "It's fine. You're excited. I am, too. After all, how many people can say they're having Santa's baby, again?"

With a chuckle, I lean forward and touch my forehead to hers. As far as I'm concerned, she can have Santa's baby as many times as she wants. I should have known that first night that we were destined to be Santa and his Bride again.

Only this time, I can guarantee she'll go through with the wedding before sleeping with Santa Claus on her wedding night.

THE END

Thank you so much for reading Santa's Baby. I hope you had as much fun reading it as I did writing it. I'd love if you could leave a review on Amazon or Goodreads.

Want to know more about the guys in Sleeping Dogs and the women they love? Check out the Sleeping Dogs series.

If you're interested in being updated when future books are released (ahem Xena and Devon, Eric and Charlie, Kaden and ?) sign up for my newsletter

Read on for an excerpt from Second Chance (Sleeping Dogs Book 1)

Excerpt From Second Chance (Sleeping Dogs Book 1)

Chapter One – Shitty Jobs and Shittier Boyfriends

Alex

"Son of a bitch." I stomp my way to my car after slamming the door behind me. I rip off my chef's jacket and throw it into the passenger seat, along with my knife roll. These assholes may have sent me home, but I should have left long ago. And not just for today, but permanently.

I've had it up to my ass with my latest clients, the dirty old pervert and his not-quite-young-enough-to-be-a-trophy wife. He keeps trying to grab my ass, and she keeps trying to blame me for it. I really need this job, but I'm not sure how much longer I'll be able to keep my mouth shut about the harassment.

I pull my hair out of its high bun and scratch my fingers along my scalp to help ease some tension. It's amazing the stress a tight hairstyle can cause. Once I'm mostly calm, I turn on some angry music to finish soothing me—what can I say? Angry music calms me—and drive home to the apartment I share with my boyfriend. Well, it's probably more accurate to say I live in his apartment, rather than share it with him, considering he's been there for years and I recently moved in. It doesn't feel much like mine since almost everything in it belongs to him, anyway.

I stop to check the mail in the lobby on my way in before taking the elevator to the fourth floor where our apartment is. Since I'm off work early, I think I may as well put the time to good use. I'm distracted with thoughts of the hot bath I'm going to take and the amazing meal I'm going to cook when I put the key in the lock of my apartment door and find there is no resistance when I turn it. That's weird. I'm pretty sure I locked it when I left the house this morning. Or am I remembering yesterday?

A loud bang from inside the apartment makes me jump.

Oh Shit! Someone's in there! I'm being robbed! What do I do? I can't let someone take all of Derek's stuff that he's worked so hard for. Holding my breath, I reach for my phone as quietly as I can and call my best friend Becca.

"Becca, it's me. I got home early and there's someone in my apartment. I think I'm being robbed," I whisper.

I inch open the door and creep in, reaching for the first weapon-like item I can find when my fingers wrap around a curved handle. Looks like the cute ladybug umbrella I keep for rainy days is about to see a different kind of action. I suppose I could use one of the knives I'm already carrying, but like hell I'm going to get dirty burglar blood on one of my professional knives and risk it being locked up as evidence.

I couldn't afford to replace it if that happened. Working as a personal chef hasn't been as lucrative as I'd hoped, but it sure beats the long hours of grueling labor I'd have to put in working in some other chef's kitchen. When you're not partaking in illegal stimulants, kitchen hours are unmanageable and, unfortunately, I've always preferred coffee to cocaine.

"What? Did you call the police? Get out of there, you're going to get hurt. I'm serious. Don't do anything stupid."

"I'm fine," I whisper, hoisting up my umbrella. "I have a weapon."

"Like what? I know for a fact you won't dirty up one of your work knives, and those are the only things you'd have with you that could work." She knows me too well.

"I have an umbrella. I'll be fine, promise."

I hear another loud bang coming from somewhere in the back of the apartment, so I tiptoe in that direction.

"An umbrella? Have you lost your mind? Get out of there, Alex. I swear to god if you die trying to catch a burglar, I'm going to kill you!" Becca shrieks as she attempts to talk me out of what I'm about to do.

Also, threatening to kill me if I die? Not the smartest thing she's ever said. Of course, attempting to catch a burglar in the act instead of waiting for the police is far from the smartest thing I've ever done, so I'd say we're even.

"Shhhh, he'll hear you, and I need to catch this asshole intruder by surprise." Nobody messes with me and Derek and gets away with it. "This guy's going to feel my wrath and that of my ladybug umbrella."

I creep forward, choosing the placement of each foot carefully so I make the least amount of noise. A giggling sound stops me dead in my tracks. It's coming from further back in the apartment, like from the bedroom.

I groan inwardly and lower my umbrella. *Oh, come on, not again. I thought Derek was different. I mean, sure, he works a lot and barely has time for me and he thinks my cooking is a hobby, but still. He asked me to move in. I thought he was serious about me. Apparently, though, he's just like all the rest of them.*

My mind quickly races through all the boyfriends who've cheated on me. Which is all of them, in case you were wondering. I refuse to relive the shitty details, but yes, I caught most of them in the act, and yes, I ended it with all of them.

It's exactly as depressing as it sounds.

And now Derek is fucking someone in our bed when he's supposed to be at work. When we're both supposed to be at work.

"That motherfucker," I whisper yell into the phone. "Becca, come over, now."

"I'm already on my way. What is it? What's wrong? Are you hurt? Should I call 911?" Becca is freaking out. If she doesn't lower her voice, all the neighborhood dogs will come running. Actually, now that I think about it, that could benefit me. I've never had a pack of dogs attack a cheating boyfriend before. It might be fun to watch.

You might hear that and think I'm being callous and, well, you would be right. I am. I've been through this so many times now I almost find it enjoyable to find new and clever ways to get back at the cheaters once I've caught them. Not that I want it to keep happening for that reason, but you know what they say. When life hands you cheating lemons, beat the shit out of them until you get lemonade. Or something like that. I'm not great with sayings. The point is, putting my heart on the line for the chance of getting revenge isn't something that interests me. Sadly, I actually kind of like the guys before they end up cheating. But I suck at picking them.

Becca's car revs in the background. Good. If this is actually happening, I'm going to need backup. I creep up to the bedroom door and stop outside of it. I force myself to stop breathing and try to listen closely, my ear pressed to the door.

"You like that, huh? You like my cock in you, you dirty slut?"

Well, fuck. That's Derek, alright. He likes to talk dirty, even though I've never thought he's all that great at it. My body gets numb all over, and then a burning rage sears a hole in my chest. You think I'd be completely numb to this by now, but the betrayal always hurts at least a little.

"Becca? It's happening again."

"That asshole! I'm five minutes away, Alex. Make sure you save some for me. I'm going to take pleasure in beating his ass."

"He won't last another five minutes, Becca. I need to go in now. He doesn't have that kind of stamina. Believe me, my less-than-satisfying love life is proof of that."

She chuckles a little at my confession. Maybe she thinks I'm making a joke at Derek's expense, but I'm really not. He's not quite a two-pump chump, but he's pretty damn close.

"Yeah, Derek, harder, harder! It feels so good, your cock is so big," the dirty slut, his words, not mine, screams as I continue to listen at the door. Derek's dick is mediocre on a good day so either this chick has the tightest pussy on earth or she's lying.

I'm going with lying.

No one's pussy is *that* tight. Plus, I'm pretty sure I can hear a hint of sarcasm in her voice even from out here.

"Are you gonna come for me, baby?"

Shit, that's Derek's way of saying 'I'm coming soon and if you don't, that's your problem.' Ever the selfless lover, that Derek is. That means if I want to surprise him in the act, I need to get in there fast.

"Becca, are you almost here?"

"On my way up. Is the door unlocked?"

"Yup, come right in. I'll be the one in the bedroom swinging the umbrella."

I turn the doorknob to the bedroom, careful not to make any noise. It opens to the sound of moans and grunts. Fucking Derek and his grunting. He's facing away from the door, pumping into Miss dirty slut from behind, so I sneak up on him while raising my ladybug umbrella. From this angle, I can see his hairy balls flopping around. Gross. I can't believe I actually found him attractive. And that was this morning.

"It's happening baby, I'm gonna come now, it's happening... ungh, ungghhh," he groans obscenely.

I creep closer to the bed as Derek thrusts erratically and grunts some more. This angle is not exactly flattering and again I wonder what I ever saw in him. Whatever. That doesn't matter now. What matters is teaching him a lesson. I grip the top of the umbrella with both hands, step right into it, and swing that ladybug like I'm Babe Ruth, nearly breaking the handle off on Derek's cheating ass.

"And it's a home run! The crowd goes wild!" Becca yells from behind me. Looks like she got here right on time. She puts her hands up like a megaphone and imitates the sounds of a crowd cheering for me. Derek's screaming nearly drowns her out, though. He throws himself off the bed, leaving Miss dirty slut exposed. She's as scared as Derek is, but I'm guessing her reason differs from his.

Becca is in the room, still cheering as she pretends to run the bases while collecting the other woman's clothes from the floor.

"You have a girlfriend?" miss dirty slut screams at Derek. She frantically tries to cover herself with the sheet. "You fucker!"

"He *had* a girlfriend," I correct her, while Becca passes her clothes to her. "But good news. It looks like we broke up. He's yours if you want him. Though I have a feeling that you no longer do."

Derek's eyes are wide and he looks like a fish with the way he keeps opening and shutting his mouth. He's sitting on his hip on the floor while he rubs his umbrella-imprinted ass cheek gingerly, wincing every time his hand grazes the hook mark left by the handle. Good. I hope he can't sit for a month.

"I am *so* sorry," the girl says to me. Her eyes are wide and her lip quivers a little. "I didn't realize he had a girlfriend. This is what I get for day drinking to forget my problems, I guess."

"No worries," I tell her, heaving a sigh of relief. It's so much easier when the other woman feels bad about being the other woman. "I've been through this enough times that I know the side chick is rarely aware of the situation. I can't blame you for trying to have an orgasm with someone who told you he was available. All the blame lies with that asshole over there." I point the broken carcass of my umbrella, all bent metal and ripped canvas, at Derek. "Isn't that right, Dickhead?"

Derek flinches a little and scoots back while I point at him. He probably thinks I'm going to break the rest of this umbrella over him, which, I have to admit, he sorely deserves. The girl stands up, holding her clothes to cover her body as best she can.

"Um, so yeah. I think I'm going to get dressed in the hallway and go if that's cool with you?" She points to the door behind me and I nod. "So, I'll leave you and Derek to work this out." She looks over at Derek. "Don't call me," she says. "Ever."

She takes tiny shuffling steps past both me and Becca to get out the bedroom door. I hear her stop and get dressed in the hallway, and shortly after that, the door to the apartment opens and closes as she leaves.

"Alright, let's get to work, shall we?"

"You bet," says Becca, shooting a dirty look at Derek. "Be right back."

"Please don't hurt me Alex. I'm sorry, I love you. I'll never do it again. I didn't mean to do it. She meant nothing to me."

Tears fall down Derek's cheeks as he crawls around looking for his underwear while continuing to spew the typical cheater's bullshit apology: *I love you, I'm sorry, it was an accident; I tripped and landed dick-first in her vagina. Blah, blah, blah.* I've heard it all before. I kick his boxers over, not because I care about his dignity, but because I don't want to see his dick and balls flopping around anymore. I can't believe I ever thought he was cute.

Of course, crawling around on the floor while crying probably isn't a good look on anyone.

"Quit being a little bitch, Derek. I'm not going to hurt you more than I already have. Probably. One never really can tell what I'll do once I've discovered my boyfriend cheated on me. But then again, I've already ruined a perfectly good umbrella. I don't really feel the need to break anything else trying to teach you a lesson that I don't actually care if you learn. I'm sure you will cheat again, because once a cheater, always a cheater. But I can guarantee you won't ever cheat on me again. Want to know why?" I taunt him by spinning what's left of the umbrella around my wrist. "Because I won't give you that chance. Now get the fuck out, I have packing to do. I'll leave the keys with security."

All the boyfriends I've ever had may have cheated on me, but at least I'm smart enough to never give them a second chance.

Now, if I could figure out what it is about me that makes them cheat on me in the first place, I'd know what to avoid next time.

Derek begins to protest right as Becca returns with some boxes and a little something extra.

"Here slugger, catch." She winks and tosses me a baseball bat and I drop the umbrella to catch it. "You know, in case you're not done with batting practice."

I bounce the bat up and down, testing the weight of it, before making a practice swing. "Nice. Thanks."

That kicks Derek into high gear. He scrambles to pick up his clothes and keep an eye on me at the same before practically sprinting from the apartment in his boxers. "I'm going, I'm going," he's saying as the door closes behind him.

"I've got a few more boxes in my car. I'll grab them and make sure he leaves at the same time."

"Hey Becca?" I call out, causing her to turn around before she gets to the door. "Thanks."

"No problem, girl, that's what besties are for," she says with a sad smile.

I nod and turn away. I can't stand to see the pity in her eyes. Again.

I'm not sure why Becca had boxes in her car, but I'm thankful she did. I'll be able to pack and get out of here right now, and I'll never have to come back. I should have known Derek would cheat.

Because in my experience, all men do.

***

"Well, look on the bright side," Becca says, while packing my clothes into a box. "A few more shitty boyfriends and your batting skills will be good enough to join a major league baseball team." She can barely contain her laughter.

Becca's been my best friend ever since I moved to this city when I was sixteen, and she's been there to help me through my breakups with all my previous unfaithful boyfriends. Not to mention Connor, the boy I had to leave when we moved. My first boyfriend and first love. And the only man who never cheated on me. Despite how it ended, he's the only boyfriend I ever look back on fondly.

"I can't believe you broke an umbrella over his ass. That shit was hilarious. He's going to have a hook shaped mark on his cheeks for at least a month."

I snicker a little at that. "I feel kind of bad for the girl. I'm amazed she actually apologized. Usually they get embarrassed and run. She seemed pretty cool. I mean, it's not her fault Derek fucked her while he was still living with me, right?"

"Funny you should mention that. I ran into her outside when I went to grab more boxes from my car. She was waiting on her cab out front. She asked me to apologize to you again." Shit. That is cool. Under other, less adulterous, circumstances, she might be fun to hang out with. "And then Derek came over." I look over at her like she's about to tell me that miss dirty slut (yes, I know, it's not nice to call her that. Sue me, I found out my boyfriend was cheating. I can't help that I didn't get her name) had made up with him, but I see Becca struggling not to laugh. "And then she kicked him in balls and kneed him in the face!"

A snort of laughter escapes me, and I double over. Fucking Derek totally deserved that. That chick *is* so cool. Now I really regret not getting her name. I laugh until my stomach hurts before I get myself back under control.

"Okay," I say, pulling my long hair up into a messy bun on top of my head. "Let's get the rest of this shit packed up. You know the drill, all my kitchen shit, clothes, bathroom stuff, and recipe books."

"Got it, boss." Becca gives a salute while kicking her boots together, like some kind of army cadet. Not that she'd ever join the army. She's way too punk rock for that. I swear that girl has more ink than regular skin. When I met her, she was sixteen and already had two full sleeves and a chest piece. Now she's thirty-five , and most of the rest of her body is tattooed as well. I've noticed some scarring under the color, but I've never asked her about it. It's not my business unless she wants to tell me, so for now I admire the artwork and hope it's helping her.

Becca grabs a big box and takes it to the kitchen to get started on the pots and pans. I paid a shit ton of money for them and they come with me every time I move. I always work professional cookware into my contracts for working as a personal chef, too. It's hard to prepare food exactly the way I want it when I don't have the right tools. I could do it if I had to, but it's much more enjoyable with the right gear.

"So where are we moving this stuff to, anyway?" Not sure why Becca is asking. She already knows the answer to this question. "Want to be roomies again? I promise I won't cheat on you like all these dudes. Well, unless some sexy tattooed guy comes along and waves his big fat pierced cock in my face. No promises then." She waggles her eyebrows at me.

"I wouldn't blame you at that point. I might be tempted to cheat on myself if that happened to me." I laugh.

The rest of the packing goes quickly and I'm completely moved out of the apartment in less than an hour. We have an absurd amount of practice with moving me out of places, which is pretty sad, but it makes for much faster moves when the time comes. How I always get myself into these relationships is beyond me. I seem to attract all the assholes and then I move in with them. I guess I just love love and love really hates me.

"Let's go back to your place and chill for the rest of the day. You know, the usual breakup routine of bashing men, eating ice cream, drinking too much, and watching chick flicks." This is literally the last thing I want to be doing today, but it's become a sort of tradition. Becca has been with me through all my break-ups and if she wants to get shit-faced and eat ice cream with me, I won't argue.

Becca's phone rings from where she left it on the counter. Probably a client. She has her own photography business and makes most of her money shooting weddings, but occasionally she's booked for other things. She talks on the phone for a few minutes while I double check I have all my stuff. I refuse to see Derek ever again, so I don't plan on forgetting anything.

"Change of plans, Alex; no pity party today. I have to go shoot a promotional thing for the radio station tonight. Some local band is doing the last show of their tour and having a special meet and greet afterward. The station wants me to shoot the meets for people who won some call-in contest."

"Oh, no worries. I'm sure I can find something to do" I'm a little relieved. This has happened to me so many times now that I don't even care about the breakup ritual. It's like my heart doesn't break anymore, it's too strong. Either that or it's been broken since the first time and has stayed that way ever since.

She grins at me. "Actually, I convinced them I will need to bring extra equipment so they're giving me an extra press pass for my 'assistant'."

"But you don't have an assistant," I point out, confused.

"Congratulations," she says to me, throwing fake confetti. "You're hired. There is no pay, and the boss is a huge bitch. What do you think?"

I laugh, finally figuring out what the hell she's talking about. "That sounds like a much better breakup ritual. Thanks."

"No problem. Now let's get this shit back to our place and figure out a plan for after the show. Oooh, you can have hot rebound sex with someone in the band. I'm sure they fuck a lot, so it's possible they're awesome at it." She wiggles her eyebrows at me while walking backward toward her car. "Of course, it's also possible they're terrible and groupies are telling them what they want to hear. It could go either way."

"Ha, yeah right!" I flip her off as I get into my vehicle. "I'm not exactly rockstar girlfriend material."

"Who said anything about girlfriend? I said rebound sex. Get your mind *into* the gutter, girl," she yells from her open window while pulling out of the lot.

I shake my head and chuckle. She's such a bitch. That must be why I love her.

Hopefully, this band tonight is good. I might not be completely heartbroken, but I could use something to distract me from sitting around trying to figure out why I've been cheated on. Again.

***

Chapter Two – Family Is Overrated

Connor

"No, Mom, there won't be another show for a long time. We've been touring off and on for almost fifteen years and you haven't been to a single show. Tonight is the last night of the tour before we head back to the studio. Please come see me play." I pinch the bridge of my nose in exasperation. We have this conversation every time I ask her to come see me play. I've purchased plane tickets for her to come to other cities for fuck's sake, and she *still* hasn't bothered to show up.

I grab a smoke from the pack in my pocket and light it, taking a long drag. If I exhale with a little more force than necessary, that's my frustration manifesting as furious smoking.

"Connor, I don't think we'll be able to make it. I mean, I don't even have anything to wear." My mother is whining again, and I can tell she's angling for me to offer to buy clothes. And I'm a sucker, so of course I do. I've always done everything I can for my family, but I'm getting pretty fucking sick of it. It sucks doing shit for people who don't appreciate it, and my mother doesn't know how to show appreciation for anything.

"I'll call a shop I know and give them my credit card number. You go, bring your boyfriend, and Sadie and Amanda, and get something to wear. Hell, buy all new wardrobes if you want. I don't give a shit. I want you guys here tonight." Somehow she always gets something out of me just to perform what you would think is basic mothering. It's like I have to pay her to be a mom. She's lucky my band turned out to be so successful or she would have to actually work for a living instead of sponging off of me.

"Oh? Well, I guess it wouldn't hurt to have a look around. Ted needs some new clothes, too. He has nothing nice to wear when we go out to dinner and to the theater and such." Dinner and the theater on my dime, you mean, right Mom? Ugh, it pisses me off that I have to pay for that leech Ted, too, but Mom wouldn't come if I didn't include him. Him or whichever other "boyfriend" was currently mooching off her (and by her I mean me).

"Great. I'll leave your tickets and backstage passes at the box office. Get them and come down to the stage and Devon or one of the other security guys will show you where to meet me. I'm glad you'll finally be seeing me play."In all the years I've been doing this my own mother hasn't been to a single show, but tomorrow she'll finally see what I've done with my life (and what affords her the lifestyle she currently lives). She may be a selfish bitch, but I still want her to acknowledge how far I've come.

"Alright, baby." Now she sounds happy, since she's gotten something else out of me. "We'll see you tonight. I can't wait for you to meet Ted. I think you're going to like him. He has some great ideas to discuss with you. Bye, Honey!" She hangs up before I can say anything else. I text her the address of the store I was talking about so she won't have an excuse to not show up.

"Fuck! Why must I have a family full of assholes?" I'm practically ripping my hair out as I throw the door open and charge back into the dressing room. I'm pissed off now. I should've known something else was up. She agreed to come because her new boyfriend 'has ideas to discuss' with me. He probably has a stupid business concept that he wants backing for. Not happening, I already give you enough money mom, no way 'Ted' is getting even more out of me.

"Ow, shit! Get off me." Ryder pushes the blonde's head out of his lap as I stride across the room to pour myself a drink. Looks like she was trying to get his zipper down and get her mouth onto his dick. I guess it's not every day that she gets her hands on the lead guitarist for one of the hottest bands in the country.

"Dude, what's your problem? You scared that chick so bad she nearly bit my dick off. Not cool bro, not cool." He's pouting now, and I can't help but snort out a laugh.

"Good. Someone needs to bite it off. Maybe then I wouldn't have to see it so much. I swear I see your dick more than I see my own." I laugh while he fakes like he's going to take his dick out again. I stab my cigarette out in the ashtray on the bar at the side of the room. All these venues are supposed to be nonsmoking, but no one has ever asked me to go outside yet. I normally don't even mind going outside, but there are too many groupies out there now. I don't need that hassle when I'm looking for a smoke.

"Oh, you love this cock. If you didn't, you wouldn't look at it so much." Oh shit, I was wrong. He wasn't faking. He's whipped his dick out again and is now waving it at every other person in this room, helicopter style. Crazy fucker has no shame. The collection of groupies someone let in here doesn't seem to mind, though. Every one of them is trying to catch his eye now that they've seen the size of his penis. The asshole is blessed in that department, even I can admit that.

Our manager, Denise, walks in at that moment. "Yes, Ryder, I believe that is a penis, albeit a little on the small side. I can get you a magnifying glass if you want to get a closer look to confirm it for yourself?" Ryder stares at her with his mouth hanging open like he's trying to catch flies. He's probably trying to determine exactly how big Denise's boyfriend's dick must be if she's saying his is small. The groupies look shocked that a woman would talk to him like that. Denise is always busting his balls and I, for one, love it. He always has it coming, and it's always hilarious.

"Now, it's time for you boys to head to the stage for sound checks. So take your dicks out of whatever wet holes you've got them in, put them back in your pants, and get moving." She turns on her heel, long black hair swinging out behind her, and opens the door while motioning to shoo us out. "Chop chop, gentlemen. The stage awaits. And you," she points to the half-naked groupies practically begging for our attention, "no sluts backstage today. The boys will find you if they want you." Denise might dislike the women who hang around us begging for any attention they can get, but she'd never break their hearts by crushing their hopes completely. They all rush out past her, giving us little waves while pushing their tits together, trying to get our attention one more time. They'll figure out soon enough that they won't be back again after the show.

Denise has been our manager since we started the band, and she's always been this way. Part sassy bitch, part mother, and part no-nonsense shark. There isn't a doubt in my mind that we wouldn't have made it this far if it weren't for her. She's never phased by any of our bullshit, including walking in on us with chicks in various positions, hence the 'dicks in wet holes' comment. As long as we wrap up, she doesn't care where our dicks go. Unless it's time to put them away and get on stage, that is.

Not that most of us have been partaking in the groupie scene much over the last couple of years. I can't remember the last time I did anything with an actual woman instead of my hand. Seems a lot safer when you consider most of these groupies will fuck anyone who gets on stage. Who'd have thought I'd have had enough of the rockstar lifestyle at the ripe old age of thirty-five , yet here we are. I started out with wanting to play music, and it seems like I'm right back where I started. This upcoming stint in the studio couldn't come at a better time. I miss hanging with the guys, writing and playing music.

"You okay, Connor?" Aiden stops in front of me as he heads out. "You seemed pretty pissed when you walked in here. Your mom cancel on you again?"

"She tried, but she'll be coming tonight, with her new boyfriend. And he apparently has 'ideas' to discuss with me." I roll my eyes. Aiden knows how my mom is, so he'll know that she and the boyfriend are after something. "I promised them all a new wardrobe to convince her to come before she sprung that on me."

"Shit dude, sorry. That's rough."

"Yeah, well, it is what it is. Everyone I know wants something from me, except you guys. You guys never ask me for anything." I slap him on the back as he walks past Denise. Aiden has his own demons with family, so I usually try to avoid complaining to him about mine. Having to buy stuff for my family is still better than hav*ing* no living family at all.

"That's not quite true." Travis gives me a shove on his way out the door. Good thing we're about to go on stage or I might have to punch him right back and start something. I'm pissed off enough that fighting him actually sounds pretty good right now. He's got a good four inches and forty pounds on me, but I think I could take him. All my time in the gym must be good for something.

"That's right." Travis' older brother, Johnny, stops in front of me as he walks by. "We ask you to sing like your life depends on it every night."

"Yeah," Ryder pokes his head back through the door with a mischievous grin. "And to shake your sexy ass so the ladies will come backstage and screw us all after the show."

"Fuck off, Ryder," Johnny yells after him. "He is such a dick-head." He grabs Travis by the back of the neck and they walk out the door. Having them both in the band can get complicated because of their brotherly dynamic. Not to mention, they are constantly arguing and fighting each other as only brothers who really love each other can.

Well, I guess it's time to head to the stage and get this over with. Mom's bullshit always puts me in a foul mood, but performing normally helps that all go away. I'll hit the gym and rid myself of this shitty mood after soundcheck so it won't affect my performance tonight. One quick look in the mirror to make sure I'm looking like a sexy lead singer and I'm out the door, too. I might not be interested in sleeping with the fans much anymore, but I gotta keep them thinking it could be possible, right? Gotta maintain the illusion of availability. At least that's what the label says.

"So Denise? What do you say?" I always ask her this before I go on stage. It's part of my "getting into rockstar mode" ritual. Over the last few years, it's started feeling more like an act, so I have to take a minute to get into character before performing.

"Time to fuck shit up, Connor" she replies with her usual answer while leading me towards the stage.

"Damn right," I mutter to myself as she walks away, leaving me with the guys. "Time to fuck shit up."

***

Sound check was great, and now we've got a few hours to kill before we're needed again. I call up the shop where I sent mom and the girls to see if they made it there already, and they have. I guess they'll make it to the show after all. Mom has a habit of saying she'll do something and then not following through, though, so I won't get my hopes up yet. I give the shop my credit card number and confirm that my family can get whatever they need before hanging up. It feels like I'm buying their affection, but I don't know how else to get them here. My sisters would come, but even at eighteen and twenty-two years old, they still do whatever mom wants. Not that I can talk. I'm the one buying them all new wardrobes to get them to come to my show, after all.

With a few hours to kill before the show, I take a car service to the gym. I've been working harder on taking care of myself, though I have held on to a few bad habits. I have the occasional drink, but I rarely get wasted anymore. I still smoke, but a rockstar needs at least one vice, right? I'm off drugs and not sleeping with groupies, so smoking is it for me. Well, some might say my workouts are not the best for me either, but I need the release.

I usually go to whichever fight gym is closest to the venue, but since we're in my hometown, I go to my actual home gym. Not that I own it, I pay my fees like everyone else, but I am friends with the owner, Mike. The gym's a little older and doesn't get as many fighters as some of the bigger gyms in town, but I've been working out here since I moved to the city and I'm pretty attached to it.

"Hey Mike, you old bastard," I yell out to the old guy standing near one of the heavy bags, surrounded by a bunch of what looks to be twelve-year-old girls. "I'm going to work out for a bit before the show tonight, cool?"

"Hey Connor! Didn't think I'd see you until after the show. Didn't think you'd want to get your pretty face messed up." Mike laughs at his own joke. He thinks he's pretty funny, so he's always cracking jokes and laughing at them himself. "There's a couple of guys in the back who might spar with you if you're up for it. But don't blame me if you're singing with a black eye tonight."

"Haha, funny Mike. You know I can hold my own with anyone you want to throw at me. Maybe I should quit the band and go pro?" I joke while he watches the girls throw combos at the bag. "Can I count on you to be in my corner?"

"Fuck that, Connor. You're too pretty to fight. Now piss off and get your workout in. I can tell you're cranky, and you're distracting my girls." It looks like a few of the girls have figured out who I am, despite my clever disguise. I guess maybe I'm finally getting too famous to wander around on my own, no matter what clothes I have on. Shit, there goes my independence. I may need to consider bringing Devon for security from now on.

Not that I really wear a disguise. I'm wearing a black ball cap over my dark brown, slightly curly hair, and a long sleeve moisture wicking shirt that covers my full sleeve tattoos. I've also got grey joggers over top of my workout shorts so I can come and go quickly without changing. I should shower before I leave, but I'd rather not confirm any suspicions about my identity, or have anyone take pictures of my junk, so it's easier to go back to the hotel to shower after a workout.

Despite my cockiness regarding fighting ability, I actually don't want to wind up with bruises of any type tonight, so I stick with jumping rope, shadow boxing, and a little pad work with Mike when he's done with the girls' training.

"So what's with the class of girls?" I ask when we're done with the pad work. "I didn't think you did classes here."

"Yeah, I didn't used to, but my friend's granddaughter got into a situation with a guy who didn't want to take no for an answer, so I thought I should show her some stuff. That turned into showing her friends stuff, and now I run free self-defense classes for middle and high school girls." Mike slouches a bit and rubs his hand over his head. "This girl got away from the asshole before he could do much, but I still feel better with showing these girls how to fight, in case one of them is ever in that situation again. I'd rather they not have to rely on luck, you know?"

"Oh shit, Mike. I'm sorry to hear that. Glad it wasn't as bad as it could've been. It's a great thing you're doing for these girls, though. If all girls had some fight training, maybe these little dickheads would finally get the message that they can't go around doing whatever they want. If you need money to hire trainers to help, let me know. I would love to get behind something like this." I've got two younger sisters and I wish they'd had an opportunity like this when they were younger. I can't help them now, but maybe I could fund some classes or something as a way to give back to the community. "We'll talk more about this. For now, I need to go get ready for tonight. You sure you don't want to come?" I wheedle. I ask him this every time we play nearby. He's been to one show, and he wasn't a big fan but at least he came.

"No thanks Connor, I need to keep what's left of my hearing intact. Plus, that shit you call music is straight up noise to me. Too much yelling, too much guitar." He grins at me as he says this, but I know he's telling the truth. He has also listened to a couple of our albums, so I know he's at least made a serious attempt. I doubt my mother has even bothered to do that.

I pull on my joggers and throw my hat back on. "Alright Mike, I'll check back in soon. Thanks for the workout." I give him a two finger wave as I walk out the door and get into the car that's waiting to take me back to the hotel. I should go to my house, but all my stuff is still at the hotel. One more show, and then I'll be back in my own home. This tour has taken a lot out of me and I can't wait to be in my own space again.

Keep Reading in Second Chance (Sleeping Dogs Book 1)

More Books by Chantal

More Books by Chantal

Sleeping Dogs the complete collection

The men of Sleeping Dogs have had their fair share of women, but now that they're a little older, and a little wiser, they're looking for something more meaningful than the one-night stands typical of their past.

Second Chance (Sleeping Dogs Book 1)

She's an unemployed chef afraid of being burned by love again. He's a world-weary rock star tired of being used. Can a second chance at first love heal them both?

Face the Music (Sleeping Dogs Book 2)

She's a serious control freak of a band manager. He's a jaded joker of a rock star. Will a jealous ex and surprise pregnancy tear them apart before they start?

Skip a Beat (Sleeping Dogs Book 3)

She's a disgraced ex-cop looking for a career change. He's a moody drummer trying to keep his demons at bay. Can vandalism and ill-conceived revenge plans be the glue that mends their lives and binds them to each other?

Only the Best (Sleeping Dogs Book 4)

He's a romantic, guitar-playing tattoo artist looking for true love. She's an emotionally and physically scarred photographer who keeps people at a distance. When one wants true love and the other wants one night, can friendship and a fake relationship ever be enough?

Way off Base (Sleeping Dogs Book 5)

She's a single mom struggling to rebuild her life. He's a reluctant rock star tired of being alone. Can they repair a foundation of lies to build the life they both want?

About the Author

Chantal Roome writes contemporary romantic comedies and is the author of the Sleeping Dogs series of cinnamon roll rock star rom-coms. She loves writing love stories with just the right mix of sweetness, humour, and sex. When she isn't writing, she's drinking way too much coffee, binge reading romance, and living out her own second chance romance with her husband. She's also a mediocre mom to two frustrating, but hilarious and endlessly loveable kids, one dog who has eaten every toy he's ever been given, and another dog who wants nothing more to use her tiny puppy shark teeth on any exposed flesh she can find.

Keep in touch with Chantal on social media

Visit Chantal's website at: www.chantalroome.com

Get the Roomie Review Newsletter chantalroome.substack.com

Join my readers' group facebook.com/groups/theromcomroome

facebook.com/chantalroomeauthor

instagram.com/chantalroomeauthor

pinterest.com/chantalroome

tiktok.com/chantalroomeauthor

twitter.com/croomeauthor

goodreads.com/chantalroome

bookbub.com/authors/chantal-roome

Made in the USA
Las Vegas, NV
14 December 2024